Deep Breathing

Deep Breathing by G. Davies Jandrey

Copyright © 2019 G. Davies Jandrey

All rights reserved. No part of this book may be used or reproduced by any means without the written permission of the publisher except in the case of brief quotation embodied in critical articles and reviews.

This is a work of fiction. Names, characters, places, and incidents either are the products of the author's imagination or are used fictitiously. Any resemblance to actual persons, living or dead, businesses, companies, events, or locales is entirely coincidental.

Cover photo of *Goddess of Agave* by Rock Martinez courtesy of Dennis Boyd.
Back cover photos by ShonEjai and rawpixel.com via Pexels
Cover design by Jacqueline Cook.

ISBN: 978-1-7320305-7-2 (Paperback)
ISBN: 978-1-7320305-8-9 (e-book)

10 9 8 7 6 5 4 3 2 1

BISAC Subject Headings:
FIC000000 FICTION / General
FIC030000 FICTION / Thrillers / Suspense
FIC069000 FICTION / City Life

Address all correspondence to:
Fireship Press, LLC
P.O. Box 68412
Tucson, AZ 85737
fireshipinfo@gmail.com

Or visit our website at:
www.fireshippress.com

*For Patti Chambers,
the daughter of my heart,
who is the hero of her own story.*

Also by G. Davies Jandrey

A Garden of Aloes
Journey through and Arid Land
A Small Saving Grace
Tortilla Moon and Other Tales of Love

Acknowledgements

Deep Breathing came into existence because I had the love, support and advice of many people during what is always a long, and sometimes tedious process. As always, my husband, Fritz, tops the list. He continues to laugh and cry in the right spots, and to show great tolerance when I am poor and distracted company. Next is Patricia Chambers, my hero. I thank her for her inspiration, courage and persistence in the face of great challenges. As is always the case, fellow writer, Veronica Robinson, was an early reader of the manuscript. I thank her for her astute observations and friendship throughout the years. For their encouragement, I am always grateful to Diane Cheshire, Mary Goethals, Ginia Desmond and Jennifer Vermich. Cameron Hintzon offered his expert advice regarding police procedures and deadly force. Michelle Kinnison and Kristen Culliney welcomed me to Caridad Community Kitchens and gave me insight into this wonderful program. Marty Marszalek was the chief medical officer when I visited Camp Bravo, a local refuge for homeless veterans. He greeted me warmly and gave me a fine tour of the facility. Garbriela E. Morales has once again made sure that the Spanish spoken by my characters is as it should be. Bonnie Lemons, supportive and talented editor and friend, has ferreted out my typos, misspellings and brain farts once again. I will love you forever, Bonnie, for your enduring willingness and good cheer in the face of my many mistakes. My thanks to Dennis Boyd for the cover photo of Rock Martinez's beautiful mural, *Goddess of Agave*. Lastly, many thanks to Jacquie Cook, production editor, at Fireship Press, for her great steady hand and head and patience.

GLFM

*Acceptance of yourself and others
as you and as they are brings joy.*
—Karma Tea

DEEP BREATHING

G. DAVIES JANDREY

Cortero
An Imprint of FIRESHIP PRESS

Part I

"Fe fi fo fum. Look out baby, 'cause here I come."
—*Get Ready* by the Temptations

Chapter 1

Tuesday, Oct. 4

At first she wasn't sure he'd seen her. She was small after all. If she could stand up straight, she might be five feet tall, but she could not stand up straight, could barely stand at all. She cleared her throat. "I have an appointment with Grace Belgrade, an interview, actually." She handed her card to the receptionist, a young man with short spiky hair and big glasses with thick black rims. Abigail Bannister, CEO and founder of GSG Gimps Serving Gimps since 2014, it read.

Smiling, the man raised the one-moment finger as he checked the messages on his smartphone. Satisfied that he'd missed nothing important, he dialed the office phone. "Ms. Bannister is here to see you. Okay, sure." He hung up the phone. "She'll be with you in a moment. If you'll just have a seat." His face reddened, but he barreled on. "I mean, well you're already seated aren't you, so anyway, she'll be right with you." He smiled again. The guy had amazing dimples.

Abby, as she liked to be called, spun her wheelchair around then whirred toward the farthest corner where she wouldn't be in the way.

Her cellphone, which she kept in a Guatemalan pouch hung around her neck, chimed the first three bars of Beethoven's 5th. She grasped the phone awkwardly, willing her left hand to behave. Squinting at the incoming number, she fetched her reading glasses from the top of her head where they rested in a nest of curly brown hair. It was a text from Robert, her oldest and best friend.

She adjusted her glasses. *Don't b nervous*, the text read. *Lunch? Meet u Cup, 11:30.*

Smiling, she typed in a single letter, K, and put the phone on vibrate. It was sweet of Robert to think of her, but Abby wasn't nervous. Why should she be? This was an interview, just a little personal interest thing about GSG for a spot on the local evening news. Presumably, she would know the answers to all the questions, since she was the founder and CEO of the company.

She shoved her cellphone and glasses back into her pouch, then absently massaged her left earlobe with its gold heart earring. When she had her ears pierced as a college freshman, she'd chosen puffy little hearts with screw backs so she'd never have to remove them. They were remnants of her youthful optimism: She often thought she should have them replaced with something more appropriate. What would that be? Two little crabs, perhaps? Or maybe a pair of tiny scorpions?

Abby combed the fingers of her good hand, which she referred to as the Mighty Claw, through her curls, then pushed herself into a more upright position with the Hammer, as she called her well-muscled right arm. Should she have worn lipstick? She had to chuckle at the notion that lipstick would make a difference. Her spine twisted by scoliosis, left her rib cage resting on her hip. Her legs, atrophied by disuse, were nearly immobile, sometimes spastic and totally unreliable.

Miraculously, the oxygen deprivation at birth that had so scrambled her brain's messages to her limbs had not harmed the apparatus that controlled speech. Abby had a nice, crisp, clear voice and loved music. Her playlist was eclectic, ranging from Mexican banda to Yo-Yo Ma, but Diana Krall was her favorite; actually Abby wanted to be Diana Krall.

Deep Breathing

In college she'd taken piano lessons—there was lots of music written for one hand. She'd splurged on a keyboard so she could practice at home. Later there had been voice lessons—one part to ease her anxiety and loneliness, one part to feed her lifelong fantasy of becoming the first pop star on wheels.

Her teacher had been one of her clients, a former local musical theater type who'd fallen off the roof while fixing his cooler. He was left paralyzed from the chest down, and though he no longer had the breath to sing professionally, he had been an excellent teacher. Abby, the queen of unrequited love, had fallen in lust with him even though he was married.

Despite the distraction of her infatuation, she'd learned from him that breath was everything. Once she'd internalized that, her life became easier. Getting in and out of bed was easier. Dressing was easier. Most importantly, she'd found that breath was essential to keeping at bay the tears that so often threatened to expose her.

• • •

Anxiety rising, Abby looked at her watch. She'd been waiting less than five minutes. To calm herself, she pulled out the newly purchased paperback from the side pocket of her wheelchair. This one she had dubbed the Chariot because it had more power than her last one, which she'd called Old Bessie.

The book, *How to Craft Your Life—Strategies for Joy and Fulfillment*, was a slender one. She'd never heard of the author, but she liked the title. Despite the fact that she had completed her MBA and owned a business and a home, Abby was both surprised and disappointed to discover that those accomplishments had brought her little fulfillment and even less joy. Chapter 1 in the book promised to help her find her luck. She turned to it now.

Often what seems like luck, Dale J. Nagery had written, *is simply recognizing an opportunity when it presents itself. Sometimes opportunity comes in the guise of misfortune.*

Abby considered that for a moment. Had she ever in her life experienced a misfortune that later revealed itself as an opportunity?

She couldn't think of a single instance. Perhaps she needed to be more observant.

The door opened and a slender, perfectly groomed woman strode over to her corner. Abby tucked the book back into the Chariot's side pocket.

"Ms. Bannister." The woman held out a hand, which looked a lot older than her face. "I'm Gracie Belgrade."

For a moment, Abby's courage faltered. Her knit tunic—she always wore stretchy knits—had ridden up over her thighs. She was suddenly conscious of her slouchy and disheveled appearance, her ugly black shoes with their Velcro straps. She hoisted herself up with her good arm then extended the Mighty Claw. "Very pleased to meet you," she said with more enthusiasm than she felt.

• • •

She stuffed the black knit sweater she'd needed this morning into the side of her chair then connected her cellphone to her earbuds. It was a typical early October morning for Tucson, dry, sunny, hot. Abby exited the TV station, then headed down Elm Street to the sweet, jazzy sound of Diana Krall and through the quiet neighborhood with its older homes, some rehabbed, others awaiting transformation as new, more affluent folks moved into the area. From a stanchion at the back of her chair flew a series of banners. The top one was the Stars and Stripes, beneath that the eagle and snake of Mexico, then, just for the hell of it, the rainbow flag. The trio snapped smartly as she sped down the sidewalk to the streetcar stop by the university. Although the Chariot was capable of doing 10 miles an hour, safety, her own and those sharing the sidewalk, dictated a more sedate pace. At her approach, passersby, students mostly, stepped aside even as they pretended not to notice her. Though this was standard, today it grated.

As she waited for the streetcar she replayed the interview in her mind. She had expected to be asked about the services GSG provided, maybe a few questions about her background, but it had taken a sudden, personal turn. Well, at least she'd been honest and straightforward. Honesty, of course, was not always the best of polices.

Deep Breathing

• • •

Abby whirred through the doors of the historic Hotel Congress. Built in 1919, it was once the playground of the notorious gangster John Dillinger. Despite the great ceiling fans that beat the air year-round, a faint but unmistakable odor of disinfectant wafted through the dim lobby, belying its faded elegance.

Robert was waiting. He waved, then lurched toward her, knees collapsing into each other in a great impersonation of Jerry Lewis doing a great impersonation of a guy with cerebral palsy. He was classic C.P. His speech was halting and sometimes unintelligible to the casual listener, but he drove a sporty red Chevy Camero equipped with hand controls and a knob on the steering wheel, was a well-remunerated engineer at Raytheon, lived in a nice condo and had a loving family that accepted him unconditionally for who and what he was. In other words, he had most of the things that Abby did not.

He involuntarily grimaced. "How'd it … go?" The "d" got swallowed, as did the final "o," and his voice sounded as though he were being garroted. This was Robert's normal.

"It went. You can see how well on the 5 o'clock news."

Robert looked her up and down, scowled. "Is that…what…you wore?"

"Yes, this is what I wore. This is what I always wear. What's wrong with it?"

"It's okay … but a little … makeup would have … helped."

"Makeup, Robert?"

"Yeah … a little lipstick. Appearance … matters, Abby."

"To you." Robert was also the board president of GSG, for which she was truly grateful, but sometimes he asserted his opinions into the little holes in Abby's confidence, and it made her want to smack the guy.

"You seem… pissed," he said, eyes swimming behind thick glasses that magnified their hazel color and gave him a misleadingly dreamy appearance.

"Not really," she lied. She turned, then whirred through the lobby toward the back entrance and the patio where there was wheelchair access to The Cup, the hotel's funky/hip restaurant.

Head wagging, Robert pitched alongside her in silence. Abby had a little problem with depth perception, and neither one could negotiate well while talking. Given her black mood, this was a good thing.

• • •

Abby picked at her cauliflower taco, while Robert tackled a pulled pork sandwich, not a pretty sight. Between them was a platter of sweet potato fries.

"So how did the blind date go the other night?" Abby asked.

Robert put the sandwich down, took a couple of paper napkins from the stack the waiter had automatically provided and wiped his hands and mouth. "Didn't." His face cracked, and he began to laugh. "I just … stood there like ah, ah, ah. Couldn't talk. Picture Frank … en … stein crossed with … God … zilla."

Abby had to laugh. Sometimes that was the only thing either of them could do.

"Well, it took guts. I'll say that."

"Guts?" He paused, gearing up for the next phrase. "More like … stupi … dity. You should … have seen … the look … on his face." He resumed the sandwich challenge.

Biting into a fry, she nodded. "You never know, you might have clicked." For both of them, "clicking" with someone was a quest on the scale of the Holy Grail, daunting, dangerous and ultimately just as elusive.

"You look sharp today," she added by way of consolation. And it was true. Robert always looked sharp, buttoned down, spanking clean. His face, like the rest of him, was lean and angular, handsome even, when he wasn't trying to talk or eat. When they were in high school they had vowed to lose their virginity before graduation. There were no takers so they had turned to each other, determined to get the deed done. At the time, sex wasn't an act of passion or even compassion, but rather a job that needed to be done, a job that had been both awkward and painful. Shortly afterwards, Robert announced that he was gay.

Still, their friendship endured despite, or maybe because of that, and the fact that in so many ways they were complete opposites. Robert was fiscally conservative, she was … well she had no real fiscal to conserve. He was a Republican, she a Democrat. She was, well, emotional, whereas Robert was analytical. And he was fanatically neat.

"So are you going to try the online dating thing again?" She asked. "I mean it's better than the bar scene, right?"

He wrestled his mouth into a frown and shook his head.

"You're not going to give up the quest, are you?" A suppressed smile twitched the corners of her mouth. "So have you thought about volunteering?" A line she knew he'd heard a dozen times from friends and family.

"Not … funny."

Abby pointed to the front of his crisp, white shirt where a blob of sauce had landed. Hands dripping, he put his sandwich down with resignation and took a couple of swipes at the spot with a napkin, then shrugged. Abby knew from experience that a brand new shirt still in the bag always lay on the back seat of the Camero for just such emergencies.

He flung the soiled napkin aside. "It's hard… putting myself out there." You should try it… Abby. When was the last time … you made an effort to get … a date? How long … has it been since you had … a relationship?"

"Pardon?"

"Sex. How long has it been?"

"Are we talking sex in the technical Clinton definition as in 'I did not have sex with that woman' or the broader definition."

"You … define it."

"Quite honestly I haven't had any since…" She shook her head. "I can't remember." This was not true. It was over a year ago. They'd met in her Conversational Spanish class. She came; he did not. She'd assumed it was first-time jitters, but when he didn't call or return her texts, she figured his apparent interest must have been driven by curiosity or worse, by pity. Perhaps he hadn't been prepared for the reality of a woman made crabbed and crooked by cerebral palsy. It must have been something like that because he never came back to class. His loss. The class had been very helpful. Her Spanish had improved a lot.

Robert wiped the last of the sauce off his hands. "You know … what I mean?" he was saying.

"Um?"

"You weren't … listening."

"Sorry I was distracted by this … canker sore kind of thing. I've tried saltwater but I …" Abby could tell by his expression, which was no expression at all, that he wasn't buying it, but that's one of the reasons they were still friends. They didn't call each other on their lies. She handed him her napkin and pointed to his chin. "So what were you saying?"

He swiped at his chin. Screwing up his face, he said, "I was saying that it hurts … like hell. Admit it. You know the problem … is public … percep … tion. Gimps aren't sup … posed to have sex. You're a good … looking woman when you… want to be. But let's … face it. People see that … chair and it never… occurs to them that you might want to … get laid."

Abby laughed then. "Jesus, Robert, you put it so delicately." She pointed to his chin once again.

He took another swipe. "Okay?"

"Got it"

Robert looked at his watch, a big, gold expensive looking thing. "Gotta get back … to work." He motioned the waitress for the checks.

"You go ahead. I'm not quite finished."

The waitress laid the checks on the table. "Whenever you're ready, guys."

Robert glanced at each. "I'll get the tip. You're too cheap."

"I'm not cheap. I'm fair."

"You're fair … ly cheap." Chuckling at his own joke, he fished out a five from his wallet and put it on the table. He patted her head. It was easier than trying to land a kiss on her cheek. "Take care."

"You too, Robert, and I am not cheap." She stuffed another fry in her mouth. It was cold, and she pushed the plate away with finality. Robert's take on the perception, or rather misperception, of people in wheelchairs was true, at least in her experience. Because she was small, people inevitably viewed her as "the girl in the wheelchair." She imagined as the years progressed she'd become the "little old lady in the wheelchair." Never would anyone see her simply as a woman, a sexual being, and no amount of lipstick was going to alter that.

• • •

Thanks to a grant she'd written for the owner of the building to make it wheelchair accessible, the automatic glass door opened at her approach. Abby whirred through and down the narrow hallway. The old brick building was a two-story converted warehouse on the fringes of the downtown arts district. The offices facing Sixth Street were pretty upscale with large windows and high ceilings. She rented an office, one of a warren of windowless spaces entered from the rear of the building. It wasn't much bigger than a cubbyhole, but GSG could afford it, just, and it was located directly across from the bathroom. Best of all, it was close enough to her house to buzz there in her chair, and it was home to Tucson Acupuncture Cooperative, where she indulged in weekly treatments that eased the neuropathy in her legs and feet.

The downside of the place, in addition to its dark and shabby interior, was that one of the spaces was occupied by the Church of the Red Word and Pastor Glorie Praise, a name she assumed when she accepted Christ as lord and master. The woman kept cheerfully pressuring her to join the congregation, which was a bit insulting in and of itself. It was as if Pastor Glorie naturally assumed that she couldn't possibly have anything better to do on Wednesday and Friday nights or Sunday mornings than hang out with a bunch of upwardly mobile homeless people and toothless ex meth addicts. Fact was, she really didn't have anything better to do, but Glorie had no way of knowing that. Moreover, Abby didn't believe that the red words in the Bible were actually Christ's and was fairly sure there was no God. Certainly, he/she'd never lifted a finger on her behalf, even after years of fervent prayers on the part of her child self and her mother's very Catholic Aunt Sally. The old lady, a spinster and a successful businesswoman, had been devoted to Abby's mother. She would have gladly paid for a visit to Lourdes so Abby could take the waters had it not been for her father's equally fervent faith in modern medicine. By the time she was 12, she'd had 14 surgeries to improve her mobility. In retrospect, Abby wondered if all those surgeries had done more harm than good. Well, she'd never know and seldom gave it any thought.

There was a second set of automatic doors opening into Abby's small office. Abby whirred through, happy and a bit surprised to see that Rita Sotomayor was actually at work. The stout Mexican matron, her silver hair freshly dressed, was called Rita by everyone but her 91-year-old mother, who called all of her daughters *mija*—daughter in Spanish—because she could no longer remember who was who. *Mija*, was an inclusive term of affection that didn't actually require one to be a daughter, so it worked well for all of the old lady's female relatives and any friends she might have that were under 85.

Rita, who at the moment was sitting at the desk drinking tea and perusing the Arizona Daily Star, tripled as office manager, accountant and plumber—the building's old toilet had a tendency to overflow at the least provocation. She'd lost a leg above the knee and a foot to a bacteria resistant infection she acquired while in the hospital for a hernia repair, then a husband to a younger woman, but was otherwise fully intact and indispensable. She put the paper down now. "*Hola, mija*. So how did it go?" she asked, dunking the tea bag in and out of her cup.

"I should have been wearing lipstick apparently."

"No, really. How did it go?"

"You can see for yourself on the 5 o'clock news. What's been going on here this morning?"

"Not much." Rita took a sip of tea and continued to dunk. "I'm trying out this new Karma tea. Each bag has a little saying on the paper thingy, so it's kind of like opening a fortune cookie." She paused to read the tag. "*You will always live happy if you live with heart.*"

"Yeah, that plus a million dollars would probably do it." Abby hung her sweater on a sawed-off coat rack standing in the corner of the tiny office. "What else is going on?"

"Your brother wants you to call." She arched one finely shaped brow. Unlike her hair, her eyebrows were dark brown. They accented her eyes, which were sometimes brown, sometimes green, but always warm and wide open. The woman missed nothing.

"Josh called? That can't be good. What else?"

"And Stewart."

"What did he need?"

"I have no idea. Couldn't understand a word, but I told him you'd give him a call when you got in."

Stewart, a stroke victim, paid Abby to handle each piece of business he absolutely had to conduct over the phone. "Okay. Anything else?"

Rita drained the last of her tea and set the cup on the counter. "Susie, that cabrona from Lane's, says she's got a first floor, wheelchair accessible condo just on the market if you know anyone who might be interested."

Abby had to smile. Rita had a dustup with Susie when the woman tried to wriggle out of sharing a sales commission. She'd never gotten over it, but Abby couldn't afford such grievances. She'd learned all the ins and outs of financing when buying her home. Next she got her real estate license. Now she worked with other agents around town, and GSG got 3 percent of the 7 percent commission on all sales initiated by Abby. Then if the house needed to be remodeled to make it wheelchair accessible, GSG got 10 percent above cost to organize the workers and oversee the project.

Rita gathered up her newspaper and purse, then shrugged her shoulders into the sweater that hung on the back of her chair. "Come on, Honey," she called, and a little dog, part Chihuahua, part something hairy, bounded out from under the desk and onto her lap. The dog sported a little vest that declared her a service dog, but she was just a mutt that Rita had picked up on the street, the vest a ruse that allowed her to go everywhere that Rita went. "And don't forget the non-medical care training for Pima Help at Home."

"Right, 10 o'clock tomorrow." The trainings, along with fees for services GSG provided, paid both Rita's and her meager salaries. Of course, Abby was GSG. She only hoped that one day she'd be able to give herself a raise so she could afford some of her own services. She had a screened-in back porch off the kitchen. When she bought the house, she had visions of pots filled with flowers, a place where she could sit with friends, maybe even have a dinner party in fine weather, but the floorboards were termite infested. She had replaced the five steps that went down to the yard with a ramp, but that was all she could afford. Each time she went out to her backyard she crept around the edges of the deck fearing the floor might collapse under the weight of her 200-pound wheelchair and she'd fall into the crawl space below. She'd love to hire herself to organize a work crew to rebuild it, but for now its main function was home to her cat's litter box.

"So, do you want me to pick you up tomorrow and take you to the training.?"

Rita was also her personal chauffer. "No. It's downtown. I can manage."

"Okay *mija*, you're on your own." Rita blew her a kiss and she and Honey buzzed out the door.

Abby took her place behind the desk. Who should she call first? On one level, talking to Stewart would be less of an ordeal. Josh's call could only be about money. That could wait.

• • •

Bruno Mars was singing *Uptown Funk* into Abby's earbuds as she whizzed down Sixth Street, bits of dust and debris swirling up around her each time a bus or truck passed. On Ash Avenue, which was actually no more than an alley, she turned north. On her right was Bica's rear entry. Housed in the basement of a crumbling old warehouse /cum artists studios, its mission was to supply bikes to the bikeless. This section of town was surrounded on three sides by recently designated "districts." There were the West University Historical District, the El Presidio Historical District and the Fourth Avenue Shopping District. All were hip and happening and rapidly undergoing gentrification. In contrast, her neighborhood, by virtue of its lack of distinction, remained low rent and quasi-industrial. The area was traditionally marginal, and its occupants embraced its marginality and abhorred the creeping affluence that threatened to displace them.

Deep Breathing

Abby passed the vacant lot with its ugly chain link fence topped with razor wire and wondered for the umpteenth time what the owner was trying to protect. Despite the fence and old warehouse, Abby loved this alley. Rarely did she encounter traffic or other people. She could buzz right down the middle of the narrow lane in high gear. At Fourth Street she turned west into the glare of the late afternoon sun hanging just above "A" Mountain.

Her house, one of many little stucco homes built shortly after WWII, was held together by chicken wire and chewing gum, she was pretty sure. Thanks to dear old Aunt Sally, who had remembered Abby in her will, it was hers—well, hers and the bank's. She had it gutted and made everything from the shower to the stovetop wheelchair accessible. Unfortunately, she'd run out of money before she'd gotten to the back porch, but one of these days, she'd get to that too.

As she whirred up the wooden ramp to her front door, she admired the bougainvillea veiling her neighbor's porch in a profusion of magenta. It bloomed its heart out from last frost to first. Though Abby couldn't see her, she knew old Mrs. Soto was tucked back into the recesses of her front porch. She took out her earbuds and called out, "*Buenas trades, Señora Soto. Cómo está?*"

"*Bien, bien, gracias a Dios,*" the old woman croaked. "*Y tú, mija?*"

"*Bien, bien,*" Abby replied, as she unlocked the door.

The moment she entered the house, Tito, the 8-year-old tabby who shared her home, leaped onto her lap. He'd been a shelter kitten, and when he first arrived he bounced around the house with such manic joy that she'd named him after the famous Latin jazz bandleader, Tito Puente.

"Hey, you," she whispered, scratching the little pleasure spots at the base of the cat's tail and under his neck. Abby whirred into the kitchen, Tito riding shotgun.

She inhaled the fragrance of Windex. Stella, a whirling dervish of a cleaning lady, had been there. The woman was mildly intellectually impaired. As her mother put it, Stella was not the brightest candle in the menorah, but she worked hard and had a sweet, docile nature. It appeared to Abby that her mother allowed the woman precious little leeway to be otherwise.

Thanks to Abby's connections, Stella had a number of clients. She wore the keys to their houses on a chain around her neck like a piece of prized jewelry. And the nice thing about Stella was that Abby rarely saw her. It worked like magic. Abby would leave forty-five dollars on the kitchen table. When she got home the money would be gone and the house clean. The two women might go weeks without seeing each other. It was the perfect arrangement.

A cellphone charger and little television were perched on a Formica-topped dinette, a chipped but cheery yellow prize she'd found at Goodwill. In fact, all her furniture—the two wooden stools tucked under the kitchen table, the tattered love seat and matching chair, none of which could she sit in, the coffee table and overhead lamp on a swag—came from Goodwill. Robert had set up board and block shelves for her books and bric-a-brac, and tacked up some old movie posters featuring Bogart and Bergman, Hepburn and Tracy, she'd found in an antique shop while still in college. That was it.

Abby put her phone into the charger and turned on the television. While she waited for the 5 o'clock news to begin, she gathered the ingredients for her dinner: two eggs, two bread heels, a nearly empty carton of skim milk and a small carton of strawberry yogurt for desert, setting each item on the counter by the stove. She made a mental note to buy bread and milk. A few vegetables wouldn't hurt either, her inner scold admonished.

"Good evening," said Brent Campbell, a stout, older gent with a mellow baritone.

She reached over to turn up the volume as the man began emoting about the city council and plans to widen Broadway as if these were matters of great consequence. Abby supposed they were to someone, but she just wanted to see her interview. Keeping an ear cocked to the news, she grabbed a tall plastic glass and whirred back over to the fridge. She poured herself a big glass from the ice water dispenser. Unlike her furniture, she'd bought her appliances new, and the fridge had all the bells and whistles.

She set the glass on the table and busied herself with pill preparation.

The pill slicer sat alongside the salt and pepper. She spilled out a dozen large pills prescribed for her spastic bladder, arranged one just so in the device, which was very much like a miniature guillotine, then pulled down the blade. She always experienced a little pulse of satisfaction when the pill fell into two perfect halves. It occurred to her that this was probably not a good thing.

Midway through the pill splitting, Brent interrupted himself with a local news alert.

"Early this morning on the side of a quiet, midtown street, a man was found slumped in his wheelchair with obvious signs of trauma. Responders performed CPR, but the man was pronounced dead at University Medical Center. Police have not released his name or cause of death, but neighbors identified him as William Strand, a 42-year-old quadriplegic who often took late-night wheelchair strolls through his neighborhood."

"My God, William Strand?" The man had been a client. Well, not a client—they never got that far. Turned out he only wanted free advice on financing his remodel. When she suggested he use GSG to oversee the project, Strand was agreeable until she mentioned the 10 percent fee. For no apparent reason, he went ballistic. Abby didn't know if it was some kind of drug thing or maybe some kind of PTSD, but Strand was a very angry man. Well, she could certainly understand why that might be, but he really was way-over-the-top out of line. It didn't surprise her that someone might want to bash his head in or whatever. Still, it gave her pause. She'd never known anyone who'd been murdered. It felt pretty creepy.

Just as she'd guillotined the last pill, Brent announced, "We turn now to 'Your Town Tucson' with Grace Belgrade. And there was Gracie, smiling sweetly into the camera, totally cool and in control. Abby's throat went dry and she took a big gulp of water.

"My guest this evening is Abigail Bannister, founder and CEO of a local nonprofit with the unlikely name of "Gimps Serving Gimps, otherwise known as GSG."

The camera closed in on Abby, hair a mass of dark corkscrews, pale face, thick brows arched over wide, brown eyes. She never plucked her eyebrows, maybe she should have, and used a little rouge and lipstick. Would that have saved her?

"Ms. Bannister." Gracie smiled her encouragement. "I understand that you're one of our native Tucsonans."

"That's right, I was born here, attended the University of Arizona. After I got my master's degree in social work, I went to work at Davis-Monthan Air Force base in hospitality for several years while I geared up to start GSG."

"Can you tell us a little bit about your very special company?"

"I'd be happy to." Abashed, Abby watched her face screw up as she soldiered on, oblivious. "GSG was incorporated in 2014 as a nonprofit. It is the embodiment of a public-private partnership model where investments from federal, state and local governments, grants from private corporations and the gifts of individual citizens play a vital and ongoing role. For most people, work provides independence and is a measure of value. This is no less true for people with physical or mental challenges."

She watched as she struggled to hoist herself upright then carry earnestly on. "The mission of GSG is to provide a wide variety of support services and employment opportunities for people who, when given a bit of help, can join the workforce and make a positive contribution to society. For a minimal fee, GSG connects people and services so that we can maintain maximum independence in a world that seems to conspire to keep us in our place—that is out of sight and out of mind."

"Ms. Bannister can you explain why you use the term "gimp," twice I might add, in the name of your company? Isn't that a word that your clients, who are all handicapped, might well find offensive?"

There was an edge to Gracie's voice, a hard glint in her eye. Abby hadn't noticed that during the interview, but she could see it now. Her chest tightened.

Again the close-up. As Abby searched for the lucky opportunity presented by this unfortunate interview, she could feel the heat climb up from her chest and into her face, which was turning red right before the camera. She turned off the television, throat aching with angry tears.

She heard the familiar commanding voice, her mother's, *Now don't cry, little girl. Don't you cry,* and she did not cry. She almost never did.

• • •

Robert paused over his dinner, two small lamb loin chops, mashed red potato with butter and chives, and arugula salad tossed with lemon and olive oil, as Grace Belgrade's focus narrowed in on Abby like a rattlesnake on a baby bunny.

"I can barely make myself say the word, "gimp." The woman said the word as if it were a turd lodged in her throat.

Robert grimaced as the corners of Abby's mouth tugged down the way they always did when she got mad. She pushed herself up with her good arm to make herself taller in the chair. "Uh-oh," he said. "Here it… comes."

"You mean because it is politically incorrect? I guess that's the point. We, people like me, are nothing if not politically, and I might add, socially incorrect. We are the proverbial elephant in the room, the one people pretend is not there."

"You go… girl," Robert shouted at the television.

• • •

Only a few women were in the common room watching the news. When she heard the name, Fey looked up from her sudoku and leaned forward. Abby Bannister -- she hadn't seen her in nearly 20 years, and there she was on television being interviewed like some kind of celebrity.

"There are many posters of children with a variety of challenging conditions," she was saying, "spina bifida, Down syndrome, cerebral palsy -- photos usually used for the purposes of fundraising. But where are the images of challenged adults? The fact is, we do grow up, most of us, but we are not in the public eye. When, if ever, have you seen a blind person or a person like me, with cerebral palsy, in a television sitcom or miniseries? Let me throw out some statistics. Characters on television with disabilities are less than 1 percent. Given that nearly 20 percent of Americans live with disabilities, that's a pretty poor showing.

"Do you realize," Abby paused again to push herself up in the chair. "Do you realize that the Americans with Disabilities Act was signed into law over 25 years ago? I wouldn't be sitting here before you without ADA, yet over 80 percent of disabled Americans are currently unemployed."

Fey could see that she was pretty steamed by the way her whole face kind of went into a spaz. She'd done that when she was a little kid every time she got mad or sad or simply tried too hard. Abby had been what, 9 or 10, when Fey left; the woman probably wouldn't recognize her if they met on the street, but Abby would remember how it had been back then. Who could forget?

Abby, the CEO of a company! She'd certainly be in a position to lend her a hand, a loan, maybe, or a job. A gift of cash would be the best thing, enough to get her off the streets so she could regroup. Tomorrow she'd go to the library, she did most days anyway, Google GSG and see what came up. Then maybe she'd just drop by Abby's office. Lay it all out for her. Maybe Abby would let her stay with her for a while. It would be like old times, almost sisters, they'd been. Maybe there would be a chance for… reconciliation would be too strong a word, but something else, that would allow her a sense of… What was it that what she wanted? Revenge? Maybe.

A woman in a Sponge Bob T-shirt got up and changed channels.

"Hey, I was watching that." The woman flipped her the bird. What a bitch, she thought, but knew better than to get into a hassle. Of all the shelters in town, this one was probably the best, but she hated the smell, hated the way people treated her as if she were a 3-year-old, or simple-minded. She was homeless, for God's sake, but that didn't mean she was stupid.

• • •

He was amazed that someone so physically disabled could be so assertive and articulate. At once, it both pained and fascinated him to watch her struggle to sit upright. There was something so moving about her appearance, her earnest expression, the tousled brown hair.

"As for my use of the word 'gimp,' I don't claim to speak for everyone who is physically or mentally challenged," she was saying. Her face contorted as she adjusted herself in the chair. "That group is too diverse, but as a teen, my gimp friends at school and I started to use the term with one another as a way to... I don't know... create a sense of community, perhaps, since we were excluded from the greater community, or maybe it was a way for us to thumb our collective noses at people who are appalled by the word, gimp, and the image it conjures."

"I see." The interview's eyes narrowed. "Still, it seems to me, Ms. Bannister, that the use of the term is insulting to people already sufficiently challenged and afflicted."

"Afflicted. Okay. Most people, Ms. Belgrade, are afflicted by something, allergies, for instance, or bigotry, say. But most people are not defined by their affliction unless they have a so-called disability. Then you become the cerebral palsied woman or the quadriplegic, or the retarded guy rather than the CEO of a company, the artist or the employee of the month at Safeway."

"I guess you've made your point. I'm just glad you don't expect everyone to use the word 'gimp.' So what do you want to be called?"

"Abby. Abby Bannister," she said looking directly into the camera.

He took out his notebook and added Abigail Bannister to the list. She was just the kind of person who deserved his help.

Chapter 2

Friday, Oct. 7

Abby had spent the better part of the morning at the caregiver training and was still mulling it over as she whirred up Sixth Avenue. Men and women who wished to become in-home caregivers had to take the training. They also had to become certified in CPR and first aid. The one class she taught each session dealt with the relationship between the person providing the care and the person receiving it. She knew firsthand how tricky it was to strike a balance between professionalism, respect and compassion. People who haven't had the experience simply did not realize that the greatest physical intimacy is not during sex but during grooming. Everybody laughed when she had said that; laughter is always a good sign, but she hadn't been joking. At any rate, her group was attentive and asked lots of questions, so she figured it went pretty well, better than yesterday's interview at least.

For a second, she squeezed her eyes shut against the vision of her contorted face as she'd struggled to explain herself to Gracie the Bitch

Belgrade. When she opened them, a guy on a skateboard was rounding the corner. He wore the usual muscle shirt. Baggy nylon basketball shorts flapped around his skinny calves and a backpack hung from one shoulder. And his hair—she imagined dreadlocks—was stuffed into one of those voluminous knit caps.

Abby eased to the right to give him room, but he continued to barrel down the middle of the sidewalk. "Hey," she shouted, but he neither slowed down nor moved over. Abby pulled as far to the right as she dared and stopped, preparing herself for the collision. At the last minute, the guy veered slightly then sailed off the curb without a glance in her direction.

"Asshole!" she yelled, but he was already out of earshot. She looked around to see if anyone had witnessed this near assault, but the only people about were across the street and oblivious. "What am I, invisible?" Slowly, she continued down the sidewalk, heart beating out of her chest, the familiar ache in her throat.

• • •

Rita was working at the computer when Abby entered the front door, still a bit flushed from her encounter with the skateboard guy. "How'd the training go?" she asked without looking up from the keyboard.

"Fine."

"You sound pissed."

"Just now, a guy on a skateboard nearly drove me off the sidewalk. It was like I was fucking invisible."

Rita nodded. "We are, apparently. Gotta drive defensively." Her fingers paused over the keyboard. "Hey, did you hear about the gimp that was murdered, William Strand. Wasn't he a client of ours?"

"Not quite. He was the one that bailed when he found out we charge for our services. Remember?"

"Oh, yeah. A nasty tempered *cabrón*, as I recall. Even so, a guy in a wheelchair? Was he robbed?"

Abby shrugged. "They didn't say on the news. But a guy like that, in-your-face angry and belligerent. Maybe it was a robbery, or maybe somebody just had enough of him."

"Maybe it was someone who just hated gimps."

Abby thought about the skateboard guy. "I guess that's possible. What do you think it means to have *obvious signs of trauma*?"

"I guess it means he wasn't shot, which makes it even more creepy somehow. Anyway, I'm packing heat."

"You're what?"

Rita pulled up her blouse, revealing a pink-handled small revolver snugged into a holster strapped over her lacy black camisole.

"Oh my God, a gun! Do you even know how to use that thing?"

"It's not just a gun, *mija*. It's a Ladysmith 38-caliber air weight snubnosed revolver. Isn't it cute? And yes, I know how to use it. Actually, I'm a pretty good shot. Since my divorce, I've been keeping it in the nightstand by my bed, but after hearing about Strand, I decided to start carrying it. Considering how you like to buzz around town at all hours of the day and night, I think you should get a gun too."

She had a sudden image of herself pointing a gun at the skateboard guy. Would that have made her visible? She shook her head. "If I had a gun, I'd probably end up shooting myself in the foot."

"You could learn. And of course, you'd need a permit, but that's no problem."

"I don't think so. I've got this depth perception thing. Besides, I hate guns and I'd appreciate it if you'd pull your blouse down. Even with the pink handle, just looking at that thing makes my stomach flip."

• • •

Rita and Honey left shortly after noon for a hair appointment. Now Abby stared at the desk in dismay. Rita had a high tolerance for clutter, and the desk they sometimes shared was covered with an assortment of knickknacks and mail, opened and unopened. An anemic African violet in a ceramic duck pot perched on one corner, and an angel-studded frame containing a photo of Rita's seven grandchildren, dark eyed cuties all, was on the other. An emergency stack of Rita's romance novels lived in the bottom drawer of the desk.

Abby was about to deal with the mail when the automatic door whooshed and an anorexic looking young woman in purple leggings entered the office. A great volume of yellow hair was stacked carelessly on top of her head and she wore too much eye makeup. She wiggled her fingers in a timid little wave and smiled. "Abigail Bannister?"

"That's me. How may I help you?"

"My name is Anûshka Sryezkeptch," she said in heavily accented English. "I saw you on the television news last night."

She felt the heat crawl up her throat. "Ah." Forcing a smile, she nodded. "The interview."

"Yes, and I am wondering if you are to be so good to help me with employment."

"Well you see Ms. Sryezkeptch… am I saying that correctly?"

"Yes, exactly, but please to call me Anûshka."

"Well you see, Anûshka, GSG…"

"Yes, Gimps Serving Gimps, such a clever name."

"Well, the 'gimp' part means we only offer our services to the physically or mentally challenged"

"But that is me exactly. I have only one eye." She leaned forward. "I bet you cannot guess which one is not for real."

Abby studied the woman's eyes. "You have a very interesting accent, by the way. Where are you from?"

"I am from Croatia." She said the word as if she had a bit of phlegm caught in her throat. "You know where is Croatia?"

Abby nodded. "On the Adriatic Sea. Part of the former Yugoslavia."

"Exactly, yes. Most people do not know where is my country. Oh how I miss the sea. It is so blue, the Adriatic, and the beaches all little white pebbles, so beautiful."

"I've seen pictures."

"In my country I was excellent gymnast. I start at age 4 so I would be to go Olympics and get gold medal, then be coach of gymnast for employment, but when was 16, I poke the eyeball in accident on balance beam. After loss of eye, I no more can go on balance beam or the uneven parallel bars, even the floor routine it was too much."

"Because of your vision?

"No. It was because I lost my, how do you say it, my nervous?"

"You had to quit being a gymnast, because you lost your nerve?"

"Exactly. You must be fearless to be gymnast and after accident, I lost my fearless. Worst thing I also lost my coach. He was like a father to me and more. I have long sad story, but now I come to the United States, here to Tucson where is brother and family to get good job."

"It was your right eye."

"Exactly," she said brushing her right temple with her fingertips. "How do you guess?"

"Only your left eye blinks."

Anûshka laughed. "Oh yes. People think I am giving them the wink. But it is such embarrassing when I'm kissing guy. I forget to close right eye. It is real off turner." She reached over and began to straighten the stack of mail on the desk.

"What are you doing?"

The woman tucked her hands behind her and stepped back. "Oh, so sorry. I cannot help but make straight. Am what you call neat nook. And your desk." She shook her head. "It gives me pain in my head."

"Yes, well my secretary and I are not neat nooks. But I must say other than the loss of an eye, you seem to be fully capable physically and mentally."

"True, but I am also readless and writeless, which is bigtime gimp. I go to school like all children but I cannot learn this. Not so important for gymnast to read and write, but for job it is too much difficult to get without. Back in Croatia there is no work, so I leave baby girl with mother. Now I need job so I can send money for my baby. You want to see picture?"

The woman riffled through an enormous faux alligator skin bag and pulled out a little rhinestone-studded album. She stroked it lovingly then passed it to Abby.

Rather than a toddler, Abby was surprised to see a dozen pictures of a little girl who was plump at age 3 and fat by age 12, she estimated. She studied the woman again; she didn't seem old enough to have a 12-year-old daughter. "Very pretty. What's her name?"

"Sonia. Look at that face." Anûshka beamed. She is my… It is for her I do everything."

Abby's cellphone chimed. She looked at the number. "Excuse me, this will only take a moment. "Hey Josh, I'm with a client. Yes, I know, but I got busy. You saw the interview? Well thanks, that's nice to hear. Ah yes. I will just as soon as I… Yes, I suppose I can do that. I'll be here until 4."

Damn, she thought, dropping the phone back into her pouch. Her brother had a decent job as a mechanic at Precision Toyota. They must pay well. Why did he always need a loan? More to the point, why did she always give it to him? She turned her attention back to Anûshka. "Have you ever been employed?"

"Oh yes. In my country I work at bakery counter. Now I have job at J.J.'s Playroom. You know it?"

Abby nodded. She imagined the whole town probably knew J.J's, one of the oldest strip clubs in Tucson.

"Am very excellent pole dancer. I demonstrate." She stepped back from the desk, and effortlessly lifted her right leg until her calf was next to her ear. From there she slid into the Chinese splits, flat chest on the floor."

"Amazing."

"Ah, but there is more." Shifting her weight to her forearms, she arched her back, bringing her legs over her head. Smiling, she continued her arch until her feet were planted on either side of her head. This progressed effortless into a back bend. Once again upright, she fluffed her hair.

"My."

"Exactly." She brushed her palms on her leggings, leaving behind dusty smudges against the purple. She frowned. "Is dirty, the floor."

"Sorry. As I said, we're not much for housekeeping around here. So you're currently employed. Pole dancers make pretty good money, right?"

"Some yes, me no," She shrugged her shoulders. When I dance, the mens say rude remarks. "Which is girl, which is pole," they yell, like this is big ha, ha, ha. They do not care about my splendid ableness to split my legs in three directions and bend my back until head is between feet. No all they care is tits and ass, of which I have too little."

"I see."

"So you will help to find good job for support my angel?"

"Do you have other skills besides your gymnastic ability?"

"I am clean."

"And can you cook?"

"You are fooling? Look at me. Food terrifies me. When was gymnast, my beloved coach tell me always, 'Anûshka, you must be thin to win.'"

Abby wondered if her beloved coach fathered her beloved daughter, not that it was any of her business. "Can you drive?"

"I am excellent driver, but no car."

"Driver's license?"

"I cannot pass test."

Abby drew a stack of cards from the desk drawer. She shuffled through them and handed one to Anûshka. This organization is called Literacy Connects. It can help you pass your driver's test, and if you want to learn to read, it can help with that too. Call them. The number is there. Make an appointment. It's free."

"Is free?"

Abby nodded. "Come back and see me when you have a driver's license and we'll talk about a job. Oh yes. Do you have a green card?"

"Of course I have."

Of course. The blond ones always did.

• • •

At 3:45 Abby pulled out a little wad of ready cash from her pouch. There were two twenties, two tens and a five, peeled off two twenties and a ten and placed them between the pages of *How to Craft Your Life*. Now she could honestly claim that fifteen dollars was all the cash she had in her pouch. One problem solved.

The other problem was stickier. Why did she continue to lend Josh money? He was a smoothie, always promising to pay her back, and with Skinnerian operant conditioning, sometimes actually did. But that wasn't it. The truth was that she didn't want to risk alienating him. He was the only family she had. Her mother, she struggled to remember, her father, she struggled to forget, and both were long dead. She did have a cousin somewhere who was probably still alive, but that didn't count because she hadn't seen Fey in ... well it had been over 20 years.

Cousin Fey. Her mother must have been an alcoholic or a drug addict. Why else would a woman allow her 13-year-old daughter to move in with strangers, related yes, but strangers still. Shortly after Abby's mother had died, Fey came to live with them to help with her personal care, Abby assumed, though she couldn't remember anyone ever telling her this. What she did remember was that for two years they had shared a room. Fey was an athletic tomboy and Abby had loved her like a big sister. Then one day, Fey simply didn't come home from school. There was no good-by, no note of explanation, just gone. After that, neither her father nor Josh ever mentioned her. It was like Fey never existed, but for Abby, it was like losing her mother all over again, tearing open again the big gaping hole in her chest. It had taken years for that hole to seal over. Cousin Fey. To this day, she felt a vague uneasiness every time she thought of her.

Again, she looked at her watch. Josh should have been here by now. She took a deep, exasperated breath and reached for her copy of *How to Craft Your Life*. Chapter 2 insisted that she was responsible for her own happiness. In theory, she agreed with that.

Do you want to be invited to a party or the movies? Dale J. Nagery inquired. *Turn that around and ask that special someone to go see the latest blockbuster that no one seems to want to miss.*

Who would she like to go to the movies with? There was always Rita or Robert, but that was the central problem, wasn't it? Other than her two best friends, there was no special someone, as DJN put it.

At the dot of 4, Josh came rushing in. Always rushing, Josh. She slid the book back into the carryall and smiled up at her handsome brother.

"Hey, babe," he said, planting a kiss on her cheek.

He was older by four years, but people always thought the reverse was the case, a fact that grated. His hair was still full and dark, while more and more gray hairs corkscrewed though hers. She already had crinkles in the corners of her eyes and two shallow trenches in between. His face was smooth and graced with a carefree smile, which he flashed at her now, big, straight white teeth gleaming. Shark-like, it occurred to her just then.

It must be marijuana, she concluded, that was keeping him young and broke, and she'd been footing the bill. She straightened herself in her chair, squared her shoulders to the degree that they could be squared. Well not anymore.

"Saw you on the news last night." He dropped into a chair, his body lithe and muscular, an antithesis to her own. "You really gave it to that bitch. What's her face? I never did like her. But you were great!"

Absurdly grateful, she could feel her resentment and resolve drain away like dishwater.

Chapter 3

Saturday, Oct. 8

Rita ferried the elderly Dodge Caravan, which she called the Iceberg for its sheer, white enormity, down Avenida Alvaro Obregón, the main southbound drag of Nogales, Arizona. It was a busy but dowdy little city that seemed mired in the '50s, with an ad hoc, Band-Aid approach to city planning resulting in a chaos of one-way streets. Even with the windows closed, the very air vibrated with the brasses of Norteño music blasting from the little shops along streets crowded with Saturday shoppers. Gripping the steering wheel, Rita pulled into the public parking lot closest to the Mexican border and the first available handicapped parking space.

"*Ay qué chingadero*! We made it, *gracias a Dios*." She sat back and closed her eyes.

"Good job," Abby said, sharing her friend's relief, though for the past 10 minutes her own eyes had been tight shut and she didn't know what kind of a job Rita had actually done. It was enough that they had arrived once again at the crossing between Nogales, Arizona, and Nogales, Sonora, unscathed.

Rita pushed a button. The side door creaked open and the ramp unfolded like the tongue of a great robotic dog. The two released their chairs from the clamps that held them in place. Abby had been riding shotgun, and it took her a few moments to position her chair for her descent. Before long, both women were headed for Mexico, SENTRI cards safely in the passport holders they carried tucked inside their T-shirts along with insurance and credit cards in case of emergency.

When they began their Saturday visits to Santa Clara Hospital last year, the two women had determined that it was worth the trouble and expense to get the SENTRI, or so-called Trusted Traveler Passes, to make the crossing hassle free.

The cityscape quickly changed once they were on the Mexican side, everything deteriorating by degrees the farther they got from the fence. Santa Clara was only 10 minutes by wheelchair from the border. The sidewalks were so cracked and crowded they were impossible to navigate so the two proceeded in high gear down the right side of the street, flags waving bravely in the exhaust-clogged air. By ones and twos a group of dark little boys and girls assembled. Windshield washers, sellers of Chiclets and bright arrays of gaudy trinkets, they began to swirl around the two women, touching their arms, tugging on their guilt strings. This was the gauntlet they always faced.

• • •

A stocky man whose only distinguishing feature was a hairline that started in the middle of his forehead, watched the two *lisiadas* from across the street, had been watching them, for weeks, in fact, as they made their way back and forth across *la frontera*. It was his job to watch, and now he motioned to a boy who looked about 10 but had the swagger of a surly teen. The boy was handsome and there were deep dimples at the corners of his mouth, as if his sly smile were a parenthetical phrase. The two engaged in a brief conversation, then he handed the boy a metal cylinder. About the size of a can of hairspray, it was equipped with a strong magnet and a GPS tracker. A smile played at the man's lips as he watched the boy run to join the children circling the crazy women, *pobrecitas*.

• • •

When Abby and Rita reached the doors to the hospital, they began to hand out the balloons, pencils, plastic barrettes and strips of stickers they'd gotten free at Trader Joe's. They tried to place one item in the hand of each child, but the clamoring mass made the task nearly impossible. When all the gifts had been distributed, Abby noticed a latecomer standing to the side, a shy smile on his handsome face. Abby gestured for him to come over. From her pouch, she extracted a ballpoint pen and handed it to the boy. In his excitement, he dropped the pen. Instantly, he was on his knees searching beneath her chair. After a moment, he rose, waving the pen in triumph.

"*Muchas gracias, Señora,*" he said, shy smile transformed into a big grin revealing two deep dimples, and then he was off.

• • •

The interior of the hospital was cool and bright, with tiled floors burnished by thousands and thousands of moppings. A bloodied and anguished plaster Christ hung from his cross on one side of the entry, a painting of a clueless Madonna gazing lovingly upon the baby Jesus on the other. Sor Juana, a slender young woman with beautiful skin and one eye that veered slightly off center, smiled broadly as they whirred up to the front desk.

"*Buenos diás, Sor Juana. Comó está?*" In college, Abby had double-minored in Spanish and American Sign Language.

"*Bien, bien, gracias a Dios, y ustedes?*" she said, nudging the sign-in sheet toward them.

"*Estamos bien, gracias a Dios.*" She and Rita answered nearly in tandem. From Abby's point of view, God had nothing to do with it, but when in Rome …

The two signed their names on the sheet and headed to the elevator. It was an elderly affair. The gate clanged shut, then rattled, both women white-knuckling it as it bumped slowly up to the third floor, which housed children so disfigured or debilitated by birth defects, disease, fire and misfortune that no one could or would care for them. For many, it was all they'd ever known.

Abby extended her foot and they powered though the double swinging doors into a vast room with row upon row of cribs, each home to a child. As they passed, an emaciated arm stuck though the bars.

Rita could have a hard edge, but Abby watched the woman's face soften as she took the child's hand.

"*Hola, Teresa. Hola chula,*" Rita crooned. The child looked to be no more than 3, but they knew her to be 8. The girl's gleaming brown eyes locked on Rita's as she wrapped her spindly fingers around the woman's hand. A bib caught the saliva that dipped from her chin. It was wet and gave off a faintly putrid smell.

This room, with its dozens of cribs, was where Rita would pass the next three hours, moving from child to child, greeting each by name in a sweet singsong, changing bibs and diapers where needed, stroking faces, arms, legs. Where allowed, she'd take a baby or a child from a crib to rock in her arms.

Abby continued on to the next room with its wall of windows where the more able children spent the day. Children sat in wheelchairs arrayed along the walls, leaving the center of the room open for play or exercise. Several children were splayed on mats waiting for their turn with Sor Felipa, and whatever helper was on hand, to provide them with the few minutes of physical therapy they received each day.

The moment Abby entered the room a boy greeted her with a broad smile. Alfonso had a long face and a slightly crooked jaw with the barest wisp of facial hair. His legs were stubby and his torso torqued to the right. Like the drunken sailor, he listed and roiled over to her now.

"Good morning, Miss Abby." With long sinewy arms, he swung himself onto her lap as if this were his due. "How are you today?"

"Very well, thank you, and you?" She'd been teaching Alfonso English and he was proving to be a fast learner.

"Very well. May I to drive the Chariot today?"

"Go for it," she said, and he carefully directed the chair toward a small group of children assembled around a table. Some wore hearing aids, all had speech problems so severe they could not communicate their simplest needs. They were waiting for her.

"*Hola, niños*, Abby said, making a gesture that looked like a little salute. Several children made the hello sign; others waved convulsively, arching in their wheelchairs. All were delighted to see her.

As Abby had learned, signing was good exercise, good for their breathing, and the first song of the day was always *Las Mañanitas*, the birthday song, just in case it was some one's special day. In the corner was an easel with the words in large print. Alfonso hopped off Abby's lap and pulled it over to the table. His job was to point to each word while Abby signed.

"*Estas son las mañanitas que cantaba el rey David*," she began in her clear warble. Though their words sounded like babble, the little group was surprisingly on key.

On the agenda for the day was *Make Way for Ducklings* and the sign for happy. Most had already learned the sign for duck, since the book was an old favorite, as well as the signs for thirsty, hungry, toilet and I love you. A few, like Alfonso, had mastered the entire alphabet, could finger spell a bit and carry on a simple conversation. If Abby allowed her mind to dwell on it, it was the lost potential of these children that could bring her to tears.

The sisters at Santa Clara's were gentle and efficient and terribly overworked. Certainly, Abby found great satisfaction in helping them, and working with the children was a joy, but it was a joy tempered by stark reality. Despite everyone's efforts, the fact was that almost no child on the third floor left the hospital, ever, unless they died.

Abby found the book on the shelf where she'd left it last week. When the children saw it, several brought their hand, right or left, whichever worked the best, up to their mouths and opened and closed their fingers and thumb, like the bill of a quacking duck.

"*Abran Paso a Los Patitos*," Alfonso read, holding up the book so the children could see the picture of Mrs. Duck crossing a busy street with her eight ducklings on the cover.

Abby signed each word then asked in Spanish. "*Cuantos patitos miran?*"

The children held up eight fingers, and Alfonso turned to the first page.

"*El Señor Pato y su señora buscaban un lugar para vivir,*" he read as Abby signed.

When they finished the book, Abby raised her eyebrows in a question, made a fist with thumb inserted between the first and second fingers, the letter t, and jiggled it. In response, heads shook side to side. If anyone had to go to the bathroom, they weren't admitting it.

• • •

The third hour on the third flood was Abby's favorite. These children were a bit older. Three were blind, but otherwise healthy and ambulatory, two had significant facial disfigurements, several had issues involving tubes and catheters. One little girl had been fed acid as a toddler and had a feeding tube in her stomach. A graduate of Group 1, she couldn't talk, but was otherwise bright, alert and now able to communicate using sign language.

These children could learn, but as far as Abby could tell, there wasn't much money to spend on their education. As far as she could tell, there wasn't much money to spend on anything. Once she and Rita had been invited to sit down with the sisters for their midday meal. If the quantity and the quality of food served was any indication, the good sisters strictly obeyed their vow of poverty.

After the children had sung *Las Mañanitas*, she took out her well-worn Spanish edition of Charlotte's Web, *La Telaraña de Carlota*, and handed it to Alfonso to read aloud as she signed. They were quite an effective duo, she and Alfonso.

• • •

When it was time to go, Alfonso swung onto her lap and directed the chair toward the door. "Today, Miss Abby, I will go home with you, okay?"

"Not okay, Alfonso," she said forcing a chuckle. They had this conversation every visit and Abby acted like it was an old joke, except she knew that it wasn't.

Deep Breathing

"Is okay," Alfonso insisted. "Take me and I help you."

"It is against the law for me to take you."

"People come here, once in a while they do, and they take a kid home with them. You could take me to your beautiful *casa* in Tucson."

"My *casa* is not beautiful," she said firmly. "It is very small and ugly. There is no place for you to sleep."

"But you have a *bañera*, yes?"

"Yes, I have a bathtub."

"I sleep in your bathtub."

She laughed then. She always laughed. There was no other way to respond.

• • •

Flashing their SENTRI passes, Abby and Rita whirred back through the pedestrian crossing with a wave and a smile. In the parking lot, Rita flipped the switch by the side door and the robot dog rolled out its tongue. It was always a relief to get back to the Iceberg.

Once in the car, the women headed directly for Zula's diner.

"I was talking to Sor Filipa," Rita said as she ferried the Iceberg down the street.

"And what did the good sister have to say?"

"She said you let Alfonso ride on your lap."

"I do."

"Well, she thinks he's too big for that. How old is he anyway?"

"Thirteen going on 10. But the big thrill is not sitting on my lap; it's the Chariot. I let him drive."

"I'm sure he loves that, but I raised two sons and I have to say, Sor Felipa has a point. Baby boys have erections, they play with their pee-pees as soon as they can find them, and it just gets worse from there. By the time they are 13, the hormonal overload is so intense it oozes through their pores. That's why teenage boys have zits."

Abby laughed. "You are such a liar."

"A slight exaggeration only."

"So what am I supposed to do the next time he crawls up into my lap?"

"Tell him the truth. He's getting too big."

Abby supposed that she could and probably should do just that, but the prospect of robbing Alfonso of the simple pleasure of operating her chair just intensified her sense of the extreme limits imposed on the children of Santa Clara. For many, like Alfonso, the limitations weren't inherent in the challenges they were born with but in the lack of a vision that it could be any other way. "Sor Felipa's probably right. It's just that …"

They exchanged looks in the rear view mirror.

"I know," Rita said. "I know."

Despite Abby's best efforts, her mouth pulled down at the corners and her chin quivered. She rolled down the window and took a deep gulp of carbon-saturated air. Radios blasted cumbias and corridos from storefronts and the sidewalks were packed with people rushing to complete lunchtime business. Alfonso. She wished she could take him home to her beautiful casa in Tucson.

• • •

Zula's had been serving up good plain food to the people of Nogales for decades, and Abby and Rita were regulars.

It was past the lunch rush and a tall woman with a white apron tied around her substantial girth appeared instantly at their table, coffee pot held aloft. "*Buenas tardes, hermanas.*" She poured a cup for Rita. "The usual?"

"The usual," they said.

Rita laced her coffee with cream then added two packets of Splenda. Stirring, she said, "I've been thinking. You know what I really want to do?"

Abby raised her eyebrows in encouragement.

"I want to go to France and take a barge trip down the Seine. They've got boats with gimp accommodations. I'll have my picture taken with the captain, if he's handsome, and post pictures on Facebook so my ex and his little cabrona will see them."

"If you can afford that, I'm paying you too much."

"If I actually had to live off what you pay me, I'd be homeless. No, I've got the money; I just have to get up the nerve. And you know what other crazy thing I've been thinking of? Legs. The other day I saw a guy walking down the street, not just walking, but walking fast. He was wearing Bermuda shorts and had two prosthetic legs. I couldn't tell if he had knees or not, and I certainly wasn't going to stop and ask. Anyway, I thought I could do that. The guy was pretty young, so maybe I wouldn't be able to walk so easily, maybe I'd need a walker or a cane at first. What do you think?"

"I think it's a great idea."

"Yeah? So if I got new legs could I still keep my job?"

"Rita, if you grew new legs you could still keep your job. GSG couldn't function without you. I couldn't function without you."

"Yeah?" she smiled. She took a deep breath and dabbed her eyes with a napkin. "That's nice to hear. And what about you, *mija*? What wild and crazy thing do you really want?"

Abby pondered that for a moment. "I guess I want to make a living. I want to work with the kids at Santa Clara's." She shrugged. "Just want to keep on keeping on, as they say."

"That's it?"

"More or less." And it was true. She liked her work, was proud of it. She liked her independence, her funky little house, loved her cat. Day to day life was … mostly satisfying. No, she figured that it was more about what she didn't want. What she didn't want was to live her life alone and die alone, but that was too depressing to share, and way too ungrateful given their morning among kids who had so little in their lives but responded to the least bit of attention with joy and appreciation. She would do well to follow their example and vowed, as she so often did, to do so.

At that moment, the waitress arrived with two big slices of apple pie a la mode. With the first bite, Abby's blue mood went up with the steam from hot, cinnamon-spiced apple meeting cold vanilla ice cream. And that was precisely why she and Rita always ended a morning spent at Santa Clara's at Zulas.

Chapter 4

Monday, Oct. 17

The radio blasted morning news, Abby's 6 a.m. wakeup call. She half-listened to the weather report, sunny with a high of 92, and ignored the traffic report. One advantage of being carless was that she didn't have to worry about things like road repair, radar checkpoints, accidents and stalled vehicles.

Tito, who always slept next to her head, stretched then took a leisurely stroll down her back before jumping off the bed, her cue to get moving. For a moment Abby lay there, simply gearing up for the day. Another Monday, she thought, as if the day of the week mattered.

For as long as she could remember, Abby had slept on her stomach, head faced to the wall. This one was papered with a cheery floral pattern, her selection. She gazed at that pattern now, a little garden on the wall, as she steeled herself to get out of bed. Inhaling deeply, she rolled from her stomach to her back to her left side, then exhaled. After another deep breath, she grabbed the chrome bar bolted onto the wall with the Mighty Claw, and pulled herself into a sitting position.

On non-shower days, it was Abby's habit to dress her torso before going into the bathroom. She struggled out of the T-shirt that served as nightgown. A three-foot-long grabber hung from a hook by her bed. She used it to snatch a pink sports bra from the pile of clean clothes on the manual chair at the foot of her bed. She used this chair when the Chariot was on the blink or on a rare night out with Robert or on the even rarer date because it could be collapsed and put in the trunk of a car. Mostly it served as a handy place to stack her clean clothes.

She'd never been able to manage the hooks on a regular bra; the sports bra could be pulled over her head. She paused a moment to gather strength. "God is with you," Pastor Glorie often told her. She shook her head. If this were true, then God was a real comedian. She had breasts most women would envy, but from the day they first erupted—practically overnight—they'd been just one more challenge.

She put her contrary left arm into the bra first, then her right. With the Mighty Claw, she tugged the thing over her head. Despite the cool morning, she'd begun to sweat. Corralling these dogies singlehandedly into a bra was a chore that would tax a seasoned cowpoke, she thought, as she wrestled first one breast then the other into place. Next she grabbed a black knit tunic, one of several nearly identical jerseys, all in dark colors, from the stack and pulled it over her head.

She rested a few beats, inhaled, then grabbed the arm of the Chariot, again with right hand. After several attempts, she grasped the other chair arm with her left hand. Deep breath now. Using both arms, she hauled herself to her feet, executed a tortured pivot, which she accomplished by twisting her torso and hips until her legs had no choice but to follow, then dropped her butt into the chair. Panting lightly, she recalled a recent conversation she'd had with Rita who was complaining about putting on weight.

"You're so trim. What do you do for exercise?" She had asked.

"I get out of bed." Abby had answered.

Unplugging her chair from the charger, Abby chuckled. Rita had thought she was kidding.

Perspiration beaded her brow as she headed for the bathroom. This is how she started each day.

• • •

Abby opened the front door. There was a cord attached to the outside knob. Before going all the way out, she put the cord between her teeth, whirred through then pulled the door closed with a yank of her head. It was a method she'd devised when she first moved into a dorm at the university. Ten years later, it still served.

At 8:45 she whirred onto Fourth Avenue right on schedule. The sky was dotted with small, puffy clouds. She squinted against the sunlight glinting off the cars parked along the street. As far as she knew there was nothing of great import going on today. She'd lined up someone who was interested in the condo and needed to call Lane's Reality and see if it was still available. There was an appointment with a potential new client. Rita had done the telephone intake on that one.

And then there was the current remodel she needed to check on again. The contractor, this one was called Frank somebody, was one in a string of contractors she'd used, and he was proving to be just as unsatisfactory as the others. It seemed the so-called able bodied didn't understand that "standard" just wouldn't cut it. One client might need a grab bar attached horizontally, another vertically or diagonally, and another might do best with a trapeze arrangement. One person might need a toilet lowered; another might need it raised. And that was just the bathroom. Abby had to watch over Frank's every modification to ensure he was doing it the way the client needed it to be done. If he told her one more time, "This is the way I always install them" she would go for his throat.

When she turned onto Ash, chair in high gear, it occurred to her that she had accomplished everything that she had dreamed of as a teen living a life constrained by cerebral palsy and the low expectations of her father and teachers. Despite everything, she'd finished college, gotten a job, owned her own home and was now the head of a company. Never mind that GSG was barely able to cover expenses, she was in charge. Why then, did she so often feel... What did she feel? Frustrated definitely, but probably lonely and unfulfilled as well, maybe all of that rolled into a hard little ball of discontent. Possibly she was just tired. In any case, the week loomed before her like a wide-open, mostly empty landscape.

As she turned onto Sixth Street she remembered the children at Santa Clara and chided herself for her lack of appreciation. It was a beautiful morning, after all, and who knew what the day might bring. In the near distance a lush, golden-skinned woman gazed down upon her. Painted on the side of the old Tucson Warehouse and Transfer Company building, she wore little but an agave on her head like a crown and an enigmatic expression on her lips. Not quite a smile, it sometimes struck Abby as seductive; sometimes it seemed like a petulant sneer. At the moment, it seemed more an expression of yearning.

The light at Stone and Sixth was red. Abby was ordering her to do list when she heard the click-clicking of wheels on concrete. She looked over her shoulder and there he was, same baggy shorts, same knit cap, coming up behind her, fast. God, not again, she thought, automatically scrunching her shoulders, as the skateboarder whizzed by so close she could feel the breeze of his passing on her face, red light be damned. Her heart raced. Who is that person, she thought, and what does he get from scaring the shit out of me?

• • •

Rita was getting caught up on the accounts when Abby whirred in.

"You're in early," Abby observed.

"Somebody has to get some work done around here," Rita said without looking up from the computer. Along with the printer, fax machine and microwave oven, it perched on a counter that spanned the room's width. Below it was a custom kick space that allowed for Rita and her wheelchair.

"Here." She held out a jar of Skippy extra crunchy peanut butter. "I couldn't have breakfast until you got here. Wow. You look whiter than usual. Are you feeling okay?"

"I was nearly run over by a maniac skateboarder, but other than that I'm okay." Using her Mighty Claw, Abby opened the jar with ease, alerting Honey, who'd been dozing in her little bed under the desk. She handed the jar back to Rita as the dog danced over, nails clicking on the cement floor.

Rita took out a spoon from her top draw and dipped it into the jar.

"You really need to start eating better." Abby put her lunch, a carton of yogurt and a banana, in the little fridge that hummed ominously beneath the counter. "Yuck. Somebody needs to clean this refrigerator!"

"Sorry, *mija*, you don't pay me enough," Rita said around a mouthful of peanut butter. "And you have no room to criticize the way I eat. Every day it's the same for you, yogurt and bananas, bananas and yogurt," she said, spreading peanut butter on a flour tortilla. "Want one?"

"No thanks. I've already eaten a well-balanced breakfast."

"Yeah? And what did you eat? Yogurt and a banana, right?"

"Toast and a poached egg."

"Liar. Speaking of poor diets, my sister-in-law made green corn tamales last weekend—she sells them out of her car in the Safeway parking lot because that *flojo* brother of mine lost his job AGAIN. She's a *cabrona*, but she makes the best tamales. Anyway there are a dozen in the freezer for you."

"Yum! How much do I owe you?"

"*Nada, mija*. My treat."

"Thanks, Rita. You're too good to me."

"*De nada.*" She broke off a piece of peanut butter slathered tortilla and offered it to Honey. "And don't forget you've got that 9:30 appointment with that guy." She checked the desk calendar. "Peter Valenzuela. Said he saw the interview last week, so that's good, right?"

Abby sighed. "I guess."

Just then the front door whooshed open and a very tall, very broad man with sparse whiskers on a dark, pockmarked face entered. A thick, black braid snaked down his back. "Mornin' ladies." He touched the brim of his cap with its John Deere logo. "I'm Peter Valenzuela. I've got an appointment with Abigail Bannister." His speech was softly clipped in the manner peculiar to those raised on the Tohono O'odham reservation.

Honey made a brief inspection, sniffing at the man's deeply cuffed Levis, before returning to her station under the desk.

Deep Breathing

"That was Honey. She's a ... service dog." Abby pushed her glasses to the top of her head and whirred over to greet him. "And I'm Abigail Bannister." She offered her hand.

He held it briefly in a loose grasp. "Nice to meet you, ma'am."

"Please have a seat," Abby said, taking her position behind her desk.

The man grunted as he folded himself into the chair.

"So how can I help you?"

He shrugged. "Used to drive a school bus on the reservation. Got something called macular degeneration. Ever hear of it, ma'am?"

Even though the man was sitting, Abby had to crane her neck to look him in the eye. "Yes, I've heard of macular degeneration."

He nodded. "I didn't want to come here, but my wife bullied me into it."

"Your wife bullied you, Mr. Valenzuela? That's hard to imagine."

"She bullies me with her sweet talk, my wife." Though he didn't smile his eyes were filled with amusement. "Anyway, she saw you on the news the other day and thought you might be able to help me find a new job."

"We might be able to help you with that. So tell me Mr. Valenzuela..."

"Um." He leaned forward, scratching at his chin. "Do you think you could call me Pete?"

She smiled. "Sure, if you'll stop calling me ma'am. Most people just call me Abby."

The man nodded. "It's Abby, then." He settled back in the chair.

"So tell me, Pete, how long did you drive a school bus?"

"Over 10 years. Before that I made deliveries for UPS. For now, I can still drive, but not for a living."

"Okay. So besides driving professionally, what kinds of things are you good at?"

"As you can see, I like to eat, so I'm good at cooking, traditional foods mostly, fry bread, green chili stew. Ever eat the buds from a cholla cactus?"

"Never."

"You pick the flower buds before they open and add them to stews or whatever. I like to pickle 'em. And I keep a garden. It's a good garden, the three sisters like it there." Again the wry smile.

"The three sisters?"

"Beans, squash, corn. I grow 'em, plus tomatoes and melons. Pretty much, whatever likes the weather in Tucson, I can grow. Got me a fig tree, a quince and a Mexican lime too."

Abby nodded. "Cooking, gardening, those are good skills to have."

"But can I get me a job, you know, with this macular thing? I've got a daughter in high school and one who's a freshman at the U. of A. Evalinda's got a scholarship, but there are still plenty costs involved. And there's my mother. The wife works for the tribe, but you know these days it's just not enough with one income. So what do you think?"

"I don't know, Pete. Have you been out to the Mission Gardens? It's part of the new historical district?"

"Been meaning to."

"You might offer to volunteer there. At least, it would be a foot in the door."

Volunteer. It was often what she told her clients to do when she couldn't think of anything else. It wasn't bad advice, but Abby felt she should have been able to come up with something better. Fact was, she had zero experience with people who were blind or, in Pete's case, perhaps about to be.

As soon as Pete left, she picked up the phone and dialed. While a disembodied voice ran through her options, she considered Pete's situation. Abby had given him the card of her ophthalmologist. Somewhere she'd read that macular degeneration could be treated with lasers. And if he volunteered his time at the Mission Gardens, it might open up some opportunities. If they were hiring, surely a person from the O'odham nation with his experience would have an advantage.

"You've reached the voice mail of…" Abby left a message and hung up. "Damn. She'd wanted to talk with someone at Pima County Rehabilitation Center to see what they might offer. In addition to a job, what Pete most needed was the training that would best prepare him for eventual blindness.

• • •

She and Rita had spent the better part of the afternoon at the South Tucson remodel. Today the workers pulled up the old wall-to-wall shag rug. The plan had been to replace it with polished concrete, a surface that was relatively cheap and held up well to wheelchair traffic, but under the carpet was a hardwood floor, so they would go with that. She had promised her client, a diabetic gentleman who'd already lost a foot to infection and was about to lose another, that the place would be ready for him and his family when he got out of the hospital. Prospects looked dim, but at the moment there was nothing more she could do about it.

She was about close up shop when a woman from Pima Rehabilitation finally returned her call. Now dusk was already settling as she headed for home, frozen green corn tamales wrapped in a plastic grocery bag perched on her lap. Tonight, she'd have something to eat other than the usual scrambled eggs and tossed salad.

Just as she was leaving the building, Pastor Glorie and five of her acolytes hustled down the corridor, each carrying a stack of big white boxes. Abby thought to slip back into her own office, but Glorie was already waving. Abby sighed. There was no way to avoid an encounter.

Next to Abby in her black pants and gray tunic, the woman looked like a large tropical bird as she charged down the hall, clunky faux diamond pendent bouncing upon substantial bosoms. Today, she was wearing a bright floral blouse and stretch jeans that fit like the casings on bratwursts. A large magenta silk flower was stuck into a purple crochet cloche and a trailing scarf, also purple crochet, completed the plumage.

"Hey girl," Glorie squealed, full of purpose as always. She planted a big kiss on Abby's cheek. "Saw your interview last week. Right on, sister. You are such an inspiration." She held up her hand for a high five. Abby gave it a weak slap. With her thumb Pastor Glorie wiped her pink lipstick smear from Abby's cheek. With the same thumb she indicated her crew, dressed in clean, but rumpled second hand. "Day old doughnuts from Le Caves," she said, indicating the white boxes. "They donate them to us and we distribute them to the homeless. We're off to Veinte de Augusto Park right now. Want to come with?"

"Got to get home, Glorie. But thanks for asking."

Glorie rained down upon her a beneficent smile. "You know, Abby, it's never too late to accept Christ as your lord and master … until it is." The smile morphed into a sad little frown. "We'd love to see you at fellowship this Wednesday," she added as she and the doughnut bearers swept through the door.

• • •

As she whirred towards home, bag of frozen tamales on her lap, Abby tried to shake off her irritation. Really, couldn't Glorie simply say *Hi. How are you?* and leave it at that, like everyone else. The sweeping Piazzolla tango she was listening to just added to her tension. She took a deep breath and removed her earbuds.

Usually Abby loved this time of day, with the clear October sky and its ribbon of crimson outlining the Tucson Mountains, but in addition to her irritation, she was feeling edgy and vulnerable. How many people in wheelchairs were looking over their shoulders as a result of the murder of William Strand? Actually, it wasn't that easy for a person in a wheelchair to look over her shoulder, she thought with a mirthless chuckle as she whirred south on Seventh Street, away from the neon lights and pedestrian traffic of the hipper Fourth Avenue area.

The sky was streaked with coppery cirrus clouds as she turned onto Ash Street, empty of traffic as usual. She whirred down the middle of the alley past an abandoned warehouse surrounded by a cyclone fence topped with loops of razor wire. Leaning against the fence was a man. At her approach, he peeled himself off the fence, waving as if he knew her. She returned the greeting, but in the dim light didn't recognize him. Earlier she'd gotten $200 out of the ATM. As the guy jogged towards her she tucked her pouch down the front of her tunic and turned her chair to face him.

He was wearing a navy tracksuit with the hood pulled up over his lank brown hair. "Hey, Abigail," he said, a bit breathless.

"Do I know you?" He was standing too close to her and she wheeled back a bit to avoid staring at his navel.

He smiled. "No, but I know you and I need a favor."

Someone else who'd seen the interview, she thought, and relaxed a bit. He had a pleasant, pimple-spotted face, young, with one of those little wooly patches under his bottom lip. "What can I do for you?"

"Don't scream," he said quietly. "That's it." He lunged toward her.

Screaming, Abby grabbed the bag of frozen tamales and whacked him on the side of the head. She got in one more whack before he yanked her out of her chair.

I'm going to die, she thought, as she lay crumpled on the sidewalk, the tracksuit man kneeling beside her.

"If it's money you want it's in the pouch around my neck."

"That's not what I'm after," he said, even as his hand shot down the front of her sweater.

He's going to rape me first, then kill me, she thought. Abby grabbed his throat with her Mighty Claw. He punched her in the face, but she tightened her grip. Above the pounding blood rush in her ears, she heard the clack of wheels on concrete ricochet off the walls of the empty buildings. The skateboard guy.

Tracksuit man hit her again. Abby lost her grip, and he staggered to his feet. She heard the snick of a switchblade. Oh God, this is it, she thought, flinging her arm over her face. She heard a crack.

"Shit," tracksuit man yelled.

Another crack and another. Skateboard guy was beating on tracksuit man's head with his skateboard. Abby scrabbled onto all fours. If she could just get back into her chair.

Tracksuit man went down and skateboard guy turned his attention to Abby.

"You okay?" he asked, hoisting her into her chair.

Abby was too stunned to answer.

Skateboard guy spotted the switchblade, picked it up, closed it and tossed it to Abby. "Come on. Let's get out of here," he hissed, grabbing the back of Abby's chair.

"Go, go, go!"

Throughout the attack, Abby had been taken little more than a few sips of air. Now she sucked in a deep breath, then plunged the joystick forward to the max and the two whirred up the alley in the fading light.

∙ ∙ ∙

Hands shaking, Abby fumbled with the house key.

"Here. Let me do it," skateboard guy took the key out of her hand.

Once inside, Abby flipped on the light. "You just saved my life," she said turning to face him.

"It was kind of fun, actually." He pulled the wool cap off his head releasing ropey brown dreadlocks that sprung up like the tresses of Medusa.

For a moment Abby stared in confusion. "My God. You're a woman?"

"So I'm told. Jesus, look at your face," she said dropping her backpack on the floor.

Until that moment, Abby'd had been unaware of any pain. Now she swiped at her bloodied nose. "Ow!" She took off her glasses, which were broken at the bridge. Her left eye was nearly swollen shut. She put the glasses into her pouch and set it on a table by the door. "You okay?"

"Not a scratch." The woman smiled, revealing a logjam of discolored teeth. She took off her hoodie and stuffed it into her pack. Her complextion was chapped and ruddy like the folks who stand on the medians for hours in the sun and wind selling newpapers or carrying signs, *Will work for food*. She was wearing a dingy white muscle shirt. On her right arm, she had a full sleeve of tattoos, on her left, a rattlesnake embraced her bicep then trailed down her arm.

"I better call the police," Abby said.

"I'll get some ice for your face."

Abby shook her head. "I don't even know your name. You've been dogging me for the past week. I mean, thank God you've been dogging me, but why?"

"You don't recognize me?"

"Should I?"

"Well, it has been a long time. I'm Fey. You know, your father's sister's daughter, that Fey."

Abby studied the woman's face. Her father had a broad, flat nose. She always thought that somebody had smashed a fist into it, but here it was replicated in the middle of Fey's face like a stamp of authenticity. And she still had that tomboy, almost boyish appearance, which was heightened by her husky voice and the baggy shorts and tee.

"Fey. My God, it is you." The threat of tears made her throat ache. "Where have you been all these years?" she said, smoothing her hand down her throat to relieve the tension there.

"Around." Fey went to get the ice. "Call the cops. We can talk about it later."

•••

A gray Ford Tauras pulled up to the curb. After a few minutes, Detective Marie Stransky heaved herself out of the driver's seat and slowly propelled her bulk to Abby's door. Ice wrapped in a towel pressed to her eye, Abby opened the door and was surprised to see a woman near middle age and well advanced into pregnancy standing on the stoop. She was wearing navy pants and a matching jacket that was open over a wrinkled white maternity blouse, and she looked exhausted.

"I'm Detective Marie Stransky," the woman said, offering her hand.

"Please come in, Detective," Abby said, and whirred out of the way.

The detective glanced around the room. "It's been a long day. May I sit down?"

"Please." Despite the belly, the woman's unadorned face and hair anchored in place with bobby pins suggested a no-nonsense competence.

"I think somebody tried to kill me this evening." Tears began to well up again. "Certainly you know about the gimp, I mean the wheelchair dependent man who was…"

"That's why I'm here, Ms. Bannister."

"Well, maybe the same guy who killed William Strand attacked me."

"What makes you say so?"

"He had a knife."

"A knife?"

"A switchblade."

"Okay, but let's not jump to any conclusions."

"And he knew my name, called me Abigail."

"He knew your name? Hmm." Marie Stransky took out her notebook. "An officer has been dispatched to the scene. I need to get your statement. Would you spell your complete name for me?"

Abby spelled out her name, still holding the ice pack to her nose. It was swollen and she sounded like she had a terrible cold.

Stransky turned to Fey. "And your name please."

"Fey Lesher." She spelled out the letters.

"She's my cousin and she saved my life." Abby wanted to blow her nose, but didn't dare.

"I see." Face in neutral, Stransky looked from one woman to the other. Just then her cellphone rang. "Excuse me," she said, slipping the phone out of her jacket pocket. "Yeah. Yeah? Too bad. Okay. Okay. No. Looks like I'll be here awhile. Oh yeah?"

She dropped the phone back in her pocket. "There was some blood at the scene.

Yours, Ms. Bannister, I presume."

"His, mostly." Fey interjected.

"And Fey got this." Abby handed over the switchblade.

Stransky's eyebrows shot up. "You disarmed him?"

"Well, he dropped it when I hit him with my skateboard."

"You hit him with your skateboard. Hmm."

"And I hit him with a bag of frozen tamales, twice, but it didn't do much to stop him."

Again the detective looked from one woman to another. "Remarkable. So Ms. Bannister, tell me exactly what happened. Start at the beginning please."

• • •

Detective Stransky stood up. "I guess that's about all for now, Ms. Bannister."

Abby followed her to the door. "So he's still out there?"

"I'm afraid so," she said matter of fact.

"What's next?"

"We wait and see."

Anger sent a flush up Abby neck. "You're awfully casual about this."

"Not at all. But right now there is nothing more to do but wait." She smiled. "I know that's hard to hear."

As the detective opened the door, a cop came up the walk. "We checked out the whole area. All we found were these," he said holding up the bag of tamales.

"Those are mine! Can I have them back?"

The cop looked at Stransky. She shrugged and he handed them over.

Chapter 5

Tuesday, Oct. 18

Before she left, Detective Stransky had given each of them her card. Now the two women sat in silence. Abby, stunned and exhausted, stared into space, while Fey rooted through her backpack.

"What now?" Fey asked, pulling a sweatshirt from her pack. "I mean, I can't just leave you here alone. I should stay, at least tonight."

Abby shook her head then winced. Her eye was swollen shut, her nose throbbed and her whole face ached. She just wanted to take two Tylenols and crawl into bed. "I'll be okay. Where are you living?"

Fey stood up and started to put on the sweatshirt, then sat down again. "Not far from here actually. The truth is, I've been going through a little rough patch lately, couldn't make the rent. I've been staying at the Hospitality House, just over on 11th Avenue. That's where I saw your interview on television. Sounds like you're doing great."

"I'm doing okay. So… you're homeless?"

"It's only temporary. You got any masking tape?"

"Yeah, what do you need it for?"

"To fix your glasses."

"It's in the top drawer to the left of the sink. So what about all your stuff?"

"Everything is in my backpack."

"Wow, Fey, that's not much stuff!"

The woman looked down at her worn black Converse tennis shoes. "I like to travel light." She began to wrap the bridge of Abby's glasses with a strip of tape.

"Well, I guess you can sleep on the couch. But first explain it to me. You were like stalking me. I was actually terrified of you. Why the hell didn't you just come up and say …"

"Say what? What was I supposed to say after all these years?"

"I don't know. You could have started with *hello*."

It sounded so lame, both women laughed.

"You know," Abby continued. "After my mother died, I was so lonely. Then you came to live with us. You were like my big sister sent from God. I really believed that God had sent you. I was in awe of you. Then one day I come home from school and you're gone, no good-by, no explanation, gone, just like my mother. Why?"

"I had to get out of there. You know… your dad."

"I do know. Dad was a drunk and you left me there alone to deal with him."

"You weren't alone. Josh was there."

"Josh, well. At least you could have said good-by."

"You're right but…"

Abby was suddenly angry and way too tired. "Look, Fey, I can't have this conversation right now. We'll talk about it tomorrow, okay? Are you hungry? I can microwave some tamales. They're green corn."

"Yeah, thanks. There's still so much to talk about. Lots of memories, right?"

"I guess." Abby didn't actually have many clear memories of her childhood other than feelings of loss, loneliness and a vague sense of unease.

Tito, who had spent the evening under the bed, was now curled next to her head, purring loudly, a sound that usually lulled her to sleep, but the tracksuit guy wrenching her out of her chair, the switchblade, the crack of the skateboard kept flashing through her mind. Wide-awake, Abby forced her mind away from her attacker and turned it instead to the reappearance of her cousin. It was hard to reconcile this woman with her tats and dreads to the girl she remembered and loved like a sister. And homeless! How much do tattoos like that cost? Lots of money, she figured, given their number and complexity—money that could have gone toward rent or clothes that were suitable for work.

In her line of business, Abby couldn't afford to be judgmental—well, she was judgmental, she just couldn't afford to let it show—but this was not her work; this was her home, her life. Still, she shouldn't judge Fey by her appearance. She would not do to Fey what others did to her.

But those teeth! She'd seen teeth like that on street people carrying little cardboard signs: *Hungry. God bless.* Except when they got money they didn't buy food. They bought booze or meth that rotted their teeth.

Abby's own teeth were straight and unstained by bad habits—cerebral palsy didn't allow any room for bad habits. She'd never had a cavity and was never sick. Her immune system was of iron; figured she'd probably live to be 90. Sixty more years alone. It was a sobering thought. Maybe Fey could stay with her for a while. Maybe she could help her find a job. Was the woman actually committed to getting off of the street? Was she using and if so, what?

She closed her eyes hoping for sleep, but an image of tracksuit man wrenching her out of her chair sent a shot of adrenaline through her bloodstream. One thing she did know for sure was that she'd have to arm herself with something more effective than a bag of frozen tamales.

Abby took a deep breath and started to spell out the Twenty-third Psalm, the sleep inducing method of last resort. T-h-e l-o-r-d i-s m-y s-h-e-p-h-e-r-d, she began. She used to just say the prayer over and over, but sometimes it would take 30 or 40 repetitions before sleep would overcome her. With this spelling method she often dropped off before she got to the part about g-o-o-d-n-e-s-s a-n-d m-e-r-c-y.

When Abby finally dragged herself out of the bedroom the next morning, the pillow, sheet and blanket she'd given Fey were neatly stacked on the couch. There was no other sign that her long lost cousin and rescuer had even been there.

Abby ate a cold tamale and a carton of strawberry yogurt while she tried to determine if she was sorry or not that Fey had gone, once again, without saying good-by. Given the woman's situation and the strong possibility that she was addicted to something, part of her was relieved. But while she was getting dressed, Abby had already spent a good deal of time thinking of ways to get Fey back on her feet and fantasizing about the friendship the two of them could share once she was.

Well, back to reality, she thought as she dialed Rita's cell.

"Good morning, *mija*," Rita said brightly. "How are you today?"

Abby hadn't felt like crying until she heard her friend's voice. "Not so good." Abby spent the next five minutes filling Rita in. "Can you pick me up?"

• • •

The sky was overcast and the air smelled of trapped exhaust as Abby waited by the curb. She'd read somewhere that sound traveled farther though humid air. She could believe it. The train tracks were a quarter mile away, but last night each train that passed, and there had been many, sounded as if were about to come through her back door.

"*Mija, mija,*" Mrs. Soto called from her porch. "Are you alright?"

"I'm okay, Ms. Soto."

"*Gracias a Dios*, but what about the police? You're not in trouble are you, *mija*?"

Abby really didn't want to be having this conversation, but there didn't seem to be a way to avoid it. "On my way home from work, someone tried to rob me but I hit him with a bag of frozen tamales."

"Good for you, *mija*. And the man who stayed with you last night?"

Abby did not bother to correct Mrs. Soto's gender confusion. "My cousin."

"Ah, your cousin. but *mija* ..."

Just then the Iceberg pulled up. "I've got to go Mrs. Soto. Have a nice day."

"You too, *mija. Ten cuidado.*"

"I will. You take care too." The robot dog tongue unfolded. Abby whirred up the ramp and maneuvered her chair into the shotgun position.

"Good God," Rita offered.

Abby shook her head. Her eye was no longer swollen shut but it was still looked like a blueberry puffed pastry. The masking tape holding the frame of her glasses together completed the picture. "Do I look as bad as I feel?"

"Hard to say. How bad to you feel?"

"Pretty bad."

"So where are we going?"

"I need to get something for protection."

"I told you. So, Liberty Pawn Shop's just down there on Fourth Avenue, or there's EZ Money Pawn on Sixth. Both sell guns cheaper than you can buy new. We might have to shop around a bit to find the right one for you. You know, something small that …"

"I don't want a gun. I'm thinking if I'd had a hammer instead of a bag of tamales, I could have nailed that sucker."

"If you'd had a gun instead of tamales, we wouldn't be having this conversation. Besides, if you can't stand the thought of shooting someone, do you think you could hit a person with a hammer? That's way more… well, hands on."

Abby tried to visualize herself actually hitting someone with a hammer, saw herself raise her Mighty Claw, saw the hammer crack through the skull and into the mush within. She winced. "Okay you're right. What about pepper spray? Closest Wal-Mart is on Grant Road."

"You want to go to Wal-Mart? Okay, you're the boss. You're nuts, but you're the boss."

While they waited for the clerk, the two women perused the items locked in a glass case behind the counter.

"They look kind of small," Rita said, tapping her nails on the counter.

"Small's good. It would fit in my pouch. Besides, it only takes one squirt."

"But what if you miss? Is there a second squirt in there? And you'd have to wait until the guy was right on top of you. I still think what you need is a gun."

The clerk, a woman well into her 70s, slipped behind the counter. She had tightly curled black hair with white roots at the crown. "What can I get for you girls today?" she said looking down from one to the other. Her thin, black eye brows had been penciled in with a shaky hand. She raised them now in concern. "My goodness! It looks like you ran into a door."

"Actually, I ran into a fist. That's why I'm here."

"Imagine someone hitting a person in a wheelchair, and a woman to boot! Well, you've come to the right place. Wal-Mart has an excellent selection of self-protection items."

"I'm thinking pepper spray," Abby said.

The woman nodded knowingly and unlocked the case. "This is a popular item." She placed a lipstick-sized object on the counter. "The Ruger Stealth, ladies. Perfect size for your pocket or handbag."

"Cute." Rita reached for the pepper spray. "What's its range?" she asked, turning it over in her hand.

"Up to 15 feet."

Abby looked doubtful. "It's awfully small. I mean, what if I miss? Is there a second squirt in there?"

"Depends on how much you used up in the first squirt." The clerk placed the Ruger Stealth back on the shelf. "Maybe what you want is the Ruger Pro Extreme. It's top of the line. Shoots a stream up to 15 feet, or up to 30 bursts at close range, and it's still a nice size for a lady."

Abby picked up the Ruger Pro Extreme and read the fine print. "I don't know. It only holds 1.4 ounces. I'm not a very good shot and I'm not likely to get a second chance."

"Well maybe you want something in a stun gun." She exchanged the Ruger Pro Extreme for another small device. "The Guard Dog Electra

Concealed Lipstick Stun Gun. It's got a really bright flashlight too, which comes in handy if you just want to temporarily blind someone. What do you think?"

"How much is it?"

The woman squinted at the price. "Looks like $43.17. Not too pricey for a stun gun and it comes in red, pink or black."

"Still, the attacker would have to be right on top of me before I could use it."

Squinting her eyes, the clerk studied Abby for a moment. "You know, for a woman in your… with a need for…" Suddenly the clerk seemed to be at a loss for words. "Oh, shucks." The clerk came out from behind the counter. "Be right back."

In a few minutes she reappeared with a canister about the size of a can of spray paint. She handed it to Abby. "This should do it, Real-Kill wasp spray. It won't fit in your purse, but it'll stop a bear at 20 feet. And it's so cheap, you could buy two and use one for practice."

• • •

Exhausted but wired, Abby whirred through the door of the Tucson Acupuncture Cooperative, Real-Kill tucked next to her thigh. What she needed at the moment was the shelter of the big dimly lit room with its friendly circle of enormous faux leather recliners draped in comfy chenille. She needed the restorative calm of Gordon with his soft voice and sharp needles and the music. Playing faint, tuneless and mentally numbing in the background, it never failed to put her to sleep.

"Good morning," she said to the slight young man sitting at the reception desk. This was not her regular day and she didn't know him.

"Good morning and how are we …" He paused when he noticed her puffy black eye.

"We've been better."

"I can imagine. Do we have an appointment?"

"No we don't."

"No matter." He said studying the appointment book. "We can fit you in. And how much would we like to pay this morning?"

Deep Breathing

The fee slid from $15 to whatever amount above that you were willing to dish out. Usually, Abby paid $20, since she was pretty sure there were others who paid nothing at all. She rummaged around in her pouch and pulled out a little wad of cash, an assortment of ones, a ten and … she counted them … six twenty-dollar bills. Yesterday she'd taken out $200 from the ATM. She'd used one twenty to pay for the wasp spray. There was $60 missing. She searched though the pouch again. Nothing. "Damn," she whispered.

"Do we have a problem?"

"Yes we do," she said and handed him a twenty.

• • •

First thing the next morning, Abby had gone to get her glasses replaced. The optician had told her that it would be at least 10 days before the new ones would be ready. As a temporary fix, the woman had kindly and expertly applied Krazy Glue to the broken frame, a big improvement over the masking tape.

Now as she waited for the bus, Abby patted the can of wasp spray that lay against her thigh. It occurred to her that her life had completely changed, and not for the better. Only last Monday, though she hadn't been giddy with happiness, her life seemed well ordered, moderately satisfying and relatively quiet and secure. Forty-eight hours later, she'd come close to death, found and lost her cousin who saved her life then stole $60 from her, and had become so fearful for her own safety that she was now armed with a weapon. Though it wasn't lethal, Real Kill wasp spray was capable of inflicting great harm. Was she capable of inflicting great harm? Forty-eight hours ago, Abby would have answered no.

The bus pulled up. Abby rolled the Chariot onto the lift then took her usual position behind the driver. She extracted her copy of *How to Craft Your Life* from the pouch in the side of her chair, wondering what suggestion Dale J. Nagery might have that could improve her outlook. She opened the book to Chapter 3. *What You Want Is Not Always What You Need*, the title read. Abby did not agree. She both wanted and needed her old life back, not to mention the 60 bucks Fey had stolen.

It was nearly noon when Abby rolled into the office. On her desk, there was a small, square cardboard box sealed with packing tape. "Where did this come from?" she asked Rita.

"Where did what come from?"

"This package. It didn't come through the mail. There's no address or return address, no postmark on it, just my name.

"I don't know. Maybe somebody put it on your desk while I was in the bathroom. Why don't you just open it and see?"

Abby looked at the package with suspicion. She didn't know whether to be irritated or concerned. In this business, there were a lot of malcontents and downright crazy losers who thought she owed them something. Well, she owed no one; she owed nothing. To be on the safe side, she put on a pair of rubber gloves she used to clean the toilet before ripping off the tape with her Mighty Claw. Inside the box was a small canning jar. She removed it from the box. Small, perfect capital letters printed on the lid identified the contents as pickled cholla buds.

She opened the jar and plucked one out. It had the sweet, sour, salty combination of Mexican candy and a sticky, chewy consistency. Delicious, she concluded. What a nice gesture, she thought, smiling for the first time that day.

"So?" Rita asked. "What is it?"

"Just a little jar of pickled cholla buds. That new client, Pete Valenzuela, must have left it here."

"Watch out, *mija*. A man starts giving you his cholla buds, what's he going to want in return? Your prickly pear?" Rita chortled.

"Very funny," Abby said dryly.

"Come on, Abby. Where's your sense of humor?"

"Right where it always is."

"So why don't you laugh. You know I've been working here for over a year and I've never heard you laugh, really laugh."

Abby allowed herself a little smile. "Well, the prickly pear comment just wasn't that funny. Besides, if every time you laughed you slid out of your chair or wet your pants, you'd learn not too."

"You're exaggerating."

The corners of her mouth tugged down involuntarily. She shrugged. "Not much."

• • •

When Abby got home, Fey was sitting on the stoop puzzling over a well-worn paperback book titled *Extreme Sudoku*, cheap mechanical pencil at the ready.

"You took $60 from my pouch."

"Nice to see you too," she said, poking the pencil into her dreadlocks.

Abby buzzed around her and unlocked the door.

"So can I come in?"

Nodding, Abby left the door open behind her. Fey stuffed the puzzle book into her pack, picked up her skateboard and followed her into the house. "I didn't think you'd miss the money."

"Didn't think I'd miss $60? Who do you think I am, Warren Buffett?"

"Who?"

"You've never heard of Warren Buffett?"

"Suck my dick."

"In case you haven't noticed, you don't have one." Abby paused. Cousin Fey had a deep, raspy voice, the kind you get from years of smoking unfiltered cigarettes, and she was a bit on the androgynous side.

Fey rolled her eyes. "You know if I was going to steal from you I would have taken the all the money and I wouldn't be standing here. I just needed a little cash. I'll pay you back once I get a job."

"And just how are you going to do that?"

"I'm looking for employment."

"Oh yeah? How's that working for you with your dreadlocks and tattoos and your … muscle shirt?" She stopped just short of mentioning her teeth.

"You're being such a prick about this."

"Wait a minute. You steal my money and I'm the prick? Never mind. What did you do with it? Did you spend it on drugs?

"No."

"Are you sober?"

"Yes."

"What was your addiction?"

"Love." Fey said it with a little smirk.

"Love?" Abby chuckled, thinking if the woman were lucky enough to land a job, the smirk alone was enough to get her fired. "And what else?"

Eyes narrowed to angry slits, Fey cocked her head to one side. "I was addicted to crack, if it's any of your business and but like I told you, now I'm clean. I've been clean for over three years."

"So if you didn't spend my money on drugs, what did you spend it on?"

"Went to McDonald's."

"Okay, that accounts for about 10 bucks if you supersize. What did you do with the rest of it?"

"Spent it on my kid. I had a visitation this afternoon so I got him a Happy Meal then I went to K-Mart and got him two T-shirts and a *Thomas the Train* book."

It took Abby a moment to process the words. "You have a child?"

"Yes, I have a 3-year-old son, Francisco."

"Wait a minute. Before we go on, I need a cup of tea." Abby buzzed into the kitchen and turned on the electric teakettle that sat on the little yellow table. "You want a cup? All I have is herbal."

"Thanks." Fey pulled up a chair and sat.

While she waited for the water to boil, Abby considered her cousin's plight. It was nearly impossible for a homeless woman to get even a temporary job; a homeless woman with a child was simply shit out of luck. She closed her eyes for a minute, sighed, then said, "Francisco, you say? Did you name him after his father? I mean is his father anywhere in the picture?"

"Nope." Fact was, Fey didn't know who the father was, hadn't realized she was pregnant until she was too far along to do anything about it, much less remember who the father might be. She'd named her son after Francisco "Pancho" Villa who rode his rearing bronze stallion in perpetuity in a park downtown. She had no idea why there was a stature of this man in the park, but loved his mustache, his big sombrero and the belts of ammunition x-ing his chest. "I call him Frisco," she continued. "Like San Francisco, the city. Anyway, he's in foster care and I need to get him back. I'm clean and sober, but that's not enough. I have to get a job and find us a place. Can you help me?"

Abby shook her head. "Having a kid just complicates everything."

"You think I don't know that?"

Abby poured boiling water over the bags of Karma tea, then handed one to Fey. "What does your tea bag say?"

"What do you mean?"

"Your tea bag. It has a little saying on the taggy thing. Mine says: *Truth is everlasting.*"

Fey turned the tab over so she could read it. "*If you have nothing to give, give a smile.*" She tossed off a wide grin. "How's this?" she said through clenched, brown teeth.

Once again, Abby was struck by Fey's appearance, which was more like a teenage boy than a 34-year-old woman. Everything about it shouted arrested development. "So what kind of work experience do you have?" Abby asked, even though she figured Fey would not get a job, would not secure housing and would never get her son back.

"The usual. McDonald's ... bussed tables at Famous Sam's. I worked for Walgreens for a while. I was at Whole Foods for over a year."

Abby could imagine Fey in Whole Foods where tats and weird hair were the rule rather than the exception. "What happened?"

"Ten bucks went missing from my cash register, but I didn't take it."

Abby raised a skeptical brow.

"Swear to God, I didn't, but they canned my ass anyway despite the fact that I'd memorized most of the bar codes and was the fastest cashier. I really was good at that job."

Abby nodded, thinking no recommendation there. "Anything else?"

"I worked at IHOP, but I got the flu and missed work for a week. When I came back I'd been replaced. Oh yeah, recently I had a pretty good gig with the city. Twice a week, a bunch of us were paid $9 an hour as day labor, raking leaves and picking up trash, general cleanup in public areas. We also went through a program to help us find full-time jobs."

"So what happened?"

"Nothing. The program lasted six weeks and then I was cut loose. In six weeks they expected me to do what I hadn't been able to do in nearly a year."

"Anything else?"

"Nothing I could put on a resume."

Abby sighed. "Did you ever get your high school diploma?"

Fey shook her head."

"Graduate Equivalency Degree?"

"Nope."

"You really should get your GED. It says to the potential employer that you have…"

"You're right. I should get my GED. I'll get right on it as soon as I have a job and an apartment and have my kid back. I'll have plenty of time then to get a G.E. fucking D. while I work two maybe three part-time jobs because no one wants to hire full time and pay benefits." She shook her head. "How can I explain so you'll understand? It's like I'm trying to climb this big old ladder, but somebody's got ahold of my ankles. For each rung I climb, I'm yanked back two. Can you relate?"

"Actually, I can. I find it works better if you grab two rungs at a time," she said dryly.

Fey just glared at her.

Abby's body began its downward slide. She took a deep breath for strength and patience then pushed herself back up. "Can you drive?"

"Of course. Who can't drive?"

"Me, for one, and many of my clients. Do you have a driver's license?"

"Yes."

"Current?"

Fey hesitated for a beat too long.

"When you get a current license and a pass the GED, maybe I can help you."

"That's like saying when you slay the dragon and bring me his head you can have the keys to the kingdom. Besides how am I going to get a job with these teeth?"

"You can get dental care through AHCCCS public health care."

"I've looked into it. AHCCCS will cover pulling them out, it's cheaper than fixing them, but they won't give you dentures. What can a person do without teeth? Hold up a cardboard sign that says, *Anything helps, God Bless*, that's what. And I swear to God I'm never going to stand on a median all day holding up a sign. It's like you said on TV, when people look at you all they see is your chair and all you are is a disabled person. When they look at me, they see my teeth and all I am is a homeless drug addict.

"The teeth are the least of your problem," Abby said, although there was truth to Fey's observation. "You need to build a resume, and you could start off right now by volunteering someplace. You might also consider getting rid of the hair."

"My dreads are clean, they don't hang down in my face, and when I interview, I wear a headband." She pulled them back from her face by way of demonstration then fingered the thick locks. "They are like who I am, and when I'm 70, my hair will be snowy white and I'll still have my dreads."

Abby sighed deeply. "Then I don't know how to help you."

"You could help me by getting me a job."

"I have a responsibility to my clients, Fey. I don't just take anybody off the street, somebody who took $60 from me I might add, and send them into a client's home."

"I'm not just anybody off the street, I'm your cousin and you owe me."

"Owe you?" Abby grimaced as heat rose up her throat and into her face, making her nose throb. "Yes, you saved my life. I owe you my thanks, my gratitude. You are my hero. What else do you want from me?"

"Valafuckingdation!"

"Give me your ticket. I'd be happy to stamp it."

"What the hell are you talking about?"

"Sorry, just a bad joke. But what can you do to make me believe in you, trust you, have faith that any efforts on my part will produce results. Make me believe that you won't just walk out in the middle of things."

"Kiss my butt."

"Bend over. I'd be happy to kiss your butt if you think it will do some good."

"Look. There are reasons I'm the way I am."

"Oh yeah? Well, there are reasons I'm the way I am too. That and five bucks will buy me a latte. The big question, Fey, is whether you have the guts and the staying power it takes to get back on track. If you don't, there is nothing I can do, nothing anyone can do, and there is nothing a 3-year-old child can do to help you either. Get it?"

"I get it."

"Look Fey, I know it may seem like I don't care, but…"

"But you do? Not a lot of practical difference between not seeming to care and not caring." Fey stared at her, face slack. After a few moments, she picked up her pack and walked out the door.

Feeling wrung out and defeated, Abby listened to the clicking of the skateboard's wheels fade into silence. After a few moments, Tito came out from his hiding place under the bed and jumped on her lap. She stoked the cat into a coil, then whirred into the kitchen and unbolted the back door. By design, there was no door jam and it swung easily outward as Abby passed through. Carefully, she skirted the termite-rotted boards and made her way down the ramp and into the backyard.

It was a traditional Tucson yard, mostly packed dirt walled by a combination of rusted corrugated metal panels and concrete block. There was a rickety back gate that opened onto an ally, but Abby rarely used it. In the middle of the yard stood a big chinaberry tree. In the spring it was covered with pale purple blossoms that smelled like lilac. But now its leaves had turned and were beginning to carpet the ground in yellow.

Gilberto, one of her clients, came by once a month to rake, trim and neaten what little there was. He was handsome and well built, Gilberto, and just smart enough to manage his little landscaping business. He owned a truck, a battered but currently running 1992 Nissan, and was now saving his money for a leaf blower. Life was simple, but good, for Gilberto. He'd recently built her a raised flowerbed. She'd filled it with Limbo White petunias because of their fragrance. To the west a pearly eyelash moon was setting into a scrim of clouds along the Tucson Mountains. Her petunias fairly glowed in the dim light, their fragrance intensified by the cooler, damp air. She breathed in deeply. Limbo. What would that be like? If it were anything like those petunias, it would be a better place than here.

She swatted at what was surely the last mosquito of summer. In Tucson, summer was five months long and defined by the arrival and departure of the first and last days of 100-degree weather. Sometimes the thermometer was kissing 100 well into October, but this evening was blessedly cool with a bit of moisture riding in on the tail of a hurricane in the Gulf of Mexico.

Earlier it had sprinkled, nothing more than God's raspberry. Abby took another deep breath. Beneath the aroma of Limbo, there was the scent of dust and wet pavement, evoking a bit of nostalgia, not for anything in the past—there was little there to feel nostalgic about—but a familiar longing for something in the future that she would probably never have. Somewhere a cricket played the first four bars of chopsticks again and again.

"Well, Tito, I guess it's good riddance to Cousin Fey." By experience, Abby knew that people who felt so entitled to her help were very poor risks. So why was she feeling so guilty and bereft, so misjudged? She did care about Fey, cared very much, in fact, but what was she supposed to do, write her a check for 50 bucks? That was about all the charity she could afford. What good would that have done? The cat jumped off her lap and ran to investigate a rustle under the porch.

The can of Real-Kill wasp spray still pressed against her thigh. She studied the label on her practice can. In bold print it promised a 20-foot, non-staining jet spray. The corners of her mouth twitched up. Non-staining, she thought, a nice quality in a weapon of self-defense. She positioned herself to within an estimated 20 feet of the back wall. Shutting her still puffy left eye, she pointed the nozzle and depressed the button, releasing a very satisfying stream of foamy liquid that would stop a bear.

Chapter 6

Wednesday, Oct. 24

As she whirred through the door, Abby looked at her watch. Late! Well, she was the founder and CEO. At least she didn't have to worry about getting fired.

Rita looked up from her romance novel. "There you are, *mija*. I was so worried."

"I couldn't seem to drag myself out of bed this morning. Sorry."

"Never mind the sorry. Did you catch the news this morning?"

"I had the radio on, but I wasn't paying much attention. What's happening?"

"It was on the TV. Another gimp has been killed."

"Jesus! Anyone we know?"

Rita shrugged. "Did you know a woman by the name of Blancher, or Dancher? Maybe it was Francher. Something ending in cher."

"Doesn't sound familiar. When did this happen?"

"Last night. They're not releasing the details, except that she was found dead in the parking lot of that big Cineplex thing at the Foothills Mall with signs of obvious trauma. Again with the obvious trauma. Why don't they just come out and say how she was killed? Anyway, I'll see if I can stream it."

Abby peered at the computer screen while Rita's nimble fingers worked their magic on the computer. Abby was fairly proficient one-handed, but doing anything on the computer was pretty slow going. GSG had a little slush fund she hoped would get fat enough to buy a voice activated computer, but she kept having to dip in it for emergencies like keeping the old toilet operational, making it more of a flush fund.

"Got it." Rita sat back in her chair.

The anchor, this one a hip young man with a tousle of glistening dark hair, straightened a stack of papers as though he weren't reading the news off of a teleprompter.

"The police are seeking witnesses to the murder of quadriplegic Coralee Fancher," he began. Few details have been released but investigators report that Fancher was attacked while getting into her van sometime around 9 p.m. outside the AMC Loews Foothills 15 Theater on La Cholla Boulevard. This is the second homicide of a person in a wheelchair. On October 23, William Stand was found dead in his quiet midtown neighborhood, the victim, it is thought, of a robbery attempt. Police have refused to comment on whether someone is stalking the handicapped, but a reward of $10,000 has been offered for information about the two Tucson homicides, which they believe may be related.

Rita looked up from the computer. "What do you think?"

"About somebody stalking gimps?" She shook her head. "I suspect that Coralee was an easy target to rob."

"I don't know, Abby. Another gimp with obvious signs of trauma? Maybe the guy who attacked you was the same guy who killed Coralee and that Strand guy." She went over to the counter and poured water from a plastic jug into the electric teakettle.

Abby shrugged. "Detective Stransky didn't seem to think so. People are killed just about every week in this town. Gimps are easy targets.

We don't even know how Coralee and William died. If the killer used a knife, then you have a point, but if that were the case, I think Detective Stransky would have said so."

"Well, I still say you should get a gun."

Too tired to argue, Abby changed the subject. "What else is going on?"

"Nada. Want a cup of Karma?" Rita held up a box of tea. "This one's Peachy Green Slimliner. I hope it lives up to its name."

"Just half a cup for me. I don't want to have to pee."

Rita extracted a tea bag from its wrapper. Rita read the aphorism on the tag. "This is a good one for you."

"What's it say?"

"*Avoidance of pain is not the path to joy.*"

"And it's a good one for me because?"

"Simple. You never have any fun because you never go out. You never go out because you never take a chance, and you never take a chance because you're avoiding getting hurt."

Abby was too tired for this conversation too. "Rita, I love you to death, but can we skip the lecture."

"I'm just saying …"

"Well, stop just saying." Abby whirred towards the door.

"Where are you going?"

"To clean the john. Better that, than listening to you."

• • •

Abby shut the door behind her. "Now that was just wrong," she said to the reflection in the mirror. Annoying as Rita's advice was, she had nothing but good intentions and she was right. Certainly, avoidance of pain is not the path to joy, but it is the path to take if you want to avoid pain.

Right or wrong, now Abby would have to apologize and she hated it when she had to apologize. She covered her face with her hands. *Don't you cry, little girl.*

She took a deep breath and another then got the blue rubber glove out of the bucket in the corner and pulled it over the Mighty Claw.

Cleaning the toilet as penance. It wasn't a concept new to her.

• • •

When Abby got back to the office, Rita was not at her desk. "Rita?" she called. "Honey?" Both gone. "Damn it, Rita. I'm sorry," she said to the empty room.

She listened to her messages. There weren't that many and none needed her immediate attention. Writing grant proposals was a constant. There was an unfinished draft of a proposal to the U.S. Small Business Administration to provide funds for modification and accommodations to make existing housing assessable, with GSG as the overseer. Written on a yellow notepad, it nagged at her from the third drawer of her desk. She should work on that. She checked the calendar on her phone. Nothing compelling. She could just go home, but there was nothing compelling to do there either. Maybe some fresh air.

She was nearly out the door when the police car pulled up in front of the building. After a few moments, Detective Stransky hauled herself out of the car and waved.

"Sorry to interrupt your work," the detective was saying as they made their way down the hall to Abby's office. "But I'd like you to look at some photos."

"Sure." Abby hoisted herself out of her slouch.

The detective pulled a manila folder from her briefcase and dropped into a chair.

"I have to warn you, they're not pretty." She took a dozen photos out of the envelope and fanned them out on the desk.

Abby hesitated then picked up a photo. In it a man with lank blond hair and a wooly patch under his bottom lip lay with a sheet tucked up to his chin. There were abrasions on his cheekbones, a pronounced yellow lump on his forehead and cuts above each brow. He looked just like someone who'd been beaten with a skateboard. Quickly she flipped through the other photos.

"Do you recognize that man?"

"It's the guy who attacked me. He's dead?"

"Very. An apparent overdose."

"When?"

"That's the problem. The body was found yesterday, legs sticking out of a dumpster downtown."

"So why is that a problem?"

"There's been another homicide. Did you know a Coralee Fancher by any chance?

Still gazing at the photos, Abby shook her head.

"It's a problem because your attacker was already dead at the time Coralee Fancher was murdered."

Abby pointed to one of the pictures with her chin. "So that means the tracksuit guy was not the person who killed Strand either, right?"

"For now that's our assumption. I don't know whether that's good news or bad news."

"Bad, I'd say. Assuming William Stand and Coralee Fancher were killed by the same person and that person was not the tracksuit guy, someone is still stalking people in wheelchairs."

"The two homicides could simply be a coincidence."

Abby gathered the photos into a stack. "Were they killed in the same manner?"

"At this point in the investigation, I can't discuss that."

"So what happens if there's a third?"

"Three homicides with the same M.O. means we've got a serial killer on our hands."

Abby nodded her head, pretty certain the detective already had a serial killer on her hands and damn well knew it. "Tracksuit guy was just after my money after all."

"Looks like he was an addict trying to finance his next fix. His name was Roland Hecker, by the way, and he was 19 years old."

"Just a poor sick kid." She pushed the photos towards the detective. "So if he died of an overdose, how did he end up in the dumpster?"

"That, Ms Bannister, is something we still need to find out, but it looks like it no longer concerns you."

Abby was not reassured. "Now what?"

The detective shrugged. "Back to work." She gathered up the photos. Grunting she hoisted herself out of the chair. "In the meantime, you keep safe. Whether or not we have a serial killer, don't go out alone if you can help it. If you do, vary the route you take to and from work. Keep your doors locked. Maybe get a big dog."

Abby nodded, though she had no intention of getting a dog and no means of altering her solo status. Raising her brows she smiled. "So, detective, when's the baby due?"

Stransky returned her smile. "Not soon enough."

"I bet. Got a name?"

"Francis Harold, if its a boy. Teresa Marie if it's a girl."

"Lovely."

She smiled again. "Thanks. We thought so. You take care now."

Abby watched the woman lumber out the door. She liked the detective, liked her straightforward manner, liked that Stransky focused on the facts, looked at her face, not the chair, as she would any other normal human being, though from Abby's perspective, normal was more of a mathematical construct than a human condition.

She looked at her watch. She still had most of the morning to go and after talking to the detective, fresh air seemed less appealing. Reluctantly, she took the yellow notebook out of the third drawer. Just as she was reviewing the first paragraph of her proposal, the phone rang.

To give the caller the impression that GSG was a much busier place than it was, Abby let it ring three times before picking it up. "GSG Abby Bannister speaking."

"Ms. Bannister, I'm the social worker at St. Mary's Hospital and I have a woman here by the name of Fey Lesher. She says you're her sister."

"Cousin, actually."

Abby jotted down a few notes while the woman filled her in on the salient details. She hung up then speed dialed Rita.

• • •

As Abby waited in the parking lot for her ride, she thought of Fey, the bad penny. Abby didn't know what actually constituted a bad penny unless it was one you laid on the tracks just before a train rolled over it. A penny like that can't be spent. Her mother had once given her a penny she'd gotten at the Pima County Fair when she was a kid. It was flattened into a thin oval and embossed with the Lord's Prayer. You couldn't spend that penny either, but it had great sentimental value. What was Fey's value and why did she keep showing up?

The Iceberg pulled up and Abby whirred in.

"It was some sort of bad trip, apparently," she said in answer to Rita's furrowed brow.

"What a pain in the *nalgas*, that one. I thought she was supposed to be clean."

"So she said."

"Was it crack?"

"No. Something called Spice, apparently. Ever heard of it?"

"Never."

"From what I understand it's a synthetic marijuana. Very popular with the homeless crowd because it's cheap and can't be detected in your urine if you're on probation, or in Fey's case, hoping to get your kid back." She secured her chair in place and Rita ferried the berg away from the curb.

For a while they drove in what seemed to Abby like a long, leaden silence. "Listen, Rita," she said looking out the window. "I'm really sorry about this morning. Your thoughts and opinions are of great value to me and…"

"So how did she end up in emergency?"

It was unclear to Abby whether Rita had forgiven her or given her the brush-off. Either way, Abby responded without missing a beat. "You smoke this Spice stuff like marijuana, but it's unpredictable. Sometimes you get brilliant hallucinations, sometimes you have convulsions, vomit and pass out."

"Well, that sounds like a hell of a lot of fun."

"Doesn't it? But I guess if you want to forget about how awful your life is, Spice will erase your tapes. Anyway, someone just dropped Fey off, literally, unconscious in front of St. Mary's emergency entrance."

Again silence filled the air like a noxious fume. Abby, feeling increasingly abashed, turned to her friend. "I truly am sorry about this morning."

"Forget *mija*. You were just tired."

"That's no excuse."

"You're right, but nobody's perfect, not even me, though I come close. So what do they expect you to do with your cousin?"

"I'm her only living relative; they expect me to take her home. Anyway, I just can't leave her there, can I?"

"If you're asking for my permission to do just that, you've got it." Rita pulled into the parking lot of St. Mary's Hospital, a big beige complex with as much charm as a stack of cracker boxes. "You don't owe her anything,"

"Except my life."

"Yeah and you can be sure she'll suck that titty dry."

"Jesus, Rita."

"What? It's an old Mexican expression I learned from my nana."

"So do you want to come in with me?"

"I'll wait for you and dear Cousin *Fea* in the Iceberg."

Cousin *Fea*, Cousin Ugly. Under other circumstances, Abby might appreciate the play on words, but at the moment she felt offended by proxy. Rita hadn't even met the woman but had unwittingly nudged a sore spot. Although Fey was not exactly ugly, she was no beauty, not outwardly or inwardly, as far as Abby could tell, and nothing like the girl she remembered when they lived together, close as sisters. It was the memory of that girl that now propelled her towards the emergency entrance.

Fey was sitting in a wheelchair in the lobby wearing a hospital gown. Her own clothes, in a plastic bag on her lap, must have been too soiled to wear.

"Where's your skateboard and backpack?"

Her face, which had the pale sheen of a blanched almond, looked dazed and haggard. Fey barely lifted her head.

"Can you walk?" Abby took her cousin's hand. "Fey? Anybody home?"

She looked around for an orderly to assist them to the car. A heavyset nurse in Scooby-Doo scrubs—it embarrassed Abby to think she even knew who Scooby-Doo was—hurried by. In fact, any number of scrub-attired people rushed by with great purpose. None met her eyes, she supposed, because then they'd have to actually do something to help her.

Abby whirred with deliberation up to the reception desk where a woman was busy entering data into a computer. Abby was too short to see the woman at the desk and she was pretty sure the woman couldn't see her either. "Hey!" she shouted. "We need a little help here."

The woman peered over the counter, pushed a clipboard with a sign in sheet toward Abby, and turned her attention back to her computer.

"Wait a minute! You don't understand. My cousin is unable to walk. Can we get help out to the car?"

"If you'll take a seat, ma'am someone will be with you in… well… what is it you want?"

"Someone to help my cousin to the car."

"Who is your cousin?"

"Fey Lesher."

The woman entered the name into her computer."

"Fey Lesher was discharged over an hour ago."

"But she's still here in the lobby." Abby raised her voice as if she were speaking to someone who was hard of hearing. "I've come to get her, but need help getting her to the car."

"You don't have to yell, ma'am. Have seat and someone will be with you shortly."

Abby waited for what seemed like way too long while Fey dozed next to her. "Fey!" She shook her shoulder. "Wake up!"

Fey managed to swim back up from where ever she'd been. "Hmm?"

"Do you want to come home with me?"

"Um hm."

"Then you have to grab the back of my chair. Can you do that?"

"Um hm." It took her two tries, but she managed to grip the back of Abby's chair."

"Hold on tight," she said and slowly whirred both chairs towards the door. Abby was sure that would grab someone's attention, but no, they sailed right out the door into the dry autumn air and golden light of late afternoon.

After a dinner of scrambled eggs, toast and canned peaches—Abby figured Fey could use a shot of glucose—they had settled in the living room. Tito was adjusting to the presence of a third being in the house and was sprawled awkwardly across Abby's lap in a doze.

"So what about your stuff?" Abby asked.

Fey shrugged. "One of my friends, either Gramps or Gentle Ben or maybe Li'l Jenny will watch it for me, or maybe somebody took off with it." Looking as if she'd been washed and left in a heap to dry, she shrugged. "I'll go back to the park tomorrow and ask around."

"Which park is that?"

"Santa Rita."

"Santa Rita, of course. You think that's a good idea? I'm mean, wouldn't you be better off staying away from places like that?"

Again the shrug. "Got to get my stuff," she said then added as if it were an afterthought. "Thanks for letting me stay the night. If you hadn't come to get me they would have sent me to CRC."

"What's that?"

"The Crisis Response Center and for sure they would have notified my social worker."

"Maybe that would have been a good thing."

Fey shot her a look that communicated Abby clearly didn't know shit.

"Look. You say you want to get your kid back but you have done nothing as far as I can tell to make that happen."

"I'm looking for work."

"At Santa Rita Park? And you're smoking Spice?"

"Only once in a while and it's not addictive."

"No, you just pass out and end up in emergency. When was the last time you had a heart to heart talk with your social worker?"

"My social worker hates me."

"No she doesn't. She doesn't have the time to hate you!" Exasperated, Abby paused for a moment. Clearly she was not getting through to her cousin. She took a deep breath and softened her tone. "Look. I'm just saying your social worker could help you get into treatment."

"And I'm just saying I'd rather be dead."

"Okay. We'll take that option off the table for now. So what else?"

The woman's face went blank.

"Well, maybe in the morning we can talk about options."

Fey started to laugh then, not a hearty laugh, nor a happy one, but the kind of laugh one makes in response to the inane and ludicrous.

Chapter 7

Thursday, Oct. 27

Looking only slightly less fried, Fey leaned awkwardly over the low sink Abby had installed for her own use. She rinsed the few plates and flatware they'd used last night and this morning, then handed them to Abby to load into the dishwasher. A nice quiet moment, Abby was thinking as she put the spoons with the spoons and the knives with the knives.

"What's your dad doing these days?" Fey asked.

"Dad died nearly 10 years ago."

Fey's mouth dropped open. For a moment, Abby thought she might cry.

"Dead. I always thought somehow..." For a moment she was silent. "How?"

"Liver."

Again there was a long pause as if Fey were considering the significance of this information. "I'm sorry," she said at last.

"Don't be. I'm not sorry, at least not very. I do wonder how things would have turned out if you'd stayed."

"You mean when we were kids?"

"Yeah. If you'd stayed and finished high school, maybe things would have turned out differently."

Fey shut off the water and turned to face Abby, a funny little smile on her lips. "Yeah, if I'd stayed maybe I would have graduated from high school, gone on to college and become a CEO of a nice little nonprofit company like yours, but at age 15, I guess I just didn't want to fuck your dad anymore."

"What are you saying?"

"You know very well what I'm saying. We did share a bedroom, Abby."

"My dad was a drunk, but he wasn't a child molester."

"Gee, I guess I never thought of him as a child molester, just a horny old dude who left five bucks on the bedside table every time he fucked me."

"I don't believe you. I was in the room, Fey; I would have heard you struggle."

"I didn't struggle."

"You didn't struggle? Well, I would have heard something. I was, what, three feet away."

"Yeah, you were three feet away with your little face pressed against the wall. Don't tell me you slept through all that grunting." Fey ran hot water into the frying pan they'd used last night, scrubbing at the dried egg. "Yup, five bucks a pop. I saved up $200, big bucks for a 15-year-old. Let's see, 200 divided by 5. I'll let you do the math. I thought it was enough money start a life on my own." She handed the pan to Abby. "What did I know?"

Stunned, Abby put the pan down and backed her chair away from the counter. This time it was her turn to run away.

• • •

The sun, just peaking over the Rincon Mountains, hadn't yet warmed the air. Abby had left the house without a sweater, but she had no intention of turning around. Despite her agitation, she remembered Detective Stransky's advice and headed east on Fourth Street, south on Echols Avenue, which was really just another alley, then east again on Fifth Street. The route was a bit convoluted, but she was in no hurry to get to work.

At this hour, the neighborhood was still quiet, no traffic, pedestrian or otherwise. Her mind buzzing, she took a curb cut off the sidewalk, which was cracked and uneven, for the smoother ride in the street.

She didn't know what to think. Their twin beds were only separated by a nightstand. The nightstand, if she were to believe Fey, on which her father deposited his token payment. How could she have slept while her father raped Fey, because that's what it was despite the five bucks, not once, but 40 times over the course of two years? And why should she believe a drug addict and a thief? Except there was this familiar little gnawing in her gut, the one experienced almost she every time she tried to revisit her childhood.

She paused for a moment, took out her cellphone and punched in her brother's number. After half a dozen rings, the answering machine kicked in.

•••

The man fingered the heavy gold chain that ringed his thick neck. He was paid to monitor the location of the canister, had been doing that ever since that fuck-up loser had botched what should have been an easy piece of work. Now he motioned to a slender young man with slicked-back hair and sideburns ending at the jawline who was sitting at a bus stop across the street. The plan was simple. Grab the canister under the wheelchair and get the hell out of there.

The slender man crossed the street and joined him in the shade of a recessed doorway. He was sweating, even though the morning was cool.

The stocky one pointed to a blip moving slowly, but steadily across the little map on his cellphone. "There she is. When she rounds that corner in her wheelchair," the stocky man was saying.

"Wait a minute. Nobody said anything about a wheelchair. Jesus."

"What difference does it make? Just pull the gun on her. The shit is in a canister under the chair. If you do it right, she won't get hurt."

"What if she resists?"

He shrugged. "Would you resist?"

"No, but what if she does?"

"Don't mess around. Shoot her in the face and grab the cylinder. Quick and easy. Probably doing her a favor."

"I don't like it. It's definitely not my style to shoot a cripple. And what are you going to be doing? Why don't you go after the shit?"

"Don't be a such fucking pussy." He peered down at the cellphone. "Hang on a minute. She's stopped. Why did she stop? Shit, I guess we better go to her. Remember, this is your big chance. Don't blow it. Just cap the bitch if you need to. And if you see a guy on a skateboard, or anybody coming your way, cap 'em too. No hesitation. Got it?"

Frowning, he shook his head. "You do it, if you think it's so easy to shoot a bitch in a wheelchair.

"You fucking fag."

"What did you call me?"

"Oh, shut up asshole. Don't fuck up, or we'll both end up like that stupid cunt, what's his name. I'll be right behind you. Remember, he who hesitates ends up head down in a dumpster. Now let's go!"

• • •

"Something major has come up," Abby was telling the answering machine. "I need to talk to you right away. Please, meet me at my office. Listen, Josh, I really really need to talk to you." She dropped the cellphone into her lap when she saw the two men bearing down on her, each with a gun pointing in her direction.

Her first thought was to try to get away, but they were too close. Grasping the cold metal cylinder of Real Kill, she tried to estimate the moment the men would be within 20 feet of her. There would be only one chance and she had to get it right the first time. She glanced down at the nozzle to make sure it was pointing in the right direction and waited. "Just a little closer," she whispered. "A little closer still." Squinting, she raised the can in her Mighty Claw, depressed the button then raised her arm a bit to redirect the spray. The men kept coming even as the white foam covered from their faces. Abby kept up a steady stream. Suddenly they began to howl.

"Hah!" she cried in triumph, but didn't stick around to gloat. As she whirred away, she'd punched 911 into her cell. "Pick up, pick up," she begged. Finally the dispatcher answered.

"Men with guns, close to the corner of Echols and Fifth Street," she said.

"Are you safe?" the despatcher asked.

"I don't know. I'm headed to 439 North Sixth Avenue. Yes, I'll stay on the line," she said and pressed on, full throttle.

The front door of the building was still locked. She pressed the electric key that controlled the door. Once inside, she relocked it and waited. Within moments, she heard screaming sirens, a sound sweeter to her ears than the angels' choir.

• • •

Officer Steadman, a middle-aged black guy with big biceps and a considerable doughnut lapping over his thick belt, loomed over her. "Now, where did you say this attack took place?"

"Like I told the dispatcher, I had just turned south on Echols Avenue when these two guys started towards me. They had guns and they were pointed at me."

"Officers checked out that entire block. Talked to people on the streets. Nobody saw anything, and there was no sign of… What did you use to scare them off?"

Abby either had to crane her neck painfully or worse, look at the officer's big belly. "Excuse me, officer. Would you please sit down? It's hard for me to carry on a conversation when I have to always look up."

"Sorry, Miss." He took a seat on the couch. "I didn't realize."

"Thanks. That's much better." She handed him the half-empty can. "This is what I used."

"Wasp spray?"

"It can stop a bear from 20 feet."

"Okay, Miss, I'll take your word for it. Two men with guns you say?"

DEEP BREATHING

The man's expression, brow furrowing to the hairline, communicated his skepticism more eloquently than words. "Yes." Abby pressed on. "If you didn't find them that means they are still out there. I assume you're aware of the two wheelchair dependent people who have been murdered in the past month right here in Tucson."

"Yeah, I know all about that, Miss, and…"

"And are you aware that 10 days ago I was assaulted by a man with a switchblade?"

He looked down at his paperwork. "That was you?"

"Yes that was me! He did this," she said pointing to her face.

"Still, I wonder if, well, maybe in your … let us say, in your heightened sense of awareness …"

"The men were real, officer. The guns were real and they were coming after me. They dropped the guns when the wasp spray got in their eyes. Maybe the guns are still there someplace, and what about the foam? There must be some of it in the street. I can take you to the exact spot."

"I assure you, Miss, the area has been thoroughly checked out. No guns. As for the wasp spay. Well we didn't look for that, but I can't say it makes much difference."

"Do you know Detective Marie Stransky?"

"Yes I do, Miss. "

"Can you call her?"

"I'm pretty sure she began her maternity leave yesterday or the day before."

"She had the baby?"

"That I do not know."

• • •

Fuming, Abby rummaged around her pouch until her fingers nudged the detective's card. Heightened sense of awareness! Bullshit. Clearly, the cop thought she were just some pathetic handicapped woman wanting attention.

When she heard Stransky's recorded message, she was fighting tears. It took her a moment before she could trust herself to speak.

"This is Abby Bannister. It happened again." She took a big gulp of air and continued. "Two men with guns this time, and the cop, officer I forgot his last name, thought I was making the whole thing up."

• • •

Abby had called Rita who wanted to come and get her, but she told her to stay away. After all, she'd reasoned, those men were still out there somewhere, maybe even watching the building. Locked in her office she was safe as she would be anywhere.

There was nothing to do but wait.

It was still early. Robert, who got all his news from Fox and ESPN, probably had not even heard about the murders. I should warn him, she thought. She dialed his number, but hung up as soon as she heard his recorded message.

She looked around the office for something that needed doing. The grant proposal was still in her desk drawer, but she was too distracted to deal with it. There was the fridge. She could start there.

After she ate the container of strawberry yogurt, which was a week past its use-by date, she sprayed Lysol on all the surfaces. Using paper towels, she swiped at the little black specks she guessed were mold. After she finished the fridge, she cleaned the microwave then scanned the Arizona Daily Star online to distract her from the anger and anxiety that kept bubbling up from the pit of her stomach. It wasn't until late morning when she saw Marie Stransky pounding on the glass door that the miasma of anger and fear parted.

• • •

"And he kept calling me Miss. Miss!" Abby was saying. "It's not the word per se, that was so insulting, but the way he said it, like, 'Now, now little miss what you have here is a heightened sense of awareness.'" Gently, she took a little swipe at the bridge of her nose, which was still tender from the last attack. "I'm sorry, you don't need to hear all this."

"It's okay. I know Officer Steadman well. He's actually a good guy, a good cop, but old school."

What old school would that be, Abby thought, but kept her mouth shut. "I'm sorry to interrupt your maternity leave. I didn't know who else to call. Can I get you some tea or a glass of water?"

"No thanks. I'd just have to pee."

"I can relate. So anyway, thank you for coming. I'm just so scared all the time now and the cop implied that I was making the whole thing up. I mean, do you believe me? You must or you wouldn't be here, right?"

"I believe you, Miss Bannister."

"So what do you think now?" she said, adjusting her glasses.

"Now I think there is something you have forgotten to tell me."

Abby was so taken aback she banged her glasses into her nose. "Ouch! Damn it." She pushed the glasses to the top of her head. "What do you mean? I've told you everything exactly the way it happened."

"Okay, but here's my thinking. You have been attacked on two separate occasions. It doesn't appear that either attack is related to the recent homicides of wheelchair-bound persons. Though at this point, I'll leave that possibility on the table, I want to approach this from another angle. It seems someone is out to get you. From my experience, I would say that you either know something you shouldn't or you have something they want."

"Me? I don't know anything that would cause someone to want to kill me, and other than the little bit of cash I carry with me, I don't have anything anybody would want."

"Let's take another tack. Tell me more about yourself, your job."

"I'm the CEO and founder of a nonprofit called GSG."

"Ah yes, Gimps Serving Gimps." A little smile slid across her lips and was gone.

"Lord, is there anyone who hasn't seen that interview? Do you think this has anything to do with my work?"

"Might. What else? Have you ever been involved with drugs even peripherally or any illegal activity?"

Abby thought about Fey. "I've never used drugs in my life, but my cousin Fey, you met her last Tuesday, used to have a crack addiction." She decided to leave out Fey's recent escapade with Spice. "As for illegal activity." She shook her head. "I've done nothing that I'm aware of. Not even a parking violation. I don't drive."

"Okay, what else? Hobbies? Volunteer work?"

"Every other Saturday my secretary, Rita Sotomayor, and I go down to Nogales where we volunteer in a hospital."

"Nogales, Sonora?"

"That's right. Hospital Santa Clara; it's just 10 minutes from the border by electric wheelchair. There's one floor that serves only children with serious developmental challenges. That's where we volunteer."

"Every other Saturday? Hmm, that's interesting. By any chance do you have one of those trusted traveler passes?"

"A SENTRI card. Yes. Why do you ask?"

"I remember hearing about this man, I wasn't involved with the case, but he did frequent business in Sonora, Mexico. He had one of those passes so he could come back and forth without a hassle."

"Yeah. It's really great. We just wave our cards and buzz right across."

"Yeah, convenient, except it's also convenient for drug dealers. They slapped a magnetized container filled with heroin and rigged with a GPS under the guy's car. As you say, he buzzed right across. They figured they could pick up the heroin at their leisure. Just by chance, he found the thing and called the police."

"So you're thinking… I don't know when someone could have done that. I'm always in my chair."

"Can I have a look?"

"Can you get down there?"

"I've got four kids under 12 at home. They keep me pretty fit. Despite the belly, I'm…" She grunted as she eased herself to her knees and reached under the chair. "Ah, there is something under there. Now If I can just… Man it's not budging. Maybe it's part of your chair."

"Let me see." Abby arched her back, slid out of her chair and onto the floor. She took a deep breath then rolled onto her stomach. With the Mighty Claw, she positioned her body so that she could reach under her chair. "I feel some kind of metal cylinder thingy and it's definitely not part of my chair." She tugged at the cylinder. "You're right. It doesn't want to budge."

"I'll call for help."

"Hang on. Let me give it another try." Abby took another deep breath and gave it a good wrench. "Got it." She handed the canister to the detective.

"Wow! I'm impressed."

"I'm sort of impressed myself," Abby said, beaming. "I assume it's full of heroin."

"That's a pretty safe assumption. Can I help you to your feet?"

"Thanks, no. It will be easier on us both if I do it myself." Using the Chariot, Abby took another deep breath and pulled herself to her knees. After a second deep breath, she pulled herself to her feet, pivoted, then flung her body into the chair

"Wow, so that's how you earn your Wheaties."

"Pretty much," Abby said panting. The front of her knit tunic and pants was gray with dust. She took a few swipes at it and made a mental note to get someone in to clean the place. "What's that thing attached to the canister?"

"Some kind of Global Positioning System."

"GPS? My God. That means they know exactly where I am right this minute."

"I'm afraid so."

"But if you take the canister …"

"That doesn't mean you're off the hook."

"So what am I supposed to do? Just wait until they kill me?"

"Settle down." Stransky put her hand on Abby's arm. "At least now we know what they're after."

"Well, that's a relief," she said, clapping the dust off her hands. "Now I'll know why they killed me."

Another smile made a brief pass over Stransky's lips.

"And who are they?"

"Guys from some Mexican cartel would be my guess; there are several to chose from. You surprised them with frozen tamales and a skateboard. Then you surprised them again with wasp spray. I think you're all out of surprises now and these guys are seriously pissed at you. Next time, and it will be soon, they will simply shoot you from a safe distance."

"So what am I supposed to do?"

Stranksy scraped at a bit of what looked to be dried milk on the lapel of her navy jacket with her blunt fingernail. "The way I see it there is only one option," she said and continued to scrape.

Chapter 8

Friday, Oct. 28

Detective Stransky had laid out the plan. Tomorrow she and Rita would go to Nogales as if nothing had happened. At the border there would be a very public search, involving drug sniffing dogs and mirrors. Detective Stransky had arranged for an undercover cop to watch over Abby until that happened. Rita would pick her up at 8 sharp tomorrow morning. Unmarked police cars would escort them to the border. After tomorrow she would no longer be of any interest to whoever planted the heroin on her in the first place. At least that was the plan.

Everything, Stransky had promised, was arranged to assure her safety, but as she whirred home she felt like a slow moving target. And the undercover cop? She hadn't seen anyone who looked the part, but supposed that was the whole idea.

Once inside her house, she locked the door and closed the blinds. As she expected, Fey had taken off again.

She whirred through the kitchen. The back door was unlocked.

Abby felt little electrical charges of fear run down her arms. Quickly she turned the dead bolt. Where was the cat? "Tito? Come on, sweet boy," she called, but no cat.

In the bedroom she checked the windows. Both were closed and locked. She pulled the shades. The closet door was ajar. Again the electricity charged down her arms. With her trigger finger on the remaining can of wasp spray, she flung the door wide open. Tito sat blinking at her from the top of the dusty keyboard she'd long ago abandoned. He stretched, yawned and jumped onto her lap, a sure sign that all was as it should be.

Abby went back into the living room and nudged the curtain aside. She stroked the cat. Was there really someone out there watching over her?

God, she did not want to be alone. Even Fey's company would be better than nothing. But Fey was gone, perhaps for good this time.

Her cellphone chimed. She checked the number. Josh. She had not told him about the first attack and didn't intend to tell him about the second. She liked to think that she was being stoic and protective rather than withholding. "Hey," she said, welcoming the distraction. "What took you so long?"

"Sorry, I got busy."

"Tell me, Josh, what were you so busy doing?"

"Fuck you, Abby!"

"Right. None of my business." She whirred away from the window.

"You're always so fucking judgmental."

"Judgmental because I have expectations?"

"Judgmental because you think everybody has to be just like you."

He had a point, her inner scold reminded her. She took a deep breath. "Right again. Sorry." Unable to stay still, she went into the kitchen.

"So why all the urgency, anyway? What's the big deal?"

"The big deal is our cousin Fey. Do you remember her?"

"Hard to forget."

"Yeah, well, to make a long story short, she saw the interview last month and just showed up… well, on my doorstep, sort of. At the moment, she's homeless and angling for some help from me." Abby was a bit surprised at how adept she was getting at skirting the truth. The cat kibble was on the counter. She scooped out a quarter cup. Tito jumped off her lap and waited by his blue ceramic bowl with little red hearts circling its rim.

"My advice would be to avoid her."

"Oh? And why is that?" She put the food in Tito's bowl and watched the cat pluck a single piece of kibble from the bowl with his paw and bat it around the kitchen floor as though it were little hockey puck.

"Because she was a little slut back then and I don't imagine she's changed much."

"Slut? And what do you base that opinion on?"

"To put it bluntly, she told me for five bucks I could put my finger in her hole."

"You didn't, did you?"

"Abby, I was 13. I stole the five from Dad's wallet."

"You molested your cousin?"

"She was what, 17?"

"Fifteen when she left."

"Well, if anybody was molested it was me. Sure, I was a willing participant, but she was calling the shots. Remember how she used to walk around with nothing on but panties and a towel?"

Abby didn't. "So you think Dad ever?"

"Dad?"

"Yes, Dad. You think he had sex with her?"

There was a long silence on the other end of the line. "Josh?"

"You should know, Abby. You two shared a bedroom."

"That's what Fey said, but I don't remember anything like that. You'd think I'd remember."

There was another long pause before Josh responded. "You'd think."

"What are you saying?"

"Just that I think you would remember if Dad was fucking Fey in the bed next to yours. You weren't a baby, Abby. So is that it?"

No, that's not it, she wanted to scream, but what else was there to say? How could she begin to put into words the sick-to-her-gut turmoil she was feeling at the moment?

"So is that it?" he repeated.

"Yeah, I guess that's it. There's some other stuff going on right now too, but I'll wait to tell you about it the next time I see you."

"Okay."

Abby was disappointed, but not surprised, by his lack of curiosity. "So, I'll see you later."

"Okay. And don't loan that bitch any money. You'll never see it again."

She had to bite her tongue. She hung up then plugged her phone into the charger. Josh had left little doubt that her father had in fact raped Fey 200 divided by 5 times. Though logically at age 7 or 8 she could not be held responsible, she must have known and then conveniently forgotten all about it.

She closed her eyes, trying to conjure up an image or a memory of that period after her mother's death. She remembered a father who was angry much of the time. Remembered worrying she was the source of that anger. She remembered a man with no patience, and though her father never hit her, he did hit Josh.

Her mother had endless patience. She had taught her to dress and feed herself, but those feats required time and her father was always in a big hurry. After her mother's death, he'd stuff her feet into the high-topped orthopedic shoes she wore as a child, twisting her foot painfully this way and that. He was so impatient with her snail's pace that he usually just picked her up and slung her wherever she was supposed to be—in the car, on her bed, at the dinner table or on the toilet. And clearly, she remembered a morning when they were running late. Her father shoveled spoonful after spoonful of cold cereal into her mouth until she gagged.

"Swallow it! Swallow it!" The voice still rang in her ears.

When she threw up, he hurled the bowl against the wall and stalked out of the room. No school for her that day.

And there were some nights after Fey left, when her father would stumble into her room. She could smell his whisky breath as he stood there while she pretended to be asleep, as she must have pretended to be asleep on those nights he raped Fey.

Her stomach gnawed. She hadn't had anything but the yogurt at the office, but she didn't think she could eat without begin sick. She stared into the refrigerator: eggs, skim milk, more yogurt, two black bananas she was saving or a smoothie—nothing that appealed.

Abby remembered that when she was sick enough to stay home from school, her mother would make her a hot eggnog with a pat of butter melting on the top. She served it to Abby in a big blue cup, steamy and soothing. Right now she needed to be soothed.

She cracked an egg into a saucepan and added skim milk. As it heated, she scooped in a tablespoon of sugar. She had neither butter nor vanilla, but she sprinkled cinnamon over the top.

As she stirred the heating mixture, she tried to conjure up an image of her mother. Her mother used Jergens hand lotion and smelled of almonds, but she could not clearly remember what she looked like. Patient, but also demanding, she would sit for what seemed like hours watching Abby struggle to dress herself, her only assist a wooden dowel with a little brass hook at the end that her mother had made for her. "Someday," her mother had told her, "you'll remember this and understand how much I love you."

The struggle to learn to dress herself hadn't felt like love when she was a little girl, but she was grateful for it now.

The concoction was steaming. She poured it into a mug, waited a moment and took a sip. Watery and bland, it was nothing like the drink her mother had made for her. She dumped it into the sink, a painful knot in her throat. *Don't you cry, little girl*. She took a deep breath and another and another until her nerves quieted and her stomach settled. Now she was simply hungry. She retrieved her cellphone from the charger and punched in a number she knew by heart.

As she waited for the arrival of her large pizza with everything but pineapple, she plugged in her earbuds, closed her eyes and tried to calm herself with some vintage Simon and Garfunkel.

Forty-five minutes later, there was a knock on her door. She pulled the curtain aside. Officer Steadman was standing on her stoop. He was wearing navy blue sweat pants and a gray hoodie emblazoned with the

University of Arizona's red, white and blue logo, and had her pizza in his hands." She opened the door.

"Detective Stransky says I owe you an apology, Miss Bannister."

For a moment, Abby thought her head was going to explode.

•••

She fetched another Kleenex from the box on the bookshelf. Though she was no longer actively choking back sobs, her tears continued in an embarrassingly steady stream. "I apologize for being such a wimp. It's just … it's been a very hard day, very scary," she said, her voice quavering.

Steadman nodded. "And I didn't make it any easier."

"No you didn't, but when I saw you there with the pizza…well, it was too much. For the first time in a long while, I felt…" She took a deep, shuddering breath. "Sorry, I usually don't lose control like this."

Looking awkward and abashed, Steadman turned his attention to the ceiling. He hated it when things turned personal.

Abby fetched yet another Kleenex, wiped her eyes and blew her nose with a determined finality. "Ouch!" Oddly enough, the pain in her nose had a calming effect. She took a deep breath. "There. That's better. I think I can eat that pizza now."

"Good. Just remember even if you can't see me, I'll be right outside."

"No wait. I owe you for the pizza."

"Pizza's on me."

"You don't have to do that."

"Already did."

"Well, thank you. That's very kind of you. And thanks for your patience." She dabbed at the tears that once again threatened to overflow. "Just knowing you're out there really helps."

He nodded then started for the front door. "Good night, Miss. Enjoy your pizza."

"Wait, Officer Stedman! Don't you want some? There's much more than I can eat and it's got everything but pineapple."

•••

Deep Breathing

As Rita steered the Iceberg off I-19 at the Nogales exit, Abby stared out the window, bleary-eyed, but resigned. "Are you sure you're up for this?"

"*Seguro, qué si!*"

She sounds more like a Samurai than a middle-aged double amputee, Abby thought. Unfortunately, she didn't share her friend's equanimity. She was simply too tired and scared. Well, in a couple of hours it would all be over. At least that was the plan. She looked at each car they passed, but didn't see anyone behind the wheel that looked like a cop. "Can you tell if anyone is following us?"

Rita studied the review mirror for a moment, shrugged. "Everything looks just like normal. But isn't that how it's supposed to be? Undercover escort means you don't know they're there. Don't worry *mija*. Last night I put a candle by Guadalupe and one by my little Flaquita."

"Flaquita? Who the hell is Flaquita?"

"Flaquita, the skinny one, you know, Santa Muerte."

"I thought you were a good Catholic. Don't tell me you believe in Santa Muerte."

"Why not?"

"Isn't she worshiped by drug dealers?"

"I don't know, maybe, but to me she's just a fallen angel who's trying to get back to God. And she does perform miracles."

"I don't believe in miracles."

"Two tries on your life and you're still alive. That seems like a miracle to me. Maybe it was La Virgin de Guadalupe, maybe La Santa Muerta, maybe both. It's good to keep an open mind. You should remember that, Abby. You believe in nothing. What good does that do you?"

Abby sighed. There was no use continuing the conversation. "So how was your date?"

"Hardly a date. Just breakfast at Jerry Bob's. Norberto said he wanted to see how I looked first thing in the morning. *Qué tontería!* Was he thinking I would just fall out of bed and roll into Jerry Bob's? I almost told him to forget it right there and then."

"But did you have a good time?"

"The strawberry waffles were good."

"That's it? The waffles were good?"

Rita looked the rearview mirror and smirked. "Well, I got a little dab of whipped cream on my chin. Norberto just reached over and wiped it off with his thumb as if I were a child. I didn't expect it, but when he touched my face, I got this little jolt of electricity, you know like you do when there's that kind of sexual, what do you call it?"

"Magnetism?"

"That's it and he's got it."

"Well, good for you."

"Yeah, good for me." She reached over and patted Abby on the knee. "I just wish you'd find someone with a little of that magnetism, *mija*."

Abby sighed. There was no use continuing this conversation either. She closed her eyes and pretended to sleep. After a few minutes, her head fell back, then from one side to the other, until finally it came to rest against the window.

• • •

The man with the low forehead, studied their progress, a little blip on his phone, as the *lisiadas* made their way through Nogales towards the border. It would only be a few more minutes, now. He stationed himself in an alley that she would have to pass on her way to the hospital.

Some, whose little manhood had been insulted by *la pobrecita*, wanted him to kill her outright. Others thought she was protected by Santa Muerte and should not be harmed. Personally, he would have loved to see her in action, but to him it didn't matter one way or the other. In this business, it did not pay to have an opinion. He had one job to do. He would do it. If *la lisiada* got hurt in the process, too bad.

Ah, the car has stopped, he noted. After a few minutes he began to track her as she proceeded towards the American Customs. He could imagine them smiling as they wheeled past the checkpoint, but no. They stopped. Now why would that be? He stared at the screen, waiting for her to resume, but the blip did not move. After 15 minutes, the blip still did not move. It could only mean one thing.

"*Ay, chingado*, she'd been caught!" he whispered. Well, none of this had been his idea, he was only the watcher, but somebody was going to suffer. Ah well, *no esta me pedo,* he reasoned. It wasn't his fart so the stink wouldn't be coming from him.

Part II

"Tweedley dee, tweedley dum
Look out baby 'cause here I come."
—*Get Ready* by the Temptations

Chapter 9

Monday, Oct. 31

Anûshka's stomach burned as she stood in front of the refrigerator. There was orange juice. Here it came from a carton and tasted nothing like the freshly squeezed juice she would make in her mother's home by the sea. There was a gallon jug of 2% milk, a loaf of bread that she imagined tasted like cardboard, a head of lettuce that had no taste at all, a few little tomatoes, also tasteless, a red onion and a Ziploc bag with a few hot dogs left over from the dinner her sister-in-law served last night, which Anûshka had refused to eat. From her corner of the refrigerator she took out a carton on nonfat Greek yogurt, a half-empty can of stewed prunes, a bag of chopped kale and one of the three small green apples stored there.

Using the blender her brother had bought her for her birthday, she pureed the apple, exactly three prunes, two fistfuls of kale and 1 cup of yogurt. To this she added a tablespoon of protein powder and ½ teaspoon of flaxseed, pressed pulse a half dozen times, then poured the

Deep Breathing

contents into a 12-ounce glass. She chugged down the turbid liquid without tasting, then removed the rubber band from a of pile index cards that lay on the counter. She flipped over a card. "Yield." She pronounced it "gield." She flipped over another card. "No left turns." Flipped another, "No U Turns." She continued until she had read all the cards, the started over from the beginning. Smiling, she wrapped the rubber band around the index cards and dropped them in a drawer.

Anûshka looked at the clock: nearly 2. Her shift began at 3 and ended at 6. She should be going, but first she washed her dishes and then sprayed down the counters with a mixture of warm water and bleach. Surveying the kitchen, she was satisfied that all was clean and tidy.

She patted her concave stomach. "Well, I should go then," she announced to the empty room, but the image of leftover hot dogs snugged in in their Ziploc bag flashed before her face. For several moments she wavered in front of the open fridge, chill air washing over her body, then eased a hot dog out of the baggie. Over the sink, she took a bite. After a second bite, she threw it in the garbage pail. For a moment, she stood before the sink, savoring the taste of fat and salt. Against her will, she picked the half-eaten hot dog out of the garbage and took a third bite, chewed it then spit it into her hand. Quickly she poured soap over the remains, wrapped them in a paper towel and stuffed down deep into the pail.

In the bathroom she washed her hands and mouth to rid them of the tantalizing stink of hot dog. Now she would really have to hurry.

• • •

Anûshka climbed onto the bus that would take her within a block of the club. She chose a seat behind the driver where she felt safest and gazed out the window as the bus swung onto Miracle Mile. An ugly street, it was populated with raggedy people, stealthy people. An old woman pushed a grocery cart piled high with plastic garbage bags. What might be in those bags, Anûshka wondered. Nothing of value certainly, nothing that had meaning to anyone but the poor, crazy soul pushing the cart. One man stood against a low-slung building dressed in a heavy coat and knit cap even in the full warmth of the sun. Another danced down the street to the music that played in his ears only. Legs splayed as if he had testicles the size of grapefruit, he was gesticulating happily to people only he could see. High, she concluded, and turned her attention to the letter she wrote daily in her head.

Each letter always began with *Sonia, my darling, beautiful angel daughter* and ended *with kisses from your mother who loves you more than the sea, the sky and the stars.* In between she filled the invisible lines with the lies she wanted to believe.

•••

As usual, there were only a handful of men in the audience when Anûshka stepped onto the stage wearing her baggy warm-ups. First she did a few leisurely stretches, touching the dirty floor with her palms. How she hated touching that dirty floor. She did a backbend, a walkover and turned a few perfect cartwheels. *Play for childrens*, she thought, but there was no way she could bring herself to flip through the air as she once had done with such joy and confidence. That was why the pole was such an ideal vehicle for her talents.

She drew her hand across her forehead dramatically. "Phew! Is it hot in here or is it just me?" she said in a breathy Marilyn Monroe manner. She slipped out of her sweats and flung them to the side, then gave her hair a toss. This was the cue for the stage manager to turn on the synthesized thumpa, thumpa that could hardly be considered music.

Wearing nothing but a leopard print thong, she wondered what her beloved gymnastics coach would think if he could see her now as she leapt onto the pole, breasts, bottom and thighs barely aquiver. Clutching the pole with the steel grip of her thighs, she swung languidly a few times about the pole then climbed hand over hand to the top. As the pole spun, her legs, split 190 degree, beat slowly against the air, pliant and graceful as the wings of a swan. The pole, now tightly grasped between her rib cage and thigh, appeared to impale her through the middle as she executed a rapid downward slide. She did not bounce when she hit bottom. Turning her head toward the audience, she winked her good eye then climbed back to the top. Legs split vertically along the pole; she spiraled back down, blond frizz flying. Halfway to the bottom, her legs jackknifed. Bare toes, daubed with fire-red polish, pointed toward the ceiling as she spun around the pole a few more times. For the grand finale, she threw her legs over her head, toes pointing toward the floor, careful to make sure her bum was toward the audience. Only this and the wink were choreographed. The rest was an uncalculated act of pure joy.

From the back the room, one man clapped loudly, stood up and clapped some more. A few others offered a less enthusiastic response. Anûshka smiled and waved at the audience as she once did as a girl following a perfect 10 performance on the balance beam.

• • •

Some were still in the showers. Fey had showered and done her laundry while everyone else was in chapel or watching TV. Now she sat on the edge of her bunk, erasing her solutions in the book of Sudoku puzzles so she could do them again. Usually, she could go through a book three times before the paper began to soften and tear. She hadn't finished erasing Page 3 when the loud speaker announced 10 minutes to lights out.

"Come on ladies." The voice of Jolene, the night supervisor, echoed down the hall. "Get those fannies washed."

Her job was to make sure the women at the shelter behaved themselves, no drugs, no alcohol, no bed hopping. Fey heard Jolene had been in the Marines, which would explain a lot.

"Chop, chop, ladies," Jolene shouted, clapping her hands. "Get the lead out."

Fey tucked the Sudoku book and her pencil into her pack then stuffed the pack into the plastic bin provided to keep the sleeping area neat and tidy. One thing Fey could say about the Hospitality House was that it was neat, tidy and clean, clean, clean, not a hair or a speck of dust on the concrete floors. But from the moment she was buzzed into the glass-enclosed entry, it was always a challenge. First she was hit by the smell, a strong floral with an underlying stink of disinfectant.

Then there was the breath test and the metal detector. Security cameras were everywhere. You couldn't pick your nose or scratch your butt in privacy. To Fey, it felt like she had to leave her soul out in the parking lot in exchange for a clean, warm, safe place to stay and a decent meal.

One thing the shelters, the parenting classes, the counseling, all "voluntary" training programs had in common was the unspoken threat that you needed to do what you were told, or else. If she did not do as told there was a long list of things she'd lose: her spot in line, her access to a shower and laundry, her dinner, her bed for the night, her visitation rights, and the ultimate loss, her son. Throughout her childhood it had been that way too. Do what you're told or else and she wanted so badly to be done with it. DONE WITH IT!

Tomorrow was a visitation day and she was supposed to provide a healthy snack for Frisco. She had no money to buy an unhealthy snack, much less a healthy one, and it would count against her if she didn't. Now what was she going to do about that?

She thought about Abby. No way would she go to her again. The bitch was in denial. Though Fey wasn't a virgin when she'd come to live with them, she wasn't a whore either, not then or ever. Fact was, if she could avoid it, she didn't do sex at all. She'd had enough of it when she was a kid. But sometimes she was overwhelmed by such a hunger she couldn't help herself. It wasn't lust though, more like this scary need to be held, to be soothed by someone's skin against her own, to be warmed from the inside out.

But that had nothing to do with what Abby's father had done to her. For years, Fey had taken great pleasure constructing scenarios in which they would meet and she would confront him. With each new scene she could feel her doubts about her own culpability diminish. In her favorite, he was on his knees, tears streaming. He offered her hundreds of dollars, but she just turned her back and walked away, righteous, dignified, vindicated.

Now that he was dead, there would be no more imagined apologies. But Abby had known. How could she not have? More than money or even a job, what Fey needed most from her now was a simple acknowledgement of this fact, a proxy apology for what her father had done. One way or another Fey would get it.

She took out her wallet, empty save for a baby picture of Frisco and her all-important IDs, tucked it into the pillowcase then pulled the covers over her head. Eyes closed, she said a brief prayer. If prayers counted for anything, she would get her act together. If she was going to get her son back, she simply had to.

The lights went out, but it was not dark. It was never dark, and none of the windows opened so there was no fresh air, not a breath of it. That was another thing she hated about being in a shelter, that and the constant nighttime noises, the coughing, the snoring, women moaning and talking and sometimes yelling in their sleep. Never would she get used to it. She rolled onto her stomach, pulled the pillow over her head and willed sleep to come.

•••

Fey added four packets of creamer and four of sugar to her coffee. Jolene, who was standing guard over the food, was giving her the old hairy eyeball as if she personally paid for each packet.

Sometimes there was a nice hot breakfast, eggs and bacon or pancakes, but this morning they were serving only bananas and cold cereal. Fey put on her best closed-lip smile. She held up a banana. "Can I take extra for my son?"

"Sorry, honey. If I let everyone take an extra there wouldn't be enough to go around."

Fuck you, Fey thought as she tossed one back. She put the other into her pack. Everyone had to be out of the shelter by 8 and it was 10 minutes after 7 already. She needed to be at the Department of Child Safety for the visitation at 11:30. She took a moment to calculate. It was maybe 30 minutes by skateboard from the shelter to the plasma bank. The plasma draw took a couple of hours, plus or minus, depending on the line. She could grab a bus to the DCS offices, another half-hour give or take. She could do it, might even have time to pick up a carton of chocolate milk to go with the banana. Frisco loved chocolate, and milk was healthy -- lots of calcium, right?

On her way out, she paused at the sign-in desk, where a young woman was eating one of Jolene's precious bananas. According to her nametag, this was Esperanza. Again, Fey arranged a sweet smile. "Excuse me, ma'am. I wonder if you could spare a few sheets of that Xerox paper." She pointed to the printer.

Wordlessly, Esperanza gave her two pieces.

"Hate to trouble you but could I have two more? It's really important."

Esperanza sighed then handed over two more sheets.

"Thanks so much, ma'am. You're so kind." Kind of a bitch, Fey thought turning toward the door. She folded the paper and put it carefully between the pages of her Sudoku book.

• • •

CSL Plasma Bank occupied a small single-story building on Fourth Avenue just south of Broadway. Fey knew it well. It was only 7:45 when she arrived, but there were already a half-dozen people, men mostly, sitting in the waiting room. Not bad. Sometimes the line was out the door and down the block.

The girl at the reception desk was no more than 19 or 20. She was new, but as Fey approached the desk, she smiled as if they were old friends. One thing Fey appreciated about the plasma bank was that people here treated the clients like regular human beings. The business could not survive without the homeless and the down-and-outs, and the employees, probably no more than a paycheck or two away from dire straits themselves, knew it. As a consequence, they ignored the bad teeth, the dirty fingernails and were kind.

"I'll need to see your three IDs, ma'am."

Fey dug out her driver's license, Social Security Card, the TB card Gospel Mission required when she stayed there and shoved them through the little window. The girl examined each carefully then typed Fey's name into the computer. "Any changes in your health?"

"Nope."

"In the past 6 months have you had any new tattoos or piercings?"

"Nope."

The girl's face reddened. "I hate to ask, but it's required. Have you been in jail in the past 6 months?"

"Nope."

"That's it then. Hmm." She held up Fey's driver's license. "Did you know that your driver's license has expired?"

Fey's eyebrows shot up in surprise. "Really?"

"Yes. Nearly a year ago in fact." She passed the IDs back to Fey with a conspiratorial little smile. "Have a seat. It won't be long."

Irritated, she took a seat. It occurred to her just then that she'd come to a place in life where even kindness grated. Her chest tightened. A place like that would have to be called hell, she thought, then took a deep breath to dispel the notion.

• • •

The technician, a big, muscular black man with a sleeve of blue tattoos on each arm beginning just above his gloved hands, handed her a little rubber ball.

"Do me a favor and squeeze the little ball a couple of times."

Fey squeezed then concentrated on the complex designs, as he patted her inner elbow to locate the vein. With a swab, he spread iodine generously over the area. It felt cool, nice. Starting at the wrist a python, she supposed it was, wound around his arm until it disappeared into the sleeve of his purple scrubs. There was a fish, or maybe it was a dolphin jumping from a frothy wave, rain falling through rays of sunlight, a heart pierced by a dagger, Batman and what looked like a parrot, but was probably an eagle because it had a thunderbolt in its talons.

He patted her inner elbow once again to make certain he had the right spot. "Nice tats, by the way." He nodded at her arm.

"Thanks." Fey's face reddened with pleasure and embarrassment. "Yours are awesome."

"Ready now?" he asked softly.

Fey nodded. Prepared for the worst, she closed her eyes. This time the needle slid in almost painlessly and she was awash with gratitude.

At the front desk, Fey collected her money. The plasma bank paid by the pound, in cash. Weighing in at 125 pounds, Fey collected 22 bucks then checked her watch. Nearly 3 hours start to finish, less than minimum wage. She rolled the one-dollar bills into a tight tube and slipped it behind her ID cards as if to hide them from herself, then headed out into the sunshine to wait for her bus.

It was nearly 10:30 when the bus pulled up, on time for once. As she swiped her bus pass, she gave the driver a closed-lip smile then took the nearest seat. There would be just enough time to zip into the Quick Mart for the chocolate milk. She felt a sudden but familiar post-donation wave of lightheadedness. She put her head back and let it wash over her, the sun warm on her eyelids. Today was turning out to be a good day.

...

Pressing her back against the warm stucco wall facing the little patch of grass, Fey glanced at her watch. She was early; she hated to be early even by a few minutes. Hated waiting. It seemed much of her life was spent waiting, waiting for breakfast, lights out, her turn at the computer, the washer, the telephone, waiting for the line in front of her to grow shorter.

A neatly dressed woman, probably a social worker, glanced at her as she passed by. Fey considered her baggy basketball shorts, the hoodie. At least they were clean. She might have worn the black pants and long-sleeved navy T-shirt that she kept carefully rolled in the bottom of her pack, but she was saving them for a possible job interview. After her visit with Frisco she planned to swing by the library and fill out three online job applications. Sometimes she'd just go from place to place, McDonald's, Safeway, Whataburger, and ask to fill out an application. Each week she had to show that she was actively looking for a job, but rarely did she get an interview. It was tricky. She could get phone messages at Casa Paloma, but then the potential employer knew from the get-go that she was homeless or in rehab.

Shading her eyes with her hand, Fey looked out toward the parking lot. It was a beautiful day, which meant she and Frisco could stay outside, much nicer than meeting in the visitation room, which was close and unwelcoming. She heard his voice out in the parking lot before she saw him, then he was there clutching the hand of the woman who transported him to their visitations. Her name was Elena, and her other job was to watch, watch and take notes.

"Hey, Buddy." Fey opened her arms and the boy, ran into them. She swung him around, kissing his cheeks, his chin, and forehead. "Did you miss me?"

"Yes!" He patted her cheek.

"New haircut?"

The boy rubbed his hair, which was black and shaved close to his scalp. "Yeah."

"Looks good, buddy," she said, hating that some woman had done this to his silky black curls. She took his hand and walked him over to a little picnic table on the edge of the grass. "Hungry?" she asked, her own stomach rumbling.

Smiling, he nodded, teeth, white and shiny, perfect.

Fey put a granola bar, banana and carton of chocolate milk on the table. While he ate, she unfolded the sheets of Xerox paper. Today she would teach him how to make paper airplanes, then they would read the book she'd checked out at the library the other day, *The Runaway Tortilla*. Perhaps he'd fall asleep in her arms, that was the best, and then it would be time for him to go. Fey looked up at the note-taking woman, who smiled her approval. It really was a very good day.

• • •

The woman was smartly dressed. She looked down at her freshly manicured fingertips. A large emerald surrounded by diamonds graced the middle finger of her right hand. "My real problem is that I have OCD, ADHD, and PSTD, she was saying. "I'm not all these letters all the time, but I'm some of these letters all of the time. You might think I'm making fun, but there's nothing funny about my life, which is not to say that I don't have any fun." She raised her eyebrows then added, "If you know what I mean?"

Abby did not. She glanced at her watch. For the past 30 minutes this woman had prattled on about her mother, ex-husbands, her brief careers as an actress, a Toyota saleswoman and a sculpted nail artist.

"Unfortunately, my OCD and my ADHA kept me from becoming a certified aestheticist, but I'm as good as. Did I mention that I'm also a trained parfumier? Anyway, despite my broad skill sets, I can't seem to find a job commensurate with my ability. So often the disabled have an advantage, I just thought…" She let her words trail off. "I don't know what the problem is."

Abby willed patience. "If the so-called disabled have an advantage, I'm sure I don't know what it is. No, your problem…" She looked down at her notes. "Ms. Pomeroy is that you have a 15-year gap in your resume.

Bristling, she said, "I told you that when I was married to numbers two and three. During this time, I was well-cared for and…"

Thinking the woman could add another acronym to her list, NPD, narcissistic personality disorder, she stopped listening. When the woman finally paused for breath, Abby quickly cut in. "I understand, but marriage doesn't count as a job." She smiled and added. "No matter how much work it is."

The woman did not return her smile.

Abby shuffled through the papers in her in-basket. As far as she could determine this woman's OCD, ADHD and PTSD were self-diagnosed. By her own account, she wasn't under a doctor's care for these disorders and the only prescription meds she was taking were for insomnia. To Abby's mind, there were some people who were so tedious and so clueless, they should qualify as disabled. This woman was clearly one of them, so it was a relief when Officer Steadman appeared at the door.

"I'm sorry, Ms. Pomeroy. I'm going to have to cut our interview short." The woman's face became rigid and Abby sensed a hissy fit coming on. "But before you go, let me give you a bit of advice." Abby smiled her warmest, most assuaging smile. "Volunteer. Use your time to do good for others. You'll feel good about yourself AND have something to put on a resume. Come back and see me then and we'll talk some more. Now I have to talk to this police officer. Bye-bye and best of luck."

The woman looked from Steadman to Abby and back to Steadman

as if to confirm that she wasn't being giving the bum's rush, then left without a word of thanks or good-by.

"Officer Steadman." Abby smiled, genuinely pleased. "Nice to see you. What's up?"

"The good news is that Detective Stransky had a baby girl and both are doing well."

"That is good news. What's the bad news?"

He looked puzzled for a moment. "There really is no bad news, I guess. I was just passing by on my way to… another place and I remembered that you'd asked if Marie, that is Detective Stransky, had had her baby."

"That was very thoughtful of you." Sensing that there was more to Steadman's visit than that, she added. "Do you have time for a cup of tea?"

"Tea? Nice of you to offer but the fact is I was on my way to lunch."

For a moment Abby thought he might ask her to join him. When he didn't, she started to straighten the papers on her desk as if this needed to be done at once. "Well then, enjoy your lunch."

"And everything is okay with you? No more stalkers?"

"Not that I'm aware of."

"I'll be on my way, then." He headed for the door, hesitated then turned back. "Still have that can of wasp spray?"

"Right here next to me," she said patting the arm of her chair.

"Well, keep it handy. You never know. And one more thing. The other night I noticed you were wearing earbuds. When you're out and about, you might want to put your tunes aside. You need to stay alert, young lady, and those ears of yours are your first line of defense."

"Good point, Officer Steadman. I'll take your advice."

"Glad to hear it. By the way, my first name is Torrance, Miss Bannister."

"Torrance, not Terrance. I like that. Most people call me Abby."

Steadman smiled. There was a slight gap between his front teeth. Abby hadn't noticed that before.

At the door, he stepped aside with a little bow to allow Rita and Honey to pass, then he was gone.

Glancing over her shoulder Rita said, "*Muy caballero*, that one. Who is he?"

"The cop who was assigned to watch over my house the other night."

"Oh yeah? What was he doing here?"

"Not much. Said he was just in the neighborhood."

"I've heard that one before." She set a brown paper bag down on Abby's desk. "Brought you a Sonoran Dog from Nene's."

"Thanks for thinking of me, but you know I shouldn't eat hot dogs. Why did you get me one?"

"Because you need to live a little. You don't go out, you eat nothing but yogurt. Where's the fun?"

"Like you're have such a great time."

"I don't tell you everything I do."

"I thought you did," Abby said slipping the hot dog from the bag.

"Well, I don't."

"Great. So you're having more fun than me. Congratulations."

"Thank you. Did I miss anything?"

"Not much," Abby said, but Steadman's behavior had set off her alarm bells. "Did you catch the news while you were out?"

"No. I was listening to *Radio Caliente*. Why?"

"Torrance, Officer Steadman, that is, wanted to know if I still had my wasp spray handy."

"Torrance, is it? Hmm. That's an interesting development."

Abby shrugged. "Purely professional. Something Detective Stransky probably put him up to." She removed the hot dog from the bag. It was nestled amid beans, onions, cheese and salsa in a slipper-like bun. She should not eat it, wasn't even that hungry, but she was surprisingly disappointed that Officer Torrance Steadman had not invited her to lunch. She retrieved a plastic plate and a bunch of napkins from her desk drawer. Nene's hot dog, Sonoran style, was not as good as a lunch date, but not a bad second. She promised herself she wouldn't eat the bun, a promise she always made and never kept.

• • •

Trolling, he called it. Might be at a Safeway or the Cosco. Reid Park was sometimes a good place. Usually a bar was not a good place, but the fact was he never knew when or where he might meet the next one. Sometimes they just fell into his lap—an act of God. That's the way it had been with Coralee. He'd been following her for some time waiting for the right moment, but she was a woman who followed no particular routine and it seemed he was never in the right place at the right time. Then one evening he had been shopping for shoes at the mall and there she was getting out of her van. He simply followed her into the theater then followed her out after the movie. Now William had been a creature of habit so that had been an easy one.

There was still Abigail to consider. Her dark curly hair reminded him of his sister. Of course, they all reminded him of his sister in a way. He hadn't decided what his approach would be with Abigail. At first he thought she'd be easy. Unlike Coralee, she was a creature of habit and there were a variety of quiet little alleys she took to and from work. But she was also cautious and alert. Every day she chose a different route. Rarely did she go out at night, and never by herself. He had considered simply going to her office and offering to hire one of her gimps. Such an awful word, he thought, but a smile crept over his lips despite himself. But going to her office would be an unnecessary risk. It might take planning and finesse, true, but some opportunity would present itself. All he needed do was have faith and wait.

He looked around the Shanty. Close to the University of Arizona and downtown, it was a popular hangout for both students and professionals. If Tucson had an inner city, which was debatable, its epicenter would be just about here.

He glanced at his watch. He'd been nursing a beer for the past hour. He tossed down the last of it. Maybe take a walk through the university, he was thinking, when a man lurched in the door. Poor guy. Cerebral palsy would be his guess.

He was about to join him at the bar, when a young Latino, handsome kid, kind of swishy, sat beside him. After a brief conversation, the two got up and left.

Imagine that, the man thought. Not enough to have cerebral palsy, the poor devil was gay to boot. His heart went out to him. It really did.

•••

Robert and the boy, this one was André and he looked to be no more than 20, 21, had exchanged fewer than a couple of dozen words. In the bar, he'd offered to buy him a drink but André had declined, anxious, Robert supposed, to get this transaction over so he could move on to the next.

As Robert dressed, the familiar sinking feeling and nausea descended. He took off his glasses and splashed cold water over his face. Was sex worth the feelings of self-loathing and fear that followed? It was not that Robert was ashamed of being gay, not anymore, but this hunger that sex with strangers could never satisfy overwhelmed him. Like everyone else, he needed to be held and desired. His greatest fear was that he'd just continue to stagger and stammer through life, essentially untouched and unloved.

"I'm a human being, damn it," he said to the blurred image in front of him.

Wanting something more—he always did—he had asked André if he could buy him dinner, but no, he had another date. Another date? Had they just had a date? Robert took a deep breath and splashed more water onto his face.

Chapter 10

Tuesday – Sunday, Nov. 1-6

Fey knew she had to claim her spot before sunup, so she'd asked for an early wake-up and left the shelter at 5:30 a.m., met the guy who sold copies of the Arizona Daily Star to the homeless—six bucks for 20 newspapers was the going rate—then took a bus to Orange Grove and La Cholla, just outside the Tucson city limits where it was still legal to stand on the median and solicit motorists with a cardboard sign or newspapers for sale. Now she perched on her skateboard shivering in the thin morning sun while she waited for the signal to change from green to red. The traffic was heavy and exhaust formed a gray layer between pavement and milky blue sky.

    With a little luck, Fey had hopes of turning her $6 investment into $20 or even $30. As the cars waited for the green arrow, she arranged her face into an expression of despair and walked down the medium, trying to catch the eye of each driver. Most were texting or deliberately looking in every direction but hers. The next hour she tried upbeat, waving and smiling as if she hadn't had a care in the world, but with little success. So far, she'd been given a banana, a box of apple juice and a bar of soap, but had sold only three papers. As the light tuned green, a lady in the fourth car back rolled down the window and flung out a handful of change. Fey smiled and waved, then picked up the scattered coins, a quarter, two dimes and a nickel. It was going to be a long day.

The light changed, she hopped up, offering a fresh newspaper and a gloomy expression to those waiting for the green light. You had to be quick if you wanted to make a sale.

• • •

"Today's the first day of November," Rita announced. "Soon as it warms up I'm going to South Lawn to visit my *nana, tata* and mother. You know, clean up around their graves, put new silk flowers. Want to come?"

"I'll pass, thanks."

"Aren't your parents buried there?"

"Yes, but I don't feel the need to visit them." Abby had never discussed her parents with Rita except to say that they were dead.

"You should come. It's feels nice to spend a little time with the dead, peaceful. I just hope I don't run into my father and his wife."

"Why?"

"He remarried not one month after my mother passed. Mom had been gone mentally a long time, so I can understand his quick rebound, but I simply can't stand the sight of him with that woman. It's not that I don't want him to be happy, but she's a *gringa* and..."

"Hold on. You dislike her because she's a *gringa*? I'd like to remind you that I am a *gringa*."

"Look, I don't have anything against white people except when they marry into a Mexican family. It's like they are doing us a favor. Improving the genes, or something."

"That's not true."

Rita shrugged. "So you won't come with me?"

"No." The word sounded angrier than Abby actually felt.

"Don't get your *chones* all in a bunch. You know I am forever grateful to you, love you like a daughter. Too old, no experience and no legs, you hired me when not even Walgreens would give me a call back."

"My *chones* are not in a bunch and I know you love me, despite the color of my skin, apparently. I love you too, couldn't get along without you, but I don't want to go to the cemetery. Okay?"

"Okay. So did you get any trick-or-treaters last night?"

"Not too many kids in my neighborhood. You?"

"Went through two bags of mini Snickers and one of gummy worms. Fun, all the little Batmans, zombies and princesses running house to house, so excited."

"Speaking of which, I've been thinking about the kids at Santa Clara. I miss them and feel so guilty that we haven't been back."

"Me too, but we don't dare. Besides, most of the kids probably haven't even noticed."

"You can be sure Alfonso has noticed. He must be wondering what happened to us. It just makes me feel so sad and… powerless. Anyway, I've been thinking…"

"It never hurts."

Abby glared at Rita. "Never mind."

"Why are you so touchy this morning?"

"Why are you so sarcastic?"

"Sarcastic? I thought I was being funny. Anyway, tell me what you've been thinking."

Abby hesitated for a moment. Rita would think she was out of her mind.

"Come on, *dígame, mija*."

"I was just thinking that there must be a way to get Alfonso out of that hospital. If I offered to sponsor him, maybe he could get a visa and come up here to go to school. He could stay with me and…"

"Are you out of your mind?"

Abby felt the familiar heat crawl up her neck. Now on top of feeling guilty and powerless, she was suddenly furious. "You don't understand," she said, the corners of her mouth tugging down. She pushed herself up in her chair. "Alfonso's bright and capable. He already speaks some

English and he's just… just rotting in that place."

"Yeah, you're probably right about that, and the United States is always looking for opportunities to help poor Mexicans make a better life for themselves in the land of the free."

"There you go again with the sarcasm."

"*La cara del realidad no es algo que anhelemos saludar.*"

"What?"

"The face of reality is not one we long to greet."

"Teabag wisdom or an old Mexican saying?" Abby knew her voice was reaching critical whine, but she couldn't help herself.

Rita folded her arms across her chest and smiled. "I made it up, actually, and since I'm an old Mexican that would make it an old Mexican saying."

Abby, who was never as quick witted as Rita, opened her mouth then closed it. She drew in a deep breath while searching for a stinging retort. Before she could exhale the door whooshed open and Anûshka stepped into the office, a space so small that the poor woman couldn't help but feel the bite of tension in the air. She looked at Abby and then at Rita and started to back out of the room. "Later, I come back."

"No, no. Ms…"

"Sryezteptch, but please to call me Anûshka."

"Yes, I remember, Anûshka. Come in." Abby smiled, relieved to have an excuse to end what was threatening to become a shouting match, at least on her part. Rita, who tended to quietly smolder, never blew her top.

"I'll be on my way to the cemetery, *pues*," Rita said.

Anûshka frowned. "Someone has died; I'm so sorry."

"Several people have died, actually, but none recently," Rita said.

A look of confusion passed over Anûshka's pale face.

"The first two days of November are the Dias de los Muertos, days of the dead," Rita explained. "It's a custom, at least among us MEXICANS, to visit the graves of our LOVED ones as an act of GRATITUDE and RESPECT."

"Ah, so beautiful a custom. Some people in my country have like custom too."

"Well, I should go. Come on, Honey." The dog crawled out from beneath the desk, tail between her legs. Eyebrows arched, Rita turned to Abby. "It's okay," she said to the dog. "She's only mad at me." Honey jumped up on Rita's lap and they were gone.

Abby took another deep breath. The tide of anger was quickly receding, but the sadness and guilt remained like a clump of sodden debris. "So Anûshka, what brings you in today?"

"I have progress to report thanks to you, Ms. Bannister, my very excellent sponsor."

"I can't take any credit for your progress, but I'm glad to hear you're making some. Did you get your license?"

"I am to take the test for driver's license tomorrow, thanks to the excellent persons you sent me to for literacy."

"That was fast work."

"Ah, but I need only to read the traffic signs. My reading coach, she give me cards with the words. I study to get each word tight in my brain, then we go in to driver license place, me and my coach who is to read test to me. It is called oral test. Isn't that so clever?" She reached over and ran a finger through the dust on Abby's desk then wiped her finger on the side of her pants. "Sorry. It's what you call compulsion."

"I should be so compulsive. Anyway, I do hope after you get your license you will continue to work on your reading."

"But, of course I will do it. My beloved reading coach tells me I am to make great progress. But there is a problem that I have."

"And what is that?"

Anûshka stroked her throat then pushed a few frizzy blond wisps back from her face. "The cost for the oral test and test that is behind the wheel. You know what that is behind the wheel?"

Abby nodded.

"Total cost for tests is $25. This Department of Transportation and Motor Vehicles must think I am maked from money. I have so many expensives. Money goes to my mother for to take care of baby, I have much rent to pay to my brother and even I have to eat."

"Well, maybe you could put a little aside each night from your tips?"

"From my tips I put aside for rent and put aside for daughter and put aside for my grocery. There is no money left to put aside for anything else. That is why I come here to you, my sponsor, for help to get better job, so I have something more to put aside."

"But just save one dollar a day, you would have the money in three weeks."

A little flush colored Anûshka's cheeks. "Three weeks and three days it would take. But if you could give money now I have license tomorrow. You tell me I am to get license for to drive, I want to do this, but I need help to pay. I return this money to you when I get good job."

"I'd like to help you, Anûushka, I really would, but I run a business and …"

"You do not trust that I pay back to you the money?"

"It's not a question of trust, it's that you must try…"

"Try, you think I do not try? I try too hard every day. It is not me for you to judge," she said then frowned. "Did I say that correct?"

"I think you meant to say: It is not for you to judge me."

Left eye closed, she whispered, "It is not for you to judge me." She opened her eye then pointed to the ceiling. "It is not for me to judge you. Only God knows the insides of my heart and how I try hard every day to make better live for my angel child."

Defeated, Abby took another deep breath. Anything to bring this conversation to a natural death, she thought. "All right." Pulling her stash of cash from her pouch, she peeled off two tens and a five. "Here's the money. I'll add it to the finder's fee, assuming I can get a job for you."

"What is finder's fee?"

"A small percent of your first month's paycheck."

"How big is small percent?"

'Fifteen percent."

Anûshka took a moment to calculate then her eyes grew wide. "So if my first pay check is five hundred dollars, you would take from me seventy-five dollars?"

Abby sighed. "That and an additional twenty-five dollars to repay the loan. Take it or leave it."

"What do I have for choice, but you are highway robbery." Anûshka removed a tissue from her pocket and began wiping the surface of Abby's desk.

"What are you doing?"

"But is clean the tissue and look how dirty is desk." She shook the now grimy tissue in Abby's face. "Here's good deal. I clean office. You pay twenty-five dollars."

Abby sighed. This was not the way she liked to do business, but the office was very dirty. "Including the floors?"

"Of course including floors. Now where is supplies?"

"Is under... the supplies are under counter."

Anûshka peered under the counter and pulled out a nearly empty can of generic multipurpose cleaner. "You call this supplies? Where is Windex, where is Clorox and little scrubbing bubbles. And what is this?" she said holding up a desiccated item that looked like an aged Portobello mushroom. "You call this sponge?"

Abby shrugged. "The broom, mop and bucket are in the bathroom across the hall. There's a bottle of some kind of industrial strength cleaner in there too, and be sure to use the rubber gloves."

•••

It was after 2 p.m. when Fey sold the last newspaper. She emptied her pockets and counted. There were two fives, 13 ones, 18 quarters and an assortment of dimes, nickels, pennies and the little bar of soap—she'd eaten the banana and drunk the juice long ago. Minus the time it took to pee at the gas station, she had been standing on the median for five hours straight. Not as good an hourly wage as the plasma bank, but good enough. She counted out six ones for tomorrow's newspapers and stuck those in her bra. She dug out the $2 from the plasma bank she'd squirreled away behind her ID cards and replaced them with the fives. That left her with $22 plus change, all disposable income. She'd have to think long and hard about how best to use it.

As she walked to the bus stop, she thought about Abby. All day off and on she'd been thinking of her. Was she in danger? Did Fey care? She did, and it made her tired and angry.

When they lived together, Abby'd thought the sun rose out of Fey's backside. Now in her eyes, she was just a worthless, stupid piece of shit. Fey hated that, wanted to change it, but how? There was so much she needed to do every day just to stay alive. How would she prove to her that deep down she was still the same person Abby'd loved and trusted with her life. How would she prove it to herself?

Dark thunderheads bloomed far to the south, an unusual sight for November. The wind was already whipping up and Fey prayed the storm would veer off or at least hold off for a few hours. She needed to make a urine drop, find three jobs to apply for at the library and get back to the shelter by 6.

She looked at her watch. The bus was late. Fuck Abby, she thought. Fuck her.

• • •

Two or three times a week it was his habit to take a walk after dinner through the university campus. He especially liked the older parts of the campus, loved the old brick buildings and the enormous old trees, so unlike the rest of the city. People were hurrying toward Centennial Hall. Itzhak Perlman was performing there this evening. He'd tried to get tickets, but they were sold out.

The wind was beginning to pick up. Overhead, thick clouds had begun to gather. Reflecting the city lights, they were a rather poisonous looking sulfur color. The weatherman on the 5 o'clock news had predicted rain, but he was so often wrong, his predictions were generally ignored.

He had just turned onto the path that paralleled University Avenue when he saw her. The first thing he noticed about the woman was her slow, awkward gait, feet splaying outward with each step. Even from a distance, he could tell it pained her to walk. When he came within a few yards of her he noticed the shoes, ugly black boxy affairs with thick Velcro straps. How she must hate them.

"Maybe we'll get some rain this time," he said as he passed.

Smiling she waved an unfurled umbrella. "We always need it."

From the looks of her hands—fingers warped, knuckle joints big as cherry tomatoes—he would guess rheumatoid arthritis. Very painful. And she was young. At least she was young to be so disfigured by the disease. His heart went out to her.

• • •

The dregs of a late hurricane in the Gulf of Mexico blew in sometime after midnight. Now high winds buffeted the walls and rattled the windows. The bedroom lit up as lightening flashed. Once again Abby began the count, 1,001, 1,002. Before she could get to 1,005, she heard the thunder. The lightening was now within a mile of her house.

Some nights her mind was wound so tight it took hours for it to spin out. Tonight was one of those nights. It was going on 2 a.m. She'd counted her breaths up to 100, masturbated twice and spelled the Twenty-third Psalm a half-dozen times, but the little voice in her head continued yammering on and on. Usually it was the voice of reason and all things in moderation, but tonight its focus jumped from guilt about Alfonso to her personal failures as a human being then on to the latest homicide victim. This one, according to the 10 o'clock news, was another woman, a university student, ambulatory but already hobbled by severe rheumatoid arthritis. She was found earlier this evening, no cause of death given other than "evidence of severe trauma." Now the victims numbered three, the magic number that Stransky said changed coincidence to serial murder.

Abby'd always been a fearless sort. But the events of the past month had changed that. How had Anûshka put it? She'd lost her fearless. Sounded something like losing her virginity, except Abby didn't miss her virginity.

"All right, all right, let's change the subject," she whispered in the dark.

If the voice had eyes, it would be rolling them right now, she thought. The lightening and the thunder were now nearly simultaneous. If someone were to jimmy the lock on her front door, she wouldn't be able to hear it. Before she'd gotten into bed, she'd set the can of wasp spray on her nightstand. Now she reached over and nudged it. Satisfied that it was still half-full and easily accessible she settled back into her grim reveries.

Maybe I should just go stand under the chinaberry tree and wait for lightening to strike, she thought. The problem was, of course, that by the time she could manage to get outside, the storm would have moved on to the next county.

And what was she going to do about Alfonso? She had called the Citizen and Immigration agency of Homeland Security to find out about getting a visa for him, but had given up after being placed on hold by a robot for 15 minutes.

And what about Robert? He only listened to Fox News and probably hadn't even heard about the murder. This latest victim made it clear that not only were people in wheelchairs targeted, but people like Robert were also vulnerable. Definitely, she would call him tomorrow, would like to call him right now, but then they'd both be awake all night. And who was this man, if the killer was a man? How did he choose his targets and why? Was it hatred that drove him, or was he some kind of warped mercy killer? And they still had not revealed how each victim had been killed. Could it be worse than being struck by lightning? Probably not.

And then there was Fey. Josh had made it clear that her cousin had been telling the truth about their father. What was still unclear to Abby was whether she'd actually known what was going on in the bed next to hers. How could she not? It had been nearly a week. Where was Fey tonight? She should have done more to help, but now it was too late. Guilt washed over her like rain.

The room lit up again. Abby counted 1,001, 1,002, 1,003, 1,004, 1,005, 1,006. The lightning was over a mile away. Another opportunity missed.

Chapter 11

Monday, Nov. 6

Abby whirred into the office, bringing with her a blast of cool damp air. Putting her book down, Rita took a moment to appraise her friend. "Well, you look like caca."

"Thanks. That's pretty much how I feel. I assume you saw the news."

"Yes." Rita lifted her blouse to expose her little revolver. "I just wish the son of a bitch would come after me."

Abby pulled off her wet, bright yellow poncho and threw it over the chair to dry. "You're nuts. You know that, don't you?"

Rita shrugged. "Have you had breakfast?"

"I'm not hungry."

"On the way to work, I stopped by La Estrella for *empandas*."

"As I recall, that bakery is not on your way to work."

"True, but La Estrella is worth going out of my way for. So you want one?"

"What have you got?"

"Three mangos and three apples."

"Mango I guess."

"Thata girl." She whirred over to the counter and selected two of the Mexican turnovers from a box and popped them into the microwave. "This will only take a sec."

"I was planning to go check on that remodel job. Frank was supposed to put in grab bars around the toilet and I want to be sure he did it the exact way I told him to, otherwise Missy Clapman won't be able to use them."

"We could do that."

Abby shook the rain out of her hair. "I don't want to go back out into that wet.

"Just as well. A fellow called a few minutes ago, a Mr. Grady, no wait, that's his first name." She looked down at her note pad. "His name is Grady O'Riley. Nice Irish name." She took the empanadas from the microwave and put them on a paper plate.

Abby made a half-hearted attempt to fluff her damp hair. "Is he looking for a job or hiring?"

"Hiring, thank God. Wants someone to clean his house and chauffeur him around." She passed the plate of warm turnovers to Abby. "He said he'd be in at 9:30."

Abby studied the *empanadas*. "Which one is the mango?"

"Three holes on the top."

Abby looked at her watch. "He should be here any minute." She took a couple of bites of the *empanada* and fluffed her hair again. "I must look like a drowned rat."

"More like a drowned poodle."

"First, I look like shit; now I look like a wet dog. Make up your mind."

"Okay. I'll go with the poodle. So, *mija*, I guess you didn't sleep so well last night. Me neither, and not only that but…" Rita's eyebrows shot up. "*Híjole!*" she whispered.

He was bent over nearly double, his back round like the cap of a giant mushroom. It occurred to Abby that if Mr. O'Riley had two more limbs he'd look like Kafka's giant beetle.

Deep Breathing

Abby shoved the *empanada* into the top drawer of her desk. Swallowing, she waited for Mr. O'Riley, who walked with a cane, to inch over to her desk, then extended her hand over the desk. "Abby Bannister."

He lifted his head a few degrees so he could see her then took her hand. "I recognize you from the interview. I'm Grady O'Riley."

"Would you like a cup of hot tea, Mr. O'Riley?"

"Do you have a straw?"

"Can you find a straw, Rita?"

• • •

Though she was soaked to the skin, Fey blessed the rain. People were kinder or maybe guiltier on rainy days. Whichever, it had taken Fey only two hours to sell 19 newspapers—she'd saved one for herself for the Sudokos in the comics section—and the whole day was still before her. She'd scored $42 bucks plus change, a pretty serviceable jacket and another bar of soap.

Now she stepped out of the wet and into the fragrant warmth of Domino's Pizza. While she waited for the pimply boy in a hairnet to take her order, she peeled off six ones for tomorrow's newspapers and put them in her bra.

Pulling off his latex gloves, the hairnet boy asked, "What will it be?"

"A slice of pepperoni, please, and a cup of coffee."

"That will be $5.18."

Fey put five ones on the counter, pulled out a fistful of change from the pocket of her new jacket to make up the difference, then dropped the pennies and a few nickels and dimes into the tip jar. "And can I change these ones for a twenty?"

While she waited for her order, she counted the rest of the change. There were 7 quarters, 11 dimes and 4 nickels. She took her pizza and coffee to a chair by the window. Before eating, she rolled up the twenty into a tight tube. From her wallet she extracted the two fives and replaced them with the twenty. That brought her disposable income to $45 and change.

As she ate, she paged through the damp newspaper, scanning the headlines. It was there in the upper lefthand corner of page five, under the Law and Order Briefs section. *Handicapped Homicide on U of A Campus*, it read. Her chest contracted and she felt a thud of foreboding. Holding her breath, she quickly scanned the article for a name. It was in the second paragraph. Not Abby. She exhaled. That makes three, she thought, and wondered if Abby knew. Well, there was nothing she could do about that.

Bolstered by coffee and greasy food, Fey pulled on the jacket and stepped into the drizzle. A little puff of confidence filled her lungs as she hopped on her skateboard and headed for the bus stop. Just yesterday, she would have been mighty tempted to use the money to score some pot or whatever was available for $34 dollars, but today she was done with that. She knew it in her head and felt it in her heart. She couldn't say what had changed so radically in the past 24 hours, but it had. She had a plan. Today, not tomorrow or the next day, she would begin to build her resume.

• • •

Abby dialed Anûshka's number. The woman picked up after two rings. "Did you pass your driver's test?" she asked.

"Both tests were so excellent, but the picture on my license to drive is too terrible.

"They usually are, but I have some good news. I have a job interview for you."

"A job! Soon I have with me my angel and it is all because of thanks to you," Anûshka said with what seemed to Abby as both premature and excessive enthusiasm. But Abby did think this was a match made in heaven.

"Mr. O'Riley needs someone three mornings a week to keep house and drive him to appointments, which would allow you to continue working at J.J.s while you build your clientele."

"This job fits hand like... like. What fits hand?"

"A glove."

"Ah yes. This job fits hand like glove."

"That's what I thought." Of course, Abby had no idea what kind of a driver Anûshka was, and that could be a deal breaker. Mr. O'Riley had a late model Lexus that he was no longer able to drive due to the ever-increasing curvature of his spine, and he repeatedly used the words "cautious" and "experienced" as qualities he demanded in a driver.

"So I'll set up an interview and get back to you," Abby said. She put the phone back in its cradle then looked around the little office for another distraction. Rita had gone off to meet her daughter-in-law, the one she did like, for an early lunch, leaving Abby feeling vulnerable. Abby considered locking the door, but lectured herself out of it. This was a business; it was supposed to be open from nine to five, Monday through Friday. The recorded message on the office phone said so.

She dialed Robert's cellphone but got his voice mail again. "Damn him," she said softly. This was typical Robert behavior. Sometimes he wouldn't check his personal email or his phone messages for days. Abby suspected it was his way of coping with rejection or maybe some sort of self-punishment for perceived transgressions. Whatever the reason for his lack of response, part of her was mad at him and part of her was worried about him. In addition to the crazy guy stalking people who didn't conform to his standard of physical normality, there were other reasons to worry about Robert. He worked 12 to 14-hour days to prove he was as good as everyone else at Raytheon, engaged in risky sex and then got depressed about it. Once he'd threatened suicide, but Abby had talked him through it. Regardless how lonely and work obsessed he might be, Abby was pretty sure Robert was way too adoring of his family to ever deliberately harm himself.

As she stared out the glass door into the dark and empty hall, Abby could feel her heart banging against her ribs. She closed her eyes and took a deep breath, inhaling through her nose, exhaling through her mouth. She counted the breaths. When she reached 59, she remembered the *empanada* in her desk drawer, now cold. Two more were still in the box sitting on the counter. She shouldn't, but she would.

She jumped when the microwave timer went off. "Jesus, get a grip!" She took an additional five complete breaths before slipping the warm *empanadas* onto a paper plate.

Just as she was about to take a bite, Officer Steadman walked through the door. The wave of relief she felt came as a bit of a shock.

She smiled. "Want an *empanada*?" she said by way of greeting. "It's warm."

He returned her smile. "Do I look like the kind of man who would turn it down?" The automatic door shut behind him and in two steps he was at her desk.

"Please sit down, Officer Stedman. "Just throw that poncho …" She looked around the room. "Here, give it to me." He handed her the poncho and she stuffed it under the desk. "Phew. I have to admit I've been a bit tense since I heard the news last night."

"That's why I'm here, Ms. Bannister." He took an *empanada* from the plate and eased his substantial self onto the chair. "What kind?"

"Mango."

"Never had one of those." He took a bite, closing his eyes as he chewed. "Umm umm, mighty good on a rainy day." He smiled his gap-tooth smile. "And by the way, the last time we met, I thought we had agreed that it was Torrance."

"And Abby. So Torrance, three homicides makes it official, right? There's a serial killer on the loose."

"I don't know about official, but I'd say somebody out there has a strong dislike for disabled folks and you, little lady, need to be on the lookout."

For some reason the labels *disabled* and *little lady*, hardly rankled. Maybe it was because Torrance was just… how had Detective Stanksy put it? Old school. Maybe it was his gap-tooth smile. Whatever, at the moment, she was just happy to have his company in her little office located at the end of a rather long, dim corridor. "So, what's next?"

"I'm going to finish this empanada and be on my way. Just wanted to check on things, see how you're doing and all. Oh yes, wanted to tell you we've doubled the officers patrolling this area, Stransky's orders. Still, while you're about, keep those eyes open and don't plug into your iTunes, or whatever it is all you young folks listen to. You need your ears too." He chuckled. "You still got that wasp spray?"

Abby pulled out the can. "Right by my side."

"Good girl."

Deep Breathing

•••

The metal sign outside the building said Bicas, one of the many repurposed warehouses located just north of downtown. Fey had passed it many times without bothering to go in. She plugged her ears as a train rumbled not 30 feet from where she stood in the parking lot. Sculptures made from pieces of rebar and old parts filled the yard in front of the building, and colorful, crazy, bicycle-themed art covered the crumbling plaster walls. She had heard that a person could volunteer there and get $9 an hour credit toward a recycled bicycle.

As she entered the basement/bicycle workshop, she liked the funky feel of the place, even liked the way it smelled like grease and damp cement. There were rows of bikes, four and five deep, and bins filled with what she presumed were bicycle parts. Fey knew nothing about bicycles, hadn't even ridden one in over 20 years.

A young woman with what looked like a set of miniature cow horns piercing the septum of her nose was busy texting behind the counter. In addition to the horns in her nose, her earlobes were stretched into long loops. Attached to each was an array of small discs, washers perhaps, or maybe some small, but important, bicycle parts.

The girl looked up and smiled pleasantly when Fey approached the counter.

"Zero carbon footprint," she said, pierced chin pointing to Fey's skateboard. "Cool."

"Yeah thanks." Fey returned her smile. "I try to be earth friendly. No carbon emissions except when I fart."

The girl laughed at that. "My name is Tanya."

"Fey." She slipped her backpack off her shoulders and rubbed her neck. "So I'm interested in the volunteer opportunities here."

"Do you know how to repair a bicycle?"

"No, but I could learn."

Tanya pointed to a sign written in pink chalk on an old blackboard hung on the wall: *Bicycle repair class, Saturdays, $20.* It's really worth every penny."

Twenty dollars, one trip to the plasma bank, Fey was thinking. "I'm a little short on cash at the moment."

"There's also a Women's Trans Femme workshop every Monday from 3 to 7. It's awesome and all you need is your bike."

"Well, see here's the thing. I don't own a bike, but I heard that a person can earn $9 an hour credit here towards a recycled bike. Plus, I'm trying to build my resume and volunteering for Bicas will give me something to put on it. See, it's been a while since I've worked and… well you know."

Running her pierced tongue over a gold bead pierce in her bottom lip, Tanya looked Fey over as if seeing her for the first time. She nodded her head. "Yeah, I do know. So, awesome! You can learn as you go."

"Can I start today? I mean, since I'm already here."

Tanya shrugged. "Don't see why not." She pushed a clipboard towards Fey. "Sign in and I'll get you started."

• • •

Ball cap pulled down to keep the rain out of his face, he had been waiting in the doorway for the past 20 minutes or so. His mission required patience and restraint, but even more, it required faith. He had no control over those God chose to put in his path, but he was a very intuitive person and could tell when a person was in great physical and emotional pain. He knew when a person had been placed in his hands by God.

He smiled when she emerged from the office building in her yellow poncho –yellow, such a bright and cheery color. He checked his watch. It was just after five, but he'd discovered that Abby never kept to any exact schedule. He'd been observing her for some time now and could see that despite the brave face she put out to the world, she was suffering, suffering like his sister had suffered, and he would do whatever was in his power to help her.

• • •

Light, on and off again rain had continued through the day. Now, as Abby sped down the alley toward home, the sun was beginning to break through the clouds, creating pastel swirls in the oil-tainted puddles. To the west, the rain, backlit by the setting sun, became of shower of confetti. Normally, she would have taken a moment to enjoy the fragrance of wet pavement and the amazing light, but her attention was narrowed to dark doorways and spaces between buildings. Every parked car was a possible point of ambush. To assure herself, she touched the can of wasp spray snugged against her thigh.

As she whirred up her walkway, a little bolt of electricity shot up her arms. The front door was ajar. She gripped the can as she entered the house. There on the couch a woman dozed, Tito tucked into the curl of her slender body. He blinked at her as if to say, *Sorry boss, I had no other choice.*

"Stella?"

The woman shot up. "Oh, sorry, Abby. I didn't mean to fall asleep." She was slim, delicate with short auburn hair and lovely pale skin. Her eyes were slightly protuberant, the lashes flocked with repeated passes of the mascara wand. At first Abby didn't take in the swell of her waist, hardly noticed the little bump beneath her skin-tight tee. It took Abby some moments to understand that her prized cleaning person par excellence and mainstay miracle worker was pregnant. "Oh, God," she said, still not quite believing what was right before her. "What did your mother say?"

Stella's hands flew to her face. She began to weep then sob, shoulders shaking, while Abby stood, dumbstruck. Because of her chair, she was unable to give the poor woman the reassuring embrace she so badly needed. "Does your mother know you're here?" It was all she could think to say.

Fingering the Star of David that hung from her slender neck, she shook her head. Mascara trailed down each smooth cheek, underscoring her misery.

"Okay. It will be okay." Though knowing Stella's mother, who in Abby's opinion was at once controlling and dismissive of her daughter, it probably wouldn't be.

• • •

Willing the bus to appear, Fey peered down the street. "Come on. Come on." She looked at her watch. It was quarter till 6 already. She looked down at her hands. Though she had washed them with borax soap before leaving Bicas, grease inked in the whorls, creases and cracks in her chapped hands and was thick under her nails. After she had cleaned the bathroom and swept the floor, a 12-year-old kid named Jake or Jack taught her how to take the wheels off a bike, pack the whatevers with grease, and put the wheels back on. She had accrued $54 toward a bike and was already thinking about how much she could sell it for, but now she was running late.

For the past few months, Fey had been alternating between four women's shelters around town. She had been at the Salvation Army Hospitality House for the past seven days, the limit allowed each month, and was headed for Gospel Rescue Mission. Their limit was only four days and it was farther away from her downtown base of action, but it was her best bet at the moment. If she wanted to get a bed, she'd have to be there by 6, and if she didn't get a bed there, it would be too late to get one anywhere else.

Stomach growling, she considered her options—homeless people always had to consider their options. If there was no room at Gospel Mission, she'd have to try Camp Bravo. It was run by veterans for homeless veterans, but she'd heard they allowed women, if there was room, even if they hadn't served. It was safe, she'd heard, but it was way in the opposite direction and she really wasn't keen about sleeping in a tent. It was nearly dark, the rain had finally stopped, but it was getting colder by the minute. Fey pulled her jacket out of her pack, tugged it on and thrust her grimy hands deep into the pockets. Where was that bus?

• • •

It was settled, barely. Stella would spend the night with Abby and her mother would be by early to pick her up. Throughout the brief conversation, Abby sensed that Stella's mother could barely control her rage, sensed that a good deal of that rage was directed at her. Odd, she thought. Not odd that the mother should be mad, but odd that she should be mad at her.

"I won't go with her." Stella filled the teakettle.
"We've been over this again and again, Stella. You can't stay here."
"Please, Abby. I'll clean for free."
"I'm sorry, Stella, but you can't stay here."
"Why?" Her eyes, encircled in black smears, pleaded.
Abby shook her head as she searched for a plausible answer to that question. "Because your mother won't allow it."
"My mother's not my boss." Her voice had an uncharacteristically hard edge.
"But she is, sort of."
"No she is not!" The word *not* trailed off in a whine and Stella was crying again so loudly that it was hard to discern the whistle of the teakettle from her shrill wail.
Abby waited. "So who's the father?"
The wailing stopped. "My boyfriend, of course."
"Of course," Abby said. "But who is he? Where did you meet him?"
Stella looked into her lap.
"Stella?"
"I met him here." Her voice was barely audible.
"Here? What do you mean, here?" she asked, but already she knew the answer. "Gilberto is the father of your baby?"
Stella nodded miserably. "We love each other."
No doubt, Abby thought. An image was forming in Abby's mind of the two young lovers going at it hot and heavy on her own bed. She winced. Stella's mother sounded so pissed over the phone. Did she think that Abby had played nurse to the star-crossed lovers?
"She said I can't marry him unless it's over her dead body. She said I don't know how to take care of a baby, said that I'd have to give it away. I'm not giving my baby away, Abby."
Abby patted her hand. "Tea water's boiling," she said, for lack of anything more comforting.

• • •

The Gospel Mission had no empty beds and by the time Fey got off the bus at 22nd Street, it was dark. Camp Bravo was located on a formerly vacant lot just north of Santa Rita Park, a place she was all too familiar with. Rather than shortcutting through the park, it would be safer to skirt around it. Shivering in her damp clothes, she got on her skateboard, head down and grim. Speed was her ally and her left leg swept rapidly over the pavement.

She didn't know what hit her, but a blow to the side of her head threw her off balance. She stumbled then tumbled to the ground. Without pausing to assess the damage, Fey quickly picked herself up. For a few minutes she peered into the dark, brandishing her skateboard, a proven weapon. The rock thrower, if it had been a rock, could be a druggie who wanted to steal her backpack, a would-be rapist, or simply some asshole who hated who he thought she was. She'd been victimized by all three over the past months. "I'll kill you, mother fucker," she growled into the dark then got back on her board and sped away.

• • •

It was past 9 when she got to Camp Bravo. There were maybe a dozen big tents, army surplus she supposed. Several of them glowed like lanterns and there was a campfire blazing. She'd heard about that campfire, how people would sit around it at night for warmth and company. Now as she approached, she was relieved to see one of the people sitting around it was a woman. Her stomach fluttered from nerves and hunger as she surveyed the camp from a discrete distance. What were the sleeping arrangements here, she wondered, and who was the dude marching around with the American Flag?

This place was undoubtedly full of druggies, alkies, chronics, crazy-assed sign carriers and beggars of the first order. Well, whatever, whoever, this was where she'd be spending the night. She put her hand on her stomach to quell the dread that had settled there, then pulled her cap low over the stinging wound on her temple. Fey never thought she'd end up in a place like this. But a year ago, she never thought she'd ever be homeless again either, thought she'd left that behind with the crack cocaine.

"Hey," she said, stepping into the firelight. "I'm new. Can someone tell me how things work around here?"

One of the men pointed to a sign, which read: *22 Suicides a day among Vets. Camp Bravo is Tucson's camp, no drugs or alcohol allowed.* "That pretty much sums it up. Those guys with the American flags make folks behave. If you do, you can stay as long as you want. If you don't, the sons of bitches will kick your ass to Mars."

"Don't believe him," said the women at the fire. "Veterans on Patrol is what they are and they've been goddamn good to me." She was scrawny and weather-worn with scruffy, iron gray hair. "Still, I wouldn't want to buck 'em, if I was you." With a grunt, she rose. "These goddamn knees." She rubbed them back into service. "My name's Angie." She held out a veiny, thick-knuckled hand. "I'll show you where the porta-potties are located and take you to the women's quarters, less you want to sit around all night with these goddamn bums."

• • •

Shivering, Fey looked around the tent. She'd gone from no windows that opened to no windows to close. She dropped her pack onto a cot, one of a half-dozen set up in the tent reserved for women, then sat beside it to take stock. At this point, she was exhausted, cold, and beyond hungry. She pulled the black, job interview pants out of the bottom of her pack. There was no way around it, she'd have to sleep in them tonight. She was about to pull them on over her shorts when there was a rustling outside.

A tall, burly guy appeared at the entrance of the tent. Despite the chill, he wore a muscle shirt revealing thick arms, a bull-like neck and substantial belly. He held an American flag on a pole and there was a gun on his hip. One of the Veterans on Patrol, she assumed, keeping America safe for Americans.

"Knock, knock," he said before entering. He placed his flag on an empty cot, gently as if it were an armload of long-stem roses, then dropped two wool blankets and a sleeping bag on her cot. "I was told you don't have any gear." He handed her a hot Cup O Noodles and a bottle of water. "All the folks who stay on base have to register, but I guess you can take care of that tomorrow. Just ask for Doc."

"You Doc?"

"No. I'm Friday. Doc's the chief medical officer. He's here every day, all day and sometimes into the night depending, but he lives off base."

"My name's Fey." She rolled the Styrofoam cup of soup between her hands to warm them.

"Welcome to Camp Bravo, Fey. Oh, and I brought you these. Angie said you were wet." He put a pair of sweats on the bed. "Gonna be to too big for you I see, but at least they're clean and dry."

"Well, I thank you."

"One more thing. These tents are kind of transparent, so you might want to turn off that light before you change clothes."

"Thanks for the heads-up," she said wanting him gone.

"Oh yeah. Bed hopping is against the rules here, so you don't have to worry about that."

It occurred to Fey that a person would think more than twice before breaking the rules with Friday on guard, but somehow the muscles and the gun did not make her feel safer. She turned out the light. Appreciating the near solid dark, she took a deep of breath of cool fresh air and chuckled. Unlike the Hospitality House, Camp Bravo sure had plenty of that, and the only sound was the roar of traffic over on 22nd Street.

• • •

When Fey awoke just before sunup she became aware of a small, warm lump nestled against the curve of her body. Pleasantly surprised, she stroked the creature into a purr. How long had it been since she had the simple pleasure of petting a cat?

After some minutes, Fey sat up and the cat hopped down then scurried out of the tent. Robed in blankets and still hooded, she sat on the edge of her cot looking much like a monk praying for divine inspiration. Though she was not praying, Fey was seeking inspiration. If she wanted to regain custody of her son, she needed a job and an apartment. At the very least, she needed to prove that she was making progress toward those goals. The next dependency hearing was looming in the near distance like a funnel cloud, and the judge would not consider the sale of plasma and newspapers progress. Time was running out.

A groan rose from a pile of quilts. Angie's feet hit the floor and she groaned again. "Morning." She wiped her face with her hands and smiled revealing a near absence of teeth.

"Morning, Angie. How are you?"

"Alive, as near as I can tell. I'll gain a clearer picture after I have my coffee."

"There's coffee?"

"You bet. Doc's always got a pot going." Angie struggled to her feet. Squinting, she asked, "What's that you got all over your face? That blood?"

Fey pushed back the hood of her sweatshirt and lightly brushed her fingers over her temple. The blood had dried and but the wound still smarted. "Some son of a bitch threw a rock at me, at least I think it was a rock."

"Well, Doc can take a look at that too."

• • •

The tents at Camp Bravo weren't all for sleeping, Fey realized. On the way to the tent that presumably housed the coffee, Angie pointed out the medical tent, which was under Doc's direct supervision, and a tent housing a common area equipped with a couple of battered couches and a surprisingly, large flat-screen TV. There was a makeshift kitchen with a pantry full of packaged and canned food, free for the taking, apparently. At least it wasn't locked up.

Doc stood over a camp stove tending a large pot of oatmeal. He was a stringy old dude with all the signs of addiction and homelessness. What little hair he had was white, but the clothes hanging off his bones were clean.

"Morning ladies. Coffee's ready," he said, pointing his spoon in the direction a big electric coffee urn.

His eyes were a clear, intense blue and when he smiled, Fey saw a mouthful of well cared for teeth. Whether they were his or not, the teeth meant access to a dentist, which meant stability, which meant that this man was no longer a homeless addict.

He balanced the spoon on the edge of the pot. "Name's Doc. I'm the chief medical officer on base. Looks like you've got an owie young lady."

The words *owie* and *young lady* struck Fey as hilarious. "I guess you could say that," she said, covering her grin and rotten teeth with her hand.

"We'll take a good look at it in a bit, but first things first." He took two cups from a drainer sitting by a large plastic tub. "Coffee?" He passed out the cups. "Creamer and sugar's on the table. The oatmeal won't be ready for another..." He looked at his watch. "Seven minutes. It's steel cut."

•••

"You can sit over there." Doc indicated an old chair with stained upholstery. "It doesn't look clean, but it is, sort of." He slipped on a pair of wire rim glasses then pulled on a pair of latex gloves. "Now lets take a look." He removed an antiseptic wipe from a package and dabbed at Fey's wound. "I think it would be best if I took a few stitches."

"Stiches!"

"Just a few, otherwise it might heal kinda lumpy." He took out a ring with an impressive number of keys on it, selected a small one then opened a padlock on a metal cabinet. Inside were shelves stocked with medical supplies.

"All donations," he said, selecting a couple items. "Veterans on Patrol doesn't accept any cash—not one cent—but we do accept donations of material. In fact, everything you see, the chair you're sitting on, the tents, the food, these medical supplies were all donated." He selected several items then closed the cabinet and snapped the padlock. "When we finish here you're welcome to go check out our boutique. Pick out a new-to-you outfit." Chuckling, he peeled off the old gloves and put on a fresh pair.

"Cool." Fey found it interesting that the medical supplies were locked up and wondered what besides bandages and the like were kept in there. "So do you live here?"

Deep Breathing

"Used to. Got my own place now."

Fey wanted to ask him how he'd accomplished that, but didn't want to appear nosey. At that moment, the cat appeared at the entrance to the tent and sat as if waiting patiently.

"Hold your horses. I'll be with you in a minute," Doc said. "That's Sara, the base mascot. She's not allowed in the medical tent and she knows it."

"We've already met," she said as Doc swabbed the wound then made several Novocain injections around it. Fey winced.

He patted her shoulder. "Steady on, girl," he said leaning into his work.

"So do you like working here?" she asked in order to distract herself, then closed her eyes.

"Don't work. I volunteer my time, every day, Monday through Sunday, 7 a.m. to 7 p.m. Keeps me sane and sober, and you'd be surprised what comes up. I've treated everything from corns to stab wounds. Just last week I stitched up a guy who'd been hit over the head with a pipe." He sat back. "There, you're all set."

"Really?" Fey gingerly fingered the now cleaned and closed wound on her temple.

He put his glasses in his shirt pocket. "So darlin'—do you mind if I call you darlin'?"

"I've been called worse."

He tossed her a little smile. "You planning to say awhile?"

"If it's allowed."

"You a vet?"

Fey shook her head.

"Doesn't matter. Women can stay as long as they obey the rules. Speaking of which." He pulled out a couple of sheets of paper from a one of the two filing cabinets that supported an old door that was his desk. "Lewis Meyer, our base commander, is in Phoenix this week, at Camp Alpha, so as temporary officer in command, I need to go over a few things with you." He handed her a sheet of paper. "Read that."

Fey scanned the sheet. Veterans on Patrol Bravo Base Rules, it read in bold print. The rules were simple:

1. Respect Others and Their Belongings
2. No Drugs or Alcohol
3. Residents Need to Help Around Base Daily
4. No Fraternizing. Only Men Allowed in Men's Tents and Only Women Allowed in Women's Tents.
5. Personal Area Is To Be Kept Tidy
6. Visitors Not Allowed in Tents at Any Time
7. Base Locked Down at 10:00 pm
8. No Smoking

"Two fewer rules than God." Fey smiled behind fanned fingers. "I can live with that."

Doc handed her the second piece of paper and a pen. "Then you need to fill out our intake form."

Fey looked it over. "I don't have an emergency number."

He jotted something on a piece of paper. "Now you do, darlin'. Here's my cell."

Chapter 12

Sunday, Nov. 6

Robert slid into the pew next to his mother. Every Sunday he joined his parents for worship at Saint Phillip's Episcopalian Church. Though he wasn't particularly religious, he enjoyed the tradition, enjoyed the breakfast of waffles with hot maple syrup and bacon his dad would make after the service.

His mother patted him on the knee. "You look very handsome today."

She said that every Sunday, but he did like to dress well. He'd tucked a white handkerchief into the pocket of his navy blazer, and a very nice silk tie with a subtle stripe lay flat over his light blue Oxford-cloth shirt. He would have preferred a shirt with French cuffs, but couldn't manage cufflinks. His gray slacks were sharply creased though, and he'd recently had a manicure.

Across the aisle a family with two small boys, twins who looked to be about 4 or 5, were settling in somewhat noisily. They had recently joined the church and Robert found husband and wife a curious match. The husband, a man he'd guess to be in his late 30s, was a bit paunchy and had a shaggy head of hair, the wife looked worn-out and disheveled. She wore no makeup, and her hair was pulled back in a ratty ponytail. Obviously the woman didn't own an iron. The man's shirt and the boys' matching polos looked as if they'd been pulled out of the bottom of the laundry basket.

As if he could feel Robert's eyes on him, the man looked up and smiled. Robert felt himself blush, but he managed a smile of sorts, then turned his attention to the church bulletin. The topic of the sermon was to be "Allhallowtide, Its Meaning for the Modern Christian."

The organist, a plump woman who wore wigs in an assortment of colors and styles and had an affinity for pastels, began to play *Jesu, Joy of Man's Desiring*. He thought about Abby and felt a stab of guilt. Sometimes he'd ignore his messages for days at a time, too busy or too discouraged to bother. This morning, he'd been checking though a backlog of messages and there was a bizarre series of them from her about a long lost cousin, serial killers knocking off gimps, and something about a drug cartel planting heroin under her chair while she was in Mexico. One of the things he always appreciated about Abby was that she wasn't constantly emailing and texting him, so he was curious and more than a little concerned. He took out his phone now, texted her briefly, then turned it off.

• • •

"Well that was an interesting little sermon," Robert's mother said, slipping her arm though his as they walked the down the maroon carpeted aisle towards the vestibule.

"Inter… esting as in shitty?"

"Interesting as in interesting."

In his sermon, Father Olmsby had urged his congregants to celebrate the season of All Souls Day because death connects us with the resurrection. Robert felt no connection with either death or resurrection. Other than his grandparents, Robert didn't know that many dead people. In college, a gay acquaintance of his had committed suicide when he was outed on Facebook, but it had made Robert angry rather than sad and motivated him to tell his parents the truth about his sexuality. Turned out they already knew.

"Your father and I want to go to fellowship this morning."

"But I'm… starving," Robert complained. The fact was that he hated fellowship, all the phony smiles and glad-handing. And he was hungry. All through the Gloria his stomach had rumbled.

"It will only take a few minutes, I promise." She gave him the pleading smile that never failed to force him into compliance.

• • •

Fellowship hall was a dreary, windowless affair with concrete floors. Metal chairs and collapsible tables were stacked against the wall. One of those tables was set up to hold a large coffee urn, paper cups, napkins and an assortment of store bought cookies. Robert didn't want to risk spilling coffee on his shirt, but he did scoop up several cookies, oatmeal he thought they might be. Immediately, he stuffed one in his mouth to preclude conversation while he waited for his mother to make the rounds. Across the room, she was already carrying on a jolly conversation with the new couple, each of whom had a restraining hand on the shoulder of a squirmy twin.

His mother motioned for him to join her. He pointed his index finger to his mouth signaling that he couldn't possibly talk with it full, but she gave him that smile. He chewed, swallowed, chewed, swallowed then dutifully lurched over to meet the newcomers.

"This is my son, Robert," his mother announced. "And this is Nelson Armbruster. He's a teacher at a Montessori school. Isn't that interesting?"

Robert offered his hand, thinking that his mother, who was a redder Republican than he was, would find teaching in a Montessori school not only uninteresting, but possibly subversive.

"Nice to meet you," the man said, gripping Robert's hand. His broad smile revealed a row of very straight, very white teeth in an otherwise ordinary face. "And this is my sister, Mary Ellen, and her boys, Tom and Ted."

Just then it occurred to Robert that whether Nelson Armbruster realized it or not, there was a conspiracy afoot, and the look on his mother's face, at once sweet and knowing, confirmed it.

• • •

Abby kept nodding off as she tried to study the plans for a kitchen remodel. Now that Stella was staying with her, she thought that sleep would be easier, but nothing so positive, as yet, had come out of this new arrangement. She felt just as alone as ever but had less personal space to be lonely in.

It was only Tuesday, she thought. How would she make it through the week? More to the point, how would she get rid of Stella? Her mother had picked her up Saturday morning as planned, but Stella had run away the next morning, if you could call it running away when you're 28 years old. Her plan had been to marry Gilberto and live with his family. No dice. Though Abby didn't know it for a fact, she was pretty sure that Gilberto's very Catholic mother was just as firmly against this union as Stella's very Jewish mother.

Stella had another explanation. "We can't get married because he has to save up money for a leaf blower." She had told her this as if the logic of it were perfect. Then when Abby suggested that Stella go home to her mother, the woman had wailed so loud and so long, Abby had caved. What else could she have done? Put her out on the street? Well, she was stuck for now, but she was actively looking for a solution. Tonight they would talk finances, figure out how much money Stella earned each week, how much she should put aside in savings, how much rent she could afford. Abby would not encourage Stella with a place to stay, however humble, rent-free.

She turned her attention back to the plans. The stove and sink were probably too high. The drawing began to blur and she could not keep her eyes open a moment longer. Abby's head popped up when Rita whizzed in the door in a burst of frigid air and energy.

"Sorry I'm late, *mija*." Honey peeked out from the folds of the red wool cape that served as Rita's winter coat then hopped off her lap and onto Abby's.

"No problem. Nothing's going on this morning anyway," Abby said, squeezing her eyes shut as the dog licked her face, the little pink tongue a wet blur. "Okay, I love you too," she said before giving the dog a gentle shove.

Rita shrugged the cape off her shoulders, flung it onto the coat rack then held out her hands, fingers wiggling. "What do you think?"

Her fingernails were midnight blue, each with a tiny lightening stroke of silver. Abby had never known Rita to paint her nails. "Sexy. What's the occasion?"

The woman smiled. "Got a date Thursday. He's picking me up after work. Well I'm driving of course, but he's meeting me here."

"A date? I'm jealous. Who's the lucky guy?"

"Norberto, the guy who took me to breakfast last week. Remember, he's the father of Alma's daughter's husband's cousin. You remember Alma. I took you to her granddaughter's Christening."

"Oh yeah, cousin Alma. But doesn't that make Norberto his uncle?"

"Whose uncle?" Rita filled the electric teakettle with water.

"Alma's daughter's husband."

"No, because they're second cousins or something. Anyway, we're sort of related but not, so it's okay to date."

Abby nodded, too tired to untangle the convoluted relationship

"Where's he taking you this time?"

"Someplace nice I hope. The manicure cost me 30 bucks. You should treat yourself to a manicure. It's so relaxing." She paused, lifting an appraising brow. "You look beat. If you had a gun, you'd sleep better."

"Please don't get started."

"Okay, I won't. But I sleep like a baby." She dropped two bags of Karma tea into two mugs. "Anyway, you need to get out more. Go to a movie."

"Like Coralee Fancher?"

"I forgot about Cora. What you need to do is go out and have a little fun with somebody nice and safe."

"I'm having lunch with Robert tomorrow."

"Robert doesn't count."

"I'm sure he'd be happy to hear that. Anyway, not everyone has an enormous herd of relatives to set them up."

"There are other ways to meet men."

"Join a club. Go to church. Get a hobby. Volunteer. Look online."

"Why not look online? At least you could…"

"The water's boiling."

Rita poured hot water into the mugs, then plunked them, one at a time, on the desk.

Abby reached for a mug then read the tag. "Oops. I think I got your teabag."

"Oh yeah? What's it say?"

"*If you think you have the key to someone else's happiness, try turning it in your own lock.* Yours?"

"*If you are focused on what you are missing, you are missing what you have.*"

They traded mugs.

• • •

Anûshka slid down the pole one last time, legs in what was now her signature 190-degree split. When she reached the bottom she did a walkover then waved to the audience, a smile broad upon her lips after what she considered another near 10 performance. He was there again this evening standing and clapping wildly. She bowed at the waist, blew him a kiss, bowed once more then skipped off the stage, waving as if she were once again a 16-year-old, medal-winning gymnast.

In the cubby that was a communal dressing room, Anûshka counted the tips from her three sets. There was one twenty, 14 ones and a single quarter. A quarter! Was this insult? she wondered. Who would be so cheap, so low and mean to leave a quarter only? But there was also the twenty-dollar bill. As she pulled on her sweats, she thought of the man who had stood and clapped, the man of the twenty-dollar bill.

Anûshka didn't glance in the mirror or smooth her hair before leaving the club. What would be the point? She was only going home to her brother's house where she would drink another protein smoothie and watch on TV whatever her sister-in-law was watching. Her life, it was really too boring.

By the time she got to the bus stop, it was already dark. She sat on the cold metal bench to wait. Though this area of town, with its strip joints, prostitutes and drug addicts, was not a place a lady would choose to find herself, the bus stop was well lit and the wait would not be long. She closed her eyes and allowed her thoughts to stroll down the well-worn path to her daughter, the reunion they would have. She smiled, thinking how she would take her angel to the zoo. She herself had never been, but would once her Sonia joined her.

Anûshka stiffened when she heard the sound of rapid footsteps on the sidewalk. She sprung to her feet, ready to run if necessary.

"Excuse me, miss," he said, a bit breathless. "I didn't mean to startle you."

He was wearing a baseball cap that obscured the upper part of his face, but she recognized him immediately by the oversized Hawaiian print he wore to disguise his paunch. Definitely him, the man who appreciated her great ableness with a twenty-dollar bill. She smiled. "It is you from the club, the man who claps too much for me."

He smiled. "Well your poll dancing is amazing. Really, you could win prizes. My name is Howard Grosman." He offered her his hand. "And you are?"

"Anûshka Sryezkeptch."

"Anûshka, that's a Russian name, isn't it?"

"It is popular name in my country as well."

"And what country might that be?"

"Croatia."

"Really, that's someplace in Europe, isn't it?"

"Yes, it's on the beautiful Adriatic Sea."

"Yeah, the Adriatic Sea. Anyway, Anûshka, I was wondering if I could buy you a cup of coffee. There's a Whataburger. See, it's just across the street. We could talk."

• • •

After Abby had told Robert about the sudden appearance of cousin Fey, after she had told him about her attackers, the frozen tamales and the wasp spray, after she had told him about Detective Stranksy and the canister of heroin, after she'd told him of the murders and how the number three meant a serial killer was on the loose, after she had lectured him about the very real danger of picking up strange men in bars and after he had wiped the hamburger juice and ketchup from his face and hands, a little smile rippled across his mouth and he said, "I... got some news... too."

"And what would that be?" Frustration edged her voice. Had the man heard a single thing she said? Did he understand the danger?

"I have... a date."

"A date? Well... that's just great," she said, trying not to sound as though she gave a fart. "Where did you meet?"

"In church."

"No, really. Where did you meet?"

•••

Anûshka walked into the office wearing a conservative pants and blouse combo. Her makeup was subtle and she'd wrestled her blond frizz into a chignon. She twirled in front of Abby's desk then took a little bow. "What is it you think?"

"Very professional," Abby said. Without the gobs of makeup, Anûshka looked quite pretty, softer and younger. "You will inspire confidence."

"Confidence, I do not feel it. In my stomach is butterflies."

Abby too was nervous. Brady O'Riley struck her as a taskmaster and she wasn't sure Anûshka was up to the task. Cleaning, of course, would be no problem, but ferrying the man around town in his expensive car might well be. If she failed, Abby doubted that GSG would be given a second chance to fill his employment needs. She looked at her watch. "Mr. O'Riley probably won't be here for another 20 minutes. Would you like a cup of tea while you wait?"

"That would be very nice, Ms. Bannister."

"Call me Abby, please, otherwise I'll have to call you Ms. Sryezkeptch."

"But you say Sryezkeptch so perfectly. Most people have great difficulty to pronounce my name."

"Yes, but Anûshka is such a pretty name and suits you so well."

The woman's cheeks colored and she smiled. "You are too kind." She drew a tissue from her purse and flapped it in the air. "Do you mind I make little touch up before arrival of Mr. Riley?" Without waiting for permission, Anûshka began dusting the top of Abby's desk. "I clean office for you. I give for you good discount on my excellent services.

Abby laughed. "Discount? How much?"

"For you, my excellent sponsor, I give 20 percent discount." Anûshka moved on to the counter where she quickly straightened stacks of yet to be filed folders, paper plates and napkins and printer paper. She gathered up dirty plastic spoons and forks, old crumbs and wrappers and threw them in the trash. "I clean office and bathroom bottom to top. Two hours I could do it for total of only $24. Is good deal, once a week."

"It's not in my budget."

"Your budget is too much small."

"That's because my income is too much small."

"Okay. You don't charge finder's fee. I clean office how many times, I don't know until first pay check."

Abby had to hand it to the woman. She was always angling. Still, she liked her persistence, up-beat confidence and straightforward manner. She only hoped Mr. O'Riley would appreciate these qualities. "I'll think about it," she said, pointing to the mug of tea on the counter. "Now sit down and drink your tea."

Abby took her mug to her now dustless desk and opened an email from Susie at Lane's Realty. Attached were photos of another condo that had just come on the market. It was a single story. With little modification, the kitchen and bathroom would accommodate a person in a wheelchair. She had a client who'd broken his back in a biking accident. There had been a settlement, and he and his wife had been looking for an accessible home to buy.

Slim hips leaning against the counter, Anûshka blew on her tea, then took a small sip. "I have one other news."

Without looking up from the computer, Abby smiled encouragement.

"I have date with very nice man!"

• • •

"The sooner the better," Abby was saying. "My assistant won't be in until this afternoon. I could meet you at the condo, say at 4. Will that work for you, Susie? Great. See you then."

She put the phone back in her pouch. Sighed. Took a sip of now tepid tea then read the aphorism on the tag. *Sow kindness and reap love.*

Was that her problem? She pulled out the teabag, dribbling tea over her computer, and flung it in the trash. "Damn!" she hissed. She wanted to scream. Really, it would feel good to scream, pull her hair, and beat her Mighty Claw against her head.

Of course she was happy for Robert, happy for Rita and for Anûshka. Happy, happy, so happy she could spit. It wasn't simply that she wanted to meet someone; but that THEY could meet someone and she could not. Besides the obvious, there must be something wrong with her. Something she was doing wrong, but a failure to sow kindness? She thought of Fey. She had been honest, or at least she thought she was being honest at the time, but unkind? And Stella, she'd been kind enough to allow the woman to stay even though it was an invasion of her space. She's made a bad business deal with Anûshka out of kindness. Didn't that earn her a few Karma points?

Robert had a date, Rita had a date, Anûshka had a date, and she had Stella. Taking a deep breath, she closed her eyes, took another deep breath and another. She opened her eyes, looked around the office, which was now neat as a pin.

"Shit!" she yelled "Shit, shit, shit!"

There. That felt better.

CHAPTER 13

Thursday, Nov. 10

Rita looked nervously at her watch. She was wearing a deep blue sweater with some kind of sliver thread woven through that glinted when it caught the light. "You know you don't have to wait," she said to Abby.

"Of course I have to wait. I want to meet this guy. You look great, by the way, very sexy."

Rita gave her a dazzling smile. "Thanks, *mija*. The sweater matches my nails. Did you notice?"

She nodded, though she hadn't. "So what's the plan?"

"I drive to wherever we're going. We have a nice dinner. If all goes well, we'll be eating chilaquiles for breakfast. At my age, you I don't want to waste any time."

"Kind of slutty, but I see your point. So do you have a sexy nighty all picked out and ready to go?"

Before Rita could answer, the door swept open and there was Norberto. The first thing Abby noticed about the man was that he had a full head of mink brown hair, a color, she was fairly certain, that was natural only to a mink.

Rita whizzed out from behind the desk "Norberto, I'd like you to meet my boss and good friend, Abby Bannister."

"A pleasure to meet you," he said, but didn't offer his hand.

It's not catching, Abby was tempted to say. Instead she smiled. "Nice to meet you, too."

• • •

Anûshka sat on the couch, holding tight to her own hands, knees nudging a glass-topped coffee table. Layered across its dusty surface were bits of paper, envelopes with hastily written jottings—names and phone numbers mostly—an ad announcing a sale at Sears, an electric bill. On top of last Sunday's sports page was a dirty coffee cup and next to that a laptop computer.

Howard emerged from the kitchen with two glasses of white wine. He shoved the paper pile to the floor and set the two glasses on the sports page. Anûshka pressed her lips together and tightened her grip on her hands. He was hatless now and she couldn't help but notice that long strands of blond hair starting just above his left ear were carefully combed over a wide swath of pink skin and held in place by some stiffening agent.

"This is why I invited you over tonight," he said, rapidly entering words she could not read into the little box at the top of the screen. "It's amazing."

Anûshka took a sip of her wine as she waited for the amazing event.

"Watch this." He sat back, arms folded across his chest.

A woman in an orange bikini and amazingly high platform shoes was ascending a slowly spinning pole, hand over hand, while executing the Chinese splits.

"That's Anastasia Sokolova. She reminds me of you except she's more..." he gestured toward his chest. "They say she's the greatest pole dancer in the world."

Unimpressed, Anûshka said, "But I can do that no problemo." Then the woman in orange gasped the pole between her waist and thigh, torso and arms appearing to float on thin air. "And that I have done many times." The woman continued to writhe and twist. Her body, amazingly supple and strong, assumed a position akin to a pretzel while the pole slowly spun. "Well, I have never done that, but I could do it."

"Better. You could do it better than Sokolova."

"So why you show me this?" She nodded her head toward the computer.

"The "Ms. Pole Dance Arizona" is why. I think you could win it."

"Is there medal for winning?"

"If you win, you get $5,000."

"So much money!"

"But there is an entrance fee of $500."

"I don't have $500."

"Neither do I, but I could probably pull together $250. If you could lay your hands on the other $250, we'd be in business."

"And when is contest?"

"December 1. But you have to register by November 25."

"So soon. I need new routine. I need new costume and those big shoes. Shoes like that cost much money. Allow me to thinking." Mr. O'Riley was to pay $20 an hour, nine hours guaranteed per week, but that was only $180. Where would the rest come from? There was money put aside for Sonia, but was contest wise investment? What were chances of winning gold?

Anüshka studied the man's face. "So you loan me $250? Why do you do this?"

"Because, Beautiful, I think you're a winner."

She took another sip of wine and set the glass back down on the sports page. Really, she could think so much better if she could just wipe dust from the table. She made a few quick calculations in her head. "Okay," she said at last. "Here is excellent deal. If I win, I return $250 investment plus 15 percent of prize money. That is $1,000 profit for you and $3,750 for me."

"No way. You're the one with the talent; you keep all the prize money. My reward is giving you a nudge toward your destiny."

"Let me see again this woman, Sokolova. Are there other such womans for me to look at?"

Suddenly, he pulled her to him. "You are so beautiful, baby." He planted a big wet kiss on her mouth. As his hands moved over her body, she remembered to close both eyes, but couldn't stop thinking of the piles of paper, the dirty cup and the dusty table. She could only imagine what the bedroom would be like. And the sheets! She did not even want to think about the sheets. With some force, she pushed him away. "No way, José. I am not this kind of girl."

The door whooshed open and Rita whirred in looking tired. A good sign, Abby thought. Then Honey jumped off her lap and scurried under the desk, tail between her legs. Not a good sign.

"Sorry I'm late, *mija*."

"You're sorry to be late every morning. More importantly, how was the date?"

"That's why I'm late." She hung her cape on the coat rack.

"Oh?"

"He took me to El Coral. It was so noisy I couldn't hear a thing I said." She waited a beat then added, "That was a joke Abby; you're supposed laugh."

"Sorry. So go on."

"Anyway, all I can say is that if your *novio* is over 60 and you want to get laid, don't order a bottle of wine at dinner."

"So what happened?"

"So I invite him in for a nightcap."

"And?"

"And I go in the bathroom, you know, to freshen up. By the time I come out, he's asleep on the couch."

"What did you do?"

"I went to bed. I did put on my sexy nightie in case he woke up and wanted to join me, but no, when I got up this morning, he was still snoring on the couch. I gave him a cup of coffee and shooed him out the door. No way was I going to waste my chilaquiles on a man who can't stay awake long enough to take care of business."

"Poor guy."

"Please don't defend him," Rita said, filling the teakettle.

Abby started to protest, but thought better of it. "Put my name in the pot, please."

"So what's on the agenda for today?"

"Same old, same old. I finished the grant to the SBA. I'd like you to go over it before we send it out. There's the remodel. I want to check up on the new guy, see how he's doing. After that I was hoping we could go to Food City. With Stella eating for two, I have to make sure there's something more in the fridge than yogurt and eggs."

"So what are you going to do about that?"

Abby sighed. "I'm working on it."

The door whooshed open and a middle-aged woman stepped into the office holding a vase of red long-stem roses. "These are for Rita Sotomayor," she said looking from one woman to the other.

Rita's hand went to her throat. "Roses for me?" She read the card and smiled. "Well, looks like Norberto gets a second chance."

• • •

As soon as she had gotten to the DCS office Fey checked the visitation room, but Frisco and Elena were not there. Even though it was chilly out, she'd gone back outside to wait for her son, preferring the little grassy courtyard to the dreary visitation room.

The stitches on her temple were beginning to pull and itch. She resisted the urge to scratch them. It had been five days since Doc had stitched her up. When she got back to camp she'd ask him if he could take them out. Absently, she flipped through the library book she'd brought to read to her son. Frisco had recently developed a fascination with Thomas the Train. In this one, Thomas encounters a Tyrannosaurus rex. Frisco would love it.

Setting aside the book, Fey opened her wallet. She'd been back to the plasma bank this morning and she reckoned she was finally far enough ahead on her funds. From behind her ID cards she extracted the bills she'd hidden there, two twenties, one ten and a five and put them in her pocket. She pulled a wad of bills, her seed money, from her bra and sorted through them, peeling off a limp five-dollar bill. She put that in her pocket with the others, refolded the wad and tucked it back into her bra.

After 20 minutes, Frisco and Elena had still not shown up. Had she gotten the wrong day? Fey went back into the building to the receptionist's desk. "Hi," she said. "I'm here for a visitation with my son ..."

"And you are?" The woman asked, eying her tattoos.

"Fey Lesher."

"Hang on a minute." The woman gazed at her computer. In sharp contrast to Fey she was soft, round, her face was dusted with powder, lashes mascaraed and lips freshly lipsticked. Fey took an instant dislike to her, though she wasn't sure if it was because she wanted to be like her or because she didn't want to be like her.

"Francisco Lesher?" She said at last. "Oh, he's not coming in today."

"Why not?"

"His foster mom says he's got a little cold so she's keeping him home."

"She can do that?"

"Yes, she can."

Anger, punctuated by disappointment shot through her body like twin lightning bolts. Fey started to protest, but caught herself knowing that this woman would report any bad behavior to her social worker. Defeated, she was about to leave, then paused. "Excuse me ma'am."

The receptionist looked up, red slash of a mouth drawn into a firm straight line.

"Do you have an envelope I could have?"

Wordlessly, the woman shoved an envelope at her.

"Thanks. And could I borrow a pen for a minute?" The woman handed her a pen and Fey jotted a brief note on the back on the envelope. "Thanks, that's very kind of you." She smiled sweetly, congratulating herself on her control. A few months ago, she'd have let the bitch have it. One thing Fey had learned from being in the bottom of the heap was that a person needed self-control to crawl back out of it.

Deep Breathing

• • •

Fey had just put in two more hours of sweat equity at Bicas, earning another $18 toward her bike. She was getting pretty fast at cleaning parts and dismantling bikes. Now, as she tooled down Sixth Street, skateboard wheels clicking on the sidewalk, her thoughts turned to Abby as they so often did. At this time of day, her cousin should still be at work and that was for the best. Though Fey would like to see the expression on Abby's face when she read the note on the envelope, she really did not want to see her. It wasn't just that Abby had denied any awareness of what her father had done to her time after time, but Fey was also deeply ashamed. She was ashamed of her lack of progress and ashamed of her appearance, but there was something else. As Abby had pointed out, Fey never once put up a struggle. Instead of screaming and fighting off the old bastard, she'd let him have her, accepted the money and then pretended it hadn't happened. How was she supposed to explain that?

But her life was far from over. Unlike poor old Angie at Camp Bravo whose only concern was getting out of bed each morning, Fey needed a plan. She had her work at Bicas, and was close to earning her own bike, which she could either sell or use for transportation, and there was the growing wad of seed money, now over $70. It wasn't much, but it was more cash than she'd had in months. More importantly, she hadn't wasted it on drugs, wasn't even tempted.

Yes, she was ready to take back the controls. All she needed was a little luck, a chance to wedge herself back into the life she wanted for herself and her son. She imagined a small apartment—one-bedroom or even a studio. They wouldn't need much. There was a fridge full of food, good food, healthy food for her boy who stood by the door patiently waiting for her to take him to preschool. There was a broad smile on his sweet face, and he was wearing new clothes and those shoes, the kind with little lights that blinked with each step. She remembered that once Frisco had a tantrum in Target over shoes like that, shoes she couldn't afford to buy for him. She understood his tears of want and rage. Understood that it was not just the shoes he wanted back then, but a mother that could feed, clothe and protect him from all harm. She knew the feeling well. Her own mother had failed her in the same way time and again. It was what had landed Fey in the bed next to her cousin Abby so many years ago. A dark cloud of reality settled over her. If she managed to regain custody of her son, what made her think that this time around she would do a better job than her own mother?

Sure, she'd passed all her recent urine drops and had started to build a resume by volunteering. So what? She was still jobless and homeless. In the past two months she'd had only three interviews and no callbacks. She was on the waiting list for subsidized housing, but couldn't afford even minimal rent on plasma bank and newspaper hawker wages. Her social worker was getting impatient, and the next dependency hearing was coming up to determine if her parental rights should be severed. Severed, that was the term they used. And it was fitting. If she lost Frisco, they might as well cut off her hands and feet and let her bleed to death. With her fist, she beat on her chest as if to break up the congestion of anxiety that had lodged there.

Across the street, a bigger than life woman smiled down on her from the side of the crumbling Tucson Warehouse and Transfer Company. A desert goddess, she was surrounded by juicy prickly pears and an agave grew out of the top of her head. She was lush and sexy and was appeared to look right a Fey. "Listen," she seemed to say, "I've got to go around with this stupid agave growing out of my head, but you don't hear me complaining."

Fey considered the mural for a moment. "Okay," she said to herself as she sped down Ash, then onto Abby's street. "At least I don't have an agave on my head. I guess that's something."

Browning crabgrass fringed the ramp up to Abby's front door. For the past three weeks she had looked forward to this moment, but now she wasn't sure. Was this really the best thing to do with $60? What, if anything, did she owe Abby? She was about to get on her skateboard and roll back down the ramp when the door swung open, and a slender woman with a ruffled cap of auburn hair said, "Can I help you, sir?"

Fey was so startled that she almost stumbled off the ramp. "No, I… Who are you?" she asked, not bothering to correct the woman's confusion over gender.

"I'm the cleaning lady." Smiling, she stepped forward. "What do you keep under there?" she asked, pointing to Fey's voluminous knit hat.

"My hair." Smiling, Fey pulled off her hat and her dreads sprang up like trapped rodents.

"Whoa!" Stella stepped back and a young man came forward. One arm cradled Abby's cat. The other he placed protectively on the woman's shoulder.

Fey noticed that both had the sweaty sheen and guilty expression of lovers caught in the act. By the look of the cleaning lady's belly, they had been going at it on Abby's dime for at least five months. Before she could change her mind, Fey reached into her pocket and handed the woman the envelope. "I'm Abby's cousin. Would you see that she gets this?"

• • •

Friday afternoon was probably the worst time to grocery shop, but sometimes Rita and Abby couldn't avoid it. As was their habit, once they got to Food City, each went their separate way, respective grabbers ready to retrieve items from the upper shelves. Arguably, this store had the best and biggest produce section in town. Serving a largely Hispanic population, it offered at least 15 varieties of chilies alone and lots of fruits and vegetables Abby didn't have names for.

She put half-a-dozen plump Roma tomatoes into a bag and laid them gently among the yellow onions, zucchinis and bell peppers already in the little wheeled cart she used for grocery shopping. Cooked with a pound of hamburger then poured over spaghetti, that would be dinner for the next few nights.

As she maneuvered her cart toward the aisle where the pasta was, it occurred to her that at least she was eating a better diet now that she was cooking for Stella.

From the middle shelf, Abby plucked a bag of pasta. On the shelf above, she spotted jars of marinated artichokes. They would be great in the sauce. She extracted her grabber from her cart. Awkwardly, she maneuvered it into position, squinting to improve her depth perception. She hesitated, as she envisioned glass jars crashing to the floor. Just how much did she want those artichoke hearts?

"Excuse me, Miss. Could I get that for you?"

Not waiting for an answer, the man reached for a jar of artichokes hearts.

A blocky man of middle age and height, he was clad in Bermuda shorts and Birkenstocks. A black long-sleeve T-shirt was his only concession to the cool weather. He put the jar in her basket. "Is one enough?"

Abby tilted her head back so she could look in his eyes, which were deep-set, brown and fringed with amazing lashes. Only his prominent nose saved him from being handsome. He smiled warmly.

Abby returned the smile. "Yes, one's plenty, thanks. I appreciate the help."

"So, do you always shop here?"

"I do," she said. "And you?"

"I'm new in town, but I heard that this was a great place for produce. I'm trying to learn to cook Mexican food. This week it's pozole."

"Hmm. Pozole. Your wife is a lucky woman."

"My wife and I are divorced, unfortunately."

A spark of interest ignited and she searched for something interesting to say. As usual, nothing came to mind.

"Say, is that a can of bug spray there?" He pointed to the canister of Real Kill resting by her thigh.

She chuckled. "It's wasp spray. Can stop a bear at 20 feet."

"You got a wasp problem at your house?"

"Sometimes," she said, not wanting to go into detail about why she carried wasp spray with her everywhere she went. Again she searched for something less complicated to prolong the conversation. In addition to the tomatoes, chilies, tomatillos, cabbage, cilantro, limes, oranges and a package of hominy in the man's cart, Abby noted a big bag of cat kibble. "I see you have a cat."

• • •

"Mike's originally from Minnesota," Abby was saying. "He's retired Air

Deep Breathing

Force, was stationed at the base here over 20 years ago, so after his divorce, he decided to move to Tucson. Oh yeah, and he's got three cats, Juniper, Frank and Bess."

"Boy, you certainly wasted no time in the pasta department," Rita said as she pulled up in front of Abby's house. "Did he ask for your number?"

"No, but I gave him my card."

Rita turned to face Abby, left eyebrow sharply arched. "You gave him your card?"

"Well, he offered me his, but when he looked he couldn't find one, so I just gave him mine. You think that was too forward?"

"Not at all. I'm proud of you for taking the initiative. As they say, *Solomente elle que persigue, consige.*"

"Only she who does what?"

"*Only she who pursues, gets. Now if he wants, he can get in touch.*"

Pleased to have earned Rita's approval for once, Abby released the apparatus that secured her chair in the Iceberg and smiled. "That's what I thought."

• • •

As Abby wheeled in the groceries, she was imagining a coffee date with Mike Brown and how they would exchange funny stories about their cats.

Stella was sitting at the kitchen table watching *So You Think You Can Dance.* "You want some help putting those away?" she asked without taking her eyes off the screen.

"You can put the eggs, yogurt, cottage cheese, milk and bread in the fridge. The rest is dinner."

Stella began unpacking the cart. "A guy came by to see you this afternoon."

"Did the guy have a name?"

"No, but he said he was your cousin. He left that envelope." Stella pointed to a long white envelope on the dinette.

Abby turned the envelope over in her hand, saw the note on the back: 12X $5 = $60, it read.

There had been a dozen or more times over the years when Abby thought her life could not get worse, but she had to wonder if she had hit an all-time low. Fey's terse message on the envelope containing the $60 had hit her like a gut punch, causing a crashing wave of guilt-induced nausea. By repaying the money, it was as if Fey had passed off a burden of debt to Abby. Because of Abby's earlier denial, it was a debt with compound interest and she didn't know how to manage the payback. She didn't even know where Fey was.

From the moment Abby had walked in the door, Stella, oblivious, prattled on about how her mother would not allow her to withdraw money from her savings account even though she had earned that money and how her hot boyfriend needed a leaf blower and she was getting fat and needed new clothes. On and on she went until Abby could not listen to another inane word. "Sorry Stella, but I'm worn out. I just want to go to bed."

"What about dinner?"

"Too tired to eat. You're welcome to make a hamburger for yourself, or anything else that appeals." She whirred into her bedroom and closed the door.

Abby hadn't lied. Guilt had exhausted her. She'd crawled in bed fully clothed. After she'd played and replayed the Fey record, her unresolved guilt over the abandonment of Alfonso resurfaced. Sleep seemed improbable, if not impossible. As if he were doing her a favor, Tito crawled alongside her chest so she could pet him.

It struck Abby as patently unfair that she should be so afflicted by guilt. Hadn't she suffered enough affliction in her life already? Wasn't it enough that she was born with cerebral palsy? Wasn't it enough that she lost her mother and had to suffer the verbal and emotional abuse of her alcoholic father? Shouldn't there be some sort of quid pro quo here? You endure X amount of suffering and hardship and in exchange you get Y amount of little tokens that you can spend to avoid feeling guilty. One would think, but apparently not.

Abby didn't know how long she'd been in bed before she heard a soft knock on the door. She sighed deeply then told Stella to come in.

Deep Breathing

"I made you some cinnamon toast and hot milk with honey." She nudged Tito off the bed unceremoniously. It wasn't that Stella didn't like Tito; it was just that she didn't like him that much, didn't like his hair everywhere and really didn't like cleaning his litter box. She put the tray on the bed. "This is what my mom always makes for me when I feel bad."

There was a wistful tone in Stella's voice that Abby hoped was homesickness. She drew in a lungful of air then pulled herself up into a sitting position. "My mom always made me a hot eggnog."

"That's nice," Stella said, settling on the edge of the bed.

Abby took a bite of toast then a sip of warm milk, grateful now for the distraction of food and company, even Stella's.

...

On her way to the office, feeling no less guilty and wretched, Abby had come to a clear understanding that there was nothing to be done about Stella or Fey, at least nothing she could think to do at the moment, but she could try again to find a way to bring Alfonso to Tucson. She'd given up too easily the last time, but now was determined. It was the only thing that might ease her misery.

She looked at her watch—9:42—then went to the website of the Citizenship and Immigration Services of Homeland Security, which led her to the National Customer Service Center of U.S. Citizenship of Immigrations Services website and a telephone number. After five minutes of the menu merry-go-round and several false starts, Abby heard the longed-for words, "How may I help you."

"Yes, I would like to arrange for a handicapped but highly intelligent child who is currently in a ... well it's a hospital, but also a kind of home for orphans with medical conditions. Anyway, I want to arrange for this boy to come to Tucson, Arizona, for the purpose of education and rehabilitation. How do I do that?"

"Well, the child will need a visa, but you will have to go to the Department of State website to determine what else is needed."

"But I was hoping…"

"I'm sorry, you need to go to the Department of State website for further information."

"Thank you," Abby said, though gratitude was not the emotion she was feeling at the moment. She hung up the phone and googled Department of State. After a bit of searching, she found another telephone number. Again the menu choices, none of which seemed to be exactly what she needed, so she just pressed 2 and hoped an actual person might help her narrow her search.

"All of our representatives are busy helping others." She checked her watch. It was now 10:07. While she waited, Abby held the phone away from her ear so she wouldn't have to listen to canned music. After a mere four minutes, another real human, this one male, came on the line.

He listened patiently as she described her quest then said in a pleasant baritone, "I can walk you through it."

Hallelujah, Abby thought. "I'm ready when you are."

"Okay, what you need to do is go to Visa-info.com."

Abby entered the website. "I've got it. Now what?"

"Now click on nonimmigrant."

She did. "Now what?"

"Well, what does it say; there should be a pull-down of choices just below."

Abby searched the screen. "There are no choices."

"They're right there, just below nonimmigrant."

"Not on my screen."

"That's funny. Okay, here's what you gotta do then. Go to the website of the National Customer Services Center of U.S. Citizenship Immigration Service website."

"God help me, not another website."

"Hang on there. I'll give you the phone number."

He did and after more menu choices and canned music, Abby discovered that Alfonso would have to go to the consulate in Hermosillo, Sonora, to apply for a passport. Once he'd been issued a passport, it would take 160 nonrefundable dollars to apply for an F-1 nonimmigrant student visa. That meant that Alfonso would have to be told of her intention without being assured that her efforts would result in a student visa. Abby sighed. Well, there was no way around it, but first, she needed to make her case to Sor Felipa, whom she suspected would not be a big fan of the plan.

Abby looked at her watch. It was now nearly 11. She was about to put in a call to Sor Felipa when the door whooshed open. A man, supported by Canadian crutches, hesitated a moment as if to regain forward momentum. He reminded her of the scarecrow from *The Wizard of Oz*. His skin looked more like canvas than skin, the slash of a mouth, even his hair, what little there was of it, resembled straw. He staggered forward, one painful step at a time, right knee caving into left. A cloth satchel hanging from one shoulder swung with each step, threatening to upset his tenuous balance. When he reached Abby's desk, he held out his hand, or what was left of it. "Barney Franklin," he said.

Training her eyes directly into his, the only part of him that seemed unscathed by fire, Abby took the disfigured hand in hers, "Abby Bannister. How may I help you, Mr. Franklin?"

"I saw your interview on TV several weeks ago. I've been meaning to come by and introduce myself. I'm a local contactor and I'd like your business. He smiled, or at least Abby thought he did. "My partner and I do quality work, remodeling as well as custom home construction."

"Would you like to sit down, Mr. Franklin?"

"Thanks no. Once I sit, it's hard to get up."

She smiled. "I completely understand. So I'll need some references and I'd like to see your work."

He rested a crutch against the desk, then pulled a portfolio from his satchel and handed it to Abby.

Abby slowly paged through the plastic enclosed photos of bathrooms, ramps, kitchens, several entire houses. "These look great, Mr. Franklin. If you can give me a list of clients I could contact for references. Are you currently working on a house?"

"A remodel just over on Third Street."

"I'd like to stop by and see it, if that's possible."

Again the tortured smile. "You can do that. We're not the fastest in town, but folks are happy with our work."

"Does your company have a name?"

He handed her his card. "Franklin and Son, General Contractors. No job too small," was it's modest message.

Part III

"Get ready, get ready. I'm on my way."
—*Get Ready* by the Temptations

Chapter 14

Monday, Nov. 14

Abby had awoken in an uncharacteristic bubble of optimism. Even the morning grind of dressing and grooming hadn't burst it. Stella had made a big pan full of scrambled eggs with toast and jam and half a grapefruit, food that had bolstered this strange feeling that her luck was about to improve.

Now, as she rolled down the ramp and onto Fourth Street, she vowed to follow Dale J. Nagery's advice and keep a sharp eye out for hidden opportunities to make her own happiness.

It was a beautiful morning, clear and sunny and windless. She missed listening to her music on her way to work, but knew she couldn't risk the distraction. Full of renewed purpose, she could almost feel the warmth of the agave woman's approval as she sped down Sixth. In addition to starting a new grant application, this one to the Arizona Department of Fair Housing, she had plans to visit Barney Franklin at his remodel and a determination to call Sor Felipa about her plans for Alfonso.

As Abby entered the building, Pastor Glorie and four members of her congregation were on their way out. Each was carrying a box filled with what Abby assumed to be day-old doughnuts. This morning, Glorie was sporting a black and white ensemble with red accents. On each thick wrist there were several red plastic bangles, on her feet, red tennis shoes. A wide-brimmed black hat adorned with a red ostrich feather completed the picture. Before Abby could duck, the woman planted a big red kiss on her cheek. "Blessed morning to you, sister."

Abby wiped her cheek with the palm of her Mighty Claw. "And it's a beautiful day." She was determined that even Pastor Glorie's kisses would not dampen her spirit "Looks like you're on one of your good deed rounds."

"Camp Bravo this morning."

"Camp Bravo?"

"You haven't heard of it? It's a little tent city for homeless veterans mostly, but women can stay there too. It's just north of Santa Rita Park. Once a week they get our doughnuts and a little prayer service. Care to come with?"

"Thanks, no. I have to get to work."

"Well, you have a blessed day."

• • •

As usual, Abby was the first to arrive at the office. She put water into the electric teakettle. While waiting for it to boil, she dumped out the stack of cards that were in a small basket on her desk. She sorted through them trying to locate one of her own, on the back of which she had written the number for Hospital Santa Clara. While she was sorting, it occurred to her that Rita would be a better person to petition Sor Felipa. For one thing, Rita's Spanish was much better than her own. For another, Abby suspected that the good sister did not quite approve of her relationship with Alfonso, and was afraid she'd reject her proposal out of hand. Rita was never that late and Abby could wait.

She selected a tea bag. Its tag read *A fool and his money will soon be parted*, reminding her of the money she'd have to spend on the passport and visa application. She found the card with the hospital's number and set it aside. As she gathered the cards back into their basket, the office phone rang.

Abby let the phone ring the customary three times, hitched herself up a bit straighter, then picked it up. "GSG, Abby Bannister speaking. How may I help you?" Then, "Oh, yes, Mike, how could I forget? You saved me from being pelted with jars of artichoke hearts." She felt a pleasant little flutter in her chest. "So what can I do for you?" Then, "Lunch? Well that would be lovely," she said, and the flutter intensified to near fibrillation.

They'd settled on a time. Abby had suggested they meet at the Shanty, which was in striking distance by Chariot. By the time Rita arrived, Abby was in a state of nervous agitation, a condition that her friend picked up on at once.

"*Que passa?*" she asked, unwrapping herself from her bright red cape. "You look like you're holding back a fart, and what's that red blotch on your cheek."

"Charming, Rita, and how are you?" Abby said, trying to rub the residue of Glorie's kiss from her cheek.

Rita nudged Honey off her lap. She cocked her eyebrow then and said. "*Dígame.*"

"There's really nothing to tell. Mike Brown just called and asked if I could meet him for lunch is all."

"Ah, Mike Brown of the too many cats? No wonder you're blushing."

"I am not blushing and it's really no big deal."

"*Mentiras.*"

Though Abby wasn't lying exactly, she was not telling the exact truth. The fact was, she really didn't want to make a big deal out of a lunch date. If she'd learned anything from past experience, it was not to get herself all worked up over a date, which would ultimately lead to disappointment.

"*Pues?*"

Abby looked the woman straight in the eye. "*Pues*, I have nothing more to say on the matter."

Rita smiled. "Have it your way."

Abby shrugged. "There's hot water in the kettle. Oh, and I need a favor."

"*Dígame.*"

"I need you to call Sor Felipa. I'm going to try to bring Alfonso to Tucson so he can go to school. He'll need a passport before he can apply for a student visa and …"

"You think Sor Felipa is going to go for that?"

"That's why I want you to talk to her."

"What? You're too chickenshit?"

"Not at all," she lied again. "It's simply that your Spanish is so much better than mine." She handed Rita the card with the phone number.

"I know you think Alfonso is a genius with great potential, but I certainly don't see it." She shot Abby a look, mouth pulled down in a frown conveying great skepticism. "Personally, I think the whole idea is nuts. The visa alone will cost you over a hundred bucks."

"One hundred and sixty actually. Now would you just make the damn phone call, please?"

"Yes, ma'am. You're the boss."

Abby hated it when Rita pretended to take orders. "While you make the call, I'll make you a cup of Karma," she said to demonstrate that they were equal players.

After 10 minutes of rapid fire Spanish, much of which Abby could not understand, Rita hung up the phone. "She agreed to do it on the condition that Alfonso attend Catholic school. Now I think you're both nuts."

"We'll see." Abby handed Rita her tea. "Read your tag."

"*The difference between a flower and a weed is perception.* So?"

"When you look at Alfonso, you see a weed. I see a flower."

• • •

After checking out a new Thomas Train book for Frisco, Fey took her place at one of the computers to fill out her three applications as she had done once a week for the past three months. She was about to Google Whataburger to see about openings when Frances, the librarian she liked best, placed her hand lightly on Fey's shoulder.

"Have you seen this?" Francis put a flyer beside the computer. "I thought you might want to apply."

Prepare for a Career and Become a Culinary Professional, the flyer read.

"Can't afford to go to a cooking school."

"But look." Francis pointed to the *please read* section at the bottom. "It only costs $25."

Fey was suspicious. "Caridad Community Kitchen. I've never heard of it."

"Look." Frances again pointed to the pertinent information. "It's a program sponsored by the Community Food Bank. You've heard of that."

She had. Fey quickly read the requirements applicants needed. She certainly met the one for low-income.

Frances gave her shoulder a little nudge of encouragement. "At least you should fill out an application. You can do it right now online. And Fey?"

Fey angled her head so she could look directly at Frances. There was nothing but kindness to be found in that plain, round face.

"It matters less where you've been than where you're going. This is a program for people who need second chances. Be totally honest in your responses to the questions, and here." She placed her card next to the computer. "You can use me as a reference. You'll need two."

Fey nodded. "Thanks, Frances. I'll fill it out." She reread the flyer. There were only two requirements that she didn't meet. Drug-free and sober for 180 days and reliable housing during program. She could lie about the drug-free part, since she was now, which was what really mattered. Would Caridad Community Kitchen consider Camp Bravo reliable housing?"

For over nine months now, she had worked the program, gone to parenting and work training classes, done her urine drops and filled out countless applications, all so she could get her son back, but without a job that would never happen. With the passing of each month her hopes faded and with that, there was a bit of relief. If there was no hope that she might succeed, she could stop trying. Day after day, she tried so hard, but other than her pitiful seed money, now totaling $37 and change, and a bike that she might earn in some unpredictable future, there was nothing to show for it.

Keep your eye on the prize, she told herself. For a moment she closed her eyes and imagined herself lying on a big bed next to Frisco. He was wearing the puppy dog PJs he loved; a Thomas Train book lay open between them.

Fey took a deep breath and started in, line by tedious line. She paused when she came to emergency contact information, hesitated a moment then wrote in Abigail Bannister.

She hesitated again at the bottom of page three. *Please write a 3-5-sentence paragraph explaining why you are interested in this program.* How could she possible explain her situation in three to five sentences? She made several false starts then decided to come back to it later.

Though Fey had finally asked Frances for help with the essay, the application had demanded so many dates that she could only guess at and reasons and explanations, it had taken her well over an hour to complete. When at last she hit *submit*, Fey pulled her cap low over her brow and began to cry. The application was the longest, the most detailed she'd ever filled out, and, as Frances had advised, she'd been totally honest, almost. Her whole adult life was on that form. It was proof of her worthlessness.

• • •

Both women were at the counter trying coax the old printer into service when the phone rang. Rita whirred over to the desk, paused to let it ring a third time then answered. "GSG, Rita Sotomayor speaking. How may I help you," she said, in her professional receptionist tone. "Just one moment, sir."

"Mike Brown," she mouthed to Abby then passed her the phone.

"Hi, Mike. What's up?"

Rita sat back to listen to the one-sided conversation.

"Oh. That's too bad." Then, "Well it can't be helped." Then, "No, not at all." Then, "Sure, when you get back. Bye-bye."

"So?" Rita asked.

"So he has to go out of town on business."

"I thought he was retired."

"Retired from the Air Force, but now he works for some medical supply company. He usually can work from home, but he's been called into the corporate office."

"Where's that?"

"Pittsburg."

"How long is he going to be in Pittsburg?"

"He wasn't sure."

"Well, he called once. He's interested."

Abby wanted to believe that, but reality had burst her bubble.

• • •

Anûshka, who had talked Abby into letting her clean the office instead of paying the 15 percent employment finder's fee, was mopping the office floor. "Howard wants me to gain weight," she was saying. "Just 10 pounds, he wants. But that's…" She took a moment to calculate. "Four point five kilos, which is as much as a great sack of potatoes or a big tin of lard. He says I'm all bone and muscle. Says I'm like giant praying mantis. What is praying mantis?"

"It's an insect." Abby paused. "But it's a very helpful insect and I think quite … handsome."

"Awk, is insult. He says to compete as pole dancer I must do it. But I am too terrified. If I start to eating I will not stop until I am fat as a… as a…"

"Pig?" Rita suggested.

"No I was thinking of the one with the big nose."

"Elephant."

"Yes, elephant." She dipped the mop in the bucket and wrung out with furious energy. "And breast enhancement, he wants I should do that too. Breast enhancement, that is disgustive. From when I was child, I pray that my breasts do not grow big and bouncy. Gymnasts do not have big bouncy breasts. God answered this pray and now Howard wants that I should have such breasts."

"Actually, silicone doesn't bounce," Rita offered.

"No? Well, it does not matter, even if I wanted, I could not afford."
"You know, this guy sounds kind of... well..." Abby began.
"Abusive," Rita finished.
"Abusive? What is abusive?"
"Let me field this one," Rita said, warming to the conversation. "Abusive means someone who hits you or forces you to have sex."
"Howard never has done such things."
"Right, but it can also mean a person who doesn't accept you the way you are. An abuser is a person who says things that hurt your feelings or makes you feel that you are not good enough. I was married to one of those."
"But he thinks I am enough good to be Ms. Pole Dance Arizona. He will give to me half of money I need to enter contest. That is no small thing. Besides," she said pointing to the ceiling beyond which God resided. "I believe that there is reason why things happen. Howard comes into my life for reason. It can appears this reason is stupid and has many harms, but in a future time, it becomes all for better."
Abby and Rita exchanged looks. Abby shrugged. "How's the reading coming along?"
"My beloved reading coach say to me that progress is excellent."
"And your new job? Is Mr. O'Riley happy with your driving?"
"Yes. He say to me I am excellent driving."
"Wonderful. I'm proud of you."
"Yes, everything is good, expect for the wife of my brother. She hate me. She say I take so much room. Look at me? Do I look like I take up so much room? It is she that take up so much room with the fatness of her bottom. And now she is with baby and when born, I must to move. If I had money I would to move last week."
"Could you move in with your boyfriend?"
"He is manager, not boyfriend."
"Ah, well ..." Abby looked at her watch. "It's getting late, Rita. If we're going to see Barney Franklin's remodel this afternoon, we'd better get going."
"So *dígame, mija*, is this Barney Franklin cute?" Rita wrapped her cape around her shoulders, cuing Honey to scrabble out from under

the desk and leap onto her lap.

"He is the opposite of cute, but even if he were, this is just business, Rita." Which was essentially true. Business and curiosity.

"We'll see you later, Anûshka. Keep up the good work."

"Okeydokey," she said, without looking up from her mopping.

• • •

Rita pulled the Iceberg into the drive. In front of the sprawling sixties ranch-style house, a well-built young man dressed in a snug T-shirt and well-worn Levis was throwing strips of rolled carpet into a dumpster.

"I thought you said Barney Franklin wasn't cute."

"That's not Barney Franklin," Abby said. "Are you going to let us out, or are you going to sit there drooling?"

By the time Abby rolled down the dog's tongue, the man was waiting for her. He pulled off a pair of leather gloves and offered his hand. "You must be Ms. Bannister. Barney's expecting you."

"Where is he?"

"Up there," he said, pointing with his chin.

Abby followed the line of his chin to the top of the roof where Barney Franklin, legs and arms splayed like a giant starfish, was inching along the eaves.

"My name is Brad. I'm the son in Franklin and Son."

For the next 10 minutes, they watched the man creep toward the ladder that leaned against the roof, then make his painstaking descent. At the bottom, he retrieved the Canadian crutches that he'd left hooked onto the ladder. Abby could understand now the man's earlier caveat that they were not the fastest contractors in town. Having spent her childhood moving through life at the pace of a snail, Abby understood that fast was overrated.

• • •

"This is the part of the house I wanted you to see," Barney was saying as he led them into the kitchen. "Custom cabinets are my specialty. My son does the counters, tile, granite, whatever surface the customer chooses. He can install it."

Abby gazed at the beautifully crafted wooden cabinets. "Oak?"

"Oak. That's my preference, though I can provide maple, cherry, what have you." He opened a door. "Lazy Susan. There's one in each corner." He gave the circular shelves a spin.

"Well, you do amazing work. I wish I'd known you when I was remodeling my house."

He turned, catching his right foot behind his left. "Oops," he said grabbing the counter for support. "This damn leg doesn't always do what it's told."

Abby smiled. This was a man she could work with.

Chapter 15

Wednesday, Nov. 16

Torrance Steadman, siren whooping and lights twirling, pulled over the old truck with the cracked taillight. While he ran the plates, he considered the truck. Whips of tar like dribbled chocolate syrup crisscrossed the sides and one door was so dented, he doubted it would open. Three small men were sitting shoulder to shoulder in the front seat. Roofing was a shit job, but these guys were willing. He had to give them that. He got out of the car and slowly approached on the truck's passenger side. It would make his job a lot easier if these folks would just fix their goddamn taillights.

"*Buenas tardes, amigos,*" he said, sticking his head into the window on the passenger side. There was no whiff of alcohol or dope in the cab, just three tired men in soiled clothes, illegals, most assuredly, with kids waiting for papa to come home and one lousy broken taillight.

"Good afternoon, officer," the driver said in heavily accented English. "Is there a problem?" The other two men kept their eyes tight

Deep Breathing

on the windshield as if there was a *telenovela* playing out just beyond the hood of the truck.

"Left rear taillight's broken."

"Humm. That's very strange. It was okay this morning."

Steadman's grandmother was a Mexican who came up from Chiapas when she was 12 back in the day when the question of legal or illegal didn't seem to be one many people cared to ask. But now he was supposed to do just that. Screw it, he thought.

Steadman usually did things by the book, but sometimes the page he was on was not in the book and he had to wing it. Sometimes he got caught, more than once he'd been demoted, but never did he regret the times he acted as a human being first and a cop second.

"I'm going to give you a warning. Get that light fixed."

"Yes sir. Thank you, sir. I'll take care of it."

"If I were you, I'd take care of it right now." He checked for oncoming traffic. When it was clear he waved them on.

He looked at his watch. By this time of the day, Abby was usually home. Since he couldn't get the captain to assign him to her case he had unofficially assigned himself. Maybe he'd drive by, let her know he was still keeping an eye on her. That page wasn't in the book either.

He'd gotten a text message earlier. It could only have been from his daughter, Cara. Currently, she and her four-year-old daughter, Linetta, were living with him. It was only temporary. It was always only temporary. Cara and Linnie would come and go, depending on love and finances. He didn't mind, liked the company, liked the fact the Cara preferred his company to her mother's. He especially liked having his granddaughter around. Saucy and too smart for her own good, the child reminded him daily why life was essentially good.

Before pulling back out into the traffic he read Cara's message. It was a simple one. *Hey Pops, Milk, hamburger, Pepsi. Love ya.*

• • •

Stedman was surprised when a young pregnant woman opened the door. "Who are you?" he asked. The words sounded rude even to him and he quickly amended them. "Sorry, is Miss Bannister in?"

"I'm Stella, the cleaning lady, and Abby should be home any minute. I'm not allowed to let you in, but you can wait outside if you want."

"No, no. I was just in the neighborhood and thought I'd drop by to see how she was doing." There was something a little vague about the girl and he supposed she was one Abby's special employees. "Just tell her Torrance came by. Nothing to worry about. Tell her I'm keeping an eye out for her. Can you remember that?"

"Torrance came by. Nothing to worry about. You're keeping an eye out for her."

"Good girl." Now he sounded condescending and he quickly added. "Thank you, miss, and what's your name again?"

"Stella."

"Thank you, Stella."

As he walked to his car, Stedman felt oddly deflated. Now what was that about? A little white lady in a wheelchair and a big fat black man. An image came to mind. He winced. If Stransky had even the slightest hint that things were getting personal, well ... he'd probably be in trouble again.

They went back a long ways, he and Stransky. She'd always had his back and had taken his side when he'd been demoted for failing to get a search warrant and call for backup. He'd made his case to the board of inquiry, explained that he'd seen the perp go into the apartment, knew the guy was armed, knew the woman that lived in that apartment, knew this guy was neither boyfriend nor husband, but a very bad-assed dude. He was pretty sure the board had been on his side until Chief Charles Lindgren claimed that his concerns had been overblown and boom, he was busted back down to patrolman.

Maybe it was because Lindgren didn't like the fact that Stedman had the trust of the black community, which gave him an insider's advantage. Maybe it was because he just didn't like fat black cops. Whatever the reason, Stedman had gotten under his very thin white skin. In many ways and on numerous occasions Lindgren had come just short of calling him a cocky nigger.

He wasn't cocky, not back then or now, but Stedman firmly

believed that in certain circumstances rules were best ignored and one's sense of right and wrong, and the risk to civilians needed to be factored into actions taken. That had been one of those circumstances. What he did not factor into his decision was his own personal interest. Had he done that, he'd still be a detective, but the woman and her kids might be dead now.

Stransky had borne witness to it all, the veiled insults and the inquiry. She'd done what she could, which hadn't been much—was pregnant with number three at that time and was going through her own little hell at the department—but in this case, she would not take his side and rightfully so. No, no, there wouldn't be anymore welfare checks on Little Miss Abby. Still, that didn't mean he couldn't cruise her neighborhood to keep an eye out. Nothing wrong with that.

• • •

He'd been out for his evening troll, but now it was getting late. On his way back to the car, which he'd parked in the far, southwest corner of the Food City's parking lot, a van caught his attention. The grocery store was nearly empty, but he figured that's exactly why some folks liked to shop late. Though it had a handicapped license plate, the driver didn't bother to park in one of the spaces reserved, but pulled in diagonally beneath a struggling mesquite not far from the entrance. After several minutes, the door opened, and a greatly obese guy came down the metal ramp on one of those little motorized scooters.

God help him, he almost laughed at the sight of that enormous ass slopping over the impossibly small seat of the scooter. What a hell of way to live, he thought. As he made his way along the periphery of the parking lot toward the van he pulled a pair of leather gloves from his jacket pocket. When he stepped into the shadow of the mesquite, he noticed that in addition to the little wheelchair on the license plate, there was also a Purple Heart. Well, they had that in common.

It wasn't long before the guy came out of the store. He wasn't carrying a grocery sack, just a carton of cigarettes. The guy must have run out. Never would he understand how some folks could eat and smoke themselves into such misery.

The scooter was now so close he could hear it purr. He waited until the guy entered the shadow of the mesquite, waited another beat for the scooter to come to a stop. He slipped up behind him, the stink of old cigarette smoke filling his nostrils. Quickly, he thrust his arms beneath the fat arms and locked his hands behind his head. He threw all his weight forward and waited for the snap and waited. Again, he threw his weight forward. Still no snap. The guy was scrabbling and tearing at his gloved hands. He bore down, but the fat neck would not break. He was sweating now from exertion, but he couldn't let up the pressure. After several minutes, the massive body went limp.

"God rest your soul," he whispered, lips grazing the dead man's ear.

• • •

Breathless, he tossed the gloves onto the back seat and slid behind the wheel of his car. A guy that big, he should have anticipated trouble. It was supposed to have been a quick and painless release, but clearly the man had suffered. Pressing his forehead against the hard cool plastic of the steering wheel, he began to weep. He felt so terribly alone. He had no one but God and He seemed so far away.

"Oh Lord," he whispered. "Haven't I proven myself to you time and again? Why are you still testing me?" For a long time, he sat there, tears wetting the collar of his shirt, then a sudden calm settled over him like a net cast from the sky.

Before turning the key in the ignition, he looked into the rearview mirror. Nothing. Hands shaking, he took out his handkerchief and wiped the tears and sweat off his face. Control. He needed to regain control. He took a deep breath and another, then pulled out of the parking lot and onto St. Mary's Road.

The light ahead turned red and he slowed to a stop, stomach sick. It was supposed to be quick and easy, just like the first time. Back then he'd had to act so fast that he hadn't had time to think.

The Army recruiter had told him with his test scores, he'd definitely go to Europe, most likely Germany. When he ended up in Afghanistan, he was definitely pissed, but in time he recognized it as God's will.

The supply truck was the first in the convoy. He'd been in the one behind. The undersides of those trucks were reinforced with steel plates, but when they ran over an IED, it didn't seem to make much difference. The soldier, he was just a kid too, was still fully conscious when he pulled him from the truck and laid him on the ground to assess the damage.

Dazed, the guy looked at what had once been his right arm and asked. "What else?"

As he'd been trained to do, he was already starting to apply a tourniquet to his shredded leg when he saw the blood soaking through the front of the guys pants.

"What's fucking left, man?"

The kid must have read his expression.

"Please man, not like this," he said, groping his bloody crotch with his left hand, his eyes wide and wild.

He knew he had to act fast before the medics got there. He didn't remember the thinking, only the doing.

Just as he heard the snap, there was an instant of white heat slamming into his shoulder, hurling him forward over the kid's body.

He'd gotten a Purple Heart and a Silver Star, for that one. The light turned green and he shook his head at the crazy-sad irony.

Feeling calm now, wrung out but calm, he turned on the radio. A cool sax riff washed over him and his thoughts returned to the guy at Food City. His life was hell, clearly, he could see that, and there were worse things than a few moments of pain, things much worse than death. His sister had taught him that and he knew better than to ever second-guess God.

Chapter 16

Thursday, Nov. 17

Stella's mother was waiting outside the office when Abby whizzed up. The woman wore a sour expression and Abby wished that just once Rita could get her ass to the office on time. She smiled even as she braced herself for the explosion.

"Ms. Boom, I mean Ms. Bloom. It's nice to see you."

"I know that's a lie."

Ignoring the statement, Abby unlocked the door and both women stormed through. "So, what can I do for you?" She asked as she hung the thick wool poncho she wore in cool weather on the coat rack.

"You can stop enabling my daughter."

Feeling vulnerable, Abby whirred behind her desk. "I'm not enabling her."

"You are letting her stay in your home where she continues to see that boy. If that's not enabling I don't know what it is."

"I'm merely allowing her to figure out what she wants to do next."

Deep Breathing

"She wants to marry…"

At that moment, Rita wheeled in, the Arizona Daily Star tucked under her arm. In an instant, she appraised the situation. "Darn, I forgot to pick up the empanadas," she said and backed her chair out the door.

Without pausing for breath, Ms. Bloom continued. "…that boy and have his baby, and that can't be farther from what I want for her. You seem to forget that Stella is not the brightest candle in the menorah."

"So you've said." Abby took a deep breath then changed tack. "I know that Stella's happiness is… "

"There's happiness and there's security, Ms. Bannister. In my experience, when there is security, happiness will follow." Arms folded across her ample chest, she leaned forward in the chair. "And who is this boy, this what's his name?"

"Gilberto."

"Does this Gilberto love her? In my book, love means marriage, something he is not offering. In his estimation, Stella and his unborn child rank somewhere below a leaf blower in order of importance. This is not a recipe for happiness."

Abby had to admit the woman had a point. "I agree that getting married doesn't seem…"

Ms. Bloom raised her hand, palm outward. "Allow me to finish. There's a woman I know at Jewish Community Center, we work out together in the gym. She's got a nephew who's a… well…like Stella, a few cents short of a dollar. His family is well off and the boy needs a wife, but not a pregnant one or at least not one pregnant with someone else's baby. You see where I'm heading here?"

Hoping for a moment to regroup Abby asked, "Would you like a cup of tea, Ms. Bloom?"

"Thank you, no."

Abby gathered together a few random papers on her desk and put them into a folder as if they were all part of a bigger plan. "So Stella has to give up her baby because you want to marry her off to this friend's nephew? Has she met this nephew? Have you? And what do his parents think of this plan?"

"Thanks to you, everything is now on hold."

Taking a deep breath, Abby pushed herself upright in her chair. "Sorry, Ms. Bloom. I'm not accepting any responsibility for Stella's pregnancy or for her refusal to put her yet to be born child up for adoption."

"You know, I could have her declared incompetent."

"That's not as easy as it used to be, but let's say you find a judge that would declare Stella incompetent. You become her guardian so you can tell her what to do for the rest of your life. Then what?" There was a satisfying silence as Ms. Bloom chewed on that for a moment. Having scored a point, Abby continued. "I will say this, and I speak with the authority of experience: With a little support from you, Stella is bright enough to make a living, live independently and raise a baby." As her body once again began its downward slide, Abby looked the woman as squarely in the eye as she was able. "Given a little time and space, you might find that what she wants for herself is not so different than what you want for her. I'm pretty sure she misses you, by the way."

Ms. Bloom looked skeptical. "What makes you say so?"

Abby shrugged. "She made me hot milk with honey when I was feeling like I was coming down with a cold."

"Really?" She thought about that for a moment, sudden tears filling her eyes. "You know I love my daughter, but this is not about love. It's about my duty to make sure her future is secure. Sure, I'm not old, but I'm not young either. I could have a stroke and die tomorrow. What would happen to Stella then?"

"And Stella's father? Does he have a role to play?"

"As you may or may not know, Stella's father and I have been divorced for years and he rarely sees her. Sure, he's a generous man. He'd be happy to pay the costs of what? A group home? That's not what I want for Stella."

"That's exactly why it's in Stella's best interest to help her prepare for independence." Abby studied Ms. Bloom's expression, which was skeptical at best. "You know," Abby continued in a softer tone. "I think you're looking at this situation as a loss, but maybe it's an opportunity in disguise. Sometimes you have to let go of the wheel to gain control. Jumpstart your vehicle to a more joyous and fulfilling… ah…"

"What are you talking about?"

"Well…" Abby was not quite certain herself where the combined wisdom bytes of Dale J. Nagary and Karma tea tags were taking her, but she soldiered on nevertheless. "You might think about guiding her rather than trying to control her. Stella has developed a backbone; I suspect she got it from you—a single mother of a … challenged daughter. Stella is having your grandchild, Ms. Bloom. You can fight it or embrace it, but you can't change it."

That last bit sounded surprisingly wise, but it was mostly just words and cynical ones at that. She wanted Stella out of her house; at least she had until lately. Now, thinking back on the warm milk and honey, she wasn't so sure.

• • •

Moments after a somewhat mollified Ms. Bloom left, Rita appeared. The newspaper was still tucked under her arm. Honey jumped off her lap and immediately scrabbled at Abby's shins with her dull little claws.

"Good timing, you coward," she said patting her lap. The dog jumped up, little pink tongue darting at Abby face. "You must have been hiding out across the street."

"Not at all and here's the proof." Rita waved a bag of *empanadas*. "Want me to heat one up for you?"

"A mango and a cup of tea, if you don't mind."

"So?" Rita asked, filling the electric teapot.

"So, she's going to think about doling out some of Stella's savings; they are co-signers on the account. If she does, Stella can start looking for an apartment. I think she should qualify for Section Eight housing, so that will help."

"Good job."

"We'll see. Ms. Bloom is not wholly convinced that Stella can survive without her constant supervision and advice. The woman's a bit of a control freak."

"No wonder the two of you got along so well."

"What's that supposed to mean?"

"Come on, Abby. You know how freaked out you get whenever someone else has their hands on the reins."

Abby had to think about that for a moment. Rita was probably right. All her life she'd had little control over what happened to her body. So many things, from major surgery to kind of shoes and bra she wore, had been determined by cerebral palsy. Was it so surprising that she wanted to have control over what was left? Still, she didn't appreciate Rita's tone. "Freaked out? When have I been freaked out?"

"The time your brother bought that junker?"

"Well, he'd paid way too much money for it and most of the money was mine!"

"How about the time the contractor installed the grab bar on the wrong side of the toilet."

"Sure I was pissed, but freaked out?"

"Then there was the time the bank called because you'd overdrawn your account. And what about that time Pastor Glorie wanted to sing Christmas carols in the hall?"

"I was not freaked out."

Smiling, Rita put a cup of tea and a warm *empanada* down on the desk. "Just saying."

Abby read the tag on the bag. "'Let go, let love.' How many bags of Karma did you have to go through to find this one?"

"First one out of the box. I hate to change the subject, but have you heard anything from your cousin?"

Abby had never mentioned the missing $60, or their return. "I don't know where she is, but I think of her every day." A partial truth was better than a total lie. "I'm kind of worried about her actually."

"Well, I'm sure she'll resurface. You know what they say: *Una manzana podrida eventualmente se cae de arriba de montón.*"

"What?"

"A rotten apple eventually falls from the top of the pile."

"You don't know the first thing about her, Rita. She's had a hard life."

"Who hasn't?"

Abby didn't want to get into a discussion about Fey's hard life and the role her father had played in it, nor did she want to talk about her own part as unwilling witness. "Well, Fey is not a rotten apple."

"If you say so."

Abby had just taken a big bite of *empanada* to avoid further discussion when the phone rang.

Rita waited for the customary three rings. "GSG, Rita Sotomayor speaking. How may I direct your call? One moment, sir, she's on another line." Eyes wide, she whispered. "Mike Brown."

Abby swallowed, took a sip of tea then swallowed again before picking up the phone. "Mike, what a nice surprise. How was Pittsburg?" Then, "Oh. So who's taking care of Juniper, Frank and Bess?" She turned to Rita and mouthed, *He's still there.* "Oh? Well, that's good." Then, "Just same old same old, which is a good thing actually. Is it cold in Pittsburg?" Then, "I hope you brought an umbrella." Then, " Me too." Then, "Me too." Then, "See you when you get back." Abby chuckled. "No really. I'm looking forward to seeing you."

"Juniper, Frank and Bess?"

"His cats."

"You remembered the name of his cats? You must be in lust."

"I don't even know the man," she said, trying not to smile. "Anyway, he said he'd call when he gets back."

"And when will that be?"

"I didn't ask." She took a bite of *empanada* to quell her jittery stomach. "Don't give me that look," she said around the mouthful. "I didn't want to sound all forward and anxious."

"You're probably right, *mija*, but for him to call from Pittsburg just to say he misses you… "

"He didn't say that."

"Then why would he have called all the way from Pittsburg? You must have made a hell of an impression on him in the pasta aisle."

Abby smiled then shrugged. She took another bite of *empanada*, chewed then washed it down with tea.

Rita had left the newspaper on the counter. She retrieved it now and scanned the headlines. "Uh oh," she said.

"Uh oh?"

"Another gimp was murdered last night?"

"Where?"

Rita drew her finger down the column. The parking lot of the Food City on Saint Mary's."

"That's our Food City! That's way too close to home."

Deep Breathing

Chapter 17

Thursday, Nov. 17

Fey and Tanya had spent the afternoon dismantling old bicycles for their parts. Now they stood shoulder to shoulder at the grimy little sink in Bica's bathroom. Other than the sink, which was hopelessly stained, the bathroom was clean, thanks in no small part to Fey's attentions.

"Try using a little Boraxo on your hands," Tanya handed Fey a stiff cuticle brush.

"Thanks." She scrubbed at the black beneath her fingernails while studying the other woman's reflection in the mirror. Tanya's dangling earlobes arced back and forth slightly as she wiped her hands on a paper towel and the gold bead in her lower lip gleamed with saliva. Though she'd like to, Fey couldn't say they were friends. Still, Tanya had been kind and helpful right from the first. She didn't judge, and Fey felt she could trust her. Even so, all afternoon she'd been trying to find the courage to ask her for a favor, something that would be no big deal for anyone else. She took a deep breath. "Umm," she began. "I need to ask you for a favor."

"No, you cannot borrow my vibrator," Tanya said, lips twisted into a playful half smile.

Fey laughed and her hand flew up to cover her mouth. "Even if I promise to wash it afterwards."

"Even if you scrubbed it with Boraxo."

"Okay then. Let me ask you another favor."

"Shoot."

"Could you write a recommendation for me? You can do it online."

"Easy. Let's go out front and I'll do it right now."

"Really."

"Sure. I know just what an employer wants to hear."

"Like what?"

"Like Fey Lesher is a willing worker and a team player who learns quickly and can accept criticism. Can you accept criticism? I mean, it's never come up."

Fey snorted. "If I couldn't accept criticism I would never have survived my childhood."

"I hear you."

"Really?"

"Really. To this day my mother and I can hardly be in the same room."

"My mother and I couldn't even be in the same city." It was something that one friend might say to another. There was a moment of silence and Fey was afraid she had said too much. "Anyway," she added. "I really appreciate everything you've done for me. It's... it's." She had the terrible feeling that she might cry and that would really mess things up. "Well, it means a lot."

"No biggie," Tanya said, earlobes swaying like twin tire swings. "Give me the info and you can watch me write it."

Biting her lower lip hard, Fey just nodded.

• • •

Before returning to Camp Bravo, Fey swung by Casa Paloma, which was not too far out of her way. Though she wasn't staying there, if she needed to wash her clothes, which thanks to Camp Bravo, were now in greater number and variety, she could. If she wanted to take a shower there, instead of the dicey outdoor shower at Camp Bravo, she could. If anyone, a potential employer or her social worker needed to contact her they could leave a message for her there. The only problem was that the hours the doors were open to drop-ins was limited to midafternoon.

She stood in front of the intake desk waiting to be acknowledged, her dreads still dripping from the shower. Dreadlocks took forever to dry; it was their only drawback. They didn't get in the way and were easy to maintain, but the thing she liked most about her hair was the way people stared, half-surprised, half-scared as if her hair could bite. It always gave her a pleasant little surge of power. Yes, her dreads suited her well.

Fey didn't expect an interview, but there might be a message from Abby. It had been four days since she'd left the envelope at her house. Plenty of time for Abby to think things over; reconsider the part she'd played. Fey could almost see her lying in the next bed, hardly breathing, her little nose pointing toward the wall. The image left a metallic taste in her mouth, as if she'd been sucking on a penny. She used to do that when she was little, suck on a penny to see if it tasted different than a nickel or a dime.

When the receptionist looked up, she offered her closed-lip smile. "Fey Lesher, she said, pushing her ID over the counter. "Any messages?"

The woman returned her smile. "Telephone message." She handed Fey a small piece of paper.

Fey scanned the message. Not from Abby, but Caridad Community Kitchens. She was to call for an interview. She slipped the note into her pocket then exhaled. Fey hadn't even realized she'd been holding her breath.

• • •

Anûshka hesitated in front of the door to Howard's second floor apartment. The building was rundown. No one had bothered to sweep up the blown trash that had collected against the building, the wood on Howard's door was warped and splintery and she had noticed on her way in that the water in the swimming pool was a suspicious green color. Two hundred and fifty dollars was a lot of money, nearly all her savings, and it worried her that she was about to hand it over to someone who lived in such a dirty place. Through the door she could hear the television. There was yelling and she suspected some kind of a sporting event. She almost turned to go, but then she thought of her angel daughter. With the money from the Ms. Pole Dance Arizona contest she could have her daughter by her side. *You must recover your fearless*, she told herself. She took a deep breath in the same manner she did as a girl just before her performance on the balance beam then thumped on the dry wood with the side of her fist.

Howard opened the door. "Hey, Gorgeous." Patting her fanny, he pulled her into the room.

...

"Knock knock," Fey said as she entered the medical tent.

Doc was lying on a cot reading a paperback. He tossed it aside and sat up. "Evening, Fey," he said pushing his glasses up on his forehead. "What can I do for you?"

She held out her hands. "Do you have anything that could remove the grease from under my nails?"

He pulled the glasses down and took her hands in his. "I don't know. They're pretty raw. What did you use on them, steel wool?"

"Boraxo and a nail brush."

"Well, honey, if that didn't get it… "

"I've got to do something. I've got an interview for a culinary training program at Caridad Community Kitchen. Ever hear of it."

"Back in the day, I picked up many a sack lunch there."

"They have training for low-income folks to help them find jobs in the food industry and I've got this interview. Anyway, I can't show up with grimy nails."

"Let's see what I can do." He took out a pair of small scissors. "Use these for removing sutures. Now hold still. Expertly, he cut each nail just shy of the quick, but a slender crescent of black grease remained. "Okay. I've got another idea."

He rummaged through a drawer then produced two half empty bottles of nail polish. "Do you prefer red or green?"

"Nail polish is kind of a strange thing to keep with your medical supplies."

"You'd be surprised at the stuff that ends up with my medical supplies. I found these in a box of donations. I thought they might come in handy sometime and I was right. So what will it be?"

"I guess the red."

He hummed tunelessly as he started to paint her left thumbnail.

"You don't smoke, do you Doc."

"Used to, but I had to quit when I moved here. You can't smoke anywhere but the front tent. Well, that's where all the vets gather to talk trash. See, I liked to have my smoke and my coffee in the wee quiet hours while I contemplate the movement of my bowels." He looked up at her and smiled. "Anyway, there's always a lot of yap in that tent about the Russians, the Iranians, the Mexicans, the Iraqis, everybody talks about their war, if they've been in one, as if it were the only war and then they bad mouth the president of the United States." He picked up her right hand, applying smooth deft strokes of red as if he did it for a living.

"Now, I'm not a man to get into a heated discussion about who's the idiot," Doc was saying, "so I just decided to quit smoking. Did it cold turkey same way I did alcohol. Of course I had pneumonia and was in the VA hospital at the time, which made it lots easier." Again the smile. "But when I got well, I stayed off 'em. The way I look at it, these guys who sit around on their asses smoking like chimneys, what they're doing is committing suicide piecemeal. I know because I was at that point. The only thing that kept me alive was inertia."

He applied polish to the last nail. "What do you think?"

Fey examined the stubby nails under the light. She was experiencing a rare moment of relaxation, grateful not just for the manicure, but for Doc's gentle attention. There weren't many men in her life who'd been gentle with her. At the moment she could not think of a single one. "Maybe a second coat." She closed her eyes and let his words wash over her without paying much attention.

He took her left hand in his and continued. "Don't get me wrong. I'm not opposed to suicide. In my view, pills, injection, a bullet, electrocution, the stunning blow to the head with a hammer, for that matter, provides a death more humane than nature, which is indifferent to suffering. And since we have no choice upon entry, the manner in which we exit this world should be our own decision when possible."

"I've never giving it much thought before, but I see your point," Fey said by way of encouragement.

"And I'll tell you something else." Doc dipped the brush in the polish then picked up her right hand. "To me, evolution is like God, and Darwin, not Jesus Christ, is its prophet. Over millennia, plants and animals adapt, cells mutate. This, and not some old graybeard in the sky, determines which species move up the ladder and which go the way of Triceratops, the giant sloth and the Neanderthals. What with climate change and all, I think humans are an end-of-the-line-species. The survivors will be the ones who evolve to eat plastic. Makes me fear for my grandkids. Do you have any kids, Fey?"

"A boy. Frisco is 3, but Child Safety took him away from me. Said I neglected him but even at my worst, I never did. Anyway, I can't get him back until I have safe housing and a job. That's why this interview is so important. If I complete the training successfully, they'll help me find a job."

He patted the back of her hand. "Honey, you're a smart cookie. It didn't take you near a lifetime like me to figure out that sober is better than not."

"I hope you're right; I know you are, I mean about the sober part. Mostly I used to get high because I wanted to be somebody else, doing something else in some other place."

"But when you came back down it was still you doing nothing and going nowhere. The fix is temporary, but the consequences aren't." He smiled sadly. "I wasted my best years, but you're still young and on track, Fey. You'll ace your interview, get that job and bring your son home, not because you've become someone else but because you have become the person you are meant to be."

"Thanks Doc." She looked down at her glossy red fingernails. "So are you happy doing what you're doing?"

"Happy? No. Happiness was when I took the first sip of beer knowing there were 11 more cans to go." He chuckled dryly. "But I feel like I'm finally doing a bit of good in the world and that makes me content."

"You're quite the philosopher, aren't you, Doc."

"If you survive it, that's what sobriety will do to you." He winked. "You better watch out, or you'll become a tedious old fart like me."

She leaned over and kissed his bristly cheek. "You're not a tedious old fart. You're a sweet old fart."

A blush spread up from his scrawny neck and stopped just short of the pouches beneath his clear blue eyes. "Why thank you, honey." He opened a cabinet and pulled out a box of latex gloves. "In the future, wear these when you're monkeying around with those bicycles."

Chapter 18

Monday, Nov. 21

Abby and Rita were both at the desk, a box of Karma tea and a scattering of tea bags between them.

"It's your turn," Rita said, drumming frosted pink nails on the table.

Abby closed her eyes and picked up a tea bag and read the tag. "For those who are forced to beg, there will be bounty." She shrugged then glanced at her watch. It was just shy of half past 10, there was nothing that needed to be done and still hours left to do it in. "Your turn."

Rita hesitated a moment, fingers fluttering over the pile, then chose a teabag. "The heel that crushes the violet releases its fragrance only once."

"What time is Norberto coming?"

"About 11 so we can beat the lunch crowd. Your go."

Abby closed her eyes and selected a bag. "Practice kind listening and kind speaking." She pushed the bag aside. "This batch is really lame."

Deep Breathing

"I'm going to try one more." Rita mixed up the remaining bags like a child might mix a deck of playing cards then slid one out from the bottom of the pile with the tip of her finger.

"Ah ha! This one was meant for you!"

Abby boosted herself up and pushed her glasses back up her nose. "What's it say?"

"Be kind, but be prepared."

"So, why is that meant for me?"

"Because you are not prepared. Four murders, *mija,* and you're still carrying around nothing to defend yourself but half a can of bug spray."

"It's wasp spray and it works."

"Not as well as a bullet to the head."

"If you're a good enough shot to hit the head, or any part of the body for that matter, which I am not. You want to carry a gun around. Fine. I'm not going to and I'd appreciated if you'd just let it alone." Abby started stuffing the tea bags back into the box.

"Come on, Honey." With great care and dignity, Rita gathered her cape about her shoulders. "I think we'll wait for Norberto outside."

"Have a nice lunch."

"I think it will be a long one."

"Good. Hope you get a bang out of it." Either Rita didn't hear this last bit, or she was ignoring it. Either way, the woman sailed out of the office without responding, which was disappointing. It wasn't often Abby came up with a clever rejoinder.

Her Karma tea bag had advised kind listening and kind speaking. Well, she had not been speaking unkindly, merely assertively. Apparently Rita didn't appreciate the difference. Abby sniffed, then pulled out her copy of *How to Craft a Life* from the side pocket of the Chariot and opened the book to Chapter 7, *Seize the Day,* where she'd left off.

A cliché to be sure, Dale J. Nagery began. *But a phrase becomes clichéd because it encapsulates truth. Those who start the day with positive energy end the day with positive outcomes.*

Before Abby could ponder that bit of wisdom, the front door whooshed open and Pete Valenzuela ducked through.

"Ah, Pete. How nice to see you."

He handed her a jar then folded himself into a chair. "My wife sent this."

Prickly pear jelly was printed in block letters on a piece of masking tape affixed to the lid. She turned the jar of bright magenta in her hand. "What a beautiful color! Please thank your wife for me. And I really enjoyed the… what were they?"

"Pickled cholla buds."

"Yes, and they were delicious. So how are things going?"

"I followed your suggestion and began volunteering at the Mission Gardens."

"Great!"

"Better than great. They offered me a job. I'm now an ethnobotanical engineer."

"Really. What does that mean?"

"Means I'm a gardener."

"Congratulations."

"Yeah, thanks to you. I also went to your ophthalmologist. She told me that there was some kind of laser surgery that would improve the vision in my good eye. I'm just waiting for the insurance to kick in that comes with my new job. Then we'll see if that kind of stuff is covered."

"Well, Pete, I must say, you've made my day. I'm not just saying that either." She smiled, appreciating the long delayed positive outcome of a day seized weeks ago.

• • •

Fey pulled up her black pants. She had pressed both the pants and her long-sleeved white shirt yesterday afternoon at Casa Paloma and washed her tennis shoes as well. From her backpack, she extracted a tight stretchy black headband. Pulling her dreads back, she slipped it on. She examined her stubby red fingernails then sighed. They looked like they were bleeding. Well, there was nothing to be done about that. Just below the cuff of her right sleeve, twin drops of blue tinted venom dripped off the rattlesnake fangs that were hidden beneath the sleeve. She'd gotten that tattoo, all her tattoos really, because she wanted to feel dangerous. Well, she wasn't feeling dangerous now, only foolish and shaky.

She took a deep breath. If she didn't want this chance so bad, she wouldn't feel so ... so bad. It was the wanting and the hoping that always set off her deepest feelings of failure and worthlessness. Gently, she lifted Sara off her bed and dropped her onto Angie's cot. Her jacket remained tucked under the covers, keeping warm while she dressed. She put it on then neatened the blankets on her cot.

The appointment was at 9. It was only 7 now and still nearly dark. Yesterday, she had made a dry run. She'd skated by Caridad Community Kitchens many times on her way to the Hospitality House, but the building was inconspicuous and she'd never noticed it before. By skateboard it would take her no more than 45 minutes to get there, so she had some time to burn. Though she wasn't hungry, she thought she should eat something. Doc would probably be in the kitchen tent by now. Maybe he'd know what to say to make the hollow feeling that was expanding in her chest go away.

• • •

Doc already had the big pot of coffee ready when Fey walked into the tent. "You're up early," she said by way of greeting.

"Spent so many years sleeping out, it's hard to sleep in." With his index finger, he stirred two packs of instant creamer into his coffee then hung his skinny butt on the back of a once elegant, now tattered and stained upholstered chair. "You took totally respectable. How are you feeling?"

She shrugged. "Nervous, scared, tacky." She stuck out a foot clad in the worn black Converse tennis shoe as evidence then poured hot water over a Cup O Noodles.

"Tacky? I think you look professional in your black and white, and I've noticed most kitchen staff wear some sort of athletic shoe." He reached over and patted her hand.

Fey fingered the scar on her temple, now a small red zigzag. Steam rose out of the Cup O Noodles. Fey blew on it for a moment before taking the first salty sip. She slurped a noodle out of the cup, but could hardly swallow it.

"You know, Fey, I'm a pretty good judge of who's going to make it around here and who isn't. You've come such a long way. It takes courage to go the whole distance and I know you've got it." Doc stood and patted her shoulder. "I'll be right here waiting to hear all about it when you get back."

She smiled her closed lipped smile, though she wanted to cry, wanted to give up hope, wanted to crawl back into bed and pull the blankets over her head. Pointing to the Cup O Noodles she asked, "You want the rest of this?"

"Just put it in the fridge, honey. I can't face breakfast till noon."

• • •

Robert slid into the booth across from Nelson, who reached under the table and squeezed his knee. Flushing red, Robert smiled a goofy, intoxicated smile. Last night they'd gone to a movie. Afterwards they'd gone for coffee and after that Nelson followed him home, followed him into the house and into his bedroom, renewing Roberts's faith in God and miracles.

Hungry, he scanned the breakfast menu looking for something he could eat that wouldn't end up all over the front of his crisp white shirt.

Nelson studied the menu for a moment then sat back. "So Robert, what about this guy who's going around killing … killing all these …"

Robert waited a beat before supplying the word. "Gimps?"

Nelson flinched. "What's the politically correct word?"

"There isn't… one." It occurred to Robert that if Nelson had trouble saying the word gimp or handicapped, or disabled this relationship wasn't going to get very far.

"So what about this guy who's going around killing… gimps?"

"What a… bout him?"

"Aren't you the least bit concerned?"

Robert shrugged.

Nelson pushed his menu aside. "You're being rather cavalier, aren't you?"

Robert laughed. "Cav…lier? No one has ever…called me…cav.. lier."

"In case you haven't noticed, Robert, you are a… a handicapped person."

Robert put his menu down. He bumped his glasses back up to the bridge of his nose then focused his hazel eyes on Nelson. "Thanks for … remind … ing me, Nels; some … times I forget."

Nelson smiled. "Your welcome. My point is you need to be careful. Just because you're not in a wheelchair doesn't mean you're not vulnerable. And what about what's her name, your friend."

"Abby carries … a can of wasp spray for … pro … tection." He flailed his arm in the air for emphasis. "Not my … style."

"Oh yeah? What is your style?"

"I thought … we covered that … last night."

"I'm serious, Robert. I care for you. I worry."

"They say … gimps have … nine lives."

"Please save at least one of them for me."

Robert considered that. Maybe there was a chance for the two of them.

• • •

The woman who introduced herself as Elaine, the program manager, was sitting behind a big, messy desk, Fey's application and a yellow legal pad before her. She looked tired for so early in the day and was dressed simply, gray slacks and a floral blouse, as she scanned the first page of the application. "To be in our culinary training program, you have to have stable housing. It says here that you're staying at Camp Bravo."

Fey's hands were folded in her lap. She squeezed them now. "That's correct, ma'am."

"Please just call me Elaine." She flipped to the second page of the application. "So tell me a little about this Camp Bravo."

"It's not fancy, but it's a safe place to stay and I don't have to keep moving from shelter to shelter."

"I see. Is there a place to shower and do your laundry?"

"I've been doing that at Casa Paloma."

"Casa Paloma?"

"It's a woman's shelter."

"Yes, I know. Why aren't you staying there?"

"No beds, but I can use their facilities."

"Okay." She looked up from the application, eyes tightly focused on Fey's face. "So if you're selected for our training program, how will you get here?"

"Skateboard. Zero emissions." Fey pressed her lips into a tight smile.

With only the barest twitch of her upper lip, Elaine continued. "Camp Bravo is right by Santa Rita Park, isn't it? That's kind of a long way by zero emissions and what if it rains?"

"Then I'll take a bus. It's a pretty direct route down Stone."

"What if the bus breaks down?"

Fey felt a prick of anger. Why was this woman hassling her about transportation? She took deep breath. "I'll use my skateboard just like I did this morning. It took 45 minutes."

"Hmm." Elaine wrote something down on her notepad. "And drugs?"

"Used to, no longer. My urine drops have been clean for the past nine months."

She flipped through the application. "And how would you support yourself during training?"

"I'll sell newspapers on the weekend." Another hand squeeze.

"Newspapers? There can't be much money in that."

Fey could feel her face redden. "In the situation I'm in right now, I don't need much money."

"Really?" Her expression was skeptical. "In your essay you mention that you have a 3-year-old son? Who's going to take care of him while you're attending our training program?"

Fey's heart was clawing its way up her throat and she was afraid that she was about to cry. No, not cry. She was going to throw up. "Excuse me, ma'am. Is there a bathroom I might use?"

• • •

Fey kneeled over the toilet bowl, sweat and tears mixing and running down the sides of her face. She coughed, retched, but produced nothing but threads of saliva. She took a deep breath, spat then rose to her feet. She wanted so badly to walk out of this place, leave Elaine diddling at her desk with her applications and yellow notepad, but that would make all of Doc's words about courage and going the distance just that, words. She imagined his face, the wrinkles, the stubble and the kind blue eyes. She splashed cold water on her face and took another deep breath before returning to Elaine's office.

"I'm so sorry," she said as she took her seat.

"It's okay, Fey. Really. This process isn't easy, but there's a good reason for that. Now, what about child care?"

For the first time, Fey noted a slight softening about the woman's eyes. "My son's is in a foster home. They said I neglected him."

"And?"

"And?" Might as well get this over with, she thought, and took another deep breath. "Well, what happened was that I had to go to work; I was waiting tables at the time. Anyway the woman who normally looked after him was really sick; it turned out to be pneumonia. I couldn't call my manager and say, sorry but I have to take care of my kid. Sure, he'd have said, no problem, but what he'd mean by that was no problem because you're…" Fey searched for a better word than fucked. "You're toast. He'd give me bad hours or cut my hours or flat out fire me. I'd seen it happen to other woman, so I left my son with a friend who lived in the same apartment building." She paused to take another deep breath. "My friend, who is no longer my friend, smoked crack with her boyfriend, who started to knock her around and the neighbors called the cops."

Elaine studied Fey's face as if another version of the story might be written there. "All right." She flipped to Page 4 of the application.

"How'd you lose your last job?"

"After they took Frisco, that's my son, I did everything I was supposed to satisfy DCS."

"Department of Child Safety?"

"Yes. Anyway, I was on track for getting my son back when I got sick myself. I went into work anyway, but the manager told me to go home. Turned out I was really, really sick with the flu. I called in every day, but after a week of being out, the manager told me not to bother. He'd hired someone to replace me. Everything kind of went ... south after that."

"I see."

Face burning, Fey wondered if she did.

Elaine sighed deeply, jotted down a few more words. Leaning forward, she looked intently at Fey. "There was one part of your personal essay that struck me. I'll read it to you now."

I am committed to making a good home for my son. To do that I need a steady, fulltime job. I am ready, willing and able to take direction, learn new skills, work hard, and become a responsible parent, employee and citizen. If I am chosen, Caridad Community Kitchen Culinary Training Program will be a first positive step toward my goal."

It was the part of the application that Frances had dictated to her word for word. The librarian must have been reading her heart, because it was exactly what Fey really felt, but didn't know how to put it down in words.

"So would you say that's still true?"

Fey cleared her throat. "Every bit of it."

She made one last note on her yellow pad. "Okay, so one more thing." She reached into her desk drawer and pulled out a small black hat. "Those dreads, every last one, have to fit under this hat."

Fey considered the hat, considered her hair, took one more deep breath then asked if she could borrow a pair of scissors.

• • •

Anûshka had just dropped Mr. O'Riley off at his townhouse. She was headed to Whole Foods to do his grocery shopping, but was finding it too difficult to keep her brain on the traffic. All morning she had been so worrying. Howard had not come to J.J.'s like usual this weekend. He had been always so good to call each day if he did not come to see her dance. Now she wondered if he could be sick, or worse, if his feelings for her had changed. Could there be another woman, one with big floppy breasts? She knew she shouldn't use Mr. O'Riley excellent Lexus for her personal business, but Howard's apartment was in the direction of the Whole Foods. It was still early in the day. He should be home and it would only take one small moment.

She knocked on the door. There was no answer. She pressed her ear to the door and listened for a moment then knocked louder. Still no answer. Finally, Anûshka took off her shoe and pounded the door with its heel. "Howard! Open door! Howard?" For some moments she continued to pound. At last, a woman in a robe with curlers in her hair flung open the door to the next apartment. "He's gone, so you can stop the banging."

"Gone? Then I will come back later."

"You can come back later, but he's gone. You understand gone?" The woman said the words slowly, "As in gone for good?"

"Yes, I understand what is gone for good." And gone for good was her $250. For a moment she just stood there in confusion. Did he think she was not good enough to be next Miss Pole Dance Arizona? Had he met a woman of more excellent ability? Only slowly did it come upon her that perhaps he never intended to help her win Miss Pole Dance Arizona contest, that perhaps such a contest did not even exist, that he had use not for her excellent ability as he had said, but only wanted her money, the money that it had taken so many months to save for her beautiful angel to come to the United States.

• • •

When Fey entered the medical tent, Doc was straightening his supply cabinet. She slipped off her knit hat and dropped onto a chair.

Doc looked up from the little pile of bandages he was sorting. "Good, lord, child. What happened to your hair?"

"It wouldn't fit under the cap we're are supposed to wear during training so I cut it off right there and then."

"Does that mean that you've been accepted into the program?"

She shrugged. "I have something called a kitchen day to prove that I can take direction and be a team member, or something, but that's not until next week." She ran her fingers through her short, ragged hair. "Do you think you can fix it?"

"I'm not much of a barber, but it wouldn't take too much skill to make that mess look better. Let me get my comb and scissors."

He flung a towel around Fey's shoulders then took a long appraising look. "Not too bad," he said, running his index finger lightly over the jagged little scar on her temple, just below the hairline. "Still a little red, but I think after awhile you won't even be able to see it. "I could cut you some bangs to cover it, maybe."

"No bangs."

"No bangs." He dipped a comb in a glass of water and ran it through her hair. "So tell me a funny story."

Fey took a moment to think. There weren't too many funny stories to choose from.

"Okay, I've got one. It was just after I'd lost custody of Frisco and I was not doing all that great," she began. "A woman comes into IHOP, which is where I was working at the time, and orders pancakes, nothing else, just pancakes, the big stack. I set them down in front of her. 'Anything else?' I ask. 'No, she says.' A few minutes later she's waving me over. The pancakes are smothered in syrup but she's only eaten a couple of bites. She points to the plate, says, 'These pancakes are thicker than Kotex Maxi Pads and taste about as good.' So I ask her if she wants to order something else. She says no, but I better not charge her for the nasty pancakes either. I pick up the plate and tell her there will be no charge, like I've been told to do, but what I want to do is dump the pancakes into her lap." She made a sweeping gesture with her arm.

Doc interrupted. "Hold your head still unless you want to look like Vincent van Gogh."

"Sorry." Fey folded her hands in her lap. "Now listen to this. Then she says, 'Box them up. I'll take them home and feed them to my dog.' Can you imagine?

Anyway, I was about to tell her in so many words to go to hell, but then I see this look on her face, kind of tight and… I don't know, a look."

"Seen that look, looked that look."

Fey nodded. "Yeah. Then I notice her ragged, dirty fingernails, and it hits me that she's got no money, probably no home and certainly no dog. It also hits me that I'm not more than one paycheck away from being her."

"That's your funny story?"

"I guess it's more funny odd rather than funny ha ha."

"I guess so. What did you do?"

"I boxed up the pancakes, stuck in extra butter and a half-dozen little cream containers."

Squinting, Doc ruffled her wet hair then combed it out before resuming his snipping. "Well, as they say, what comes around, goes around. Now the good deed is coming back around to you, darlin'."

"You think?"

"I know." Carefully, he removed the towel from her shoulders, took it outside and gave it a good shake.

"How does it look?"

"Better. Not great, but it will do."

"So you believe in karma?"

"Believe is probably too strong a word."

"Well, I think it's all up to God."

He rubbed the towel over her head, made another critical assessment then took a few more snips here and there. "Seems to me that if it's all up to God, then you don't need to do anything—don't need to take any personal responsibility for anything."

"But maybe God kicks in when a person takes responsibility and starts to take positive action."

"Sounds like we're back to karma." He produced a small mirror. "Take a look."

Fey turned her head to the left and then the right. Her hair, now less than a half-inch long, stood nearly straight up. As she ran her hands over her head, she felt a little boost of confidence. "I like it, Doc." She smiled behind her hand. "Oops."

"Oops?"

"Elaine, the lady who interviewed me at Caridad, said I'd have to get out of the habit of hiding my teeth behind my hand. Says it's not professional or sanitary in a kitchen."

"There's always something to work on." He studied her for a

moment. "In a way, darlin' that hairdo suits you."

She looked into the mirror and smiled. Doc was right. It did suit her. Suited her fine.

• • •

Abby was about to pack it in when Detective Stransky walked in the door. Though her step was decidedly lighter, she still carried the bulk of her baby fat and looked more disheveled and exhausted than ever.

"Detective Stransky! It's nice to see you, but doesn't the city provide maternity leave and shouldn't you still be on it?"

"They do and officially I am on it, but I like to keep up on the cases I was working before I went on leave."

"It's so chilly outside and you look pooped. Why don't you sit down and I'll fix you a cup of hot tea. It will only take a minute."

Stransky glanced at her watch then sat down with a weary sigh. "That would be very welcome, Miss Bannister." She took a folder out of her briefcase and set it on the desk. "Another body has been found head down in a dumpster. It occurred to me that it might have been one of the men who you fended off with… what was it, Mace?"

Abby flipped the switch on the electric teakettle and put a bag of Karma tea in a mug. "Real Kill Wasp Spray. Do you take sugar?"

"No thanks." The detective opened the folder then fanned several photos out on the desk. "I'm sorry to bother you with this, but would you look at these please?"

Abby felt at once reluctant and curious. She set the mug of tea down in front of the detective then took a side-eyed glance at the series of color photos. Satisfied that they were neither gory nor sickening, she picked one up. In it a young man with long sideburns was laid out on a table, a sheet tucked up under his chin. Except for his skin, which was gray, and a livid bruise on his cheek, he looked as if he were merely sleeping. She quickly shuffled through the other photos. "That's one of them."

"You're certain."

"Yes. Another overdose?"

"Yes."

Abby thought about that for a moment. "So both guys were killed because of the heroin I was carrying around?"

"Killed because they failed to get the heroin you were carrying around, yes," she said reaching for the mug. "At least, that's my assumption."

Abby hitched herself up in her chair then nudged her glasses back in place. "You don't think I still have to worry about the drug cartel guys, do you?"

"No. I think we took care of that." She took a sip of tea. "This is nice. What is it?"

"Karma tea, Peachy Green Slimliner."

Stransky took another sip, then turned the tag over in her hand.

"What's it say?" Abby asked.

"*A thorn of experience is better than a word of warning.* Which reminds me. There's something else I want to discuss with you. It's in reference to the murder of William Strand."

A little shiver, like an insect crawling just under her skin, traveled down Abby's spine. "Okay."

"His girlfriend reported that Mr. Strand was in the habit of taking his Rottweiler out for a walk every night after the 10 o'clock news. That would be 10:30 every night."

"He had a girlfriend?"

"Yes. Why are you surprised?"

"It's just that he was a pretty unpleasant man, verbally abusive, I'd say. I wouldn't think… never mind. Go on."

"Really? Well, he's not abusing anyone now. Anyway, the girlfriend said that the dog was pretty unfriendly to strangers."

Abby boosted herself up in the chair once again. "So for someone to get close enough to kill him, he'd have to be accepted by the Rottweiler."

"Exactly. Folks in the neighborhood reported seeing a late night jogger several times. It's possible that the two men might have encountered each other on a number of occasions. I walk our dog most mornings. I don't know how it is in your neighborhood, but in mine, I'm better acquainted with the dogs than the people who walk them."

"So maybe both Strand and his dog had at least a passing acquaintance with this jogger. Maybe, if the jogger had murder in mind, he might have offered the Rottweiler treats to soften him up."

Stransky scooped up the photos. "That's my thinking."

"And you're telling me this because?"

"Because I think you need to be on the lookout for a man or possibly a woman jogging or riding a bike, maybe walking."

"That's a lot of people."

"True, but there's one more thing I want to add. Although we've been keeping this information out the papers, I think you should know that the victims' necks were broken. That's a pretty hands-on homicide, one involving struggle I'd imagine, probably some scratching, but there has been no DNA evidence found in any of the cases."

"Gloves?"

"Gloves. Be on the lookout for a man or a woman, presumably wearing gloves possibly riding a bike, walking or running. Maybe someone you've seen repeatedly, but does not live in the neighborhood."

"Where have these murders taken place?"

"With one exception, they've taken place along a corridor bordered by Alvernon to the east, Prince to the north, Sixth Street to the south and Park to the west."

"I live outside of that corridor."

"True, but not that far outside the corridor, Ms. Bannister. And there was one exception. You don't want to be the second exception. Just keep your guard up is all I'm saying."

"That's pretty much what Officer Steadman said when…"

'Wait. You've spoken to Officer Steadman?"

"Yes, twice he came by, once to tell me you'd had your baby and once to ask if I still had my wasp spray handy."

The detective released an exasperated sigh.

"What?"

"Nothing. It's just that Officer Steadman likes to do things his own way."

"Old school?'

Stransky drained the cup of tea. "The oldest."

CHAPTER 19

Tuesday, Nov. 22

Anûshka was quietly weeping as she scrubbed at the crusted cheese from the quesadillas Abby had heated in the microwave yesterday. "Two-hundred and fifty dollars. Do you know how long takes me to save so many dollars?"

Abby, slightly irritated by the woman's drama, ignored the question. "It's not the end of the world, Anûshka. Everybody has setbacks," she said, recalling the words of Dale J. Nagery. "Setbacks are the road signs that direct you on a new, more favorable route."

Anûshka stopped scrubbing long enough to glare at Abby. "This is too easy for you to say. You have nice business, nice house, nice money in the bank. Now I have nothing and my sister-in-law tells me I must find other place to live yesterday."

Rita had been Googling Ms. Pole Dance Arizona. "Well, at least the contest is on the up and up." She scanned the website for the pertinent facts. "It's on December 2 at some place called Smokey's Last

Roundup, blah, blah, blah, prize money $5,000, blah, blah, deadline November 25, entry fee $200."

"Only $200? The liar said it was $500. Oh well, that cannot matter now. I do not have $200 and deadline…" She counted on her fingers. "Deadline is two weeks and one day. I cannot save $200 in so little time. And I had such excellent routine. I call it 'I Am Beautiful for America.' And my costume, I made it. So beautiful, red, white and blue." She began to cry again. "And there were little silver stars to cover my breasts."

Rita shot Abby a look. Abby shook her head. Rita, shot harder. Abby sighed. "Are you working the club tonight, Anûshka?"

"I work club every night, but Sunday when is closed."

"Maybe Rita and I could come see your routine. Maybe …" Abby did not want to say the words."

Rita finished Abby's sentence for her. "If we like what we see, we'll loan you the entry fee."

"You would do this?"

"If we think you've got a chance to win. Right, Abby?"

Abby glared at her friend.

"Right, Abby?"

"If we think you've got a chance to win."

"Oh, how excited I am that you will see my excellent routine and beautiful costume. And my shoes, red and so tall." She held her index fingers six inches apart. "Never do I have so tall shoes, but all the most excellent pole dancers have so I must have too." She blotted her eyes with a paper towel. "My first set is 4. You, I will not disappoint, but is too bad you will not see my little stars."

"Why not?" Abby asked, though she really didn't give a shit about Anûska's little stars.

"At J.J.'s we dance without top, of course."

Rita and Abby exchanged looks. "Of course," they said in near unison.

• • •

Rita maneuvered the Iceberg into the single handicapped space at J.J's

Playhouse. "Gee, I guess even skin joints have to provide handicapped parking. Who would have thought?"

"For the horny quadriplegics."

"Do quadriplegics get horny?"

Abby shrugged. "Let's just get this over with."

"Come on Abby. This is going to be fun."

"Fun? At best, it's going to be boring; at worst is going to be... creepy and depressing."

"Have you ever been to a skin joint?"

"Of course not."

"Me neither. Think of it as an adventure."

• • •

It had taken her eyes a few moments to adjust to the dark. Now she looked around the near empty lounge. The tables were arranged in a semicircle, four deep around the curtained stage, which was elevated perhaps two feet above the floor. The bar was along the back wall. A waiter set the margaritas they had ordered on the table. "Want to run a tab?" he asked as if it were commonplace here to serve two women in wheelchairs.

"I think this will do, thanks," Abby answered before Rita could voice an opinion. "What do I owe you?"

He laid the little black book in front of her."

In the near absence of light, Abby needed her glasses to read the bill. She pulled them down from the top of her head. Aghast, she adjusted the glasses to make sure she was seeing straight. The bill for the two drinks was twenty bucks. She slipped a twenty and a one into the book and gave it to the waiter. "Ten dollars each plus the ten buck cover," she whispered. "You'd think they could afford to pay these women more than just tips." She looked at her watch and was relieved to see that it was nearly 4.

Rita, a self-proclaimed margarita expert, took a sip of her drink. "Weak," she pronounced. "And they used frozen lime juice instead of fresh."

There was some rustling backstage, then a great whirring sound as if some unseen hand had flipped the switch on God's floor fan. The curtains parted and the stage became awash in red, white and blue light. To the strains of a fully orchestrated *America the Beautiful*, Anûshka entered in a convoluted series of backbends, walkovers, splits and other things Abby had no names for, all performed in the red platform stiletto heels. Midstage, Anüshka stood for a dramatic moment, chest out, arms aloft, the American flags attached to her wrists and shoulders billowing in the stiff breeze from what, in fact, was a floor fan positioned in the wings.

• • •

He was only half-listening to the evening news. For the past few days, he'd been feeling increasingly bored and edgy. He checked the newspaper daily to see if there was any mention of the murder investigation—though in his mind he always used the word *release*. There'd been nothing in the paper lately and he felt at once reassured and vaguely disappointed.

He'd been renting a small apartment in one of the many old motor lodges that dotted Benson Highway. It was so close to the Triple T Truck Stop he could read by the light of its neon signs. It wasn't much, but he didn't need much. Soon he'd move on. Ironically, he was currently a driver for Angel Transport, a private nonemergency ambulance service. Though he had the occasional opportunity, he'd never gotten the calling to transport anyone in his ambulance farther than rehab or hospice. He'd already put in his notice—no suspicious sudden departures.

The weatherman was predicting the usual clear skies and cooler temperatures. Fall in Tucson was pretty monotonous. Now he closed his eyes against the boredom. As so often happened, the image of his sister, Josie, was instantly before him, a reminder of his promise to God.

He was supposed to have been in school that day, but Josie had a bad cold. She attended a special school for children with severe disabilities. Many were in delicate health. If his mother had sent her to school, the nurse would have called her at work to come get her. His

Deep Breathing

mother could not miss work every time Josie got sick, and Josie got sick a lot, so he was always the one to stay home with her. For as long as he could remember, he'd been caring for Josie before and after school, so he was used to it. Besides, he didn't like school that much anyway.

Though Josie was 13, she was tiny. Even though he was only 10 he could easily lift her out of bed and into her wheelchair. He would change her diaper and dress her. Sometimes he would put her in the bathtub and wash her hair. Lots of boys would have hated that, but he didn't mind. He loved his sister, loved her soft curly hair. Her eyes were brown and shiny as if she were always on the verge of tears. The way they followed his every move felt like she was smiling at him.

She watched him now as he spooned oatmeal, sweetened with maple syrup, into her mouth. The television was on, he never could remember what program they'd been watching, maybe the Muppets. Josie liked the Muppets. Maybe he was feeding her too fast. Sometimes she choked if he fed her too fast, but swallowing was always hard for Josie and sometimes she just choked for no reason. He knew what to do when that happened, knew to pound her on the back with his fist.

So maybe he was watching television and maybe he was feeding her too fast and she started to choke. He remembered pounding her on the back her but it didn't help. She struggled, arms and legs jerking. Her face turned red and her eyes got big and he was pounding and pounding. He thought about calling 911, but somehow he knew his mother would get into trouble and then she'd be mad at him.

He continued to pound until his arm felt too heavy to lift; he remembered it clearly, the sensation that he could not move his arm, and he stopped pounding. It took awhile, but Josie stopped struggling. Her shiny eyes still held his. He saw only love and gratitude there. After her eyes closed, he saw a beautiful white dove rise slowly from her chest. He watched it fly up to the ceiling and disappear. Only then did he call 911.

Before the ambulance arrived, he thought to perform the Heimlich maneuver. He didn't know why he had not tried it before. He picked his sister up, put his arms around her, fists just above her belly button then quickly squeezed in and up like a "J" just as his mother had taught him. He did it two more times, squeezing hard enough to leave a bruise. Somehow he knew it was important to leave a bruise to prove he'd tried his best. He wiped the tears and the oatmeal off her face with a washcloth, then held her on his lap until the EMTs arrived.

His mother was sent to jail for negligent child abuse. While she was gone, he lived in a group home. He hated that place, but he couldn't remember why, couldn't remember exactly how long he was there, but eventually he went back to live with his mother. It was okay, but it was not the same without Josie. When he was 17 his mother signed papers so he could enlist in the Army. Even though it probably would have made her feel better, he never did tell her about the dove. Never told anyone about the dove.

Years later in Afghanistan—it was sometime after he had taken his buddy out, maybe he was even back in the States—he couldn't remember exactly when he first realized that it had been God who had stayed his arm that day with Josie and kept him from calling 911 sooner. God wanted him to end Josie's suffering. From then on he knew he'd been given a mission in life. He would always carry with him the image of his sister's eyes. The love of Christ was in those eyes and every time he saw them, it was a sign from God that his mission was righteous.

His face was wet with tears, but he felt calm, felt filled with God's love and approval. He rose to turn off the news. There was just one more name on his list. After that, he'd be moving on, the sooner the better.

Chapter 20

Wednesday, Nov. 23

"Norberto and I are going to my Markie's house for Thanksgiving." Rita looked up from the computer where she was doing the accounts. "Want to come?"

Abby, who had been doing research for yet another possible grant proposal, this one to help finance the installation of manual controls for amputees and people with spinal cord injuries, was happy for a moment's distraction. "Is that the son who's married to the woman you like?"

"No, that's Freddie's wife Nunci. It's Lou I have a problem with."

"Now, why is it you don't like Lou?"

"Because she has no respect and no sense of decency. She and that little *cabrona* my ex is married to are like best friends now, which isn't so surprising considering that they are almost the same age, but I put up with her because of Markie and the kids. Anyway Freddie's wife, Nunci, is a doll, but she has no interest in cooking. Just gray meat, boiled potatoes and frozen green beans if you're lucky, which is why we all go to Markie's for Thanksgiving."

Abby considered the invitation. Rita's life was really too complicated and she had already resolved to spend the day alone. Stella had agreed to go back to live with her mother while she waited for her Section 8 housing to go through. Abby had bought a whole chicken, a few potatoes and fresh green beans and almost looked forward to having her own quiet dinner. "Thanks for thinking of me, but I think I'll pass."

"I wish I could. Too many kids. God love 'em, they run around screaming until one of them gets hurt, then everybody's in tears. Lou, that's Markie's wife, will be giving everybody hell, but the food's going to be great. I'm bringing my *calabacitas* and my triple chocolate cake."

"No pumpkin pie?'

"Nunci's bringing one from Costco so it should be okay, but why waste calories on pumpkin when you can eat chocolate? I'll save you some."

"Thanks, but I really shouldn't eat chocolate and I definitely should not eat triple chocolate."

Rita sighed. "Abby, you've got to live little. To my knowledge nobody ever died from eating chocolate."

"I won't die if I eat your chocolate cake; I'll just want to."

The office doors whooshed open and Pastor Glorie rushed in looking something like a huge bouquet of autumn leaves. "Oh good." She loosened a russet silk scarf from around her neck. "Phew. It's hot in here." She swept a few damp tendrils of hair back from her face, setting the plastic turkeys dangling from her ears dancing. "God is about to present you with a blessed opportunity."

Abby didn't try to mask her annoyance. "And how are you, Glorie?"

The woman didn't seem to notice the edge in Abby's voice. "Fat and sassy, praise the Lord, but we're having a little emergency."

"Which is?"

"My truck is on the blink and Christ needs your van to transport 200 hot meals to Camp Bravo tomorrow. And of course I'll need help handing them out."

Abby and Rita exchanged skeptical glances.

"Where's your usual crew?" Abby asked.

"Not available. You don't realize, Abby, because you're so blessed, that for many of my parishioners, just surviving is a full-time occupation."

Abby, unwilling to cave into Glorie's self-righteous bullying, said, "I think I do realize, but…"

"Feeding the hungry of body and spirit is a blessing, ladies, an opportunity, especially at this time of year, to thank God for his bounty." Smiling broadly, she looked from Rita to Abby then back to Rita. Not liking what she saw on their faces, the smile flipped to a frown. "Please don't tell me you are both so right with Jesus that you can forego a chance to help the homeless."

Rita was the first to capitulate. "What time?"

"Eleven sharp. We start the distribution at noon."

"How long will it take?" Abby asked, not that she had anything better to do.

"Couple hours. And you two will be such an inspiration to our homeless veterans, the way you work and get around and maintain such positive attitudes. What a blessing," she said and trundled out the door.

Abby glanced at Rita and rolled her eyes. What Glorie found so inspiring about her and Rita, Abby couldn't say for certain, but supposed the woman found something inherently contradictory and therefor inspirational in the words *women, wheelchairs and work*. If she knew one of them was having inspired sex as well, it would really blow her hair back.

• • •

The Iceberg pulled into the dirt lot on the west side of Camp Bravo. A wicked little wind caused eddies of dust and bits of trash to swirl. A plastic bag caught in the chain link fence that bordered the camp along two sides was whipped into a frenzy.

Each meal was wrapped separately and stacked into long insulated containers to keep them hot. There were coolers filled with pumpkin pies and cans of whipped cream, plus 200 bottles of water and 200 sack lunches for an evening snack, and all of it had to be unloaded before either Abby or Rita could exit the van. A neatly dressed, wiry little man led a contingent of younger, burlier and surlier looking men over to the van. Rita opened her window.

"Well, happy Thanksgiving, ladies," he said brightly. "And welcome to Camp Bravo. Folks call me Doc."

Rita offered her hand. "Folks call me Rita, and this is Abby." Pastor Glorie was already out of the van distributing hugs. "And I guess everybody knows Pastor Glorie."

By the time Rita and Abby made their way to the front of the camp where the tables and chairs were set up, men, women and children had formed a long orderly line and the veterans were setting out the hot food and pies.

Abby, Rita and Doc donned latex gloves and quickly organized themselves into an assembly line of sorts. As the three began to serve up the turkey dinner, Glorie began serving up a sermon, the apparent price of admission. "People often confuse Christ with Santa Claus," Pastor Glorie intoned into a portable microphone. "If we are nice, we'll get on the good list and he'll give us stuff."

Folks in the crowd were nodding their heads and for once, Abby had to agree with the woman. People, herself included, seemed to feel that virtue should be rewarded. Was there something wrong with that? She'd have to think about it.

At the first table, Rita was passing out the hot food. At the second table, Doc expertly cut pies into eighths, placed each slice on a paper plate and sprayed on a generous gob of cream. Abby handed out the sack lunches from a third table.

"Despite what you may have heard," Pastor Glorie continued. "The God that Jesus wants us to know is not about rewards and punishments,

The crowd was polite and surprisingly subdued given the occasion. One hugely pregnant woman with a toddler on her hip and a waxy looking girl of about 6 in hand, stood there looking at the food with exhausted eyes.

"Looks like you could use a little help," Abby observed, acutely aware of the understatement. "We need some help over here," she bellowed. In a flash, three vets sporting military surplus—a cap here, a webbed belt there and khaki everywhere—appeared. One escorted the woman and her children to a table, while the other two carried plates of food.

Swaying a bit like a snake charmer, Glorie continued to work the crowd. "But forgiveness is not your job," she was saying. "Even Jesus realized forgiveness was up to God. 'Father forgive them,' he asked, 'for they know not what they do.'"

Abby considered that for a moment. Since his death, she had worked long and hard to forgive her father, but Fey's revelations had reignited all her anger and resentment. The notion that it wasn't her job to forgive the son of a bitch held great appeal. Pastor Glorie was making too much sense this afternoon. If Abby weren't careful she'd find herself at one of the woman's Wednesday night services.

It was one of those crystal Tucson days, the sky a piercing blue. Across the street, the autumn leaves still clinging to the trees in Santa Rita Park glowed gold and orange in the bright sun. The wind had cut out a bit and Abby was feeling quite happy, grateful even, to be exactly where she was.

•••

The moment Fey had seen the big white van pull into the dirt lot, she'd ducked around the corner of the visitor's tent. Ever since she'd left the envelope with the $60 with the housekeeper, she'd been fanaticizing about the showdown she'd have with Abby sometime in the vague future. So why was she was hiding now like a scolded child and what exactly did she want to confront her about? Though she knew it was wacked out, part of her wanted revenge, not so much for what Abby's father had done, not even for her cousin's denial of it, but for something else less tangible. Was it Abby's success she found so unforgivable? Her lack of sympathy? At the moment, Fey was unsure she deserved anyone's sympathy. Was that why she was hiding? Near tears, she stepped out from the shelter of the tent and took a place in the back of the crowd. As she watched Abby hand out sack lunches, Fey was pretty sure she knew the exact contents of each brown bag. Was that why she was hiding?

Even as people began to eat, the woman who called herself Pastor Glorie was going on and on. "Judgment is not our job," she was saying. "Forgiveness is not our job. Those burdens are God's alone to carry." Then, hand over her heart, Pastor Glorie seemed to look directly at Fey. "But if you choose to take on the burden of judgment and forgiveness, just be aware that judgment closes doors, while forgiveness opens them."

• • •

It wasn't until everyone in the line had been served that the veterans, there were 12 staying at the camp, came forward. By this time, Abby was emotionally worn out, but she managed a smile as she passed out the last of the sack lunches. There were only three left when she looked up to see Fey, pumpkin pie in hand, smiling her tight-lipped smile. "Can we talk?" she asked.

"We really need to," Abby answered.

Fey led the way. When the two entered the medical tent, Doc looked up from the newspaper he was reading and smiled. "Welcome, ladies."

"Doc, I'd like you to meet my cousin, Abby."

"We got acquainted on the serving line. It's nice to meet Fey's famous cousin."

"Hardly famous." The familiar flush rose to her cheeks as she wondered what Fey might have already told this man.

He got up from the cot with a grunt. "Well, I guess I better go back outside and make myself useful."

"Thanks Doc," Fey said taking Doc's place on the cot. Abby positioned the Chariot across from her cousin, their knees almost touching. For an awkward moment neither spoke. Abby took a deep breath. "I like your hair."

Fey ran her hand over the top of her head. "I had to cut the dreads because I'm starting a training program in the culinary field and they wouldn't fit under the cap I have to wear."

Abby nodded. "Well, I think it's a big improvement and I'm happy to hear you're in a training program."

Deep Breathing

Fey shrugged. "Yeah. I'm lucky to have been accepted. Seventy people applied. Only 14 were chosen." She let that comment settle in for a moment then added. "I want you to know that I'm done with drugs."

"I'm really glad to hear that too, Fey." Abby figured it was her turn to speak up. She took another deep breath. "I owe you an apology."

"For what?"

"For doubting you about my father. Josh pretty much confirmed it, but from the start, in my gut, I knew it was true." She clasped her crabbed left hand with her right. "I'm sorry. That must have been the worst thing in your life."

"Actually, no. That came before and to be honest, if I'd known what was to come after, I'd have stuck it out with your dad. Maybe graduate high school." She covered her mouth with her hand then let it drop revealing her ruined teeth. She uttered a strangled little chuckle. "Think of the nest egg I would have had."

"Not funny, Fey."

"I wasn't really laughing."

Abby's body began its inevitable slide down in the chair. She pushed herself up again. "I just feel so... so guilty. But..." Abby was about to say that she truly didn't have a clear memory of her father and Fey, then thought better of it. Fey would never believe it. Abby could hardly believe it herself.

"You've got nothing to feel guilty for, not really. You were just a kid. I've been going over a lot of stuff in my mind lately, stuff I'm not proud of."

"Like what?" Abby was thinking her cousin was about to apologize for the $60 she'd stolen or perhaps her Spice adventure.

Fey took a deep breath, coughed. "I feel bad about how when you were little I abandoned you. You loved me and trusted me and I left you alone with him. I saw how he treated you. Sure he wasn't brutal with you like he was with Josh, but he was angry and impatient, which is just as bad in a way."

"It's okay, Fey. I've gotten over it," Abby lied. "But now..."

"Hang on. Let me finish. When I first saw you on television, I guess I somehow had it in my head that you owed me something."

"Is that why you took the money?"

"Maybe, but let me finish. I think it was because I was ashamed and angry at the same time. In some ways, one fed on the other. Anyway, I should not have left you with him."

"You had to

"You think?"

"Yes." Abby pushed her glasses back up her nose. "So where did you go after you left?"

"Back to my mother's. Big mistake. The two of them, your dad and my mom, were made of the same stuff. Both were alcoholics, not that that excuses anybody, but it does make you wonder what their parents were like?"

"I guess it does."

"You know how I ended up at your dad's house in the first place?"

"You came to help take care of me after my mom died."

"That was just my mom's excuse to get rid of me because her boyfriend liked me better than her. She wanted me gone, so gone I was. After I left your house, I went back up to my mother's in Phoenix thinking the boyfriend had probably moved on and I could stay there. I was right about the boyfriend, but practically the first thing she says to me, word for word, 'When you left, you were a skinny, homely little girl.' She looks me up and down then says. 'You've gotten taller.' This is my mother. Next we get into a big argument about some damn thing and how essentially worthless I am. When I remind her that she sent me away because Steve, that was the boyfriend, liked to fuck her homely worthless little daughter better than her, my mother just looked at me as if I had lost my mind. 'I don't know what you're talking about,' she says. Says, 'I sent you to live with your uncle so you could help that poor little motherless cripple girl.' She couldn't even remember your name."

Fey stared off into space for a moment as if composing her next sentence. She took a deep breath then continued. "I'm only telling you this now, Abby, because when I first told you about your dad, you didn't believe me. Maybe it was because you didn't hear me scream or fight when he came at me—like it was sort of my duty to resist. I just want you to understand, if that's even possible, why I didn't. I've been going over this in my head a lot lately and I think it was because at that point in my life, I saw no point in putting up a fight."

"But I can understand that, Fey. I can understand what it's like to feel tired and down and scared. After you left, there were times I just wanted to go to sleep and never wake up, I was so alone. But you were still right to leave. I only wish you'd told your teacher or the school counselor what was going on. They would have reported him to the police."

"Funny. It never occurred to me that what your dad was doing was against the law. I knew it was wrong, but to me it was also … normal, I guess, familiar, better than what I thought the alternative might be if I told. I can't even remember how or when I learned not to tell."

Abby realized with a little shock that as a child she had internalized the same message without even realizing it. She'd never told anybody, not even Robert, about what went on at home.

"Anyway," Fey continued. "Dear Mother and I parted ways. I bought my skateboard, equipped myself like a proper homeless person and joined up with some other homeless teens."

"Is that when you started using drugs?"

"Yup. Some of this, some of that. Whatever I could get ahold of cheap. I had a little window washing operation—cars in parking lots, small businesses. I was never totally broke, but never had enough money to change my luck."

"What brought you back to Tucson?"

Fey huffed then stifled a laugh. "Fear for my life. There was this guy, a big guy, older. Used to brag that he'd been a pro wrestler. Anyway, he'd show up on the weekends with a couple of cases of beer and just hang with us kids. This one time, it was one of those perfect days in February when it feels like spring and we were all down in a wash enjoying the beer and the sunshine, when the guy suddenly grabs me, says 'Come here gorgeous' and licks my neck. He picks me up like he's just playing, but his hands are all over me, under my shirt and inside my shorts, stabbing my crotch with his finger and I'm yelling and swearing, kicking and he's just laughing. Finally, he puts me down, smells his finger and pretends to faint and everybody busts out laughing. There was one boy—we were kind of buddies, like we had each other's back, but even he was laughing his head off. Well, I waited a bit until the wrestler guy had a couple more beers, then I filled my backpack full of rocks. The first swing, I missed completely it was so heavy, but the rest landed square on his head. I could have killed him, but I didn't, which meant he would probably kill me once he recovered. I figured it would be a good time to leave town. Besides, by then I was nearly 18, old enough to get a real job, which wasn't going to happen as long as I was hanging around that bunch of losers."

"Jesus, Fey."

She shrugged. "That's it. You pretty much know the rest of the story."

Abby looked around the tent. "So you're staying here now?"

"Not in this tent, but yes, I'm living in the camp for now. My training begins on Monday. It's a 10-week program. If I make it to the end, they'll help me find a job, hopefully in a restaurant kitchen where I can make enough pay to get a place for me and Frisco. My time's running out, though." She sneezed.

"Bless you," Abby said automatically.

Fey sneezed again. "Thanks. I think I'm coming down with a cold."

Abby pushed herself up in the chair again. "What do you mean your time is running out?"

"As my social worker loves to remind me, Federal law requires the judge in dependency cases to file for termination of parental rights after 15 months in foster care. It's already been over 11. By the time I finish training, it will be 13."

"But surely if you're making progress …"

Coughing, Fey shrugged.

It was colder in the tent than it had been outside in the sunlight. Abby wondered what it would be like to crawl into a cold sleeping bag each night then get up in the near freezing temperatures each morning. She was silent for some moments while she considered what it would be like to live with Fey. Her place was so small. Was her cousin truly done with drugs? Could she trust her not to steal? Guilt overcoming reason, she said, "I guess you could come stay with me."

Fey shook her head. "No. I'm good here."

Feeling relieved, Abby nodded. The fact was that she'd been so on edge these days that even Stella's company had been a comfort, but Fey? She just couldn't quite trust her. Had her cousin sensed that?

Abby ran her hand over her stomach to quell the guilt induced roiling that had started there. Fey's refusal seemed to underscore Abby's initial lack of sympathy and compassion. Robert had often accused her of being stingy. Now she wondered if her propensity for frugality had somehow gone beyond mere finances. Had she become stingy and guarded with her emotions as well? She thought to reach out for Fey's hand, but held back. "Will you stay in touch?"

Nodding, Fey pulled a paper napkin decorated with fall leaves from her pocket and blew her nose.

• • •

Abby let herself into the house. Since Stella's departure, it seemed emptier than ever. Tito, looking a bit disgruntled, appeared in the bedroom doorway, stretched then eyed her balefully.

"What?"

Rather than jumping on her lap, the cat turned and slunk back into the bedroom.

Since she had not eaten the turkey dinner, Doc had insisted that she take one of the remaining sack lunches home. Her stomach was still queasy, no doubt, because she hadn't eaten since her yogurt and banana breakfast. She poured herself a glass of milk then emptied contents of the bag on the kitchen table. There was an orange, which immediately rolled onto the floor, a granola bar, a hard-boiled egg and some sort of sandwich in a baggie. She opened the baggie. Peanut butter and grape jelly, she could smell it, didn't even have to look between the bread slices. She unwrapped the granola bar took a bite and stuck it back in the bag for later. The orange was simply not worth the effort it would take to retrieve it. Sighing deeply, she cracked the hard-boiled egg on the table, peeled then salted it. The egg was hard to swallow or maybe her aloneness was making swallowing hard. She washed the last of the egg down with milk. It was going to be a long evening.

Late afternoon sun filtered through the filmy curtains at the kitchen window. She thought to turn on the news. Instead, she retrieved the kitchen scissors from the drawer, dropped them next to the can of wasp spray then unbolted the back door. She whirred slowly through, carefully maneuvering her chair in a tight right turn and a tight left to avoid the rotten floorboards, then down the ramp into the back yard. It was chilly, but the motes of dust stirred up by the wind were backlit by the sun and the hard white berries on the Chinaberry tree glowed. Eventually they'd fall among the yellow leaves like dozens of small marbles.

The white petunias, flourishing during this period between heat and first frost, cascaded over the edge of the raised bed. Abby snipped a few and held them to her nose. The sweet fragrance brought tears to her eyes. She was simply going to have to do better, try harder, grow a thicker hide. In the past, that had always been her approach when faced with loneliness and fear. But sometime along the way—she couldn't pinpoint exactly when—it had stopped working.

When she went back into the house, someone was banging on her front door. She set the flowers on the table then went into the living room. Through the window she saw her neighbor, old Mrs. Soto, standing on the stoop in her baggy pants and brightly flowered blouse. She was holding a foil-covered plate. Abby opened the door. "*Buenas tardes*, Mrs. Soto. *Cómo está?*"

"*Bien, bien, gracias a Dios.* Look, I brought you a plate." She pulled back the foil covering a mound of food so Abby could see. "In my family we don't go for turkey, but there's *carne asada*, ham, macaroni and cheese, *nopalitos en mole*. I made the *cabalacitas* myself and they are delicious." She retucked the foil over edges of the plate then set it in Abby's lap. "Where have you been all day, *mija?*" she asked looking past Abby into the living room.

"Church," she said, trying to quickly satisfy her neighbor's curiosity. It wasn't a complete lie, since Glorie had delivered a prayer before serving the food.

"That's nice, *mija*."

"Thank you so much for the food, Mrs. Soto. It all looks delicious, but you shouldn't have gone to so much trouble."

"No trouble." The old woman turned and started to limp down the ramp. "Ay, my hips. One of these days, I'm going to get my son-in-law to build me one of these ramps. *Bien provecho.*"

"Thanks, Mrs. Soto." Abby started to go back inside, then remembered the petunias. "Hang on a second, Mrs. Soto."

Abby took the still warm plate directly into the kitchen table then picked up the bouquet, grateful to have a small gift to give in return for the old woman's kindness.

• • •

Fey was relieved to see that the light was still on in the medical tent. "Knock, knock," she said, her voice a rasp.

Doc put down his book. "You don't sound so good."

"I feel terrible, Doc," Fey said collapsing onto a chair. "I have a sore throat and a bad headache. Do you have anything for a cold?"

"Let's see what's what."

He put his hand on her forehead. It felt cool and reassuring to Fey. "I can't be sick."

"Sorry. Seems you are. Let's just check your temp." He put the thermometer in her mouth. While he waited he pinched the back of her hand. "See how when I let go, the skin stays kind of pinched. Could be you've got a headache because you're not drinking enough water. Could be you've got the flu. Did get a flu shot this year by any chance?"

Fey shook her head.

"Didn't think so." He draped a blanket around her shoulders then he removed the thermometer. Squinting, he angled the device into the light. "Says 102. That makes you a pretty sick little girl. Flu and dehydration I imagine. It's that time of year." He pressed his fingers on her neck just under her jaw. "Kinda of swollen. Let's take a look at your throat."

He shined a penlight in her mouth. "Might be strep."

"So can you do anything? I've got until Monday to get over it."

"That's not likely."

"I have to Doc," she croaked. "Trainees have to have perfect attendance for the first two weeks, otherwise they make you start over again with the next session. I don't have time for that. As it is, I have to miss two visitations with my son. Even though my social worker knows why, it still looks bad. And Frisco's next dependency hearing is in February. If I don't have a job by then, the judge will take him away from me for good. If they take him away from me, what will I do? There'll be no reason for me to… to be." She started to cry.

"Okay. Calm down." He unlocked the metal supply cabinet, selected several items, then poured water from a plastic bottle into a paper cup. "Here take these."

"What are they?"

"An antibiotic, two ibuprofen and a zinc." He watched her swallow the pills then poured another cup of water. "Drink this one down too." He waited until she had. "One thing's for sure. You can't stay in that cold, damp tent tonight. I'm taking you home with me. Go get your gear, while I bring the car around."

"You own a car?"

"Just the base heap, a 1997 Dodge Dart acquired from the Junque for Jesus folks. Don't know what we paid for it, but it couldn't have been much more than nothing. Now go get your gear."

Chapter 21

Friday, Nov. 25

Rita was off doing Black Friday with her daughter-in-law, the one she did like. How anyone could spend an entire day shopping with hordes of rabid bargain hunters was beyond Abby. Just the thought of it made her tired and irritable. The phone hadn't rung all morning and Abby did not have the willpower required to face the grant proposal for the installation of manual controls, not this morning. To fend off total boredom, she had muscled her way through Chapters 6 and 7 of *How to Craft a Life*. Chapter 8 was entitled "Gratitude."

Each day, find something to be grateful for, Dale J. Nagery advised. *People tend to think that gratitude follows happiness. But really, the reverse is true. It is gratitude that brings happiness.*

Abby considered the words. Was her problem a simple lack of gratitude? It was possible, she supposed, even likely. She took out a scrap of paper and began to make a list of things she was grateful for. It was a short list with Rita and Tito at the top and her petunias as the bottom. There must be more than that, she thought as she gazed at the mostly blank paper. After a moment, she inserted Robert between Rita and Tito. She was grateful to have a house, no matter how small, and a business, never mind that it barely brought in enough money to cover expenses. She wrote these down. If Mike Brown were to make good on his lunch invitation she could add him to the list, but how likely was that? It had been nearly two weeks since she she'd last heard from him. She would be grateful if Alfonso got a visa. His presence would not only provide her with a positive distraction, it would counter some of her residual Fey guilt. If Officer Torrance Steadmen, or just about anyone, walked through the door right now, she would be grateful for the company.

Her eyes darted around the dismal little office. All she needed was one thing right this instant to feel truly grateful for. Nothing came to mind.

Fresh air. She would take a little whir around the neighborhood, come back to the office and start back to work on the new grant proposal. Finishing a task, especially one she didn't like, would surely make her feel grateful.

• • •

He was standing in the dim hallway as she came out of the office. Hulking was the first word that came to mind, unkempt the second. He wore Levis, ragged at the knees, and a plaid flannel shirt. It fit so snugly over the slight mound of his belly, the yellowed T-shirt he wore beneath was visible in gaps between buttons and the shirt cuffs ended well short of his wrists bones.

At first it was as if he hadn't seen her, then his head snapped up. "Abby?" he said.

"I'm Abby." Her fingers brushed the can of wasp spray.

"I saw your interview with Grace Belgrade and I've been thinking about you ever since." He stepped a bit closer.

God, the interview. She positioned her finger on button at the top of the can. He was younger than she first thought and there was a vaguely familiar sour smell about him that she couldn't quite place.

Deep Breathing

"How can I help you?" she asked, forcing calm into her voice.

His eyes focused on a spot just off her right ear. She was tempted to look over her shoulder to see what he was looking at so intently, but resisted.

"I'm a plumber." His tongue made a soft tse-tse-tse against the back of his teeth, something like the sound of a little bird. He drew his eyes back to her face. "My specialty is water heaters. Where is your water heater? Tsk tsk, tsk."

Abby almost laughed. "It isn't my water heater. I don't know where it is."

"That's okay, Abby. I'll can find it, he said. "Be right back."

• • •

Calvin, and no-no-no it was not Cal, sat across from her, hands rubbing his knees. In the past five minutes, Abby had learned more about the old water heater that served the building than she thought possible to know about a water heater. "So Calvin," she said, trying not to focus on the smell that emanated from the man like swamp gas. "Do you drive?"

"Drive? No-no-no. Bad idea, bad idea. Tse-tse-tse," his words staccato. After a long pause, he continued. "I have a bicycle. Do you want to see my bicycle?"

"Not right now, Calvin." Despite his smell, Abby was warming to the interview. "Don't you need tools for plumbing?"

"Yes."

"Do you have your own tools?"

"Yes."

"How do you carry your tools to your job?"

Calvin's gaze was now focused to a spot just off her left ear. "My bike has a trailer. Do you want to see my trailer?"

"Maybe later, Calvin. Tell me, do you have references?"

"References, references. Tse-tse-tse. "Do you mean like … references?"

A smiled quivered at the edges of her mouth. "Yes, references."

Brow knitted, Calvin was silent for a moment then brightened. "I have telephone numbers of satisfied customers, but no references.

Tse-tse-tse. No references, no-no-no references at all, none zero, zilch references."

"Can you give me the name and telephone numbers of your satisfied customers?"

He took out a notebook and pen from his breast pocket and began writing with blinding speed. After he'd written a dozen or more Abby stopped him. "Which three on your list do you like the most?"

He rubbed his knees. "Like the most? Tse-tse-tse." He was silent for some time. "They are all satisfied customers."

"That's fine." She reached for the list of names. "Would you say you work well with others?"

He rubbed his knees. "Work well with others? I don't mind. No, no, no. I don't mind. I can work well with others."

"One other thing. It's important that you take a shower and have clean clothes when you go on a job. Do you have a shower and washing machine where you live?"

"Yes."

"Do you use them?"

"No."

"Why is that, Calvin?"

"They turned off the electricity."

"Why was that?"

"I didn't pay the bill."

"Why was that?"

He rubbed his knees. "Tse-tse-tse. I have no money. No, no, no money at all, none, zero, zilch money."

Only then did Abby identify the sour smell emitted by her new client. Eau de dumpster, it was. "Are you hungry, Calvin?"

"Yes."

"Me too. Let's go to get something to eat." On the way out, it occurred to Abby that the building's old toilet would prove a good test of Calvin's plumbing skills. Lately, even Rita's efforts could not stem its rising tides. "After we get back, I'll look into getting your electricity turned back on if you'll have a look at our old toilet."

"I can do that. Tse-tse-tse. Toilets are my second specialty."

Deep Breathing

Abby smiled. She had two things to be grateful for right now. In addition to a free toilet fix, she was grateful that Calvin was not the serial killer.

• • •

Morning sun was streaming in the front window when Fey opened her eyes. She picked up a glass of water from the bedside table, took a painful sip, coughed then sipped again. Doc was rattling around in the kitchen area just feet from her head. She lay back and cast her eyes around the room, there was only one. On the walls hung two large landscapes, the kind you might find in a thrift store. There was a well-worn reclining chair where Doc had slept the past two nights, a dinette and two stools. On the dinette was a small television, a radio, a stack of paperback books and two vases of red silk roses flanking a silver-framed photo of a young woman and three small children, a boy and two girls. The table was so cluttered Fey doubted that Doc ever ate a meal there. She coughed again.

Doc peeked around the refrigerator. "You finally awake?"

"Yes." Her throat was raw, her voice a rasp.

He came over to the bed, penlight in hand. "Let's me take a took." He turned on the little bedside lamp. It was the kind a woman might buy thinking it was fancy with a torn silk shade that probably was once white.

Obediently, Fey opened her mouth wide and he scanned her throat with the light. "Looks better. I think you'll live," he pronounced.

"Yeah, but will I be able to go to my training on Monday?"

"Can't make any promises." He produced a thermometer from his shirt pocket and stuck it under Fey's tongue. "Sit tight. I'll be right back."

Of course he'd be right back, Fey thought. The studio apartment was so small there was no place to be right back from. She let her head sink back into the pillow and closed her eyes. She must have drifted off, because Doc was now standing there holding a steaming bowl wrapped in a dishcloth.

"Think you could eat some soup?"

"What was my temperature?" she asked accepting the proffered bowl.

"Better. Just a hair above a hundred."

The soup, Campbell's Chicken Noodle, was hot and salty and stung on its way down. Still, the familiar flavor was comforting. Tears gathered and ran down her cheeks.

"Does it hurt?"

"Yes, but that's not it."

Doc waited to see if she had more to say, but she continued to spoon up the soup in silence, sucking in the occasional noodle. When she had finished, he gave her the pills he'd been feeding her for the past she wasn't sure how long and a fresh glass of water. "Drink the whole glass if you can."

She obeyed without question. "Gotta pee."

"That's good to hear. I was beginning to wonder."

She threw back the covers. The cool air against her hot skin caused her to shiver and her head spun. For a moment, she sat on the edge of the bed.

"Here, darlin'. Let me give you a little hand. He pulled her to her feet then guided her to the bathroom, pulled down the sweatpants she wore as pajamas and positioned her on the toilet. "I'll just wait outside. Don't faint on me."

"What day is it?" Fey called through the closed door.

"Saturday."

Oh, God," she thought, slumping on the toilet. I'll never get well in time. Again, tears ran down her cheeks. She swiped at them with a wad of toilet paper. Feeling weak and forlorn, she considered the photo on the dinette. The image had stuck with her. It was an old photo, she could tell by the woman's hair, which was long and parted in the middle. The boy wore a white shirt and a little bow tie, the girls, frilly dresses with full shirts. No one dressed children that way anymore. That old photo, the way it was framed in silver and placed between the silk roses somehow just made her feel worse. As she rolled up the legs of her too long sweatpants, she tried to ignore that familiar and scary need to be held. She pulled up her sweats then opened the door.

Deep Breathing

"Better?" Doc put his arm around her shoulder and she leaned into him.

"I guess," she said, willing it to be so.

"Good girl. Now get back into bed."

"Doc?"

Yes, darlin'"

"Who's that in the photograph on the table?"

"People I knew a million years ago."

Fey let that sink in for a moment. "I bet they loved you a lot." She felt his grip on her shoulder tighten a bit.

"Once upon a time, I believe they did."

She got back into bed and he tucked the blankets, there were three, under her chin. After she had a coughing fit that brought on more tears, Doc positioned a couple of pillows under her shoulders to ease her breathing. She lay back, exhausted.

• • •

Robert had invited Abby to Saturday brunch at the Arizona Inn so that she could meet his new crush. New crush! She winced at the snarky tone of the word. She did feel jealous, though she tried to ignore the fact that she was no longer the best friend of her best friend. And it was true for Rita too, whose daughter-in-law, the one Rita did like, had pretty much replaced Abby. Jealousy was petty and immature; she silently chided herself. She hadn't even met Nelson, maybe she'd love him too, she thought as she studied the assortment of nearly identical knits in charcoal grays and black that comprised her very practical and boring wardrobe.

And shoes were another unsolvable problem. Her feet were tiny and crabbed. To her mind they resembled the bound feet of aristocratic Chinese women in pre-revolutionary China, though she had never seen such feet. She purchased her small, boxy, black leather oxfords at great expense from a store that promised shoes to fit any foot. With their scuffed toes and thick Velcro straps, they were not suitable for the staid and snooty Arizona Inn.

She pulled a black knit tunic over her head. Settling the Guatemalan pouch on top, she noticed for the first time that it was beginning to fade and fray. Rita was always after her to accessorize. Now Abby wished she had a pretty scarf to hide the pouch and dress up the tunic, but she didn't have a scarf and her only jewelry were the more or less permanently installed heart-shaped earrings that she chosen as a naive and hopelessly optimistic college freshman. Back then she just assumed that nothing could stop her from having the same accomplishments and subsequent joy as her wholly abled peers. She felt like ripping out the puffy little suckers. Bloody earlobes! Now that would make a fine first impression. She pulled the tunic over her head, took a deep breath, wrestled it under her butt and smoothed it over her lap.

In the bathroom, she quickly ran a comb through her tangle of curls. Smiled at her reflection in the mirror. The black tunic made her already pale skin look washed out. She hunted down the lipstick, a tube of Burt's Bees one shade darker than her own lips, she had purchased after the interview debacle. Still in mint condition, she spread it evenly over her lips then blotted them on the back of her hand. "What the hell." She had nothing to lose. She made a slash of lipstick on each cheek, then rubbed it in until they glowed pinkly. She studied the effect, the lips, the cheeks, the dark mop of hair and those damn hearts and sighed. Not much improvement there. Well, she was as ready to meet Nelson as she ever would be. At least Robert would approve of the lipstick should he happen to cast his love-besotted eyes in her direction.

"Just stop it," she said to her reflection. Certainly, Dale J. Nagery would not approve of all this negativity, would tell her to get over herself and find something to be grateful for.

Well, she was glad to have Robert in her life even if she had been bumped from her place as best friend. Smiling, she thought of a conversation they'd had some time ago about climate change. He was saying he'd be dead by the time it got really bad and he didn't have to worry about the quality of his grandchildren's future. "Unless you're not telling me something," he'd added with a smirk.

Abby chucked recalling their single attempt at sex. Was there penetration? She thought not, but maybe. She hadn't bled. Perhaps she'd already lost her virginity to a tampon. The thought struck her as emblematic of her entire sex life. At any rate, she had assured him that there had been no issue from whatever union they'd had. One thing she'd always appreciated about their friendship was that they could laugh or commiserate about their shared past, and that was unlikely to change.

Robert had offered to pick her up but that would mean she'd have to use her manual wheelchair instead of the Chariot. It would mean that Robert would have to haul her ass up into the cramped front seat. She could see it now, her unruly legs, refusing her command to bend, sticking out of the door of his the sporty Camero like two dead tree branches. Robert would have to use brute force to get them to fold so he could close the door, or perhaps her legs could just stick out the window—that would be interesting—then once they got to the restaurant, Robert would have to push her chair. The inequality between the Mighty Claw and her weak and uncooperative left hand made self-propulsion painfully slow, not to mention, undignified, and Abby wanted to make her appearance at the Arizona Inn as dignified as humanly possible. No, the best option, she had decided, was to take the Chariot. She would arrive early and already be seated at the table, dignity intact and scruffy shoes hidden by the starched white tablecloth, when Robert and Nelson arrived.

She looked at her watch. Time to be on her way. She checked the back door. Satisfied that it was bolted shut, she whirred out the front door. The plan was to pick up the streetcar on Cushing and go to the end of the line. From there, it would only take her 10 or 15 minutes to get to the Arizona Inn.

It was a nice, wintery day, the sun coolly shining in a solid blue sky. It might be a really pleasant morning, one she could be grateful for right now, if she just accepted things as they were.

Cord between her teeth, Abby whizzed out the front door then pulled it closed behind her with one yank of her head. As she locked the door, her thoughts turned to the homeless Fey living in that raggedy tent city. It seemed like she was laboring hard to pull her life together, but she had such a long way to go. Really, Abby simply had to stop thinking she deserved more in her life and be grateful for what she had, which was certainly more than her poor cousin.

• • •

As planned, she was already seated at the table before their arrival. She took a sip of ice water then renewed her lipstick. She was about to peruse the menu when she noticed Robert and Nelson speaking to the hostess. Though her stomach was dancing with nerves, she smiled and waved. Robert, looking sporty in a V-neck sweater the same warm greenish-gray as his eyes, returned her wave as he lurched down the ramp. Nelson, in khaki's and a navy sport coat followed close behind.

"Nels," Robert began, his brow wrinkled in concentration. "I … like you … to me … my old … est and … best fren … Abby Ban… nis…t, queen an de… fen…der of gimps."

"Great to meet you at last," he said in a suave baritone. "Bobby's told me all about you." As he reached across the table for her hand, a brass button on his coat sleeve caught on her water glass. In one of those slow motion moments, the glass tipped, then fell, then rolled into Abby lap. "Oh my God." He gathered up the napkins and began to swab up the spill. "I'm so sorry. I'm such a klutz."

She laughed, feeling grateful, yes grateful, that it was Nelson, and not she, who'd knocked over the glass. "Not to worry, Nelson, I'm just very happy to meet you too." Happy and relieved, she thought, as water trickled down her legs and into her awful black shoes, but Bobby? Robert had always hated to be called Bobby. Must be true love. Well, she was happy for them both.

• • •

When Doc opened his eyes, the room was awash in the neon glow from the street. He stared hard at the lump on the bed, straining to see the covers move up and down. For some moments he listened for her breath. Finally, he cast the old Army surplus jacket that served as blanket aside and stepped over to the bed just to reassure himself that his patient was indeed still breathing. When he put his hand on her back, she jumped like a scalded cat.

"Sorry, darlin'. Settle down now." He turned on the bedside light. "It's just old Doc checking to see if you're still in the land of the living." He put his hand on her forehead. "How ya feeling?"

"Okay, I guess. Throat's still sore."

"It's just about time for another round of pills. Hang on." He shook out a zinc tablet, two ibuprofens and an amoxicillin then handed her the glass of water from the nightstand.

"Drink the whole thing," he commanded. As he took the glass from her she reached out encircling his wrist with her now icy fingers.

"What is it, darlin'?"

She tugged lightly on his wrist. "I just thought… you can get in bed with me if you want." She let go of his wrist, sat up and pulled back the covers. "Nobody's ever been as nice to me as you, Doc. I owe you."

Taken aback by the invitation, he chuckled. "That would most likely be deemed fraternizing and against base rules."

"But we're not on base," she said, slumped on the edge of the bed.

The look on her face, at once pleading and fearful, took the chuckle right out of his voice. "I'll get you another glass of water." While he filled the glass he considered his response. When a lady asks you to climb in bed with her, refusal is a delicate matter. He placed the fresh glass of water on the nightstand. "Technically we're not on base, but as long as I'm employing the base heap, I'm obliged to abide by base rules. Besides, the bed's a bit narrow for two." He tried another smile.

She raised a skeptical brow. "It's because I'm ugly."

He studied her face. Certainly, she was no beauty, with her cropped hair, pugilist's nose and sun-coarsened skin. Fact was, he could see himself in that face. Hell, he could see the goddam suffering of Christ in that face. Finally he said, "Honey dear, you are a sight that never fails to gladden this old man's heart. You are the sun after the rain, the clouds in an otherwise blue sky and a T-bone steak on the plate of a hungry man."

"What a load of horseshit," she said, smiling her tight-lipped smile. "So is it because you think you're too old for me, because if…"

"Not that either."

"Then why?

"Because you're sick. Now get back in bed." She did as told. "You know, Fey darlin', you don't ever have to pay for kindness."

"In my world, there's always a price for kindness."

He shook his head. "If it isn't free it isn't kindness."

She stared at the ceiling for a moment before the tears began to roll once again. "Well, could we just hold each other."

Her voice was so small he was reminded of his youngest daughter and he knew that he could safely wrap his arms around her and they would both sleep better as a consequence.

• • •

Doc shook her awake well before the first light. "What time is it?" she asked.

"Time to get up if you're going to that Caridad training. How do you feel?"

"Okay." She flung the covers back and sat on the edge of the bed.

Doc thrust the thermometer in her mouth then went back into the kitchen. The little apartment was warm and she could smell coffee and something else less definable, which meant Doc had been up for some time.

Doc removed the thermometer and held it up to the light.

"Well?" Fey asked.

"Normal enough," he said and handed her a glass of water and a bowl full of something undefinable.

"What's this?"

""Diced Spam, a can of chili, a can of ravioli and can of peas for good health. My father called it Slumgullion stew. When I was a kid, he'd make it with from whatever was left over at the end of the paycheck. It was that or nothing. It's a good test case."

"What does that mean?"

"Means if you can eat this you're fit for duty."

She had laid her clothes out the night before, black pants, the black T-shirt with the Caridad Community Kitchen's logo she'd been given, her raggedy old tennis shoes, clean socks and underwear. She had to be there promptly at 8—one minute late, she'd been warned, would count the same as an absence. She took a spoonful of Doc's stew. Except for the canned peas, it wasn't bad. For the next few minutes, she ate around them. When she had finished everything else in the bowl, she spooned up the peas and drank them down with the water.

"I'll drive you to this Caridad thing this morning since it's on my way back to base. I figure you're well enough to take the bus home. You got the fare?"

"Yes." She had a coughing fit and Doc refilled her water glass.

"Okay then. If they ask you about that cough, tell 'em Doc said you were not contagious; let 'em think you'd been to a real doctor."

"As far as I'm concerned you're real enough."

He smiled. "Thanks, darlin'; I always try my best. Anyway, you better shower and get dressed now. When you get back to the base this afternoon, we'll have a full debriefing."

Fey nodded though she didn't know what a debriefing was, full or otherwise. What she did know was now that she was no longer sick. Doc was once again just Doc, no more warm bed, no more special attention, no more Doc's arms holding her though the night.

Chapter 22

Monday, Nov. 28

Abby read to the bottom of the page then put aside *How to Craft Your Life*. In Chapter 11 Dale J. Nagrey had enjoined her to Identify, Implement and Evaluate. She wrote down the words at the top of a yellow tablet, underlining each.

Well, she had identified the problem. She hated her earrings and she needed to buy a scarf. The solution was also pretty straightforward. She would simply take the Chariot over to Fourth Avenue; pop into one of any number of little shops that sold assorted hip gewgaws, T-shirts, scarves and all manner of jewelry. Surely she'd find something there that would make her appearance brighter and her life… well… better crafted.

As usual, Rita was late. Abby should just move her hours from 9 a.m. to whenever she wanted to leave until 10 a.m. to whenever she wanted to leave. I should go by myself, she thought. It was serve her right to come to work and find me gone and the office locked.

The phone rang. "GS, Abby Bannister speaking. How my I help you?"

"It's me, babe."

"Morning Josh. Did you have a nice Thanksgiving?"

"Not particularly. I had to work. What did you do?"

"I handed out hot meals to the homeless." She sounded self-righteous, but she did feel proud of herself for choosing to spend the holiday in service to others, even though it had not been as much a question of free will as imposed guilt. Now she waited for the inevitable hit. "You still there?" she asked, sweetly in response to the silence at the other end of the line.

"I'm still here. So … "

"So?"

"I was wondering if you could loan me fifty until payday."

"Can't. I've had some unexpected expenses this past week," she said thinking of her half of the entry fee for the Ms. Pole Dance Arizona Competition.

"How about twenty-five?"

Identify, implement, evaluate. The problem was she didn't want to loan him money, but she didn't want to alienate him either. She decided to change the subject. "You know, Josh, lately I've been thinking of when we were kids." She heard Josh sigh audibly.

"Yeah? Sounds like you've been hanging around Fey."

"No. I guess it's just the holidays. I've been wondering about Mom. I really didn't get much of a chance to know her. Do you remember when she'd make eggnogs?"

"Eggnogs? She never made one for me, but then Mom was all about you."

"I'm sorry. I guess Mom was pretty wrapped up in me."

"You guess?" His voice was hard. "But that's okay. Dad was all about me. Bam! Bam! Bam!" he said then laughed. "Now that's what I remember."

"Yeah, he was hard on you. Did Mom ever try to stop him?"

Another silence followed by another sigh. "When it came to Dad, she was pretty passive."

"Passive? I've always thought of her as patient but determined. One time she was watching me dress and I was crying because she wouldn't help me. She ordered me to stop crying, said she wouldn't always be there so I had to learn to take care of myself. I couldn't have been more than 6 at the time. Do you think she knew she was dying?"

"Maybe. Mom was a traditional Catholic. Maybe she did know about the breast cancer and chose not to do anything about it until it was too late."

"Why would she do that?"

"Maybe she thought the only way out of marriage with dad was death."

"Do you believe that?"

"Not really ... sometimes." After a brief pause he said, "So what about twenty?"

Now it was Abby's turn to sigh. "Come by the office this afternoon."

Feeling deflated, Abby hung up the phone. Josh really had a pretty miserable childhood, she thought. She knew he'd both feared and hated their father. Did she hate the man? Probably, but her hatred was tempered by pity. He was a miserable father, but his life was miserable.

The door whooshed open and Rita and Honey whizzed in.

"Finally. I need to buy some earrings. I was thinking I might just whizz down to Fourth Avenue. Would you like to come along?"

"You mean close up shop on a Monday and just go shopping? Are you feeling oaky? Did you fall on your head or something?"

Abby smiled. "Wild and crazy me. It shouldn't take too long."

• • •

Smelling of patchouli oil, the shop was dark and cramped and full of objects she had no need or place for yet coveted nevertheless: faux ivory Buddhas, shimmering, spangled blouses, porcelain neti pots, chopstick holders and wooden carvings in all sizes from Asia and Africa, Christmas tree ornaments from places where, Abby was reasonably sure, Christmas was not celebrated. The women slowly whirred through the store, taking great care not to bump into anything breakable.

While Rita and Honey perused racks of bright batiks, silky shawls and all manner of tie-dye, Abby narrowed her focus on the jewelry in the display case. Most of the earrings dangled. They were exotic and beautiful and totally unlike anything she would ever wear. She could envision getting her hair or one of her knits snagged on one and having no way to extricate herself. "Do you have anything less dangly?" she asked the salesclerk.

"Let's see what I can find." The clerk unlocked a small display standing off to one side of the counter. She spun it around slowly so Abby could get a good look. "Do you like pearls?" she asked, reaching for a pair of earrings.

Abby leaned in for a closer look. The pearls were each set in the center of a silver Celtic knot. To Abby's mind, they were subtle and sophisticated. "How much?"

The woman looked at the price on the back of the card. "Fifty-five."

Disappointed, Abby sat back. "Pretty pricey."

"The pearls are cultured and the silver sterling."

"I think I'll just look at your scarves."

The clerk returned the earrings to the case.

Abby pulled a purple and blue rayon paisley scarf from the rack and held it to her face. "This would go with everything. What do you think?"

"Too dark." Rita riffled through the rack then pulled out a scarf with swirls of orange, red and yellow that looked like it was on fire. She held it up to Abby face. "This one."

"It's kind of bright, don't you think?"

"Yes, and just what you need."

Abby ran the gauzy affair through her hand. It was light and insubstantial, lovely and totally impractical. She looked at the price. "Twenty."

Rita shrugged. "Not bad."

Abby rubbed the puffy heart piercing her left ear. Did she dare?

"I'll take it, and Rita, see if you can unscrew these earrings, would you? I'm going to get some new ones."

Rita's brows hitched up in surprise. "Are you sure you didn't hit your head this morning, *mija*, or is it the patchouli oil?"

"Saturday I went to the Arizona Inn for brunch with Robert and his new boyfriend."

Rita nodded sympathetically as she worked to unscrew a heart. "Well, next time you're invited someplace nice, you'll be ready."

Abby's stomach was aquiver with anxiety over her extravagance. The last non-essential purchase she could recall was the damn pair of heart earrings.

Rita held both hearts in her hand. "Can I have these, Abby? They'd be perfect for my youngest granddaughter."

"Sure. I never want to see them again."

• • •

Back at the office, the flashing red light on the telephone announced a message. Abby picked it up, listened for a few minutes. "Sor Felipa." She passed the phone to Rita. Would you call her back?"

Rita looked at her long and hard before taking the phone and dialing.

Abby filled the electric kettle and tried to remain calm. Sor Felipa had probably changed her mind. Well, at least she had tried and maybe it was all for the better. As Rita had pointed out, it was crazy to think she could afford to take responsibility for a teenage boy. To be honest, she felt relieved.

"*Si, si, si.*" Rita was saying. Then added, "*Si, si.*" After a few minutes, she concluded, "*Gracias Sor Felipa. A usted también.*"

"Well?" Abby asked.

"Alfonso has his passport and they've applied for the visa." Rita had that *I told you so* look on her face. "I hope you're ready for your life to turn upside down."

Abby was not. In fact, she was awash with renewed anxiety. She pressed the palm of her Mighty Claw over her mouth. Her house and her budget were both too small. She knew nothing about raising a teenage boy, let alone a teenage boy with a significant physical challenge and limited English. He'd be way behind in school, a private Catholic school that she could not afford. And would he be accepted by his classmates or ridiculed and rejected? Who would befriend him? Rita had been right; she'd been crazy to take Alfonso on. Was it too late to change her mind? "Excuse me," she said whizzing toward the sink. "I think I'm going to throw up."

Before she had a chance to, Anûshka burst into the office like a white tornado, hair bristling from her scalp as if she'd just had a close call with an electric outlet. "Oh what a morning!"

"A good or bad morning?" Abby asked, her stomach shocked back into compliance.

"Is Mr. O'Riley, so unpatient and angry. Is always Anûshka take me here; Anûshka take me there. Do this Anûshka; do that Anûshka. Did you get the dusty bunnies under the couch, Anûshka? I am excellent house cleaner; of course I get the dusty bunnies. I do not argue, but I say *Does bear shit in wood, Mr. O'Riley?* and he just laughs at me as if I am clown. I am not clown. I am human woman with feelings. Oh, he make me so angry I want to yell, but I say, *Yes, Mr. O'Riley; you bet ya, Mr. O'Riley.*" She began pulling out the cleaning supplies from beneath the sink. "And never does he say a kind thanks to me. I am worn down to… I am worn down to… nibbles."

"You mean nubbins?" Abby said.

"What is nubbins?"

Abby and Rita exchanged looks. Both women shrugged.

"And then he says, Anûshka you must go back to school for CPA. Does he not think I am smart enough so I need more school? And what is CPA? Is this insult?"

"Not at all. A Certified Public Accountant has to be really good with math and money. You have to pass a difficult test to become a CPA."

"Oh. I am excellent in math, but there is no time or money for school so why does he say such a thing, but to make me feel stupid. I understand his back provides him with very much pain. For this I feel pity. So when he say a mean thing to me I put it up."

"I think you mean *I put up with it.*"

"What sense does that make? No. I put it up. I put it up to God." She shook a container. "We are near to out of Scrubbing Bubbles."

While Anûshka performed her magic on the office, Rita returned to the subject of Alfonso. "So have you made any plans for his arrival?"

"Alfonso's? Of course," Abby lied. She'd devoted many hours of fantasy to Alfonso, but had yet to come up with anything more than the vaguest of plans about how to actually make them reality.

"So I guess you'll enroll him in a Catholic school first."

"Actually, I think I'll home school him until he learns more English, then enroll him in the fall. I figure, Alfonso can come to the office with me. Most days I certainly have the time to work with him and he can use the computer when we don't need it. There are lots of programs for learning English and math and… and stuff."

"Those programs cost money and, according to you, the whole idea of bringing him up was so that he could go to school."

"What's that supposed to mean?"

"What's what supposed to mean?"

"The thing about *according to me*."

"Nothing. Don't be so touchy."

Was she being touchy? Probably. "By the time he gets his visa, it will be well after the start of the second semester. I think it would be better for him to get adjusted to his new life. Maybe he can start with a summer program of some kind."

"Computer programs, summer programs? Parochial schools like Salpointe and St. Augustine aren't cheap, Abby. How will you pay for all this?

Abby shrugged. "I have a plan."

"Don't tell me you're going to take out a second mortgage."

"Okay. I won't tell you."

• • •

Fey entered the medical tent, a plastic grocery sack hanging from her elbow.

"Hey darlin'," Doc said, putting the paperback he was reading aside. "What did you learn today?"

"The proper way to cut vegetables so you don't cut off a finger."

"Sounds like a valuable skill. What's in the bag?"

"Leftovers." She said collapsing on a chair. "Every day, we're going to be divided into teams. One team prepares lunch for all the students and staff, one team makes meals for the homeless, and one team puts together the things that are needed for the cooking demonstration. Once a team finishes their job they start helping the others finish theirs. It's pretty cool; there's enough food at lunch so everyone gets leftovers for everyone in their household so they won't have to cook when they get home. I figure you and Angie are part of my household, so I brought enough for the three of us.

"How are you feeling?"

"Okay. Tired. I'm still coughing a lot. Nobody wants to stand near me, but they're not mean about it."

"Did you remember to take your antibiotics?"

Repressing a smile, she said, "Yes, daddy."

"Good girl. So what's for dinner?"

"Something called chicken piccata, something called pilaf, which is just rice with some other stuff in it, and zucchini with lots of other stuff in it. I chopped a pile of onions and a mountain of zucchini." She handed him the grocery sack. "If you'll heat it up, I'll go get Angie. Oh. Have you ever heard of capers?"

"Heard of 'em, but I don't know what they are."

"They're pickled flower buds but look like little boogers. Anyway, heads up. The chicken thing has capers so don't freak out."

Chapter 23

Saturday, Dec. 3

Sporting her fiery scarf and pearl earrings, Abby felt well-dressed and excited as she whirred down the Iceberg's ramp. Anûshka, on the other hand, clutched the paper bag that held her costume, looking pale and anxious, while Rita just looked frazzled and annoyed. The competition was to start at 7 p.m., which meant she'd just battled Phoenix rush hour traffic.

Abby and Rita flanked Anûshka as she carefully picked her way in her enormous red shoes toward the entrance to Smokey's Last Roundup, a combination nightclub and venue for everything from kickboxing matches to mariachi conferences.

"Boy, Anûshka," Abby said. "I don't know how you can manage in those shoes."

"I pretend they are not there and walk on my very tiptoes, but is not easy. I worry too much that I will break my ankle. Ah, my stomach is flip-flops."

"Did you eat before you left the house?" Abby asked.

"Of course. I drink excellent protein shake. My stomach is flip-flops because of my nervous."

"Let's get going, ladies," Rita urged. "From the looks of the parking lot, there's going to be a full house and who knows where they plant people in wheelchairs."

• • •

"Why on earth would they plant us by the exit doors on the third tier above the arena?" Rita groused. "We'll need binoculars to see the action from up here."

Abby, having spent a lifetime in a wheelchair, was neither particularly irate or surprised. What did surprise her was that the audience was mostly woman, many sporting enormous platform shoes with stiletto heels, the apparent standard pole dancer footwear. And most were not well-endowed stripper types, as she had expected, but well-muscled athletes.

"So did you bring your gun?" Abby asked.

"Yeah. I've gotten used to it and Norberto thinks it's sexy."

"Please don't tell me you wear it when you have sex."

"Okay. I won't tell you."

Abby took a moment to glare at her friend. Her weapon of choice was definitely not a turn on, but it was a proven deterrent. As the lights when down, she boosted herself up in her chair and adjusted her glasses. In a blaze of searchlights, a tuxedoed master of ceremonies jogged onto a stage, which was bare except for two gleaming poles. "Good evening, ladies and gentlemen, and welcome to the fifth annual Ms. Pole Dance Arizona competition." There was a thunderous applause, considerable whistling and more than a few high-pitched ululations. Due to her late entry into the contest, Anûshka would be performing toward the end. The two women squinted at the stage. This was going to be a long evening.

• • •

He had parked his car down by the Shanty and walked the half-dozen or so blocks to Abby's house. He'd been studying her comings and goings now for weeks, and she was proving to be more difficult to pin down than he had initially thought. She rarely went out at night and when she did, it was never alone. Her route to and from work varied and was too public. He had faith that the right opportunity would arise, but he was getting impatient. Now that she was living alone again, he thought he'd just show up at her house. Put it in God's hands.

For a moment he just stood in front of her house. The street was dark save for the light coming from the front window. The house was so close to the street that he could easily look in. Once inside, he'd have to be careful to stay away from that window in case someone happened to be passing by. He walked up the ramp to the front door, rang the bell. While he waited he examined the sturdy cord attached to the doorknob and wondered what its purpose might be. He rang the bell again. No one home.

• • •

Before he could unlock the door, three cats ran out from the hedge that fronted his apartment and began twining around his legs. He opened the door to his apartment, blocking their entry with his leg. "Hold your horses, guys," he said and flipped on the light.

The bag of cat food was right by the door. He poured a pile of kibble directly on the stoop and watched the three cats as they ate, each purring like a little engine. He imagined they were the mother and what was left of her most recent litter. He leaned over and stroked each one in turn. If he didn't have to move around so much, he'd take them in. It would be nice having a little company. Within minutes the food was gone and so were the cats.

He was tired and it was good to be back. Though he felt a bit stymied, things seemed to be essentially on track.

He settled down on the bed to evaluate the situation. Clearly, if he was going to carry out his mandate, he'd have to move on again, the sooner the better, though it got old pulling up stakes and starting over each time. He wondered when, if ever, he'd be allowed to settle down in one place and begin a normal life. Where would his next stop be? His work required a place where people weren't always operating on high alert. In other words, a place big enough but not too big. Austin, Texas, appealed to him and university towns offered lots of opportunity. Well, it was all up to God.

Over the course of the past few years, he had been called to commit his acts of mercy in many different places. In each, he'd gone by a different name: Gabriel, Jeremiel, Azrael, Michael. Even so, he never assumed for himself the mantle of angel of death. No, his role was facilitator and healer. He smiled. When people prayed to God for a healing they never seemed to realize that death is the ultimate healing.

He imagined that there were many like him all over the world chosen by God to ease those suffering into the next world. At once God's blessing and command, he could not abandon his mission. He never knew with certainty what the next day might bring, but if it was God's will, he'd finish this healing release and move on.

This evenings plan to simply knock on Abby's door and surprise her hadn't panned out, but rather than a failure, he considered it more of a practice run. Practice makes perfect, as they say, and it was important to maintain a positive and focused attitude. Yes, things were still on track and there was always tomorrow. Smiling, he closed his eyes. God's will be done."

• • •

To the opening strains of *America the Beautiful*, Anûshka, all big red shoes and waving flags, performed the preliminary floor routine with its convoluted moves demonstrating great strength and agility, before ascending the pole. At first it was hand over hand, legs forming a simple vee, then with legs in a 190-degree Chinese split. When she hit the top, she slid down the pole as if it were greased. Legs still split, she broke her descent only at the last moment. Unlike some of the contestants before her, she hit the ground so lightly that she didn't even bounce. Again she ascended the pole, twisting, twirling, turning as she went. Halfway up, she grasped the pole between her thighs, legs extended outward like a plank, arms waving the attached American flags. The crowd cheered. To the second verse of *America the Beautiful*, Anûshka continued her ascent. At the top she flung off one shoe then the other, a totally unchoreographed move, and the crowd went wild. From this point on, Anûshka seemed transported to another world, one with no gravity. Her body pretzeled and levered and swung. For moments, it seemed to float in the air. She flipped upside down, flapping her legs like the wings of a pterosaur, then extended her upper body 45 degrees from the pole undulating seductively, and the crowd came unglued.

• • •

"There's nothing wrong with third place." Abby was saying. "Five hundred bucks and that nice bag of… What's in that bag?"

Anûshka, who had been crying, shuddered deeply. "I did not care to look."

"Let me see." Anûshka handed her a large pink sack. "I know you're disappointed," Abby continued, as she riffled though the contents of the bag. "But the crowd loved you best even if the judges didn't. Rita and I get our investment back and you're still three hundred ahead."

"You forget money I give Howard and my too expensive red shoes. I am in hole forty-two dollars and seven cents."

"Oh well," Rita chimed in. "There's a special place in hell for men like him. What's in the bag?"

Abby extracted a tube. "Body glitter and nail polish, I think it is, and maybe some lotion, stuff like that."

"Nice," Rita said, as she flipped on her turn signal. "Anybody hungry? That strip mall over there has a Whataburger and a Peter Piper Pizza. Oh and look, there's a Chinatown Buffet."

• • •

The three women sat in a booth. Abby and Rita had plates piled with shrimp fried rice, sweet and sour spareribs, eggrolls and chow mien atop crispy fried noodles.

Anûshka looked down at her dab of chow mien in a puddle of soy and sighed.

Brightening, Abby said, "I've got an idea. The office has never looked better. At $15 an hour sweat equity, you've just about paid off the finder's fee and the advance I gave you for your driver's test."

"I owe 45 minutes still."

"Well, you could keep our $200, right, Rita," she said smiling broadly at Rita who merely shrugged. "And pay us back by continuing to clean the office."

"Is deal," Anûshka said without enthusiasm.

"Good," Abby said. And it was good even though she was out another hundred bucks. It also felt good to turn the tables on Rita for once. How had Dale J. Nagery put it in chapter 11? *The return on an investment is not always in dollars.*

• • •

As Abby turned the key in the lock, old Mrs. Soto called from next door. "*Mija, mija,* there was a man."

"*Hola*, Mrs. Soto, you're up late tonight. *Cómo está?*"

"*Bien, bien, gracias a Dios,* but I wanted to tell you about the man who came to your door."

"Was he on a skateboard?" Abby asked, thinking it might have been Fey.

"A skateboard? No. He just walked up and rang your bell. It was nearly 7 o'clock. I know because my *telenovela* was about to begin."

"Was he a black man?"

"No."

So it wasn't Torrance, she thought then brightened. Maybe Mike was back in town. "What did he look like?"

"Look like? He was a white man, *mija*. That's all I know."

"Well, thank you Mrs. Soto."

"But who was he?"

"I don't know, Mrs. Soto, but thanks."

"Well, I just thought you'd want to know. Good night, *mija* and God bless you."

"You too, Mrs. Soto, and thanks again."

Once inside, she turned on the light then bolted the door. Tito blinked at her from the doorway to the bedroom as if to say *it's about time*. It had been a long night, the cat was cranky and she should have been in bed an hour ago.

She put her cellphone into the charger on the kitchen table then poured kibble into the cat's bowl. She unbolted the back door, set the bowl on the porch then closed the door. Immediately, Tito came out of the bedroom and ran through the cat door. She could hear the crunch, crunch as she threw the bolt on the door.

If it hadn't been Mike at her door, then who? Her home address was not on her card, but that didn't present a problem in the age of Google. If had been Mike, he might call her at work tomorrow and invite her out to that lunch he promised weeks ago. Running her finger over the pearl nestled in the silver knot earring, she smiled at the thought. Tomorrow she'd wear her new scarf again, just in case.

Chapter 24

Thursday, Dec. 8

It had been a long, uneventful day. Abby looked at the clock. It was nearly 5. Rita had left early so she could get her hair done. Abby hadn't mentioned her hope that Mike would call, mostly because she didn't want to seem pathetic if he didn't. Now she felt pathetic anyway. All week she'd been waiting, but there had been no phone call, at least not from Mike.

Robert had phoned to invite her over for brunch Saturday. Among other things, Nelson was a fabulous cook. Stella's mother called to say that the Section 8 housing request had gone through and Stella was now on the waiting list. Barry Franklin called to tell her that he would begin work on the new remodel she'd contracted him for next Monday. She told him about Calvin the plumber and he said he'd give him a try. Mr. O'Riley called to tell her he wanted to put Anûshka through an accounting program at Pima Collage, a pleasant surprise. She had called Pete Valenzuela to discuss boarding Alfonso with him and his wife so he could go to school at Mission San Xavier next fall. The amount they had settled on for Alfonso's room and board would be less than what she'd have to pay for his tuition at any other parochial school in town and, for the first time in his life, Alfonso would have a male role model.

She turned off her computer, unplugged the electric teakettle then pulled her poncho off the coat rack. After assuring herself that she had forgotten nothing, she turned out the lights and whirred out the door.

As she sped down Sixth Street, busy with rush hour traffic, the lush woman with the agave on her head peered down at her from the side of the Tucson Warehouse and Transfer Company. Her expression this afternoon was one of amused skepticism. Abby was beginning to hate that mural.

Layers of wispy clouds and contrails promised a nice sunset and everything seemed to be moving smoothly along. She should be grateful and she would be totally if it weren't for the fact that she was still stuck in the same lonely rut. She took a deep breath. Ah well, she thought. What was it that Dale J. Nagery had said? *What you are meant to have you will have.* Or was that Karma tea? Sometimes she mixed the two up.

This afternoon, she would take Ash to Fourth. As both Torrance and Stransky had advised, she varied her route home daily. It had been weeks since the last gimp was murdered. She wanted to believe the serial killer had moved on. Bolstered by the cylinder of wasp spray resting coolly against her thigh, she turned onto the deserted little lane then threw the Chariot in high gear, alert for any passerby, male or female, wearing gloves.

As promised, the wispy clouds were turning pink by the time she headed down her own block. Though Abby couldn't see her, she assumed Mrs. Soto was sitting on her porch behind her amazing bougainvillea. "*Hola*, Mrs. Soto. *Cómo está?*"

"*Bien, bien, garcias a Dios*," she called. "*Y tú, mija?*

"*Bien, bien, garcias a Dios.*" Another white lie, she thought, as she whirred up the ramp to her front door. Whether she felt good or bad, it had nothing to do with God.

When she opened the door, Tito was waiting for her. She threw her poncho on the couch and he jumped onto her lap, purring and butting his head against her chin as she proceeded into the kitchen. After filling his bowl, she unbolted the back door. The minute she set the food down, Tito jumped off her lap, affection and free ride over. For a moment, Abby sat in the doorway taking in the sunset. The clouds and contrails had gone from pink to copper in a sky now pure blue by contrast. While a mocking bird sang the last tune of the evening, Abby took a deep breath and let the colors wash over her until they faded to a smoky gray. In the quickly fading light, she closed her eyes feeling calm and now wholly grateful for a sunset that she was meant to have. Her life, she reminded herself once again, was essentially good and she simply needed to accept it as it was.

The sound of the doorbell snapped her out of her brief meditation. With hope and a pounding heart, she ran the Mighty Claw through her hair then headed to the living room.

She took another deep breath, before opening the door. He still sported the Birkenstocks, but had exchanged the shorts he'd worn that day in Food City for Levis. He smiled broadly and Abby's expression mirrored his. "Mike!" She had forgotten how nice his eyes were, how almost handsome he was.

"Nice to see you, Abby. I'm sorry I didn't call first, but I was in the neighborhood and just thought... what the heck."

"Well, you're back from Pittsburg at last. It's nice to see you too. Come on in."

As he stepped inside, he glanced around the room. "Cozy little place you've got here."

"It is little, that's for sure."

"If you haven't already eaten, I thought maybe we could grab a bite."

"We can if you don't mind walking."

"Not at all. As a matter of fact, I'm renting a place in Armory Park, so I just walked over from there."

Abby was impressed. Armory Park was an area of classy old homes, but it was at least a mile away. "You're renting in Armory Park? That's not what I'd call in my neighborhood."

"Yeah, well I guess you might say I just happened to be in your neighborhood on purpose."

Abby could see by his shy little smile that he was abashed to be caught in a lie, but she was thrilled. He'd gone out of his way to find out where she lived. Gone out of his way to get here. Her heart was practically defibrillating and like some goofy teenager she couldn't stop smiling.

"Anyway," he was saying. "I like to walk when I can and I thought we could just walk and… well… roll over to the Shanty. It's close by. Ever been there?"

"A few times. They've got good burgers."

"I'm a vegetarian, actually, but they've got salads too."

"Salads are healthy." The heat rose to her face as she tried to think of a more interesting observation. "So how are Juniper, Bess and Frank?"

"Who?" he asked then quickly added, "The cats. They're fat and sassy."

"Who takes care of them when you're gone?"

"An elderly cat loving neighbor came in twice a day." He shook his head, a wry smile on his lips. "The ingrates didn't even know I was gone."

Abby nodded knowingly. "I guess if you want gratitude, you need to get a dog." She looked around the room as if there might be something there worth mentioning then shrugged. "Well, I'm pretty much ready to go whenever you are."

"Good." He picked up her poncho from the couch. "Can I help you with your wrap?"

"Thanks."

He slipped the poncho over her head. There was a tenderness in the way he tucked it around her and smoothed it over her shoulders. "I see you're still packing around that can of bug spray." He nodded his head towards the can of Real Kill lying against her thigh.

Abby chuckled. "Wasp spray."

"I remember. It can stop a bear at 20 feet. What's in it anyway?"

Abby shrugged. "I have no idea."

"Are you sure it's safe to keep an open can of this stuff in the house? Let me read the label."

Still smiling, Abby handed him the canister. Instantly, she felt a little electric charge in the air and she was pretty sure she'd just made a terrible mistake.

For a few moments he squinted at the back of the can. "Damn print is so small I can't read it." He set the can on the couch and pulled a pair of leather gloves from his back pocket. "Ready?"

Abby's stomach heaved, but she managed a smile. "Great. I just need to feed the cat before we go. It will only take me a minute."

"Be right here waiting," he said with that same shy little smile.

She wheeled into the kitchen, took a deep breath, rammed through the back door and made a straight shot for the ramp. She could hear him slam through the door, could hear the rotten boards creak and give under the Chariot's weight. They held for her.

When she heard the crash, she turned to see him standing amid the splintered boards waist high in the crawlspace. The look of surprise on his face quickly changed to rage as he began to hoist himself out. Without hesitation, Abby spun around then pushed the toggle into high gear. Her knees caught him in the chest snapping him backwards before she fell, chair and all, into the crawlspace. For a moment, she just sat there in the dark, trying to assess the damage. Though she wasn't in any pain, blood was dripping from her arm. Beneath her, Mike was still. Oh God, he's dead, she thought, reaching into her pouch for the cellphone she'd left in the charger on the kitchen table. And her glasses … Where were they? "Damn!"

Abby inhaled deeply then screamed for help. She took another breath, but before she could yell a second time, she felt his gloved hand grip her ankle. "Help," she screamed, as she reached down with her mighty claw and seized the wrist. "Help!" she screamed again, squeezing the wrist until it went limp. "Help!"

• • •

She didn't know if she'd been sitting down in that hole five minutes or 50, when she heard the sound of heavy footsteps. "I'm down here," she rasped. A blinding beam of light filled the crawlspace.

"Good God, little lady. What have you gotten yourself into now?
"Torrance?"

"You just sit still. I'll call for an ambulance."

"I don't need an ambulance, but the guy underneath me does."

"There's a guy underneath you?"

"Yes. He might be dead, he hasn't moved for a while. Her bottom lip pulled down into a grimace as she fought off tears. "He wanted to kill me, Torrance. Get me out of here, please."

He knelt down and took her hand. "I'll call for an ambulance. You just hang on. We'll have you out of there in no time."

Suddenly there was a rush of feet. Then it was Detective Stransky peering down at her. "Ms. Bannister? We'll have an ambulance here in a minute."

"I don't need a damn ambulance. Just pull me out of this hole!"

"Sorry. We'll have to wait for the EMTS," the detective said firmly. "Just a minute."

Didn't the woman understand? The threat of tears now displaced by anger, she yelled. "I'm sitting on a dead guy. Get me out of here now!"

"Be patient, Ms. Bannister."

Abby was left fuming down in the hole as Stransky turned her attention to Torrance.

"You're not on duty." Abby heard her say. "What are you doing here?"

"Was in the area and heard the call."

"What? On your Best Buy Police Radio Scanner? Jesus, Torrance! Get a life. So what's this about a man under her chair."

"Looks like he might be our serial killer."

"I'll be. Well, it's going to be a long evening, Torrance. You better go home so I can pretend you were never here."

Chapter 25

Friday, Dec. 9

Robert and Nelson were dipping their toes into the waters of cohabitation. Unlike Nelson, who slept in until the last possible moment then rushed around like a madman, Robert was a morning person. He liked to have a quiet, orderly hour to himself before dealing with Nelson who, like a puppy, tended to be fun and affectionate, but was also messy and required lots of attention. As he sipped his espresso through a straw, he perused the business section then turned to the front page.

The headline story was a local one: *Bill looks at AZ Sales-tax Exemptions*. He scanned the article to see what effect, if any, it would have on him, before moving on to the others. In the bottom right hand corner of the paper, another headline caught his attention, *Death by Wheelchair*, it read.

• • •

When Fey entered the mess tent it was nearly 7:15 a.m. and she was pressed for time. Now that she had a bicycle, the commute to Caridad was faster than by skateboard, but not by much.

Doc was sitting in the overstuffed chair with the faded floral upholstery. As was his habit, he was reading the morning paper and drinking what was probably his third cup of coffee.

"Morning Doc."

"Morning darlin'. Sleep well?"

"Seems like I spent the whole night dicing mountains of onions. You?"

"Like a baby for about three hours." He took a sip of coffee. "Say, what was the name of that cousin of yours? The one in the wheelchair?"

"Abby."

"Says here, 'Abigail Bannister, a wheel chair bound woman, turned the tables on her would-be attacker, a man presumed to be the serial murderer that has been stalking the local disabled.' Seems like she somehow crushed him with her wheel chair. Says she was treated at the hospital for minor injuries and released."

"My God! Let me see." Fey quickly read the brief and totally unsatisfying account.

• • •

Earlier, Rita had called and offered to pick her up, but Abby needed fresh air and quiet to help her sort out the surreal events of the past night before facing a salvo of questions from Rita. Luckily the Chariot, like herself, was mostly unscathed, suffering only a small gash in the fabric in the back and a dent in the battery casing. Abby nudged her glasses in place. They were held together at the bridge with surgical tape.

The milky sky and cool moist air might mean rain, might not. She breathed deeply as she tooled down the ally and on to Sixth Street. Above the rush hour traffic, the agave woman, ever unperturbed, offered reassurance. Abby was not reassured. She had slept little. For hours her mind kept respinning every detail, her initial delight in seeing him, her blind trust, the gloves, the rage on his face as he began to pull himself out of the crawlspace. Though it hadn't been her intention, she had killed a man. No one would blame her. Likely she could expect just the opposite. In her mind she'd gone through a number of scenarios in which she was praised for her bravery and quick thinking. No doubt she'd be hailed a hero. Well, she wasn't a hero; she was a goddamn idiot. Judgment clouded by neediness, she'd opened the door to a near total stranger then handed him her only means of defense.

• • •

Rita had beaten her to the office. When Abby whizzed through the door, the electric teakettle was steaming and the aroma of warm empanadas filled the office. Rita spun around, plate of empanadas in hand. She set them on the desk then whirred over.

"I was so worried, *mija*," she said throwing her arms around Abby in an awkward, but heartfelt, wheelchair to wheelchair embrace, their first ever. "Oh my goodness! Look at your glasses."

"Yeah. Not sure what happed to them." She fingered the surgical tape. "One of the nurses handed them to me in the hospital. Somebody must have found them in the crawlspace."

"We'll get them fixed later. Now tell me exactly what happened and don't leave anything out."

• • •

Reviewing every detail with Rita left Abby feeling even worse than before. How could she have been so stupid and deluded? She dunked her tea bag several times then turned over the tag.

"What's it say?"

"Do not pray to be spared from life's tribulations," Abby read. "Pray instead to face them without anger, fear or resentment."

"That's asking a lot."

Abby shrugged. "Yours?"

"Friendship is a sheltering tree." She reached over and patted Abby's hand then broke off a piece of empanada. Honey did a little happy dance, took it daintily from her hand then crawled back beneath the desk with her prize. "So, if you didn't have your cellphone, who called the cops?"

Abby boosted herself up in her chair. "It was my neighbor Mrs. Soto, God bless her nosy heart. She heard me screaming. Like I said, Torrance was the first to get there, then Detective Stransky, then all of sudden the place with crawling with cops and fire fighters and EMTs. Next thing I know I'm scooped out of the crawlspace and whizzing along in the ambulance, lights flashing, siren howling. I kept saying, I'm okay, I'm okay, but nobody paid any attention." Abby tugged up the sleeve of her tunic revealing a large rectangular bandage. "Didn't even need stitches. Really, I was more worried about the state of my chair."

Rita held up this morning's paper. "Well, according to this, you're a hero."

Shaking her head, Abby read the headline, then the brief article. It was all too real. The only thing that had come between her and a broken neck were the rotten floorboards she couldn't afford to replace. The very scary lack of control she had over her life came into sudden sharp focus and her stomach turned over. Abby looked at the remains of the empanada on the plate, the sticky orange mango filling oozing out onto the plate, and thought of Mike, if that was even his real name, crushed beneath her chair. Her mother's words played in her head, *Don't you cry little girl*. Fighting for control, Abby took a deep breath, but it wasn't enough. She started to shake then cry as Rita, her sheltering tree, held her hand.

The door whooshed open. Anûshka strode in then paused. "Ah! So sorry. I am interruptering. I just empty trash and clean bathroom and come other time."

"You're not interruptering, I mean interrupting. I'm just having a little meltdown."

"What is meltdown?"

Chapter 26

Thursday, Feb. 2

Doc was waiting for her just outside the Ross's dressing room area. As a graduation gift, he had wanted to buy her a dress to wear to the ceremony tomorrow night, but the students were all supposed to wear their black pants, the T-shirt with the Caridad Community Kitchen logo, and of course, the little hats, not that Fey would have worn a dress anyway. She couldn't remember ever wearing a dress. Just the thought of nothing between her legs but air made her feel exposed and vulnerable. Instead, she had selected a long-sleeved blouse, a pair of black pants and a pair of plain, black flats so she'd have something appropriate to wear for interviews. She pulled up the pants. The blouse was made of a silky pale pink fabric that slipped over her arms and shoulders like warm water. Turning from side to side in front of the dressing room mirror she smiled at the image she saw.

• • •

As if turned out, neither Rita, who had to go to the wedding of the godson of her daughter-in-law's cousin, nor Robert, who was having dinner with Nelson and his parents, could take her to Fey's graduation. Fey had never graduated from anything before and this was going to be a big deal with a buffet prepared by the graduates following the ceremony. For Fey's sake, as well as her own, she did not want to miss it.

The ceremony was to take place in the old Dunbar School. In the days of segregation, it was once the only school for children of color in Tucson. Now the old building served as a cultural center. It was just across the street from Caridad Community Kitchen and only a few blocks from her house.

Abby had been going round and round about it all week and now it was almost too late. She reconsidered her options. Only a few months ago, she would have simply taken the Chariot, but no longer was she willing to travel alone after dark. She could call Handi Cab and arrange transportation, but did she really want to attend the event solo? She did not. It wasn't that she was risk adverse. She'd risked steady employment to start GSG. And there was Alfonso who would be moving into her life any day now—plenty of risk there. But what she was contemplating now was categorically different.

In the final chapter of *How to Craft Your Life*, Dale J. Nagery had advised her not to fear making mistakes, the very fear that seemed programmed into her genes. Mistakes, after all, could lead to loss of control, loss of control to failure and failure to…? That was where her line of reasoning trailed off. What would happen if she failed? What would happen if she failed to take another risk?

She rummaged through the top draw of her desk. It was there under the needle nose pliers she kept handy for some emergency yet to be encountered, Torrance Steadman's card. She took a deep breath and another then punched in the number.

• • •

Abby had awakened that morning with an earworm and all day she had been singing *Fly Me to the Moon* in her best Diana Krall impersonation.

Carefully, she applied recently purchased foundation, mascara and eye shadow. She studied the unhappy results, then washed them off her face.

She selected a tube of Burt's Bees Lip Shimmer, this one call Peony. "Let me know what spring is like on Jupiter and Mars," she sang as she spread it over her lips and cheeks. Better, she thought, brushing her hair back so her earrings would show.

"In other words hold my hand." She looped a scarf, this one a teal green and blue paisley, around her neck. "In other words, darling, kiss me," she sang to her reflection. Satisfied, she tried on a smile. Torrance would be by in a few minutes and she didn't have time for further primping.

She'd have to leave the Chariot home, which made her anxious. Without it, she was nearly immobile. Torrance would have to push her in her manual chair to his car and literally pack her into the front seat. She hated to give up her physical control, but if she wanted to go to the graduation, which she did, and she wanted to go with Torrance, which she did, that couldn't be helped. Not only was she letting go of the figurative wheel, she was overriding her fear of failure, making her own luck, and seizing the day. Dale J. Nagery would be proud of her, but it was a lot to ask and her stomach was doing its little dance in response. She patted it as a mother might pat the back of a fussy child.

The doorbell rang. She envisioned Mrs. Soto peering out from behind her beautiful bougainvillea and smiled. The Mylar balloons and yellow roses she had bought for Fey were by the door so she couldn't forget them. She took a few deep breaths. She was as ready as she'd ever be.

• • •

"I don't want to hurt you," Torrance was saying as he pulled her out of her chair and plunked her into the front seat.

"I don't want you to hurt me either, but I'm not delicate." Her right leg was being characteristically obstinate. With her Mighty Claw she tried to lift it in place, but the foot, encased in its scuffed and unlovely shoe, was hung up on the door. "If you could just give my foot a little twist and a push."

Gently he did as requested. "There you go. Let me just get the seat belt."

He reached across her torso, taking great care not to touch her body. "All set?"

"All set."

He started to close the door then hesitated. "I just wanted to say…" he paused. "I wanted you to know… Well, I admire you, and I'm proud to be your escort tonight."

"Thank you, Torrance. That means a great deal to me."

He leaned in then and kissed her on her forehead. It was not a lingering kiss, more like the kiss of an uncle or an old family friend, still it stung a bit like the first drop of cold rain on a hot day stings the skin.

Torrance started the car and slowly pulled away from the curb. After a few minutes, he said. "Sorry. I shouldn't have done that."

"I'm glad you did," Abby said. They rode the rest of the way in silence.

• • •

Mylar balloons flying from the back of her chair, Abby studied the crowd. Fey had told her that Frisco's foster mom had agreed to bring him to the graduation. There were a number of small boys. Any one of them might be Frisco. Her cousin had sounded confident on the phone. She already had several job interviews lined up, but housing was still an issue. Apparently, Fey had to land a job before she could get into a subsidized rental. That seemed backward to Abby. It would make it much easier to find employment if she had a secure place to live. Abby was working on that. Anûshka had moved into a mother-in-law apartment that had once served as Mr. O'Grady's office while he was still able to work. It occurred to her that Anûshka might be willing to share the space with someone who'd pay a little rent. Would Mr. O'Grady agree to that? So far she hadn't mentioned the proposal to anyone, but it was on her to-do list.

There was a rustle at the entrance to the auditorium and the graduates, there were only nine survivors, marched down the center aisle to the applause and whistles of friends and family. Once they took their places in front, Fey scanned the crowd. Abby waved and Fey gave her a big, unobstructed smile. Her face had lost its ruddy color and radiated happiness.

Her mother's voice admonished Abby not to cry, but she did anyway. Torrance handed her his handkerchief. As she dabbed her eyes, Abby imagined that her life was about to change in big ways. For better or worse, Alfonso would soon be her responsibility. She had this persistent and unrealistic fantasy. In it, Alfonso crosses through customs then runs, stubby legs churning in slow motion, toward her open arms, happy ever after. Her hopes for Fey were more grounded. Perhaps they could begin again, this time on more equal footing. She had no idea where her friendship with Torrance might lead. A peck on the forehead was not a commitment to so much as a coffee date, much less a relationship. Whatever was in store for her, she was determined not to let fears of failure and loss of control hold her back.

As an agent of change, the Karma thing had not been working very well for her. It wasn't that she even believed in Karma, except she sort of did. She blotted her tears on Torrance's nice clean handkerchief and determined to let go of notions of payback for suffering and good deeds and simply take each day as it came.

The graduates were being introduced one by one and awarded their certificates. When Fey's turn came, an entire row of people burst into applause. She recognized Doc immediately. The others included a tattooed and pierced young woman, a heavyset and dowdy matron. A Hispanic woman, undoubtedly the foster mom, was holding Frisco. He squirmed off the woman's lap into the aisle. Abby imagined that soon, Frisco and Fey would be reunited for good. At least that was her hope and at the moment, Abby was feeling guardedly hopeful.

She folded Torrance's handkerchief neatly and was about to hand it back to him. Instead, she stuffed it into her Guatemalan pouch. Tomorrow she would wash it, then invite him out to lunch so she could return it. At the thought her chest ached a little—hope mitigated by past experience. The ache soon became a coil of dread that followed the well-traveled path to her stomach. What was wrong with her? She was lucky to be alive. That's what people kept telling her and of course it was true, so why all the angst?

She searched through her ample stores of advice and wisdom: Don't be afraid to make mistakes, live authentically, the only satisfaction that lasts is derived from a task well done, it is never too late to begin your new day, live in the moment, breathe deep to clear the mind and heart of congested emotion. What the hell was congested emotion anyway?

It didn't matter. Nor did it matter that she could no longer discern the advice of Dale J. Nagery from that written on the tag of a tea bag. She took a deep breath and then another and another. As she gazed at Fey and the little boy in the aisle dancing with anticipation she felt the warmth radiating from the kind, fat cop sitting next to her. Gradually the coil loosened, displaced by a bright spot of optimism and a warm thrum. Spreading out from her core and across her blighted limbs, she guessed the thrum could best be described as happiness.

Her thoughts turned to the keyboard lying on the floor of her closet. Maybe tomorrow she'd dust it off and set it up in the living room. Maybe tomorrow she'd go through her sheet music for one-handed piano players. Definitely she could peck out the melody of *Fly me to the Moon* by heart.

About the Author

G. Davies Jandrey has lived in Tucson, Arizona, for well over half her life, which makes her a born again "Baja" Arizonan. She makes her home with her husband, Fritz, dog Tito and cat Goldie, la traviesa, in the desert outskirts of the city. Time spent coaching three lively third-graders under the auspices of Literacy Connect's Reading Seed Program brings her great joy, as does volunteering at Sister José Women's Center. She is a passionate, but not particularly gifted, gardener and canasta player.

She refers to herself as "the best southwest fiction writer you've never heard of." To read samples of Gayle's novels, both published and in progress, visit her website: www.gaylejandrey.com

Enjoy other titles from Fireship Press

Courage Between Love and Death
Joseph Pilliterri

Elspeth has recently landed a nursing position at the 1901 Pan American Exposition Hospital in Buffalo, New York. This is a big boon for her, but things are not going as expected. She has to navigate mischievous patients, egotistical doctors, rival nurses and prejudices. For an Irish girl with a temper, this is no easy feat. Now President McKinley is coming to visit the Expo and everyone is in an uproar. On the home front, her life is no less hectic as she struggles to put food on the table and look out for her younger siblings.

When the unthinkable happens, it is a turning point, not only for the medical industry and our country's security, but also for Elspeth personally. With her career and reputation on the line, will she have the courage to overcome the challenges she faces to clear her name and continue to be there for the ones she loves?

Stone Circle
Kate Murdoch

"In this debut historical fantasy, two young men become apprenticed to a seer during the Renaissance, igniting a rivalry for the man's daughter... Best of all, Murdoch delivers wisdom valuable to anyone trying to master a field: 'Those who are consumed by negative thoughts about others cannot possibly reach the level of purity required.' Despite a clever, definitive ending, readers may clamor for a sequel. Italy sparkles in this layered 16th-century romance." —***Kirkus Reviews***

Cortero
An Imprint of Fireship Press

Interesting • Informative • Authoritative

All Cortero books are available through
leading bookstores and wholesalers worldwide.